PARTING GIFTS

CHARLOTTE VALE ALLEN
PARTING GIFTS

MIRA

ISBN 1-55166-853-X

PARTING GIFTS

Visit us at www.mirabooks.com

Printed in U.S.A.
First Printing: May 2001
10 9 8 7 6 5 4 3 2 1

For my peerless friend Angelo Rizacos who insisted this book
had to be finished and who helped every step of the way;
and for all my readers/friends who've diligently stayed in touch
and been so supportive of my efforts through the years.

PART ONE
1976

CHAPTER 1

The concierge called to say two police officers wanted to speak to her. Was it okay to send them up? Kyra said yes. Was there a choice? Were there people who actually said no, the police couldn't come to their doors? Maybe, but she wasn't one of those people.

Between the time the concierge rang from the front desk and the arrival of the two men at the door—five minutes at most—she rapidly skimmed a mental Rolodex, reviewing the mishaps that might have befallen each member of the family, knowing nothing less than catastrophic news would bring two New York City policemen to call on her. By the time the doorbell sounded, her mouth had gone dry and she had a bad case of the shakes. She knew in her bones that these men were bringing the worst possible news.

And of course, she was right. So, even while they were apologetically giving her the details, eyeing her furtively for signs of impending hysteria (which she would never have allowed herself to display), she was thinking she'd have to get away—she couldn't possibly live here anymore—and trying frantically to decide where she might go.

Her husband was dead, and it was no one's fault, really. Even if there had been someone to blame, it wouldn't have done any good because Gary was gone, and only that fact mattered. Taken in the abstract, it was a given aspect of big-city life: random acts of violence and mayhem that were shocking when read about in the newspaper or seen on the evening news; sad and terrible, yet essentially peripheral, distant. Taken personally, it was immediate and shattering because there was no warning, no possible way to prepare. Who you were, who you loved and who loved you, what you'd accomplished—none of it had consequence. The wrong place at the wrong time, and life as you'd known it ended.

Gary was dead, and all Kyra could think about was running away. *This is bad, so bad. I've got to get out of here.* Her muscles actually twitched with a sudden desperate need to take flight. Instead she listened distractedly to what was said, then (everything inside her quivering, spastic) she went for her coat and accompanied the two deferential men downtown to the morgue to make a formal identification of her husband.

By the next evening her Aunt Catharine had taken charge, for which Kyra was deeply grateful, because nothing was completely real to her. She couldn't seem to get her mind to mesh with the facts of the matter, and had spent the twenty or so hours since Gary had been killed attempting to force herself to believe that her husband was dead. *This is so bad. I have got to get away.*

So while, with rare and impressive efficiency, Catharine got on the telephone and made one call after another, Kyra kept looking at her watch, thinking Gary should have called from Paris by now. Then Catharine's low, hesitant voice drifted in to her and, with a jolt, Kyra remembered why she was there in her aunt's apartment. Then she had to begin working all over again to absorb the present reality, her appalling new status as a widow. The effort to fuse this knowledge to some receptive region of her brain reminded her, crazily, of the way, as a child, she'd had to work a new strip of Plasticine, kneading and rolling it around in her hands until it had become malleable. She could, with remarkable clarity, remember the warm rubbery odor of the stuff, could even remember the way bits of it got under her fingernails, and over the course of days, would gradually get dislodged—tiny, crumbling pebbles of multicolored grit.

While she lay rigid atop the bedclothes on the too-hard bed and gazed at the blue-white ceiling, she wondered how it could have come to this. Perhaps if Gary had been a nine-to-five type, home each evening, she might more readily have accepted what had happened. But he was an airline pilot, regularly gone for five or ten days at a stretch on the European or Asian runs, and his returns were often delayed by weather, by air traffic, by mechanical problems. So, despite the fact that she'd identified the body, that she had seen what remained of the charming, dapper man she'd loved

in a kind of controlled ten-year-long frenzy, her brain had seg-
mented itself—part of it steaming like a kettle boiling, and part of
it complacently cool in its absolute denial.

Neither segment had priority; each had seemingly equal claim
on her consciousness. The overheated area seemed to favor the late-
night hours, with the result that she'd scarcely slept the night before; the cooler portion had taken over with daylight, keeping her
befuddled and clumsy. She felt as if she'd split in two, and much
preferred the long daytime hours that were relatively free of the irrational but profound fear that had kept her pacing on tiptoe
through Catharine's immense apartment most of the previous night.
Arms wrapped tightly around herself, she'd tried not to look at the
image of Gary that was seared into her memory: his face serene,
intact; his body destroyed from shoulders to knees. Odd bulges
where organs had ruptured; fractured ribs and a broken hipbone
poking through savage rents in his flesh. She'd had to look, to see
all of him, to touch those odd lumps in his midriff, the side of his
throat where she'd loved to sniff at him like a puppy. She couldn't
not have looked; couldn't *not* have brought her tremoring hands
into contact with his surfaces. It was the only way she could even
begin to convince herself he was no longer inside himself. The absence was astonishingly total. And all the while, trying to control
her palsy, the voice track kept repeating, *God, this is bad. I need
to go away.*

She thought now that she had gained some small comprehension
of those regions in outer space the scientists called black holes; she
seemed to have taken up residence in one. Her only company in the
desolation was the relentless voice: *This is bad. Where should I go?*

Her head was aching, and she debated getting up to investigate
the contents of her aunt's medicine cabinet. It was bound to contain some very interesting drugs—given Catharine's plethora of
primarily undiagnosable ailments—one of which would offer relief. But Kyra couldn't move. So she lay on the bed in one of her
aunt's three guest rooms and slowly looked around, aware of
Catharine's meticulous attention to detail in every aspect of the
decor: a quartet of small, exquisitely framed, antique needlework
samplers hung in a precise row at eye level just inside the door;
the glossy Prussian-blue enamel trim on the woodwork with not a
single brushmark or stray bristle captured like a fly in amber.

Catharine had spent years on end decorating this apartment, finding exactly the right painting for the wall over the buffet in the dining room (a quite splendid still life of blue-black plums in a deep white bowl), the right brass fender for the living room fireplace (simple curving lines enclosing the three panels of mesh), the right basket (a perfect handmade oval of woven rushes), which when painted white and lined with fine Egyptian cotton, was the ideal repository in the master bathroom for her soiled undergarments.

Kyra had often wondered what Uncle Henry thought when he sat down on the throne and found, directly in his line of vision, a basketful of his wife's worn knickers. Or did Luz, the housekeeper, rush in to empty the basket before Henry returned home each evening and again before he rose from bed in the morning? A basket, in full view, of worn lingerie. It was decadent, tasteless, crazy. But then Catherine was, on a certain level, utterly mad. The thing of it was, you had to know her to appreciate the totality, the integrity, of it. It was, for the most part, a quiet and fairly contained thing, like a kidney—or gallstone. And perhaps, in the arcane lexicology of such things, not true madness but something else, something less readily definable. Kyra loved her aunt, but sometimes found it hard to care for a woman whose existence was at best ninety percent form and ten percent substance.

Catharine was capable of affectionate displays, but usually only when she'd managed, through alcohol or some new marvelous prescription drug, to find an interior route to emotions that were primarily untapped—a child's untrammeled purity of feeling unexpectedly revealed by a woman in her mid-fifties. It was always shocking and deeply embarrassing when Catharine, in her cups, suddenly and tearfully, would begin proclaiming her depthless love for all those present. The tightly constrained, cold-sober woman was preferable, safer. Catharine, on substances, was an ambulatory land mine.

But then, who was to say she was any better? Kyra wondered. Certainly she felt immense and stupid, the brand-new widow, collapsed upon the bed and temporarily unable to move, bludgeoned by loss, able only to hear the same words repeating endlessly: *This is bad. I must get away.*

Her husband, that lovely, slightly daft man, on his way to the bank to cash a check when a cab, traveling at a speed rarely achieved on the city's choked avenues, spun out of control, mounted the curb and came to a stop only because a fifty-one-year-old man and a granite-faced building prohibited it traveling further.

A freak accident, the media called it. Kyra had unearthed the previous evening's tabloids and that morning's *New York Times,* which Catharine had hidden in the broom closet—thinking perhaps, in her addled fashion, to spare her niece further distress—and read, fascinated, the eyewitness descriptions of passersby and the garbled statement of the cab driver (who suffered a crushed pelvis). "I'm going twenty-five miles per, max, and the brakes fail! Then the steering locked up!" He felt terrible about that poor fellow he hit, and said he'd never drive a cab again; when he was back on his feet he'd take the wife and kids home to Mason City. He insisted that the cab company was at fault for failing to maintain the fleet properly, keeping cars on the road until they just fell apart. He planned to "sue their brains out," and hoped the family of the deceased did the same. "I tried not to hit him but I had no control of that lousy cab," he said. "The poor guy never had a chance, God rest his soul."

Kyra had felt an odd ache reading that last sentence, and stared at the newsprint photograph of the crumpled vehicle until the countless black and white dots deconstructed and became like TV snow. She stared at those dots, trying to remember the last words she and Gary had spoken to each other. Mundanities: Have a good trip. I'll phone you when I get in. I love you. I love you, too. Good-bye, good-bye.

If they had succeeded in adopting a child she might have felt somewhat less devastated. But more than eight years of applying had brought them only an infinite variety of rejections, from the genuinely apologetic to the outrightly dismissive. Financial solvency and an abiding love of children meant nothing. So, despite their advanced ages (she at thirty-eight and he at fifty-one were considered very old as potential adoptive parents), they were still on all sorts of waiting lists. There were hundreds, probably thousands, of couples ahead of them. They had never stopped hoping, never stopped trying. Now, that was over, too. Gary was dead, and with him had died the possibility of her ever being a parent.

After a time Kyra had helped herself to some of the coffee Luz had made at lunchtime, and was sitting at the table, gazing at the deconstructed newspaper photograph, yet again reviewing their parting dialogue, when Catharine came hurrying in to say, "Darling, I've finally managed to reach Mummy for you. She's on the line now." Lifting the receiver from the kitchen extension, a wide-eyed Catharine carried it over to Kyra and held it out importantly.

Kyra stared at her once-beautiful aunt, wondering why Catharine consistently referred to her older sister as Kyra's mummy (yet another of her demented affectations), and why she kept having cosmetic procedures that left her looking like something of durable rubber cast from a mold: seamless, lineless, lacking the flaws and folds that defined character, and with the exaggerated width of mouth that seemed to be an accepted part of plastic surgery. Up close, poor Catharine was well on her way to being grotesque; a life-size Muppet who often sounded alarmingly, hilariously like the Swedish chef.

Her aunt made an urgent gesture with the receiver and, at last, Kyra focused and accepted the instrument, held it to her ear.

"Kyra, I'm so profoundly sorry. Such an unbelievable thing to happen! How are you holding up, darling?"

Like anyone who'd ever heard that voice on stage or in a film, Kyra was enveloped in its husky, honeyed depths, and briefly comforted. "I'm not doing very well," she answered truthfully, her throat burning from the sudden effort to hold back tears.

"Of course not. How *could* you be? I want desperately to come to you, darling, but they can't stop production. I simply don't know *what* to do!"

"It's all right. I understand."

"Kyra, I *want* to be with you now," her mother said more emphatically. "But there's no sort of insurance to cover this situation. I've got another ten days on location, and they can't shoot around me, even for two or three days, so I just *cannot* get away. It's a nightmare. I've never *felt* quite so frustrated. I am truly, deeply sorry."

"So am I," Kyra said, as if to herself. *There has to be somewhere to go.*

"I've spoken to Kyle. He and Beth will be there by tomorrow afternoon. They're catching the next available flight from Heathrow."

"That's good."

"You're angry with me," her mother said sadly.

"I'm angry, but not with you." She glanced across at Catharine, who hovered by the stove, looking apprehensive and edgy, as if anxious to have some invisible crew retake the scene, shoot it more effectively. She was plainly unhappy with the part of the conversation she could hear.

"You wouldn't be human if you weren't angry," her mother said.

"Then I suppose I must be human."

"It's a terrible loss, terrible. I adored Gary. He was so..."

"I know." Kyra's voice sounded flat, lifeless to her own ears. *Death can kill you.*

"When it's over, come home and let me look after you for a bit. Will you do that?"

"Yes, all right. I have to go now, Mother."

"I love you, Kyra. I would be there if I possibly could."

"I love you, too." Choking, Kyra got up abruptly, pushed the receiver at Catharine and fled back to the refuge of the early American guest room. She carefully closed the door before dropping face down on the patchwork quilt, clutching handfuls of it while she wept and raged, scarcely making a sound.

At some point later, Catharine came to the door, in her soft, tentative voice asking was there anything she could do.

Kyra managed to say an audible "No, thank you," and Catharine had gone away.

Weary, Kyra now turned over and again stared at the ceiling. It felt as if there was a gaping wound in her chest, and each beat of her heart sent spurts of blood arcing into the air. An incredible pain. Yet when she took the flat of her hand over her chest, all she felt was the warm, wrinkled cotton of the dress she'd been wearing for the past two days. No blood, no wound. Only the pain and the sensation of blood loss. And that incessant voice murmuring inside her skull.

She was awakened by a quiet knock at the door. Her cousin, Glenna, slipped into the room and came to sit on the side of the bed. Taking hold of Kyra's hand, she whispered, "I don't know what to say. I feel so sad—for you, for all of us. Gary was the only sane person in the whole bloody family."

Kyra had to laugh (a husky half-strangled sound), and sat up to put an arm around her cousin, letting her head rest on Glenna's narrow shoulder. "He was as nutty as the rest of us," she murmured, "just less visibly so."

"Why are you *here?*" Glenna asked, still whispering. "Wouldn't you rather be at home?"

"Your mother insisted," Kyra answered, sitting back. "My brain's shut down, and it was easier to do what she wanted."

"As is so often the case. I've got the car downstairs, if you want to go home."

"Yes," Kyra said gratefully. "I do."

"I thought you would, so I told Mummy you'd called and asked me to come pick you up."

"You're brilliant, Glen. Let me collect my things and we'll go."

Catharine looked more distraught than ever, wringing her hands as Kyra said good-bye in the foyer. "Are you sure you'll be all right?" she asked, a taut, worried little furrow between her brows.

"I'll manage." Kyra hugged her and said, "Thank you for everything. You've been so kind, such a help."

"I'll ring you tomorrow," Catharine said anxiously, "see how you're getting on. Such a lot to do, so many calls..."

Glenna embraced her mother, said, "Talk to you later, dear," grabbed Kyra's arm and hustled her out. Catharine stood in the doorway, waiting and watching, her mouth working, until the elevator came.

She is so childlike, Kyra thought, as the doors closed on the image of her fashionable mannequin-aunt poised on the threshold.

As the elevator began its descent, Glenna said, "Henry was sitting in the kitchen, eating a sandwich and reading the paper while Mummy performed an entire Greek tragedy, complete with chorus. I'm sorry if I seem pushy, Keer, but I really thought it would be best to get you out of there."

"Don't be sorry." Kyra took hold of her cousin's small, warm hand. "I didn't want to stay, but I couldn't think how to extricate myself."

"My mother's famous octopus syndrome. Tentacles disguised with rings and gold bracelets, but tentacles nevertheless."

Kyra emitted another brief, strangled laugh. "You're very hard on her."

Glenna shrugged, her eyes on the floor indicator.

"This is very bad." The sentence slipped out and, abashed, Kyra turned to look at her cousin.

"Very," Glenna said somberly.

Relieved by this confirmation, Kyra fell silent.

In the car, somewhat awkwardly, Glenna said, "I can't begin to imagine how you must feel. The suddenness...the shock... I called Cliff and told him I wouldn't be home tonight. You can't stay by yourself. Is Aunt Octavia coming?"

"She's on location. Spain, I think. I forgot to ask where. It doesn't matter. And Father's on location, too. Neither of them can come."

Glenna chewed on her lower lip and didn't comment.

"Kyle and Beth are coming tomorrow."

"Well, that's good." Glenna took a quick look at her cousin.

Kyra stared unblinking out the window.

"Kyra?"

Kyra turned.

"I know it's not quite the same thing, but when Daddy died I was completely unhinged for the better part of a year."

"I remember." Kyra's mouth was dry. She stared at Glenna, a living reminder of just how lovely Catharine once had been. "I do remember. It was a—difficult time." *Bad. How it was then, how it is now. Is there a place where people like me should go?*

"What I'm saying is, it'll help if you let go. It's no good trying to hold it in."

Kyra nodded, said, "No, I know," and went back to staring out the window. It wasn't as if she was *trying* to hold anything in. It was just that she had generations of British stoicism in her genes. She'd have loved to tear at her hair and her clothes, to scream until her throat bled; she wanted to, but she just couldn't. Still, she'd have a long, long time to come to grips with it—a future of demilife, of amputation, of waiting for a man she'd adored who would never return.

CHAPTER 2

Kyra was eleven when she discovered that her mother was not English, as she'd always believed, but American. She made this discovery as a result of an article in British *Vogue* shown her by a classmate that referred to the actress as "American-born." Thrown, Kyra thought that couldn't possibly be right. Mummy was a famous *English* actress; she lived in *England,* worked in *England,* her children were *English.* If she were indeed American, why had no one ever mentioned it to her children?

Indignant, convinced an error had been made, Kyra returned the magazine to her classmate with a purposefully casual air, and when she and her brother were next home together, during the Christmas break, she asked him about it.

"Of course she is. Well, *was,* actually. She was born in New York, but she's *English,*" Kyle said impatiently, with an insufferably superior air. "*Everyone* knows that."

"I didn't," Kyra protested, deflated and hurt, and filled for the moment with dislike for her so-smug brother. "Why hasn't anyone ever bothered to tell me?"

"I expect everyone assumed you already knew."

"Well, I *didn't.*" For some reason, Kyra felt defrauded.

Kyle was regarding her quizzically, which heightened her upset. "What does it matter?" he asked. "It doesn't *mean* anything."

"Of course it does," she insisted. "It matters. It changes everything."

"Like what?"

Kyra looked around the lounge, trying to assemble her thoughts. They were temporarily alone in the house, their mother being at her rehearsal, their father at his, and the housekeeper up the road at the shops. She turned back to her brother, wondering how they could be twins and yet so utterly different. Everything she'd read had led her to believe twins were possessed of an almost mystical connection, that they could often read each other's thoughts; one could even feel phantom pain if the other suffered. Yet she and Kyle seemed to share only a birthday and a strong physical resemblance. Their interests, their personalities, couldn't have been more different.

Kyle was happy at boarding school, passionate about cricket and sports in general; he had tons of friends and regularly went off with one of them to spend school holidays rather than returning home. His grades were never better than average, despite the fact that he struggled faithfully to have his work done and handed in on time. Tall and well-built, he appeared alarmingly urbane—looking quite a bit older than his age—and had a perennially insouciant air that Kyra envied and resented because she was convinced that, underneath, he was as often confused and unhappy as she.

For her part, Kyra loathed boarding school, had few friends, and lived from one school holiday until the next when she'd be free again to go home. She was always top girl in her form, despite finding most of her studies boring. Over-tall, and over-critical, she was acutely self-conscious, and saw her family as a work of fiction, not as anything real. Although she loved her parents, her mother especially, she had felt for some time as if a thick glass wall separated her from them. On the far side of the glass, her famous parents performed in public and in private, gave interviews, entertained, got drunk on occasion and argued vociferously, and sometimes remembered they had two children who were watching their carryings-on. Since they'd turned ten, Kyra had felt that Kyle was on the other side, too. She couldn't seem to get close to any of them and it worried her.

She wished constantly that her parents were ordinary, that they went to ordinary jobs and had ordinary friends. She could remember a time, not very long past, when her family was just her family and not related cast members. But she'd been then what her Scottish-born father called a "wean" and she'd been mystified when people had come up to their table in a restaurant, asking Mummy to sign bits of paper, or when they stopped her on the street to talk to her. Kyra had actually, foolishly, thought the attention was because Mummy was so exotic and spoke in such a lovely, low voice. Fame was beyond her comprehending then. But at nearly twelve she'd come to the conclusion that being famous was dreadful, most assuredly not something she'd ever want to be.

Kyle, however, had always thrived in the spotlight. By the age of four he was doing clever little turns for the guests when Mummy and Daddy entertained. He participated in all his school plays and intended to go to theater school and, eventually, to follow his mother on to the stage. All of this alarmed Kyra because the three other lives being lived around her seemed to be extemporized productions, with one or all the others posturing and declaiming, acting out rather than truly experiencing anything. And, finally, discovering that her mother was American was a terrible blow. It was, somehow, the ultimate proof that the family really was a fiction, some feature film, perhaps, starring her mother and brother, and directed by her father, in which Kyra figured only as a dress extra, without lines.

In time she came to realize that, sultry voice, grand gestures and habitual mannerisms notwithstanding, her mother was in fact a passionate and caring person; that Kyle was undeniably gifted and legitimately belonged in the theater; and that their father, who had been divorced from their mother the year Kyle and Kyra turned twelve, was a wildly innovative and talented director, and a deeply tormented and unresolved man. In other words, they were, after all, merely people who were, in their own peculiar fashion, as engaged in life as anyone else.

All these years later, standing by her bedroom window with her back to the view, hands braced on the sill, eyes taking in the details of the room she'd shared so contentedly with Gary, Kyra felt even more shattered now than she had upon discovering that her mother wasn't what she'd always assumed her to be. She felt cheated, deprived. Without Gary's sane, steadying presence, she might very well revert to being the deeply suspicious, fundamentally unhappy woman she had been before he'd come along.

Suspicion had kept pace with her throughout her early life, gaining in size in direct proportion to the frequency of fawning comments on her looks and/or not-so-casual questions about her mother and father. Everyone, it seemed, had felt compelled to exclaim over the remarkable good looks of Octavia Bell and Richard Latimer's children. Kyle ate it up like a lavish cream tea, but Kyra became increasingly more wary. When the girls at school were unkind and even cruel, Kyra knew they felt diminished not only because she was the daughter of famous people but also by the very sight and size of her. When the boys she encountered began acting like fools in order to get her attention, she decided to put a stop to it all by making herself unattractive. So she ate stodge, stuffed herself with bread and potatoes and sweets until she was so overweight she could scarcely move. And for a time she was left alone. Which was good. Unfortunately she hated her bloated body, the rubbery rolls of flesh around her middle, and her vast flabby thighs. Which was bad. Ultimately self-disgust wiped out her appetite, and the fat gradually disappeared.

Then, in her teens, the boys didn't all act like fools, and for a time she was tricked into believing their interest in her was genuine. Inevitably it turned out their interest actually was in her parents or in her looks, in being seen with her, in taking her to bed; but none of them had any desire to know her. Through no fault of her own, she'd been transformed into a status symbol. So, to reduce her desirability, she went back to consuming stodge. She grew round, then chubby, then fat. Most people were repelled by her bulk, and, by the time she was attending art college, the smattering of young men who pursued her were actually keen to get to know her. She, however, found herself keen to get to know very few of them. But that didn't deter her. She had an affair, then another, and another, and another.

She enjoyed lovemaking, so she rarely refused an invitation. But she was always on guard, keeping her identity and her emotions hidden. Until Gary Sheridan. Then, for ten years she'd been able to relax, to be entirely herself; no longer bothered by people who stared, or by those who couldn't help blurting out some asinine comment about her height or her looks, or by asking remarkably invasive questions about her family. Gary had been her cushion, her comfort, her anchor to reality.

The telephone rang. Startled, she looked over but didn't move. Glenna would answer in the living room, or the service would. She lacked the energy to speak to anyone. Right now she wanted to explore her emotions; she had the sense of being at the outer perimeter of some vast uncharted territory, the ground solid in some spots but quicksand in others, with no ability to determine where it was safe to go.

At the age of eleven she'd wished for some means of converting what she perceived to be fiction into fact by the sheer force of her will. If she wanted it badly enough and made sufficient effort, the people she loved would become real, genuine and unaffected. At thirty-eight she longed for oblivion, or escape, or both. Part of her longed for the ability, the freedom to give vent to the grief that simmered inside her. But she couldn't allow herself to behave that way. She had long ago vowed that no one would ever be able to accuse her of being the histrionic daughter of the legendary Octavia Bell. Whatever Kyra did, it would be on her terms, and her success or failure would have nothing to do with the family.

The irony was that, as the cliché had it, the fruit never falls far from the tree. She'd studied set and costume design at art college, and ended up much sought-after as a costume designer, working primarily in theater but often on films. As Kyle was sickeningly fond of saying, it was in their blood. Except for poor Aunt Catharine.

At eighteen, with England on the brink of war, with stardom in mind, Catharine had followed her already-famous sister to London. But Catharine, despite her splendid figure and singular good looks, had no acting skills, nor had she been blessed with a speaking voice as rich in timbre and range as her older sister's. Almost the moment she set foot on British soil she acquired an odd, vaguely upper-class accent which, combined with a tendency to leap from one subject to another without preamble, invariably had people listening with faint frowns, as if to a foreign language.

After a few years of bit parts, occasional modeling jobs (primarily for obscure knitting magazines) and several walk-ons in films, she married Clive Carver, who was ineligible for military service because of some unspecified childhood injury and who had inherited an immense sum of money in his late teens as well as the family importing business. Settling into the house Carver purchased in Eaton Square, Catharine promptly became pregnant and gave birth to Glenna in 1943. She entrusted the newborn to the nanny and devoted herself full-time to decorating the gracious old house.

Young Kyra found her aunt peculiar but intriguing, and studied her surreptitiously whenever she visited. But Kyra was enchanted by Glenna from her first sight of the baby's fine, doll-like features and gold-silk hair. Whether it was a display of intuitive understanding or of sheer fecklessness, Catharine at once entrusted the infant into the child's arms. Kyra could scarcely breathe, so stricken was she with awe and a newfound sense of responsibility. She sat, rapt and unmoving, with the baby in her arms for more than two hours, determined that she would one day have a newborn of her own just like this one.

The two girls were very close until Catharine divorced Carver in 1957 to marry Henry Blaine, an American banking executive she'd met at one of the many social functions she so loved to attend, and with whom she embarked upon a thoroughly chaste affair until her divorce was granted.

Then, in 1958 (Catharine newly pregnant with her second child), the Blaine family moved back to New York. Glenna was brokenhearted at leaving everything she'd known and loved, particularly her cousin. She never fully forgave her mother for depriving her of a kind and gentle father, or for, at the embarrassingly advanced age of thirty-eight, giving birth to another child, a son she spoiled in such an odious fashion that it was nothing less than miraculous that Dillon turned out to be a sweet-natured young man no one, including his much older sister, could help liking.

Glenna was polite to her stepfather, Henry—as he was to her—but never warmed to him. He was a man to whom children (with the exception of Dillon) were small, alien life-forms—objects of curiosity primarily. To his credit, he was generous and tolerant, but he lacked empathy and it was, perhaps, this that led Catharine into her love affair with surgical procedures.

Evidently believing the stagnation of the marriage to be her fault somehow, at forty-four she announced she was going to have her face lifted and her nose remodeled. She spoke of the forthcoming cosmetic surgery in such enthusiastic and glowing terms that both Glenna and Kyra (who was spending the summer with the family in New York at the time) were caught up in her fervor, and the conversation for weeks prior to the event was of nothing else.

Both girls were alarmed and repelled by the sight of the battered, still fairly drugged woman who returned home three days after the procedures, and who ultimately emerged from beneath the bandages looking much as she had before, but with a considerably smaller, pointier, and far less attractive nose.

Baffled, the cousins speculated endlessly about what Catharine's motives might possibly have been for subjecting herself to such torture. And as the years passed, they could only stand by in fascinated horror as more procedures followed: an eyelid lift, then cheek and chin augmentation, and neck tightening. Just this past year she'd had a third complete face-lift. Now, only hints and shadows of her former beauty remained. In her permanent quest for perfection through surgery, Catharine alone seemed unaware of its loss.

Glenna tapped at the door, poked her head in and said, "It was some young woman making not a lot of sense. I told her you weren't available. She wouldn't leave her name, but said she'd call back. I'm warming up some soup. It'll be ready in about five minutes." Glenna backed away, softly pulled the door shut.

Frozen at the window, Kyra stared at the place in the doorway where her cousin had been, reviewing yet again that final conversation with Gary. It played out the same way; she remembered no additional words or gestures. After a time, she sighed wearily and headed for the kitchen. The voice track notwithstanding, escape didn't seem to be in the offing.

"Come home with me after the funeral," Glenna invited. "The country will do you good, and you need to take some time off to sort out your feelings."

Kyra's mind snagged on the word *funeral,* and she realized that from this point on her life would be broken into two segments: before the funeral and whatever was to come after. Thinking aloud, she said, "I expect I'll get back to work. I have obligations, after all." Her mouth suddenly dry, she gazed at the thick-looking surface of the cream of tomato soup—a long-time favorite of the cousins—as her eyes overflowed and she cried, "It's so *unfair!* I don't know how I'll *ever* get by without Gary."

Pressing a handkerchief into Kyra's hand, Glenna said, "You don't think so now, but you will."

Kyra clutched the handkerchief while Glenna soothingly stroked her hand, saying, "It's the truth. And the two of you had a good long run. What, ten years? That's a long time, really. More than most couples manage these days. The last thing Gary would want is for you to quit living."

"God, *please,* don't go that route, Glenna! It's so—Terence Rattigan."

Glenna stared at her for a moment, then laughed.

Kyra looked over at her, then had to laugh too, surprising herself. "Terence Rattigan?"

"Honestly!" Kyra sniffed. "*Separate Tables* or *The Deep Blue Sea.* Those hopeless, helpless women, undone by men, taking cheap comfort from hackneyed sentiments. I don't want to hear clichés about what Gary would have wanted for me. What Gary would have *wanted* is to be alive right now!"

"Your trouble is you're hypercritical," Glenna said mildly. "Of course, it's what I've always loved about you."

"I keep thinking he made the Paris flight. He'll be home in five days." Belatedly, she mopped her face. "He was going to retire in four more years. We planned to move somewhere warm—Arizona or New Mexico—round up a bunch of orphans or foster children, look after them and just laze about for the rest of our lives."

"The orphans notwithstanding, you'd both have been bored witless. Try to eat."

"I expect you're right. But it was such a lovely idea. Mother wants me to spend some time with her when this is over." Kyra studied her cousin for several moments. "Her not coming infuriates you, doesn't it?"

"Too bloody right, it does. If you were *my* child, I'd be here with you, come hell or high water."

"She can't," Kyra said quietly. "She'd get hit with a hefty lawsuit. You're a lawyer, you know it's true."

"I suppose," Glenna conceded grudgingly.

"And besides, it would turn the whole thing into a media free-for-all. The photographers and journalists would be everywhere, trying to get pictures of her, or interviews. No, it's best this way."

"Please eat. You'll get sick if you don't."

"I'm afraid I'll get sick if I do."

They fell silent, hands still intertwined.

At last, Glenna said, "Come stay with me for a while and then go to London. Let me fuss over you the way you used to with me when I was little."

"When did I ever fuss over you?" Was this going to be another snippet of revised history?

"When *didn't* you? Remember that spring I was six and had chicken pox? Mummy was smack in the middle of redecorating the dining room, I think it was, and Nanny had the flu, so I was quarantined in the nursery, itching to death. You came round and Mummy was in a flap, saying you couldn't visit, I was horribly contagious. And you said, 'I've had chicken pox. I'll go up and visit with her for a bit.' Mummy dithered on, naturally, but you insisted. I was listening at the top of the stairs, so proud of you."

"Now I remember. I gave you some sort of medicated bath, didn't I?"

"And calamine lotion. You slathered it all over me. Then we played Chinese checkers and you brought me my tea on a tray. I thought you were so grown-up, so in charge of yourself. Of Mummy, too. I did admire you."

"I was only eleven!" Kyra protested.

"It seemed very grown-up to me at the time."

"Hmmn. I suppose. My God, but you were a mess! Pox everywhere, even in your ears. And you scratched one when I wasn't looking, which is how you got that little scar beside your right eyebrow."

"No, it isn't. I got that falling off my bicycle at the country house."

"No. You got it from scratching at your chicken pox." Kyra smiled, thinking how extraordinarily elastic memory could be, and gave her cousin's hand a squeeze. "Thank you for rescuing me from your mother. My brain just didn't want to work and I couldn't think how to say no."

"She means well," Glenna said with a shrug. "It's just that she has no idea, really, how people feel. Never has had, never will."

"None. It's sad, really."

"Promise me you'll come to Connecticut after the funeral, take some time out."

Kyra pictured the handsome old white clapboard house set at the top of a grassy crest overlooking a shallow pond in the near distance. Then she thought of Roddy and Gage, Glenna's two little boys; thought of their faces and their laughter and the feel of them in her arms, and said, "All right. I will. Thank you. Yes, I will do that."

CHAPTER 3

When she wasn't twisting her wedding band around and around, when she wasn't checking the time, Kyra stared straight ahead, failing to hear much of what was said during the service; she moved when others moved, responding robotlike to what seemed to be expected of her. But she was remembering, in the minutest detail, how she and Gary had met, in the spring of 1965, on a flight from London to New York, where she was to meet with the art director of a film for which she'd been engaged to design the costumes. It was a period piece set in turn-of-the-century Manhattan, and for the first time she'd had a decent budget to work with, a good script and a gifted young director, James Elway. She'd been excited about the project and had immersed herself at once in the research.

Being a few inches over six feet, and hating being wedged into small spaces, she'd paid the difference herself—as she had for the three previous American films she'd done—to upgrade her economy ticket to first class. Luckily the section had been fairly empty, the seat next to hers unoccupied, and she'd been able to take advantage of the additional space to spread out and get some work done.

She'd been studying photostats from a 1901 Sears-Roebuck catalog, making notes on the fanciful hats, the starched shirtwaists, and the tailoring of ready-made men's wear, when the pilot came through and stopped to ask, with a singularly appealing smile and unfeigned curiosity, what she was doing.

She'd warmed to him at once. His interest was so genuine that she'd found herself explaining her job and the research involved in far greater detail than she would have normally.

A handsome, sturdily built man, with particularly well-defined features (eyes round and clear beneath naturally arching brows, nose straight and sharp with a slight flare to the nostrils, squared jaw and good strong teeth), he had leaned against the top of the seat ahead and listened attentively, eyes never straying from hers, until she'd fallen silent. Then he'd picked up a swatch of velvet samples and rubbed his thumb back and forth against the nap, saying, "I'm partial to velvet." A smile, then he'd said, "You have the most beautiful"—and she froze, thinking: *Please don't be another fool, taken in by surfaces.* Incipient disappointment like a sudden reflux of bile in her throat, she'd waited for the rest—"speaking voice. Warm and delicious, like melted butter."

Crazily relieved, she'd said, "Some people have actually said I sound very like my mother."

"When I've heard your mother, I'll let you know if you do. For now, though, I'd have to say you sound like you." The smile growing wider, he asked, "Would you be interested in coming up to see the cockpit?"

"I'd love it," she'd responded happily. "Aside from mock-ups on film sets, I've never seen the real thing."

"Then it's time you did," he'd said, returning the swatches to her.

And so it had begun. A long, laughing conversation at the front of the plane was picked up by telephone later the next day and continued over dinner the following evening. During her two-and-a-half-month stay in New York, she and Gary saw each other several times a week, and she'd learned a great deal about him and about the death of his wife six years before. He'd spoken with great feeling and truthfulness about watching someone he'd loved dwindle over the course of two years until she'd no longer been recognizable—to him or to herself. "People never want to admit it," he'd said, "but when the end finally does come, along with the sorrow there's a terrible sense of relief. We're ashamed that we're glad it's over."

After she returned to England he'd telephoned often and had come to visit whenever he got the London or Paris routes. She began to resent the distance between them, the time they spent apart, because Gary was the most lovable and confiding man she'd ever met, and the most sensuous. He seemed compelled to touch with visible appreciation the things that caught his eye—paper, fabrics, oddly shaped rocks, small children or elderly passengers aboard one of his flights, her flesh. He meant precisely what he said and had no time for psychological games; he was responsive and reliable; he had a whimsical streak, as well as a touching penchant for embarking upon conversations with strangers. He had an abiding interest in things, in people.

At his gentle but consistent urging, six months after they met, she'd started the paperwork necessary to claim patrimony through her mother and, thereby, dual citizenship. And within a year she had moved to New York to live with Gary because, without him close by, the world was predictable and gray. With him, she no longer felt freakishly oversized, or in any way inadequate. It seemed that she had many redeeming qualities. It was just that her life had lacked an appropriate audience.

Gary was unimpressed by the things that had made other men she'd dated hyperventilate—in particular her family. He'd seen the Latimers simply as interesting individuals. Staring at the back of the pew ahead of her, Kyra remembered him saying, "Your mother's got a terrific sense of humor, and a big heart. One day the two of you will sort things out and then you'll wonder why you ever doubted her." And about Kyle: "He's fine when it's just a few of us, but he tries too hard when there's any kind of a crowd. I think your brother's kind of a shy, unsettled guy, Kyra." That observation, so unexpected, made her begin viewing Kyle in a more sympathetic light—years of dry, accumulated animosity started to flake away. And following his first meeting with her father, Gary had said, "You know, I've got a hunch he secretly enjoys being unhappy." Which delighted her, because this had always privately been her opinion, too: that the essence of Richard Latimer, and the underlying cause of his great success, was his gift for turning a lifetime's inner turmoil into art.

Kyra had revered Gary Sheridan. His perceptiveness was a flensing knife, slicing cleanly through to the meat of an issue or of a person; his kindness was innate; his instincts generous, and his humor unclouded by meanness. He shared her love of children but wasn't in the least bothered by the fact that, due to a birth defect, she was unable to conceive. On the negative side, he tended to be unaware of clutter, and had a positive aversion to discarding things, especially old clothes; he was something of a procrastinator, paying bills at the last moment and occasionally neglecting to pay them at all; having grown up on a farm, his interest in food was basic and he ate, usually without comment, whatever was put in front of him. None of this bothered her. Having the electricity, or gas, or telephone shut off now and then had been a small price to pay for Gary's affectionate company. And, anyway, she was a terrible cook.

In late November 1966, with Glenna and her then boyfriend Cliff as witnesses, Kyra and Gary got married at city hall. No muss, no fuss, Gary said happily, and, after a week's honeymoon in Bermuda, where they walked, talking, for long hours every day, he flew off on the Frankfurt run the day after they returned home.

Now it was ten years later, and she was the widow at Gary's funeral, an immense black-garbed oddity who kept looking at her watch, estimating the time difference between New York and Paris. Trapped in the details of the last day of her husband's life, she'd been checking the time at regular intervals for four days now. She couldn't seem to stop, even with Gary's two younger brothers, David and Brian, and her own family (Kyle and his wife Beth, Glenna and Cliff, Catharine, Henry and Dillon) surrounding her— each in dark clothing; each with red-rimmed eyes, even Henry; each somewhat dazed with shock. The church was packed with pilots and ground crew and flight attendants; with friends of Gary's, of hers, and of the two families; with quite a number of media people; and with avid-eyed, curious strangers who'd read or heard about the accident—ghouls. She just couldn't connect herself to the event or to those present. She was waiting for Gary to arrive.

Afterward, an extraordinary number of people came to Catharine's apartment, filling the foyer, the living and dining rooms, the hallways. And everyone, it seemed, wanted to touch Kyra, to embrace her or to hold her hand while they told some anecdote about Gary and spoke of how much they'd miss him. She felt as if her exterior was actually being eroded by the handclasps, the hugs, the pats on the arm or shoulder or back; she was being worn away by solicitousness, made lonely by the anecdotes, and longed for some empty space where she could sit quietly and try to think. She either had to go away for real, or make some sort of plan for the remainder of her life. But run where? Do what? Her brain, finally, felt eroded, too.

Enisled temporarily in the eddying crowd, she watched Catharine—eternally fascinated by her aunt's behavior—as she oversaw the social aspects of the event: popping in and out of the kitchen to check on the catering staff, circulating through the crowd, pausing for a minute or two to take a few quick puffs on a cigarette and swallow what might have been half a glass of water but was more likely neat vodka, before continuing on her rounds. Catharine was perfection—wildly expensive chic clothes, soft confidential tone of voice and almost incomprehensible Anglo-American accent (Gary used to say Catharine spoke Bringlish. Kyra smiled, then almost wept, remembering), hair, nails and manner all just right—but she was slowly getting pissed as a newt and the only people who likely knew it were her two children and Kyra. It showed in a second or two of half-wild staring as Catharine paused in the midst of the crowd, clearly having forgotten the reason for this gathering. It showed in the way her right hand went to the back of her bare neck repeatedly, as if checking to be certain it was still connecting her head to her body. And it showed in her periodic, albeit in no way obvious, search through the rooms for Henry, who had slipped away and gone off somewhere after the service.

"She's afraid he's going to leave her." Coming up beside her, Glenna whispered, "She'll go bonkers if he does, because she can't bear being alone, doesn't know how to do it, and Dillon's off to college in September. She might just finally go right over the edge."

Kyra turned to regard her cousin. "Why do you think that? About Henry, I mean."

"He's satiated with drama. I suspect he regrets ever setting eyes on her. I think he's only stayed as long as he has because he so loves Dillon, and now that Dill's going to be leaving, Henry's probably afraid of finding himself Mummy's sole focus. Do I sound cruel? I don't mean to. But she's so...I don't know.... She's not unintelligent, but there's this tremendous gap between her brain and her emotions. I do so wish I'd known the grandparents, that I knew what went on in that household to make the two daughters turn out the way they have."

"Yes. Me, too."

"She's my mother, Keer, and I do care about her. But all my life I've hated being her child. She has to *imagine* how things feel because she only seems to feel whatever happens directly, personally, to her. And even then, those things aren't really *felt*. It's as if an emotional impact registers, the appropriate page of a manual pops up on a mental screen, and she then delivers the reactions described on the page. She's forever giving me these *ferocious* hugs and telling me how much she *loves* me. But no one who loved me could have cared so little about the effects her decisions made on my life when I was young. Dillon keeps his distance and lets her rattle on, but, clever lad, he's long since stopped listening. None of us knows how to get *through* to her. I keep thinking there's no *there* there. You know?" She stopped abruptly and took hold of Kyra's hand. "God! Listen to me! I'm being completely insensitive. I am sorry."

"No, no. I've thought the very same things about your mother, and I've always been impressed by your coping skills." Kyra's eyes slid over the press of people and she felt suddenly claustrophobic. "I don't know how much more of this I can take."

"Just let me know when you're ready, and we'll go."

"Perhaps another half hour? What d'you think?"

"Whenever you say. Really, I'm sorry for going on about Mummy. It's just that she's getting drunk and there's bound to be some sort of scene... Sorry. I'm doing it again. Forgive me...."

Glenna drifted off, and Kyra shifted her weight from one foot to the other, feeling huge and sweaty in her bulky black dress as she looked around, studying the faces in the crowd and, from moment to moment, checking the time.

Looking affronted, the concierge said, "That girl there's been waiting hours for you, Mrs. Sheridan. Wouldn't take no for an answer. Insisted on waiting."

Kyra turned to see a girl of seventeen or eighteen sitting on the love-seat in the lobby with a small boy at her side. Kyra couldn't think who this could be or what she might want.

"Let me handle it," Glenna volunteered and crossed the lobby, asking, "May I help you?"

"Are you Kyra Latimer?"

"No, I'm her cousin."

"I have to see Kyra Latimer."

"This is not a convenient time—"

"Look, I've been calling for *days*. I *need* to talk to her."

"What's this about? Perhaps I could help."

"I don't think so." Looking past Glenna, the girl asked, "Is that her?" Already on her feet, she picked up a small suitcase, and, towing the little boy along, crossed the lobby. "Are you Kyra Latimer?"

As fascinated now by this pair as she had been earlier by her aunt, Kyra nodded.

"I've got to talk to you." She was a pale, quite pretty girl with dark, angry eyes, a waif's short-cropped light brown hair and a long, vulnerable neck. She had on a bright green long-sleeved shiny polyester dress with a flaring skirt that barely reached the tops of her hollowed thighs. She was thin almost to the point of emaciation, with scrawny arms and the wrists of a five-year-old. The boy wore denim OshKosh overalls with a long-sleeved red plaid shirt buttoned to the neck, tiny sneakers with knotted laces, and soiled white socks. His hands were grimy, a ring of dirt was visible around his neck, his hair looked greasy. Kyra got an impression of long-term neglect and felt a quick flash of anger.

"This really isn't a good time," Kyra began, studying the tot, who looked to be about two years old. She could actually smell him; a reeking little boy with an exquisite, sweet-featured face, large, deep eyes that were fixed unwaveringly on the girl. His sister, Kyra wondered, or his mother?

"It's *important.* Okay? I think we should talk in private. Unless," the girl said tauntingly, "you want the whole world knowing your business."

Kyra looked again into the girl's angry eyes and said, "You'd better come up. But I can only give you a few minutes."

"I don't need more than that."

The four of them moved into the elevator, Glenna eyeing the teenager and the oddly docile, smelly little boy, wondering what on earth this rude and tenacious girl could possibly want with Kyra; and wondering why Kyra hadn't just sent the pair packing.

In the living room, still holding the small suitcase with one hand and the boy with the other, the girl looked meaningfully at Kyra and said, "My birthday is April the sixteenth. That mean anything to you?"

Kyra thought for a moment, then said, "No. Sorry."

"Look," Glenna cut in impatiently. "This really isn't the time to be playing twenty questions—"

"My name is Jennifer Cullen. I was born on April 16, 1955." Again she waited expectantly.

Kyra shook her head, eyes moving back to the silent boy, who stood obediently waiting, gazing now at his tiny feet. His neglected state made her very angry. What did soap and water cost, after all?

"I see. You're going to pretend it never happened. Right?"

"I don't follow." For the briefest space of time, Kyra saw herself striking this girl. Hard. A flash thought, then gone.

Setting down the suitcase and letting go of the boy's hand, Jennifer opened her bag, removed a piece of paper and handed it to Kyra. Glenna moved closer so that she, too, could look at what proved to be the girl's birth certificate. The mother's name was given as Kyra Lee Latimer. The space for the father's name had been left blank. The place of birth was New York, and the date was indeed April 16, 1955.

"You still going to pretend you don't know what I'm talking about?" Jennifer asked with a hurt-angry edge to her voice. "It's taken me a long time to find you. I had this fantasy you'd be, like, glad to see me."

The cousins exchanged a mystified look, then both turned to Jennifer Cullen.

"I'm sorry, truly. But it's an incredible coincidence...or something," Kyra said, feeling her throat thicken. The irony of this was simply staggering—her name on anyone's birth certificate was something she'd never expected to see.

"You're not going to try to tell me there could be *two* Kyra Lee Latimers?"

"No, but it's simply im—"

"What this *means*—" the girl waved the document aggressively in the air between them "—is you're my mother, and Jesse's grandmother."

"It's a coincidence, nothing more!" Glenna said firmly. "I can assure you of that."

"Glenna's right. Perhaps we should sit down," Kyra said, and collapsed into the nearest chair. Was she dreaming? Had she gone mad? If this was escape, it wasn't what she'd had in mind.

"I'll make some tea," Glenna said, falling back on what she'd always considered a fine British delaying tactic. "And then we'll talk about this mix-up."

"Yes," Kyra said distractedly. "Jesse," she addressed the boy at last, "would you like some juice?"

He looked to his mother who, busy returning the birth certificate to her purse, automatically answered, "Sure. Why not?" and glanced at her wristwatch.

Kyra noted this and wondered if Jennifer Cullen was also waiting for a telephone call, or a plane to land. "It's my understanding that adoption records are usually sealed," she said, hoping to introduce a note of sanity into the situation.

Jennifer shrugged. "Not necessarily. I always knew I was adopted. It wasn't, like, a secret or anything."

"But according to that document I would've been sixteen at the time of your birth."

"So? Lots of people have babies at sixteen."

"I was still at boarding school in England then. And I've never *been* pregnant, let alone had a child I gave up for adopt—"

"You're going to *deny* this?" Jennifer cut in again, her tone sharp.

"I'm unable to have children, you see, it's—"

"I can't get *over* this!" Jennifer near-shouted. "I've got the proof right here, but you're going to make out like it never happened. Well, if that's how you want it, fine. I could care less. But Jesse's your grandson, and I'm leaving him with you."

At this, the boy burrowed into the girl's side, as if attempting to disappear into her flesh. And inside Kyra hope flared brilliantly, as if the master switch for a massive bank of spotlights had suddenly been thrown. *Leaving him with me? Leaving him? With me?*

"Oh, no, you're not!" Glenna said from the doorway.

"What're you, her bodyguard or something?" Jennifer snapped. Turning back to Kyra, she said, "Look, I've got a chance to make a new start, but my boyfriend isn't into kids, and there's no one to take Jesse. So he's staying with you and that's all there is to it."

The boy started to cry soundlessly, his face red and contorted, and was clinging now to his mother. Astounded, Kyra could only watch, halfway convinced this was an outrageous dream.

"Cool it, Jess! You promised you'd be good. You *know* I can't take you with me."

Kyra found the boy's misery compelling; she watched him with mounting sympathy, stricken for some reason by his tiny sneakers. And wasn't this too bizarre! She'd lost Gary, but, like some sort of fatality compensation, was being given what she'd always wanted most. This dislikable girl was determined to give Kyra her child.

"You cannot simply abandon the boy here," Glenna said, infuriated.

"I'm *leaving* him with his *grandmother,*" Jennifer said with exaggerated care, as if addressing someone mentally handicapped. "That's not, like, abandoning."

"In the eyes of the law it most certainly is. And Kyra is *not* related to either of you. *How* many *times* must we *tell* you that?"

"I've got my birth certificate, and I've got his. They prove she's *my* mother, which makes her Jesse's *grandmother.* I'm *going,* and Jesse's *staying.* How many *times,*" she mimicked, "must I tell *you* that?"

"This is insane!" Glenna was flabbergasted. "Kyra, you're not actually considering this, are you?"

"What will you do if I refuse to take him?" Kyra asked Jennifer, bemused by her own calm. Aside from that moment when she'd imagined herself striking the girl, there was a dreamlike feeling of inevitability to what was happening. All her adult life she'd wanted a child; now she was going to get one.

"I'll turn him over to Children's Aid or whatever, put him in foster care. I *can't* take him and that's that!"

"What about your parents?" Kyra asked.

"Forget it! They died when our house burned down, like, five years ago. I was out past my curfew that night or I'd've died, too." She made a face as if to say her luck wasn't much but it was better than none at all.

"And the boy's father?" Glenna asked.

"Jess's birth certificate's got a blank there, just like mine," Jennifer declared defiantly, even proudly.

"Kyra, you cannot take this child!" Glenna stated.

"Yes, I can, Glen," she said, touched by the size of the boy, and by his manifest anguish. For a moment, she was overwhelmed by joy at the prospect of his being a part of her life. Then, instantly, she was guilt-stricken for that moment of joy.

"Sure you can." Jennifer jumped in in eager agreement. "I brought all his stuff—"

"Hold on just a goddamned minute!" Glenna barked. "Kyra, a word in private, please?"

The two stepped into the kitchen and in a fierce whisper, Glenna asked, "What on *earth* are you doing? We both know you're not related to those two. You can't take on the responsibility for this boy. You're not *thinking*. There could be all sorts of nasty legal repercussions if you do this."

"If I don't take him, I believe she will turn him over to the authorities. Besides, I want him."

"You're mad!"

"Probably," Kyra agreed. "But why shouldn't I take him? That boy needs someone to look after him, and I need someone to look after."

"This is absolute lunacy! Have you told her you can't have children?"

"She doesn't want to hear or believe that. I'm going to take him." Kyra started back to the living room, but Glenna grabbed her arm.

"If you're determined to do this, let me at least try to protect you. I'll draft something that'll stand up in court, should it ever come to that."

"All right," Kyra said mildly.

Back in the living room, while Kyra bent down and tried without success to get the boy to look at her, Glenna asked Jennifer, "Will you sign some documents if I prepare them?"

Again the young woman checked the time. "What kind of documents?"

"An assignment of guardianship, a letter of intent."

"Sure, whatever. Just so it doesn't take too long. I've got to get to the Port Authority. Listen, Jesse needs to go to the bathroom."

"Keer, may I use your typewriter?"

"Of course." Kyra got up to show Jennifer and the boy to the bathroom as Glenna raced to the rear of the apartment.

Kyra stood on the kitchen threshold. None of it was real, and yet she could hear the clack of the keys as Glenna began typing in the workroom, and beyond the bathroom door she could hear the angry murmur of Jennifer Cullen's voice and the plaintive notes of the boy's crying. As she checked her watch—11:00 p.m. in Paris—she thought that the Fates had a demented sense of timing. Or was this a display of their twisted humor?

CHAPTER 4

"What're you, a lawyer or something?" Jennifer asked mistrustfully, eyeing the several documents Glenna had hastily drafted.

"It so happens that I am. Now, if you're agreeable to the terms I've set out, both you and Kyra will sign—"

"Just give me a pen."

"Hold on. Don't you think you should read these first?"

"Just give me a pen. I don't *care* what's in them." Again, Jennifer checked her watch.

"You *should* care," Glenna said hotly. "Not only are you proposing to walk away from your child, you're also taking advantage of someone who's suffered a great loss and isn't thinking clearly right now." She looked at her cousin, hoping she'd snap out of the trance she seemed to be in, but Kyra was studying the boy intently and appeared not to hear what was being said.

"I can't help that," the young woman said truculently. "I've got my own life to think about." She cast a sour glance at Kyra, who was gazing sadly at the boy as he emitted hiccuping sobs around the begrimed fist he'd jammed into his mouth as if in an effort to hold in his misery by physical means.

"Kyra is *not* your mother," Glenna declared, willing her cousin to start paying attention. For a few seconds she was infuriated by Kyra's unexpected passivity. She glared at her cousin, finding her impossibly lumpish, and wondered how it was possible for Kyra to be so astoundingly beautiful—with her mass of strawberry blond hair, her round green eyes, perfectly proportioned features, and milky, flawless skin—and yet be so obdurate, so unbearably heavy, not just physically but mentally, too. Then, reminding herself of the circumstances, Glenna relented, focusing her displeasure instead on this hatefully callous young woman who patently cared about no one but herself.

"Yeah, right. All that stuff on my birth certificate, that's some *other* Kyra Latimer." She rolled her eyes in disgust. "Okay, so she doesn't want to admit it, and maybe you never knew. Man, what a goddamned joke! My whole life I wanted to meet my real mother, had the great reunion all worked out in my head. Well, this for sure isn't it. She's spaced, and I don't know *what* the hell *you* are."

Ignoring the insult, Glenna kept pushing her point. "You're taking advantage of someone whose husband just died in tragic circumstances. And how can you do this to your son?"

"I really am sorry," Kyra said quietly, her eyes still on the boy so that it was unclear to whom she was speaking. She kept telling herself to wake up, to end this crazy dream or change its direction, but it was as if she were immersed in some gluey substance and couldn't move or think without massive effort.

"Yeah, well." Jennifer shrugged; she was jittery, obviously anxious to get going, and Glenna wondered if she was on drugs. Why else would she have come here, convinced she'd be permitted to leave the boy and go off on her merry way?

"It's too bad about her husband, but she's his grandmother, so Jesse stays with her. End of discussion."

Determined not to let this odious little snip impose her will without challenge, Glenna said, "You're not going anywhere unless you sign these papers. I personally will not allow you to leave the boy here until you do."

"You're the one holding things up," Jennifer argued. "I *told* you I'm ready to sign. So let's get it done. Okay? My boyfriend's waiting. We're going to California."

"How lovely for you." Glenna didn't attempt to conceal her distaste. Thinking aloud, she said, "We need a witness. I suppose the concierge will do. Kyra?"

Kyra looked up blankly. Her awareness was centered entirely on the child, who steadfastly refused to look at her. "Yes, all right," she said, belatedly hearing the question. The boy looked as if he weighed very little, yet his presence was more powerful, more commanding, than anyone else's. He seemed to take up all the available space in her brain.

* * *

The concierge agreed to witness the signatures, and watched with undisguised curiosity as first Jennifer, then Kyra, signed the several pages. At last he accepted Glenna's pen and scrawled his name on the lines she indicated.

Irked by the fact that none of them had taken the time to read what they were putting their names to, Glenna finally signed each page as well. "I want ten more minutes of your time," she told Jennifer, "while I run down the block and make copies of these for you."

"Forget it! I don't want them. I just need to get going." Jennifer tried to free her hand, which the child had grabbed the instant she'd put down the pen, but Jesse hung on. "Let go, Jess! I'm warning you. If I miss that bus I'll *kill* you."

"It would be helpful if we could have an address or phone number where you can be reached," Kyra said, wondering how she could have thought this young woman pretty. There was a meanness to her, a visible self-centeredness that showed in her small, pale-pink-lipsticked mouth and in her somehow flat eyes that she'd enlarged with heavy black liner. All she wanted was to get away from her child, and all the child wanted was to stay with her. His suffering was awful, yet he exercised remarkable restraint for a child who, according to his birth certificate, was three and a half. He stood hanging on to his mother, eyes downcast, as if in the belief that if he didn't look directly at what was happening it might turn out to be something he'd imagined. Perhaps he, like Kyra, felt caught in a harrowing dream. Kyra found herself drawn more and more to him.

"I'll drop you a line when we're settled," Jennifer told Kyra.

"We need some means of communicating with you, the name of a relative or friend. *Something*," Glenna insisted, exasperated. "And we should have Jesse's medical records, too."

"Oh, I've got that stuff." Jennifer rooted around again in her bag and came up with a dog-eared card, listing the inoculations he'd had to date, and his birth certificate.

Glenna was relieved to see that the card bore the name and address of a New Jersey pediatrician who would, at the very least, have Jesse's medical history on file.

"Jess, say good-bye now." Jennifer bent to the boy who at once flung his arms around her neck and hid his face against her shoulder. For a time it seemed he was going to surrender without further fight. But when she attempted to get to her feet, he would not release her, hanging almost suspended from her neck as she struggled to rise. Losing her patience altogether, she ordered, "Let go right now!" He held on tighter. "I *said,* let *go!*" When he still refused, she suddenly heaved herself upright, thrusting Jesse away with the flat of her hands so that he stumbled backward, nearly falling. At once he righted himself and darted back to wrap his arms around her scrawny thigh, holding on obstinately, sobbing in big, nearly noiseless gulps. "Let the hell *go!*" She shoved the boy away and, on her perilous, cork-soled platform shoes, hurried to the door.

"*Wait!*" Kyra called. "Give us an address, or a phone number!"

"I'll be in touch," Jennifer tossed back over her shoulder, bobbling off up the street as fast as she was able, her skinny shins working like pistons.

All at once Jesse bolted, squeezing through the front door just before it closed. Experiencing a sudden rush of fear, Kyra raced after him, emerging onto the sidewalk amazed to see that he was a good half block away, small arms and legs pumping furiously, delivering an eerie high-pitched wail as he chased after his mother.

At the corner, Jennifer had flagged down a cab. She glanced back, saw Jesse and leaped into the car, slamming the door shut just as he reached the curb. He was on the verge of launching himself into the road to follow when Kyra grabbed him by the back of his overalls and lifted him to safety. Arms and legs flailing, he fought with surprising strength, the wail becoming a scream as his entire body strained toward the accelerating cab. Grappling with him, Kyra turned to track the taxi's progress. Jennifer didn't look back. The car shot through the intersection as the light turned red, took the next right with squealing tires, and disappeared from sight.

Jesse fought to get free but Kyra didn't dare set him down for fear he'd run off again. "I'm sorry, Jesse," she said softly. "I know it's not what you want, but you've got to come with me." Tucking him under her arm like an awkward package, she carried him, kicking and keening like an injured cub, back down the street. Under the canopy a thoroughly disgusted Glenna stood waiting.

"You've lost your bloody mind!" Glenna said tiredly. "Have you even the remotest idea what you're doing?"

Stopping dead, Kyra said, "Don't speak to me that way, Glenna. One unpleasant woman was quite enough for today, thank you.

Now and then, I get the impression that you think because I'm fat, or because I don't react as quickly as you'd like, that I'm stupid. Perhaps I am. It's irrelevant just now. I've been given this boy and I intend to keep him. So, in answer to your question, yes, I have a remote idea of what I'm doing." Kyra turned and headed toward the elevator with a chastened Glenna following and the boy still riding her hip, still pummeling her with his fists. "It's getting late," Kyra said with a glance at her watch. "I suppose you'll want to be on your way."

"What are you *saying?* Aren't you coming with me?" a now distraught Glenna asked.

"I've got Jesse."

"I'm all too well aware of that. Don't take umbrage, but could we discuss the situation, please? You're not equipped for him in terms of the apartment, for one thing. For another, regardless of how long and hard you've wished for it, you're in no condition just now to step into instant motherhood. And, objectively, I expect Jesse would feel more at ease in the country with the boys where he can run about, and where there's ample room in the house for the two of you. I really think it would be best if you come with me as planned."

"Perhaps you're right," Kyra said, thinking it was unlikely that Jesse was going to feel at ease, with anyone, anywhere, for quite some time. He was, she observed, struggling less, growing tired. Turning her back to her cousin, Kyra raised the boy up so she could whisper in his ear. "I know you want to run away, Jesse. Lately I've wanted to run away, too. So I understand how you feel. But please don't. I'd really like you to stay."

He remained motionless for a moment, then looked directly into her eyes for the first time.

"Please stay, Jesse," she whispered, her eyes locked to his.

He gazed at her for a few seconds with a disturbingly adult expression of exhausted resignation. She gazed steadily back at him. Then, with great deliberation, keeping watch to see how she reacted, he kicked her in the midriff with all his might. She winced, pretending for his sake that it hurt, because she knew how desperately he wanted to retaliate for the pain he was suffering. "Want to kick me again?" she asked. He shook his head once, sharply, and she set him down. He stood, fists clenched, breathing loudly openmouthed through his tears for several seconds, then began kicking the elevator wall. She placed a hand on his greasy hair, thinking to calm him. He shrugged away from her and continued punishing the wall. Awed by the energy of his upset, she made no further attempt to restrain him.

"I'm afraid you'll come to regret this," Glenna said quietly.

"I will *never* regret this."

"This is a child with problems, if that last hellish exchange with the mother, and his general state, are anything to go by."

"I'm aware of that."

"I hope to God you are." Glenna said nothing further, appalled by the fact that Kyra had acquiesced to what could only be deemed blackmail. Had there been time enough for it, a simple blood test would have proved she and Jennifer Cullen were unrelated. What a bloody mess! But if nothing else, at least Glenna had protected her cousin's rights, and the child's, as well. If that loathsome girl thought she could just one day waltz back into their lives, she was in for a very rude surprise. Without so much as a glance at the documents, she had, in the presence of witnesses, signed away any present or future claim to her son.

Within ten minutes of their setting off, Jesse was asleep in the back seat of the car, looking like a tatty abandoned doll—his head resting against the door, his tiny sneakers pointing straight up, grubby hands limp in his lap.

Kyra was making mental sketches of the layout of the apartment, trying to decide how she might alter it to accommodate Jesse. It wasn't possible. She couldn't give up her workroom, and there was only the one other bedroom. She'd have to move to a larger place.

"I'm honestly confounded by this," Glenna said after a time.

"This isn't quite how I'd imagined it, but I've finally got a child." Kyra sighed and took another look back at Jesse.

"Indeed you do. One badly in need of a bath, not to mention a haircut. Our poppet pongs rather badly."

"Yes, he does," Kyra agreed, relieved. Glenna had capitulated and accepted the situation and Jesse.

"Have you noticed he hasn't uttered a single word? Do you suppose he can speak?" Glenna asked.

"I would imagine he can, if he cares to." He had remarkable skill at making himself understood without using words. It was, Kyra well knew, the gift of all great actors. With a wry inward smile, she thought that Jesse was going to fit perfectly into the family.

Four-year-old Roddy and six-year-old Gage couldn't have been more surprised at discovering they had a new cousin. Being good-natured children, they at once invited Jesse up to the attic playroom to show him their toys. Jesse appeared bewildered—gratified to discover a pair of beings roughly his own size, but not sure he should trust his eyes. He gave the impression of having never before encountered other children. Certainly he seemed as intrigued by Roddy and Gage as they were by him. And intrigue overcoming bewilderment, he allowed himself to be led up to the boys' attic room.

"Who's that?" Cliff asked, watching the boys go off up the stairs.

"We'll explain over a cup of tea," Glenna told him as he embraced Kyra, holding her hard for a long moment before relieving her of the luggage.

"I put the kettle on when I heard you pull in. I'd have come to Catharine's if I hadn't had a court case this afternoon. I'm really sorry about that. How're you holding up, babe?" he asked with concerned fondness.

"I'm okay," she answered, managing an approximation of a smile for the only man in the world she'd have allowed to call her "babe."

"Kyle phoned, by the way. He said he and Beth were going to spend an extra night in the city and come up the day after tomorrow."

"Well, that's good news—a reprieve from the warden. An extra day to prepare ourselves for the beauty queen."

"I knew you'd be pleased." With a smile, Cliff went off to take the bags to the guest rooms.

Kyra followed Glenna to the kitchen and automatically went for the teapot while Glenna opened the refrigerator to get out the casserole the housekeeper had prepared that morning.

"Sorry about getting stroppy with you earlier," Kyra said, holding the empty teapot with both hands, as if for warmth.

"I deserved it."

"Yes, you did, actually. But we'll forget it now."

"I'd appreciate that," Glenna said, still feeling the sting of the accuracy of Kyra's earlier accusation. She *did* occasionally equate her cousin's bulk with a lack of acuity, and it was shameful both to have thought it and also to have been caught out.

A short time later, the three adults were sitting at the kitchen table with the just-poured tea when Kyra suddenly realized that it had been several hours since she'd given any thought to Gary. Stricken, she turned to look out the window at the early evening shadows on the sloping lawn. He was gone, and there would be no more calls from Paris or Frankfurt, no more last-minute cancellations due to storm fronts or icing that sent him home for an extra night. He was gone and she'd actually forgotten about him for more than three hours. It felt almost criminal, as if she were derelict in her obligations as a widow.

A touch, and she looked down to see Glenna's hand covering hers. Lifting her eyes to her cousin's, she intended to smile but her interior circuitry had gone haywire and, to her deep chagrin, she wept instead.

CHAPTER 5

Jesse seemed inclined to do whatever Roddy and Gage did. When Cliff called up to them to get washed and come down to dinner, Kyra, who was upstairs unpacking, stepped into the hall and was heartened to see Jesse follow the boys into the bathroom, where he watched each one washing his hands, then followed suit. But when everyone was seated in the kitchen for dinner, he was clearly at a loss. He stared for some time at the plate of food in front of him, then turned first to one side, then the other, to see how Roddy and Gage were managing, watching them intently. At last, Jesse picked up his fork and tried to use it as his new friends did. He stabbed himself in the lip. Eyes filling, he slowly set the fork down on the rim of the plate.

Kyra got up, took a teaspoon from the drawer, and put it in his hand, saying quietly, "Use this, Jesse."

He craned around to look up at her, his deep brown eyes surprised and grateful, yet cautious, too. She patted him lightly on the head and went back to her seat.

Obviously accustomed to using a spoon, he dug in and methodically ate everything on his plate, then sat scarcely moving, fighting to stay awake, twice saving himself as he was about to topple from the chair.

When Cliff announced, "Okay, guys. Time for group games in the bath," Roddy and Gage jumped down from their chairs and took off at a noisy gallop for the stairs.

"You come, too, Jesse," Cliff invited. "There's plenty of room for all three of you in the tub."

Jesse was instantly poised to take flight, eyes seeking the nearest escape route, as Roddy came scooting back, calling excitedly, "Come on, Jeth! It'th bubble time." Jesse shook his head, one hand fastened to the edge of the table, the other to the chair.

Wisely, Cliff chose not to push it. "Okay, Jess," he said. "I guess you'd prefer to take your bath alone."

Jesse kept on shaking his head until Cliff started to leave, pausing to scoop Roddy up and sling him over his shoulder. Jesse watched somewhat fearfully until they were out of sight.

"This is interesting," Glenna said, starting to clear the table. "We appear to have a phobia about bathing. Which is why, perhaps, we pong so."

"It's all right, Jesse," Kyra told him. "Tonight you don't have to have a bath."

He regarded her with eyes slightly narrowed, as if he didn't believe he was being let off so easily.

"It's been a long day and I can see how sleepy you are," she went on. "So why don't we go up now and get you ready for bed?" She offered him her hand. Ignoring it, he slid down from the chair and followed her up to the small guest room, opposite Roddy and Gage's room.

Lifting his suitcase onto the bed, Kyra opened it to find a mean collection of crumpled, reeking clothes, and an old, very worn and dirty teddy bear. Jesse darted forward, snatched up the bear and backed away to stand holding it tightly to his chest.

"Does your bear have a name, Jesse?" she asked, picking with concealed aversion through the contents of the bag.

She looked over but he merely gazed back at her.

"You don't seem to have any pajamas, or a toothbrush. For tonight we'll borrow a pair of Roddy's, but it looks as if we'll have to buy you some new clothes."

Jesse stood hugging his ragged bear, eyelids beginning to droop, seeming not to hear her.

"Wait here a moment," she told him, "and I'll be right back."

Jesse would have nothing to do with the pajamas. When she attempted to undress him, he shook her off and ran to wedge himself into a corner of the room, where he wound himself into a ball, all the while staring wild-eyed at her and shaking his head.

"Come on, love." She squatted a few feet away, reluctant to crowd in and frighten him more. "You can't sleep in your clothes. You won't be comfortable."

In response, he closed his eyes and bent his head over the bear.

He wasn't going to be undressed without a fight, and she had no desire to force the matter.

"Okay. You'll sleep in your clothes, but only for tonight. Shoes and socks have to come off, though." Tentatively, she reached for his foot. He allowed her to remove first one shoe and then the other, revealing once-white socks with soles stained almost black. She whipped them off before he had any chance to protest, revealing a pair of the filthiest feet she'd ever seen, "Right," she said. "Let's get you washed and your teeth brushed." She stood and held out her hand. Once more he ignored it but deposited the teddy bear on the side of the bed and went with her to the boys' bathroom.

The step stool before the sink was an object of considerable interest to him. He climbed on and off it several times, but stopped at once when she asked him to so that she could sit him on the rim of the sink. After scrubbing his feet (noting his toenails were badly in need of cutting) she patted them dry, then set him back on the stool. His expression was almost comically contorted as she applied a soapy washcloth to his face, ears and neck, but she was gratified that he permitted her to do this much. When at last she presented him with a new toothbrush from the medicine cabinet, he behaved much as he had when confronted with the cutlery at dinner.

"You know how to brush your teeth, don't you?" she asked.

He didn't reply.

"Can you talk, Jesse?"

He stared at her, eyes again fearful.

"Have you ever used a toothbrush?" He shook his head. "Fair enough," she said. "It's easy. I'll teach you. Take the toothbrush, Jesse." She held it out and he accepted it with his left hand. Then, her hand on his wrist, she directed the brush over greenish teeth that looked as if they had never received any attention.

Seeing himself reflected with a mouthful of toothpaste foam, he stopped and smiled at his reflection, then, afraid, his eyes shot to hers in the mirror.

"You do look funny, don't you?" she said, getting an altogether bleak picture of the kind of parent Jennifer had been.

After he'd rinsed his mouth, they started back to the guest room, but at the sound of Cliff's voice reading aloud to his sons, Jesse came to a stop. In a state akin to wonderment, he stood listening for a time before his eyelids once more began to droop.

She lifted him and carried him across the hall, and tucked him into bed with the bear, saying, "I always liked being read stories when I was little. Tomorrow we could get you a storybook of your very own and I could read to you. Would you like that?"

A drowsy nod.

Sensing he might fear being in a strange place in the dark, she left the lamp on the dresser lit and went to the door, where she said, "Sleep well, Jesse. I'll see you in the morning." Unresponsive, he lay with the bear's head pressed to his nose. She closed the door partway and carried the suitcase down to the kitchen, where, with Glenna looking on, she more thoroughly examined the contents of the small bag. "I suppose I'd better put it all into the wash. At least if he won't bathe, he'll have clean clothes to wear."

Nose wrinkled, Glenna declared, "This lot's going straight into the trash. There's a box of things Roddy's outgrown I was planning to take to the Goodwill store. They're in better condition than these disgusting rags. If you'll get the coffee started, I'll go fetch the box from the basement."

Cliff came down while the two women were sorting through Roddy's cast-offs. Helping himself to a cup of coffee, he sat down, watched for a bit, then said, "Mind if I ask how you came to be in possession of that very interesting child, Kyra? Assuming, of course, that he is in your possession."

"It's an unbelievable mistake," Glenna said, and proceeded to recount the details of their encounter with Jennifer Cullen.

When she'd finished, Cliff asked, "Will you keep him, Kyra?"

"Yes, definitely. And I'd like to keep the details between the three of us. I'm going to have some explaining to do to the family, and I've decided to say that Jesse's turning up now is just a curious bit of timing. I think the matter of my name on Jennifer's birth certificate would only confuse things."

"Probably the wisest course," Glenna said, still disturbed by Kyra's having so blithely agreed to take the boy.

"I suppose you've noticed, Kyra," Cliff said, "that the boy seems to have either a hearing or a speech problem."

"Perhaps," Kyra allowed. "Or it could be he's just frightened. Imagine having your mother leave you with total strangers and then literally run away from you!"

"Point taken, but I eavesdropped while he was playing with the boys and he never made a sound," Cliff said. "During dinner he was watching everyone's mouths. I wondered if he was doing a kind of lip-reading rather than actually hearing what was said."

"I don't know," Kyra said helplessly, lacking the energy to defend Jesse properly just then. "He seems to hear and understand me."

"We'll take him to see our pediatrician, have him give Jesse a complete checkup," Glenna decided.

"Why didn't I think of that?" Kyra wondered.

"You've had other things to think about," Glenna said generously. "I'll phone in the morning, see if they can squeeze Jesse in."

"Not only wouldn't he take a bath, he refused to let me undress him," Kyra said. "I had to put him to bed in his clothes."

"For one night we'll live with it, but tomorrow morning that lad's going into the tub. He smells like a goat and I don't want Roddy and Gage getting the idea being dirty's acceptable."

Amused, Cliff said, "No chance of that. They're Mr. Bubble junkies. So, ladies, I'm going to flop in front of the tube for a while, if no one minds."

"No one minds," Glenna said. "I think it's going to be an early night all around. I'm already half asleep and Kyra's showing definite signs of wear and tear."

"I am tired," Kyra admitted.

"I think you'll do well with Jesse," Glenna said out of the blue, ashamed of her behavior throughout the day.

"Really?" Kyra was absurdly pleased by the comment.

"Really. I've always thought you have a wonderful way with children—mine in particular." Glenna looked at the clock and said, "Why not go up and take a nice hot bath? I'll finish here, then pry Cliff away from the TV and drag him off to bed."

Kyra carried her cup to the sink, then came back to kiss Glenna on the top of her head, murmuring, "I'd never have been able to get through this week without you."

"Yes, you would have. And I'm very damned glad I happened to be there to help out with some paperwork today. As for the rest of it, I was rude and patronizing at a time when you needed my support. I behaved like a complete bitch and I'm sorry. You didn't deserve that. Now, don't say a word!" She put a hand over her cousin's mouth. "Just accept my apology. Sleep well, Keer."

* * *

After her bath, Kyra went to check on Jesse. As she peered into the room, her heart seized at the sight of the empty bed. She stood in the doorway, telling herself to stay calm. Jesse couldn't have left the house without someone seeing him. He had to be here. But where? And why, now that it had restarted, was her heart racing so frantically? How had she come to care so immediately for a child she hadn't known existed until only a matter of hours before? And why did the thought of him being gone from her life as abruptly as he'd entered it turn her queasy with dread? *Don't be gone, little boy.*

The bedclothes were pushed aside, the pillow missing. She moved into the room and ducked down to check under the bed. Nothing. Straightening, she looked around the room. The closet door was ajar. She distinctly remembered it being closed. Shakily, she crossed over to ease the door open further. Inside, Jesse lay curled up, asleep on the floor, the bear cradled to his chest. Exhaling tremulously, she debated whether or not to return him to the bed.

Built under the eaves, it was a low-ceilinged closet, a good five feet wide, running almost the entire length of the room. Perhaps, she thought, he felt safer within the enclosed confines of the space; perhaps the dimensions were, for some reason, more to his liking. She got a blanket from the bed, crept into the closet to cover him with it, then sat on her haunches and watched him sleep for a time, breathing in his pungent smell, touched by the way his arm sheltered the teddy bear, and by his features, refined and innocent, in repose.

There was something about this child that she recognized, although she couldn't have articulated what it was. Just a hint of a foundationless familiarity that might have been based on nothing more tangible than her deep fatigue. She was taken, too, by the glimpses she'd had of his sense of humor, by his obvious intelligence and by a certain aged aspect to his gaze. She wished he could tell her about his life, about the things he'd experienced in the three years of his existence.

She awakened just past seven to the laughter of little boys and the mingled aromas of breakfast. Rested for the first time in days, she pulled on her robe, made a quick trip to the bathroom, then peeked into the boys' bedroom. Roddy, the younger and more gregarious of her two young cousins, was acting out a story that had Gage and Jesse in stitches. The sight of tiny Jesse laughing almost soundlessly sent hope darting through her. If he could laugh with such abandon it had to mean that eventually everything would be all right.

After pausing to drag in a breath, Roddy continued his narrative. "Tho, the elephant got very angry and thaid to the mouth, 'You better watch it or I'll thtep on you and quish you flat.'" Gleefully, he stamped his foot several times. "And the mouth thaid, 'You're not very thmart! Don't you know I'm a *mouth?*' 'Oh, no!' cried the elephant. 'It'th a mithtake!' 'Too late now!' thaid the mouth." Roddy made a rodent face, twitching invisible whiskers, and turned his hands into clawed paws. His audience warbled with delight, rocking from side to side in happy anticipation.

Smiling, Kyra slipped away.

In the kitchen Glenna was busy at the stove, and Cliff, suited up for the office, was at the table, a mug of coffee in hand as he read the morning's *New York Times*.

"Sleep well?" he asked Kyra.

"Yes, thank you."

"Hungry I hope," Glenna said, as Kyra poured herself some coffee.

"Yes, actually."

"We'll eat in about ten minutes. What're the boys up to, did you notice?"

"Roddy's telling the other two a story about an elephant and a mouth."

Cliff laughed and put down the paper. "Believe it or not, that's Roddy's version of 'Androcles and the Lion.'"

"It's wonderful, complete with gestures and grimaces," Kyra said. "Are you off to work so early, Cliff?"

"Have to make up for the hours I didn't put in yesterday, and—" he cast a significant look at his wife "—fill in today for both halves of the mom-and-pop operation."

"He loves to layer it on with a trowel," Glenna said mildly. "We have two closings and a divorce action scheduled for today. The two closings are both at the office, and the divorce is a no-fault at the court in Stamford, which shouldn't take more than a minute and a half. He's grizzling in the hope of enlisting your sympathy because he knows he's not getting any of mine." In passing, she swatted her husband on the head with a pot holder.

"You get to stay home," he complained lightheartedly, "and play with Kyra and the boys."

"I'll gladly do the closings and the divorce if you'd like to ferry Keer and Young Master Pong about to shop for clothes, then do the marketing and fix dinner."

"Forget I spoke!" Cliff downed the last of his coffee and got up. "I'll see you both later." He planted a kiss on the nape of his wife's neck, kissed Kyra's cheek, then went to the foot of the stairs.

"Old Gulliver's leaving now!" he shouted. "Come kiss me good-bye, Lilliputians!"

Roddy and Gage came thundering down to fling themselves at their father. Kyra wandered over to the doorway to watch.

Jesse stood near the top of the stairs, mouth slightly open, his expression a blend of wonderment and envy as he watched the two boys climbing over each other to kiss their father good-bye. Unblinking, wide-eyed, the tiny child popped a thumb into his mouth and stood sucking on it thoughtfully.

For a few seconds, she thought how surprised Gary would be when he got home and found Jesse. Then the grief kicked in, constricting her throat, filling her eyes. She fought it off as Cliff looked up and waved to Jesse, saying, "See you later, puppy," and the thumb was instantly plucked from the boy's mouth and hidden behind his back.

Kyra wanted to say, It's all right, Jesse. Suck your thumb if you like. No one here will mind. Sadly, though, she doubted he'd believe her. She was going to have to find ways to assure him that it was okay to laugh at his reflection and to find step stools amusing; to convince him that no one would be in the least upset if he behaved like a small child.

CHAPTER 6

The three boys were in the attic playroom after breakfast when Kyra came up to tell Jesse it was time for his bath. At once he looked around for a way out. Seeing none, he ran to the far end of the attic and, as on the night before, wedged himself into a corner. Thinking this was some kind of game, Roddy and Gage chortled merrily, egging him on. As Kyra approached, Jesse took off again, heading for the stairs and freedom, and the boys realized it wasn't a game.

"What's the matter?" Gage asked, turning to see Jesse run smack into his mother, who got a grip on the boy but had difficulty maintaining it as he fought to get away from her.

"Jesse doesn't seem to like baths," Kyra answered, worried.

Ever the conciliator, Gage went to where his mother was struggling with a panic-stricken, tearfully red-faced Jesse, and said, "Baths are fun, Jess. There's nothing to be scared of. If you want, you can play with my bath toys."

"Yeah!" Roddy came loping over. "Loth of bubbleth, Jeth, and you can play with my toyth, too."

Jesse fought on, trying with all his might to free himself from Glenna's hold.

"Why's he screaming?" Gage asked Kyra, becoming alarmed. "What's wrong with him?"

"It would be best if you two went to play outside," she told the brothers, removing Jesse from Glenna's grasp and tucking the writhing boy under her arm so that his kicking feet and flailing fists could connect only with air.

"Why?" Gage wanted to know.

"I wanna thtay," Roddy said, edging closer to his brother.

"That's not a good idea," Glenna told them. "It's only going to upset Jesse more."

"But *why's* it gonna upset him?" Gage kept on.

"I don't honestly know," Glenna admitted, the three of them watching Kyra cart the now howling Jesse off down the stairs. "His mother went away and left him yesterday and that was very distressing for him. And he hasn't had time to get to know any of us, so it could be he's afraid we're going to hurt him."

"But we'd *never!*" Gage was shocked.

"Of course not. But Jesse doesn't know that. And he really has to have a bath because he's awfully dirty and doesn't smell too nice."

"Yeah." Whispering, Roddy said, "He ith kind of thtinky. But I like him, Mum."

"I know you do, and you don't want him to be upset. Do you?" Both boys shook their heads. "Of course not. That's why it would be easier for everybody if you two go outside to play while Kyra and I get Jesse cleaned up. He'll come out to join you after his bath. Okay?"

"Okay," Gage said. "C'mon, Rod. Let's go climb on the jungle gym."

In the bathroom, with Jesse continuing to struggle fiercely under her arm, Kyra got the water started in the tub. Then she stood him on his feet and, holding him firmly by the shoulders, tried to get him to listen to her. "No one's going to harm you, Jesse. It's only a bath. Look, we'll put in the Mr. Bubble now."

He heard her out, but the instant she stopped speaking he started howling again and trying to wrench himself free.

"You're going into the tub, my lad," Glenna said firmly, "so there's no point carrying on this way. Keer, you keep hold of him while I get these clothes off."

Jesse fought furiously, sobbing wretchedly as the two women undressed him. As the clothes came off piece by piece, the two women were silenced by the array of injuries and bruises that covered the boy's undernourished body—fading yellow-green bruises, newer, overlapping purple-red ones; the pronounced imprint of an adult's grip on his thin upper arm, an alarmingly large, dark blue and deep red region on his lower back that looked puffy and painful; long red weals on his upper back that might have been made by a belt, and many crusty round inflamed areas on his inner arms that looked very like cigarette burns. All over him were scars—old ones gone white, new ones still red.

"Would you ring your pediatrician, please, Glenna?" Kyra asked in a voice gone husky. "Explain, and ask if he'll see Jesse today."

"Yes. I'll...I'll phone right now." Glenna turned and raced off to the telephone.

Kyra reached for a tissue and blotted his face, saying, "It's only a bath, Jesse. No one here will hurt you."

His sobs continuing, arms wrapped around himself, his eyes would not meet hers. Confronted by the indisputable evidence of something she'd previously only read about and had never imagined she might encounter, she felt miserably inadequate. "Just a bath to get you clean," she said softly. "That's all. You have my promise, Jesse. And I always, *always* keep my promises."

He looked at the frothy surface of the water and, finally, at her.

"You'll feel so much better once you're in the tub. And wouldn't you like to be clean? I hate being grubby. Don't you? It makes me feel as if I'm the most horrible creature in the universe, as if I'm something that should be living in a cave." At this there was a flicker of something in his eyes. "It's a nasty feeling, isn't it, being dirty? Shall I help you in?" she asked, holding out her hands.

Chest heaving, clearly defined ribs pushing in and out against the scant flesh, he rubbed his eyes with his fists, and nodded in assent.

Handling him with great care, she lifted him into the water.

He sat for a time, his panic ebbing, then tentatively poked at a bubble. A quick look to see how she was going to respond. Kyra smiled. His breathing still shuddery, he allowed his hand to fall back beneath the water as if too fatigued to play.

Kyra sat on her heels, waiting for him to relax, a terrible, unprecedented anger building inside her. What Jennifer had done, or allowed to be done, to this child was indefensible, unforgivable. Kyra had never been struck, nor had she ever raised her hand to anyone, but had she known where Jennifer was, she'd have gone there that instant and beaten her to a bloody pulp with her fists.

From the doorway Glenna said, "We're set with Renny for two-fifteen." Moving to the side of the tub, she handed Kyra the soap and a washcloth, then lifted Jesse's chin and gave him an encouraging smile. "Not too bad, is it, poppet? Loads of lovely bubbles. And when you're done, we've got some of Roddy's clothes for you to wear. You like him, so it'll be fun to have some of his things, won't it?"

Jesse's eyes slid away to Kyra, who was lathering up the wash-cloth. He watched alertly, shoulders stiff with apprehension.

"I'll leave you two to get on with it," Glenna said, seeing that her presence was keeping the boy's tension level high.

Kyra longed to know what Jesse was thinking as she cautiously began bathing him. She was accustomed to Roddy and Gage, had been handling them all their lives. But they were whole, happy children who didn't require the kind of ongoing softly spoken encouragement this boy did, or the lightest, gentlest touch. It took ages to rid his body of what seemed to be weeks' worth of dirt, but finally he was clean from top to bottom, and sat with a certain glow to him, poking at the last remaining bubbles, now and again shaken by a residual sob.

"Time to come out, Jess." Kyra plucked him from the tub and wrapped him carefully in an oversize towel.

Compliant now, he allowed himself to be patted dry, his hair to be parted and combed, all the while his eyes steadily reading hers. Giving in to impulse, Kyra enfolded him in a cautious embrace. A mistake. He went rigid; his breathing turned loud and panicky. Quickly she let go, and after a moment started to dress him. He pulled away, making it clear he would dress himself. She sat back on her heels and let him, helping only when it came to the shoelaces he couldn't manage.

To her surprise, he climbed up on the step stool to have a look at himself in the mirror. He couldn't see, so she stood him on the edge of the sink for a better view.

"You look very nice, Jess."

He nodded soberly, running his palm appreciatively over one sleeve of his new yellow rugby shirt before indicating he wanted down.

For quite some time after he'd gone running off to join Roddy and Gage outside she continued to feel the impression of his hard little body, and to see the terror that had twisted his features.

"She ought to be in jail!" Kyra fumed.

"Perhaps it was the boyfriend," Glenna said. "Jesse seemed very attached to Jennifer, and she did say the boyfriend wasn't 'into kids.'"

"Whether or not she hurt him, she certainly knew it was happening and that makes her every bit as much a criminal!"

"Obviously this is why she wouldn't provide us with any means of communicating with her. She knows damned well she'd be held legally responsible for his condition."

"You're probably right. That hadn't occurred to me."

"Let me ask you something, Keer. What will you do if she turns up in a week or a month saying she's changed her mind and wants her son back?"

"I'll see her in court first, let her answer to a judge for what's been done to Jesse!"

"I was hoping you'd say that. But it'll never happen. Those papers she signed will prevent that. While you were busy upstairs, I took the liberty of phoning his former pediatrician."

"What did he say?" Kyra asked.

"He was rather reluctant to discuss Jesse with me. I could've been anyone and he does have confidentiality on his side. But when I got specific about why I was calling, he admitted that he hasn't seen Jesse in almost a year, but he saw no evidence of abuse the last time he did see him."

"So, either that was when the boyfriend appeared on the scene and began battering Jesse, or it's when Jennifer herself started."

"That's about it." Glenna glanced at the time, saying, "Okay. Why don't we round up the boys and go buy Jesse pajamas and some shoes? Then we'll take the kids to lunch at McDonald's before we see the pediatrician. Sound okay?"

"Fine."

"You're upset."

"I'm well beyond mere upset. How anyone could *do* that to a child?"

"I honestly don't know. But it infuriates me. People can be such *animals.* Now, I hate to change the subject, but if we're going to get everything done, we really should be on our way. Unless you'd prefer to put off the shopping and have lunch here."

"No, Jesse needs quite a few things. And I expect McDonald's would be a treat for him."

"Right, then. Five minutes and we're off." Glenna grabbed her handbag and keys, then went to get the boys.

Kyra remained at the table, closing her eyes as Gary suddenly strolled through her mind on a treadmill of memory. She was shocked again and again by the overwhelming fact of his absence. How could he be gone when he was still so real, so nearly tangible to her? Death was an evil trick for the Fates to play on an unprepared mind. That last casual good-bye, and the attending dialogue, ran once more, unaltered, through her brain. The words would never have any more or less significance than they'd had at the time. And all the things she hadn't said that day ate away at her like avid little rodents, using tattered fragments of her guilt to make a sizable nest inside her skull.

She knew she was indulging in self-pity but she craved the sight of her husband and the sound of his laughter, because she had doubts about her ability to provide Jesse with what he needed. What if she made mistakes that compounded the damage that had already been done? Oh, stop it! she told herself. *Her* fears were of no consequence. She was an adult, well able to take care of herself. But Jesse was completely powerless, and *his* fears were legitimate. So from this point on there'd be no more fretting about her capabilities. Whatever it took, she would keep Jesse safe.

Renny Hogan was a massive presence, tall and broad, with a headful of graying hair, a penetrating gaze, and a plainspoken, unapologetic approach that children appreciated, while their parents often did not.

He greeted Kyra with a brisk handshake before hoisting Jesse onto the examining table, saying, "My name is Renny. I'm a pediatrician. Know what that is?"

Jesse nodded.

"It's been a while since you've seen your own doctor, hasn't it?"

Again, the boy nodded.

"I know that because you've missed some of your shots," Renny said, deftly removing Jesse's outer clothes. "But don't worry. We'll save those for your next visit. Okay?"

A relieved Jesse nodded a third time.

Kyra sat quietly and watched the doctor turn Jesse this way and that, humming under his breath as he examined him, looking closely at the circular wounds on his inner arms. Several times he asked, "Does this hurt?" as he palpated areas of the boy's abdomen. Each time Jesse shook his head, no. Renny looked in his mouth, in his eyes and ears, listened to his lungs, and tested his reflexes. At last, he asked, "Anything hurt, Jesse? Anything bothering you you'd like to tell me about?"

Jesse's eyes went to Kyra and he shook his head.

"Tell you what, Jesse. You sit here a minute, and I'll send Sally in to keep you company while I have a word with your...with Kyra. Okay?" He stepped out into the hall and summoned the nurse, who came bustling in; then he showed Kyra into his office.

Sinking into a capacious swivel chair, he said, "Glenna gave me a quick rundown over the phone, so I know Jesse's only been in your care for a couple of days. But somebody's been using that child as a football and a human ashtray, and God only knows what else. It makes me madder'n hell."

"Me, too."

"If this was local, I'd be on the phone to the police so fast it'd make your head swim. But it isn't, so I won't. I'll keep records, though, in case they're ever needed."

"That's a good idea."

"I don't care for that bruising on his lower back. I'd like to keep an eye on it, make sure there's no internal damage. From the size and position of the hematoma I'd say he was kicked, and hard."

"Bastards!" Kyra clenched her fists.

"Personally, I'd like to beat the stuffing out of people who treat kids this way. And I see more of them than you'd ever believe. Glenna seems to think his hearing may be impaired. I haven't found any evidence of that, but I'd like to do a couple of tests, and while I'm at it see if I can't get him to open up a little."

"Whatever you think is necessary. I'll wait in the reception area." She went to the door, pausing to say, "As you said, it hasn't been very long, but I'm fond of Jesse. He seems very...valiant, very... I like him."

"Most people wouldn't take on a kid like him," he said. "You get points in my book for that. We'll talk some more after I've completed my exam."

Glenna was reading an old issue of *Good Housekeeping* while Roddy and Gage played with a well-used collection of oversize wooden trucks and trains.

"So?" Glenna asked, setting aside the magazine as Kyra sat down next to her.

"He's not finished yet. We agreed it was best for me to wait out here." In an undertone so the boys wouldn't hear, she said, "I don't like the world right now, Glen. I really don't."

"We have to live in it," Glenna said with a shrug. "We try to make safe islands for ourselves and the people we care about. Not ideal, but we do the best we can with what we're given."

Clichés. In the worst possible situations, that seemed to be all people could think of to say. Kyra fell silent, watching Roddy propel himself around the room atop a tractor-trailer truck, despair falling over her like a sudden ice shower as an image came to her of someone holding a lit cigarette to the tender, vulnerable flesh of a toddler's arm. She blinked back tears, pushing away the image. "This is hard," she said at last.

"That it is," Glenna said. "Bloody hard."

Jesse came running into the waiting room and went directly to Roddy, wanting to ride with him on the truck. Renny appeared a few moments later and beckoned to Kyra.

Back in his office, he said, "There's nothing wrong with Jesse's hearing, and he speaks exceptionally well for a child his age."

"He does? That's wonderful!"

"He's a *very* intelligent kid who was told to be seen and not heard, and had the lesson driven home to him in no uncertain terms. I promised him I wouldn't repeat the rest of what he told me, and I won't."

"No, you shouldn't," she said quickly. "I wouldn't be happy hearing things he didn't want me to know."

He nodded at her approvingly, then continued. "He's malnourished, but with vitamin supplements and a decent diet he should catch up pretty fast. Get him some Flintstones. The kids don't mind taking them. I'd like to watch that hematoma, so bring him back to see me in a few days. I'll give him his shots then, too. Get some Neosporin for those burns, and have his teeth checked. He's never been to a dentist. That's about it. If you have any problems, any questions, anything at all, call me. My best advice is: Give him time, Kyra, and be patient. Kids like Jesse need a *whole lot* of understanding and latitude."

"Oh, I'm prepared to give him whatever he needs. Jesse is an unexpected gift and I will treasure him."

Renny Hogan smiled for the first time. "I have a hunch he's going to feel the same way about you."

CHAPTER 7

That night at bedtime Jesse put up no fight about getting undressed although, as usual, he refused any help. It took him a while but he managed to get into the bright blue pajamas with an airplane motif that Kyra had allowed him to choose. Then he picked up his new hand-me-down clothes and draped them carefully over the back of the chair. Briefly, admiringly, he stroked the rugby shirt before making his way to the bathroom to wash his face and hands and to demonstrate his new skill with a toothbrush. He climbed on and off the step stool a couple of times, a barely discernible smile uptilting the corners of his mouth as he glanced over at Kyra to see how she was taking this. When she made no attempt to stop him, he climbed up a final time, took Gage's comb, wet it under the tap as he'd seen Gage do, then combed his hair.

"Well done, Jesse," she said as he contemplated his reflection and she studied his lovely, fresh-scrubbed face.

He turned to look at her assessingly, then, reassured by her smile, replaced the comb, got down from the stool and went back across the hall to the guest room to clamber onto the bed.

With the bear pressed tight under his nose, he listened, entranced, as Kyra read him the beginning of *Stuart Little*. When she looked up, his thumb was in his mouth and he was struggling to keep his eyes from closing. Getting up, she touched her hand to his cheek, whispered, "Sleep well," and again left the lamp on the dresser burning and the door ajar. After kissing the sleepy-warm faces of Roddy and Gage, she went downstairs.

Seated at the kitchen table, she said, "It's just occurred to me that I've got to get Jesse a passport. I promised Mother I'd come for a visit, and I couldn't possibly leave him behind."

"Of course you couldn't," Glenna said. "It should be simple enough to arrange. As a minor, he'll travel on your passport, and yours is current, isn't it?"

"I just renewed it last year."

"Good. I'll be happy to take care of the appropriate documentation for you." She paused for a moment, then said, "Look, I hate to be indelicate, but will you be all right for money, Keer?"

"I think so. I have our savings, the checking accounts. And there'll be some insurance money. Gary had several policies. I haven't looked at any of them in ages so I can't say how much I'll receive." She stopped speaking, feeling as if the temporary sutures protecting the wound in her chest had come unknotted.

Glenna saw her cousin drift away, her eyes locking on some point above the stove, and she had to remind herself of how very recent Gary's death was. Why did everyone, herself shamefully included, want people to rush through their grief? Time was needed to adapt to your new status—as orphan, or widow. So she sat in silence, observing that Kyra's face, like that of so many weighty women, was virtually without lines and, as a result, appeared almost preternaturally youthful. It was a face of such glorious perfection that Glenna had, on countless occasions, seen men so unable to take their eyes off Kyra that they'd walked smack into walls, or stumbled over fire hydrants.

"Why not turn everything over to me and let me take care of settling the estate for you?" Glenna offered, at last breaking the silence and drawing Kyra back. "I really would like to help."

It took several seconds for Kyra to absorb what had been said before she replied. "I'd appreciate it, Glen. Thank you. The very thought of sitting down to go through it all..."

"Leave it to us. Cliff and I will see to everything."

"What time did Kyle say he and Beth were arriving tomorrow?"

"They're getting into Darien at noon. Cliff will fetch them from the station while you and I put together a real Sunday lunch with a roast and Yorkshire pudding. Dear stupid Beth will whinge about how we're playing hell with her diet and eat half a potato and a few peas, while Kyle stuffs himself and waxes poetic over the airy perfection of my Yorkshire pudding."

Kyra smiled. It was true: Kyle was capable of performing entire monologues on subjects that scarcely warranted comment.

"She's such an utter dimwit," Kyra said. "I've never understood what he sees in her."

"Maybe she reflects well on him but doesn't detract attention. He *is* an actor, after all."

"I don't know if that's valid. Mother's not in the least like that."

"She doesn't have to be. She's the real thing."

"So is Kyle," she said defending her brother. "He's very gifted."

"Undeniably. But your mother is a natural. I think Kyle has to work hard to make an impact, while all Aunt Octavia has to do is walk onto a stage. People are riveted, stunned. You know that's true. We've been watching her do it all our lives. I've also seen Kyle endlessly rehearse every last little detail, right down to his vocal inflection. And that's what wows his audiences. He's a gifted perfectionist, but she's *great.*"

"Perhaps," Kyra conceded. Her thoughts bobbing haphazardly like small craft that had slipped their moorings, she said, "You know, I keep trying to figure out how my name came to be on that girl's birth certificate."

"It's not that hard to imagine. A young girl goes to one of those homes for unwed mothers, signs in as Kyra Latimer, and that's that. Who's going to insist on proof of her identity? Those establishments are concerned primarily with adopting out the babies. There's serious money in it, you know."

"But how would some girl in Manhattan twenty-odd years ago have known the precise details about my date and place of birth?"

"That, I admit, is a mystery."

"What is?" Cliff asked, coming in from the den. "Are we having coffee?"

"We are," Glenna answered, getting up to prepare it.

"You didn't have to interrupt your conversation. I could've put the pot on."

"Then why didn't you?" Glenna asked, holding the carafe under the faucet.

"I would've, but you didn't give me a chance." He went over and nuzzled his nose into his wife's neck.

"Go away." Glenna laughed.

Kyra averted her eyes, their intimacy sharpening her sense of aloneness. *Widow.* Unthinkable. Widows were elderly remains, the artifacts of ancient marriages, gradually decaying conjugal amputees. How could she be one of them? But she was. The edges of the wound seemed to be slowly spreading, the surrounding flesh beginning to tear, the resulting ache extending into her bones. Would it ever end? Catching Glenna's eyes on her and reading the sympathy there, Kyra knew she was going to have to stop her mind from its meandering or people would begin finding her tiresome. And she hated being caught in emotional displays, just as she hated the idea of anyone discovering that she'd taken to carrying Gary's airline insignia in her pocket, touching its sharp wingtips from time to time in the course of a day; or that she slept each night in some article of his clothing.

"So what's the mystery?" Cliff asked, sitting down opposite Kyra at the table.

"How my vital statistics came to be on Jennifer Cullen's birth certificate."

He sat, chin in hand, considering the possibilities. "Maybe you lost your purse once upon a time. Someone found it and made use of the contents."

Kyra thought about that, enjoying Cliff's profile as he turned to look over at his wife. If anyone had asked her to describe him, she'd have said he was as comfortable, appealing and unpretentious as a flannel bathrobe. With sandy-brown hair, he had a high forehead, round blue eyes, a longish nose, a wide mouth, and a strong squared chin. He was about six feet tall and had been stick-thin when he'd first met Glenna. In recent years he'd filled out some so that now he was merely lean. He claimed to be "anti-intellectual," yet he had one of the keenest minds Kyra had ever encountered. He read voraciously and loved all the arts, encouraging his sons to sing and dance, if the spirit moved them, as well as to play traditional sports. His, Kyra thought, was the predominant influence in this household. In his quiet fashion, Cliff served as both anchor and inspiration for Glenna and the boys.

"Recall anything like that?" Cliff asked Kyra as Glenna got an ashtray, lit one of her occasional after-dinner cigarettes and slid back into her seat.

"Kyle and I were here the summer of '54," Kyra remembered. "Mother was rehearsing a new show for Broadway and we came over to spend the summer with her. Kyle spent every free moment hanging about the theater, and I went to all the galleries and museums.

"One afternoon just before Kyle and I were due to fly home,

Mother and I went shopping. When it came time to pay, it turned out she'd forgotten her credit cards. She said never mind, we'd use the one she'd given me for emergencies. But my wallet wasn't in my bag. I took everything out, dumped the whole thing on the floor of the shop. No wallet. I was very upset. Mother kept saying it wasn't important, we'd undoubtedly find it back at the apartment. But we didn't.

"Kyle insisted that I'd been the victim of a pickpocket, but I knew I hadn't been. There wasn't a single moment that day when I didn't have a good solid grip on my bag."

"Aside from the credit card, what else was in it?" Cliff asked. "A copy of your birth certificate, perhaps?"

"No. But I did have a learner's driving permit, library tickets, bits and pieces."

"I'd say that's your answer," Cliff said. "Someone got hold of your ID and used it."

"Seems a bit far-fetched," Glenna said, getting up to pour the coffee.

"It's going to niggle me, not knowing," Kyra said.

"Now that you've got Jesse, what'll you do if you have to go on location for a movie?" Cliff asked.

"I'll take him with me, or maybe I'll just concentrate on theater work, stay in one place. I haven't thought that far ahead."

"Well, don't rush into anything. Okay? It's not a good idea to make important decisions at a time like this."

"No, I won't. I couldn't, in any case. My brain's not firing on all cylinders." Kyra sat back, thinking about that long-lost wallet. For curiosity's sake, she wished she had some answers. But now that she had Jesse, she didn't really care how he'd come into her life.

She wasn't surprised to find Jesse's bed empty for a second time. She opened the closet door and there he was, asleep on the floor, with the pillow and his bear. She got the blanket from the bed, crept in to cover him and then sat on her haunches, watching him sleep.

He touched her so, this gallant tot who had fought ferociously to stay with a mother who'd sanctioned his abuse. Understandable, she thought, with a sigh. Better the devil you know.

After adjusting the blanket so he wouldn't get chilled in the centrally cooled air, she went to her room. The light out, she lay for a long time, unable to sleep, listening to the sundry small sounds of the house. Then, as if slipping down a muddy slope, she tumbled into the grief. Glad of the thick rural darkness that shrouded the room, she turned onto her side in the too-short bed, and wept into the pillow. Eventually, the insignia clutched in her hand, she fell asleep.

She was thrown by the emphatic insistence of her brother's embrace. He held her close, whispering, "We didn't get a chance to talk at the funeral and when I tried to find you during the reception, you and Glenna had gone. I haven't been able to stop thinking about you, worrying. How are you, Kyra?"

"Oh, all right, really."

Holding her at arm's length, Kyle gazed into her eyes. She gazed back at him—endlessly intrigued by their sameness—as if into a mirror that distorted gender but little else. "If there's anything I can do, *anything,* you will let me know, won't you?"

She nodded, wondering if this was real. It certainly wasn't typical of the Kyle she'd always known.

"I've been thinking hard the past few days, about all sorts of things, and I'd like us to talk later. It's time we did, don't you think?"

"Perhaps it is," she said, aware that Beth, like a pretty but unfortunately slow-witted child, was waiting her turn to speak.

Kyra moved significantly, and Kyle, never one to miss a cue, released her. Then Beth, with a big, completely inappropriate smile that showed her flawless teeth, said, "*So* good to see you, Kyra. *How* are you getting *on? Such* a difficult time. Kyle's been terribly concerned about you. Really, *terribly.*"

Oh, God! Kyra thought. *Somebody make her stop!* "I'm quite all right, thank you," she said, her tolerance for this well-born British ninny at its lowest point ever.

"You *look* well, darling, in spite of everything!" Her eyes bright, Beth said, "Isn't it funny? You look exactly like Kyle and I always forget that. I'm *such* a silly! But, look at you! You've lost weight and it's *so* becoming. If you keep on the way you're going, you'll be normal in no time at all."

Kyra found herself fighting down an urge to pick up her sister-in-law and bounce her off the wall. She could almost see the skinny wretch colliding with the lathe-and-plaster surface before slithering to the floor in a startled heap.

"Beth, come give me a hand in the kitchen, would you? There's a love," Glenna said, taking the younger woman firmly by the upper arm and towing her off.

Kyra turned back to see that her brother looked mortified. What was going on? He seemed to have gone completely out of character.

"How can you *bear* her?" Kyra asked in an undertone. "She's such a bloody idiot!"

Taken off guard, Kyle stared at her for a moment. Kyra stared right back at him. Then something in the air between them dissolved and they both laughed loudly. Apparently pleased by this momentous departure from their usual manner of dealing, Kyle hugged her again.

"I *can't* bear her," he confessed in a low voice. "That's part of what I want to talk to you about."

"All right, then. After lunch, I promise. How was Auntie Cath?"

"Mad as a hatter—as if that's news. But Kyra, you're a mother now! Cliff was telling us a bit about one of the agencies coming through for you with Jesse. Incredible timing. And I caught a glimpse of him hiding behind a tree outside. He's an adorable little chap. I'm happy for you. Truly. I know how long you've wanted a child."

"Jesse and I are still sussing each other out, but I'm very glad to have him."

"I'm sure you are."

Again looking at her brother, she said, "It's good to see you, Kyle."

"It's good to see you, too, old thing."

"We've been doing well here, breaking down some sort of wall. If you go all public school on me now, I swear I'll do you an injury. I *hate* that 'old thing,' 'old girl' rubbish."

Eyebrows lifting, he said, "I'm not used to your saying what you think, sister mine." Beginning to smile, he said, "I like it. Keep it up, please. Now, tell me the truth. *Are* you all right?"

"No. I'm in pieces. But Jesse helps keep me distracted."

"Poor you. I'm having a hard time accepting that Gary's gone, so it must be sheer hell for you." He heard a car door slam and looked out the front door, saying, "I'd better go give Cliff a hand with the bags. Mother sends her love, by the way. She rang

Catharine last night to see how things had gone. They were on the blower for a good half hour. Henry got so bored or fed up—hard to say which—he went out to buy a newspaper and didn't come home until after midnight. There's definitely trouble brewing on that front." He looked through the door again, saw Cliff grappling with the luggage and said, "You and I have a date later. Don't forget!" With that, he hurried out to give Cliff a hand.

Through the open door Kyra saw the three boys chasing one another across the lawn. She watched for a few moments, relieved at how readily Kyle had accepted her being in possession of Jesse. One hurdle mastered. Clenching her teeth at the thought of dealing with Beth but unable, in good conscience, to leave Glenna alone to cope with her, Kyra took a deep breath and went to the kitchen.

CHAPTER 8

Kyle's relationship with his wife had puzzled Kyra from the start because it seemed so out of character for him to take up with a woman like Beth. The pampered daughter of wealthy parents, Beth had signed on with a modeling agency at the age of sixteen. Although she was only five-foot-eight, she was such an alluring example of perfect androgyny—with the wide square shoulders and slim hips of a male, and the face and full breasts of a female—that photographers and editors went mad for her. Now, at twenty-seven, she had appeared countless times on the covers of fashion magazines, and had earned and frittered away a sizable fortune.

She was best appreciated in close-ups that showed the contrast between the blackness of her hair and the pale purity of her complexion; tight head-shots that focused attention on the bright blue of her enormous eyes, on her pouty lips, prominent cheekbones, and short, chiseled nose. In person, she was painfully thin and astonishingly dumb. One could say almost anything to her, and she'd make a show of serious consideration before replying with either a non sequitur or some remarkably stupid comment. At the wedding reception, Octavia had whispered to Kyra, "The child has the face of a Botticelli angel and the brain of a kumquat."

Beth spoke in captions, favoring vocal italics on adverbs. Shoes were of singular importance to her and, according to Kyle, she had hundreds of pairs. She also had a substantial mental catalog of diets and could, without hesitation, suggest the perfect one at any time, to anyone. She herself didn't bother with anything as tedious as a formal diet, but lived on black coffee, Dunhill cigarettes, the occasional slice of unbuttered toast and, just prior to a shoot, three or four pieces of Kleenex. "They're brill!" she'd explain happily, chewing away. "They bulk up the tum-tum, so it thinks it's eaten. And then you're not hungry."

As Kyra entered the kitchen, Beth, with a vegetable peeler in one hand and a potato in the other, her face the essence of bewilderment, was asking Glenna, "How does this work again?"

"I'll do it," Kyra offered. "You sit down and keep us company, Beth. Tell us where you've been and what you've been doing lately."

"Oh, *blessings.*" Gladly surrendering potato and peeler, she looked around, asking, "Ashtray?"

"Cupboard above the stove," Glenna said, vigorously stirring the batter for Yorkshire pudding.

"T'rific!" Beth found an ashtray, settled at the table, and lit a Dunhill with her gold Cartier lighter. "*Such* a super house," she declared, exhaling a plume of smoke toward the ceiling. "And the *boys are so* heaven! Another year or two, Kyle and I plan to start having babies. Mums and Daddy are *simply* desperate for more sproggies. As if Freddy's two aren't *enough* for them!"

Working side by side, their backs to Beth, Glenna turned slightly to Kyra and rolled her eyes. Kyra swallowed a laugh and went on peeling the potatoes.

"And *Kyra!* Cliff was telling us that *adorable* sprout I saw outside is actually yours. I am *so* jealous! Oh! And guess what! I've got another cover for American *Vogue.* I'll be spending a month in Morocco. *Bliss!* If it's not too hot, of course..."

On and on she went, one thought colliding with another like bumper cars at a fun fair, while the cousins avoided eye contact for fear of breaking up. Like most egotists, Beth had no sense of humor—especially about herself. To laugh at her would be on a par with kicking a kitten.

Finally, the potatoes were in a pot on the stove, the pudding was ready to go in the oven, the roast was underway, and Beth's monologue hadn't faltered for an instant. Rinsing her hands, Kyra looked through the window and saw the boys come running across the front lawn.

Roddy was first into the kitchen, his sneakers squeaking on the linoleum as he skidded over to his mother, asking, "When'th lunch? We're thtarving!"

Gage was right behind his brother, echoing, "Starving, Mom."

Jesse was the last one in.

Beth exclaimed, "*Sweetie!*" and reached out for him, a just-lit cigarette between her fingers. Jesse flew to take shelter behind Kyra's leg, where he peered out suspiciously at Beth, his hand fiercely clutching at Kyra's dress.

Kyra casually placed her hand on top of Jesse's head, her eyes connecting with Glenna's.

Without missing a beat, Glenna said, "I'd prefer it if you didn't smoke near the children, Beth."

"Oops! Bad me!" Beth frowned but obediently put out her cigarette while Kyra gave each of the boys a carrot, then took Jesse by the hand and led him outside.

She sat down on the wide tree stump to the left of the house and lifted Jesse onto her lap, where he sat, stiffly apprehensive. So much for small gains, she thought, having been pleased at his allowing her to take his hand. She was going to have to win him over by tiny incremental degrees.

"I've been thinking it's time you and I had a little talk. It's okay to eat your carrot, Jesse. I know you're hungry, and lunch will be a while yet."

He took a small bite, his eyes fastened guardedly to hers, intelligence gleaming in their dark, bottomless depths.

"You understand that your mother has left you in my charge, don't you?"

Soberly, he nodded.

"You'll be living with me from now on. I know you're not happy about it, but there's nothing either of us can do to change things." She paused and looked around. "It's very nice here, isn't it?"

He, too, looked around and indicated his agreement.

"Do you think you'd like to visit often with Roddy and Gage?"

An enthusiastic nod.

"Did you have friends where you lived before?"

A shake of his head, no.

"That's a pity. We all need friends, and you'll make lots of them from now on. The couple who arrived a short time ago are my twin brother, Kyle, and his wife, Beth. Do you know what twins are?"

He studied her intently for several moments, then shook his head.

"Kyle and I were born together, on the same day. We are what's called fraternal twins, but we actually look more alike than most fraternal twins. Twins who look alike are called identical, but identical twins are either two boys or two girls, not one of each. Do you understand?"

A nod.

"Clever boy. So—" she paused and drew a deep breath "—a week or so from now we'll go on an airplane, all the way across the ocean to England, where you'll meet my mother and father. You picked pajamas with airplanes on them. Do you think you'd like to go on one?"

Skeptical, as if it were a trick question, he inclined his head slowly and took another bite of his carrot, his eyes reading hers, searching for secondary meanings.

"It's quite a long trip. We'll be in the airplane for seven or eight hours. Would you like that?"

His jaws working as he chewed the carrot, he nodded.

"Good. I know it must be scary for you to find yourself left with a towering great fat lady." At this, the slightest smile upturned the corners of his mouth. Encouraged, she went on. "But I'm not at all a scary person, and I like small children very much. I like *you*, Jesse, and I'm glad you're going to be living with me. It will take time for us to get used to each other, to learn the things we each like or don't like. So if there's something you're not happy with, let me know and I'll do my best to fix it. Okay?"

A quick nod, as if humoring her (he gave the impression he believed adults could and would say anything; it didn't mean that what they said was true), then he popped the last of the carrot into his mouth.

Roddy and Gage came banging out of the house just then, and, without actually moving, Jesse was suddenly straining to be away from her.

"You can call me Kyra," she said. "And you can tell me anything at all, no matter how awful you think it is. I will *always* listen to what you have to say, and I will *never* hit you. I might get cross with you, and you might get cross with me, too. We may even raise our voices and shout at each other. But even if we're cross, we'll still be friends, and there will be no hitting, *ever.*"

At this, his eyes came back to hers; and again he seemed to be searching for the hidden meanings bound to be contained in her eyes.

"You have my promise," she repeated. "And I always keep my

promises. If I'm angry with you, I'll tell you and we'll sort it out. And if you're angry with me, I want you to tell me. But I will never, ever hurt you. No one in this family will hurt you. Okay?"

Eyes widening, as if what she was proposing was the most extraordinary, scarcely believable thing he'd ever heard, he nodded a final time.

"Good." She smiled and tapped him on the nose with the tip of her finger. "I know you want to, so go on now and play with Roddy and Gage."

He hesitated for a moment, still searching her eyes intently, then he slid down from her lap and took off running across the grass. She sat a little longer, watching the three boys confer before they tore off down the slope at the rear of the house. Smaller, slower than the other two, Jesse ran after them—a little bright-colored blur flying out of sight.

The boys were sent up to their rooms to rest after the heavy meal. And Beth, covering a yawn with a silky, manicured hand, said, "*Such* a good idea. I'm for a nap, too. Darling?" She turned to Kyle expectantly.

"Kyra and I are going to take a walk."

"I really should help Glenna..." Kyra began.

"Go for a walk," Glenna told her. "Cliff will help me clear up."

Getting to his feet, Cliff saluted and said, "Yes, sir, I will, sir," and began collecting the plates.

Holding on to a petulant expression, as if in the hope of persuading Kyle he'd have a better time napping with her than marching through the dangerous wilds of Connecticut, Beth conceded defeat. "I suppose I'll go up, then," she said, in a teenager's sulky tone.

Once away from the house, Kyle looped his arm through his sister's, saying, "It's really hard to believe Gary's gone. He was such a delightfully unaffected man, so admirably his own person. It must be awful for you. I am sorry, Keer."

"Thank you." Choked, she looked ahead to the pond some distance from the bottom of the hill. "I can't believe it, either," she admitted. "For days on end, I've been waiting for him to phone from Paris. Then I remember..." Unable to say more, she left the thought dangling.

Arm in arm, they walked under the hot July sun, the sky cloudless and very blue, the breeze fragrant with the scent of freshly cut grass. The intense green of the countryside and the density of massed, elderly trees were so like home that she thought again, as she did every time she came here, it was why the first settlers called it *New* England. For a moment or two she experienced a rush of homesickness and wondered if the most sensible move might be to pack up all her belongings and take Jesse home to London. Aside from Glenna's family, Aunt Catharine and a few friends, there was nothing to keep her in New York.

Approaching the pond, Kyle said, "Let's go in."

She made a face, recalling the claylike bottom and the qualmy sensation of thick mud oozing through her toes.

"Come on. It'll be refreshing." He quickly stripped down to his boxers, took several running steps then dived beneath the surface of the water.

She stood indecisively on the bank, noting that as always he looked fit and trim while she looked like an overstuffed sofa standing on end.

He came up complaining, "It's not very deep."

"About five feet. Deep enough." Tempted, but unwilling to have him see her in her underwear, she unfastened her sandals and waded into the wonderfully cool water, her feet suctioned by the mud. Holding up her skirt, she took several more awkward steps, until the water was above her knees. Kyle was out in the middle of the pond, flat on his back, gazing up at the sky.

"Don't be shy, Keer," he called to her. "It's only me. And it's lovely and cool."

"Oh, what the hell!" she said softly, and dived, fully clothed, beneath the surface. Opening her eyes in the murky water, everything was distorted and green, dreamlike. She swam underwater, enjoying the relief of the water leeching the heat from her body, until her breath gave out. She surfaced a few feet from where her brother floated, arms tucked beneath his head as if he were reclining on a vast bed.

"Good girl," he said. "Nice, isn't it?"

"Actually, it is. I hadn't realized I was so hot."

They drifted quietly side by side for a time, feeling the sun on their faces.

After a while he said, "I wanted to tell you that Beth and I are splitting up. The marriage has been a complete farce. I don't know *what* I could've been thinking, getting involved with someone so young, and so regrettably dimwitted."

"But she was saying earlier that the two of you plan to start having children."

"Beth has a rich fantasy life," he scoffed. "The idea of having a baby with her gives me the collywobbles. It could well turn out to be a variation of that famous George Bernard Shaw story about the actress who wanted to bear his child. She insisted that with her beauty and his brains the child was bound to be fantastic. And Shaw said, yes, but what if the child had his looks and her brains. You know?"

She laughed and said, "Yes. Unfortunately, I do."

"I knew you'd understand."

"The splitting-up part, yes. What I don't understand is what attracted you to her in the first place."

"I thought at thirty-five it was time I settled, and I did want to have kids. I knew it was a mistake the instant I proposed, but I didn't have the guts to call it off. Aside from everything else, she's pissed away all her own money and would dearly like a chance to piss mine away, too. I'm sorry, but that's just not on. You know how it is for actors, Keer. We so rarely know what or where the next job's going to be."

"Surely you don't worry about that, at this stage of your career? You're never out of work."

"I do worry, actually. Always have. I keep thinking they'll get bored with me once I hit forty and can't play romantic leads anymore. They've never been willing to give me the meatier roles, Richard the Third, say, or Macbeth."

"That's only because you look young for your age, Kyle. It'll come. It's not as if no one *wants* you. What about that film you're to do in September? Isn't that still on?"

"It is. Damned good part, too."

"So you're all right, then."

"In a manner of speaking. Are you afraid of getting old, Keer?"

She turned to look at him. He was still gazing up at the sky. "To be honest," she replied, "I can't wait for it. I hated being young, being so different, being the child of Richard Latimer and Octavia Bell. I'm looking forward to wrinkles and age spots and gray hair, and a time when people will stop trying to find ways to compliment me on how good-looking I am, despite the fact that I'm so unfortunately ample."

"You surprise me," he said, turning to look over at her. "I had no idea you felt that way."

"Why should you have? It's not as if we've ever been in the habit of discussing intimate issues."

"No, but still. I mean to say, it's certainly not the impression I had of you."

"Impressions are just that, Kyle. Most of the time they have precious little to do with reality. I loathed people fussing over us as children and, later on, making endless assumptions about me because of how I looked. It hadn't anything to do with *me*. It was all about surfaces and about our parents being who they were. Most of my life I've felt it was a vicious cosmic joke—that I'd been given this face to compensate for the fact that certain vital parts of me weren't functional. I'd have been far happier being plain. At least then I'd have been certain people were with me because they liked me. I wouldn't have found it necessary to get fat in self-defense, and I might actually be comfortable with myself now, instead of filled with contempt for the monstrosity I've made of my body."

"I had no idea you felt that way," he said again with sadness. "I wish I'd known."

"Why?" she asked mildly. "What possible difference would it have made if you had?"

"It would've made a lot of difference. It was something we shared. I know you think I'm a complete egomaniac, but I very much dislike having women throw themselves at me because of how I look. It's insulting and irrelevant. If I'd known you felt the same way, I'd have made more of an effort, tried to be more open with you."

"No you wouldn't have," she disagreed in that same mild tone. "We are who we are, Kyle. You were launched on your course and I on mine. The face has served you well. It's only been a hindrance to me. Of course, once I met Gary, how I looked was no longer an issue. Now that he's gone, I expect I'm about to discover if it is once again."

"But you've got a child at last," he pointed out. "Won't having him change how you feel about yourself?"

"Perhaps, because I won't be completely alone, so I'll have a broader focus. Which is a good thing because I've got a truly terrible talent for self-hatred. Are *you* afraid of getting old?"

"I am a bit, which is why I'm ending it with Beth before it's too late. The idea of being seen as one of those middle-aged men clinging to his youth through a beautiful young wife appalls me. I hate the image, and I hate the marriage. We spend perhaps a week together out of every six, and it's seven of the longest days ever. I want to shake her every time she opens her mouth. She's so bloody *feckless*. And, since we're being so candid, I don't like making love to her. She's uninterested, in any case. I swear it's because of the vast number of tissues she's consumed. Her brain's turned to cellulose."

She laughed again, then asked, "Have you met someone else?"

"No, but I'd like to be free, in case someone does come along. The thing is, I'd rather be alone than with someone I don't like and can't respect."

"I agree completely."

"There's something more, actually."

"What?" she asked.

"The truth is I married Beth to see if I could make a go of it...I mean, I've always liked the idea of being married but...I was testing myself, so to speak."

"Testing your sexuality?"

Righting himself so that he was standing in the water facing her, he asked anxiously, "You know?"

"Kyle," she said gently, "I've always known you were homosexual."

"How could *you* know when *I* didn't?"

"I just did. It never mattered to me." She shrugged. "Why didn't you know?"

"I suppose I just didn't want to. I mean, being homosexual's never been at the top of my wish list."

"No," she said sympathetically. "I don't imagine it would be."

"Now it seems inescapable, but I don't dare come out. My career would be over."

"It might not be."

"Were we not just discussing my playing romantic leads?" he said with some bitterness. "I'd be lucky to get supporting roles, and that would kill me."

"Then I guess you'll have to stay in the closet."

"How could you know and never say anything?" he asked, stretching out again in the water, arms under his head.

"What could I have said? Met any hot new men lately, Kyle? Had any super kinky sex? Honestly! Are you really that thick?"

He laughed loudly before saying, "No. The words just came out wrong."

"Story of my life," she said tartly. "So have you had affairs—with men, I mean?"

"Not since school. I didn't dare. I was terrified people would find out."

"But you'd like to."

"I would, yes," he confessed. "Whether or not I'll ever have that sort of courage remains to be seen."

"Don't think about it that way, Kyle. Just take the chance, if it comes along, and be with someone, whoever it is, if it makes you happy. You deserve to be loved."

"Thank you. That's the kindest thing anyone's ever said to me. You're a generous woman, Keer."

"Merely truthful."

"Generous," he repeated. "And what about you? Will you be okay?"

"I'm not going to go to pieces, if that's what you're asking. I can scarcely afford that luxury, now that I've got the responsibility of Jesse."

"I know it's not an appropriate time to ask, but do you think you might marry again someday?"

"You're right. It's *not* an appropriate time. At this moment I can't conceive of being with anyone but Gary. And I can't conceive of the rest of my life without him."

"Sorry. That was exceedingly tactless."

"Oh, not exceedingly. Catharine asked me the same question less than twenty-four hours after Gary died." She smiled and shook her head.

"Absolutely bonkers, dear Auntie Cath. As usual she and Beth nattered away nineteen to the dozen, got on famously."

"They would do, wouldn't they? Neither one of them makes much sense at the best of times."

"Too true. Think you'll be able to manage with Jesse?"

"Oh, I think so."

"There's nothing...wrong with him, is there?"

"Why, because he doesn't talk? He's able to, if that's what you're wondering. He's been through a lot and needs time to adjust." She told him about Jesse's being abused, then fell silent, beginning to feel chilled. "He and I both need time," she said at last.

"It enrages me, hearing things like that. I want to gather up all the people who prey on children and exterminate them." He hesitated for a moment, then asked, "Forgive me if I'm being tactless again, but why would you take on a child with such problems?"

"For God's sake, Kyle. Given my own defects, I'd be the worst sort of hypocrite if I refused to take Jesse on because, through no fault of his own, he was less than perfect."

"I was simply attempting to express my concern—for both of you. Your lips have gone blue. Shall we start back?"

In answer, she turned and started swimming to shore.

They sat on the grass for a while, letting the sun dry them.

"Please don't take offense," he said finally. "I'm coming across very badly, but in some ways we scarcely know each other and in others we suffer from overexposure."

"Why have we talked so rarely?" she asked him as they got up to return to the house.

"I honestly don't know. Hell of an oversight, though." He again looped his arm through hers. "Let's see if we can't remedy that in the future, now that we've made such a good start. I care about you, Keer. Very much."

"I care very much about you, too. Perhaps, at long last, we'll actually get to know each other now, Kyle. I'd like that so much."

CHAPTER 9

Upon returning to the house Kyra went upstairs to shower and change into dry clothes. Kyle tiptoed along behind her, heading for his room. As he was passing the smallest guest room, he glanced in and saw Jesse sitting cross-legged on the floor, a teddy bear under his arm and a book in his hands. He was staring intently at the pages, as if attempting to absorb the meaning of the words by sheer force of will.

Pausing to study the child, Kyle felt an odd sense of recognition, as if he'd always known Jesse. Impossible, of course. Yet he knew the set of his eyes and the shape of his mouth; he recognized the potency of the boy's focus. Kyle had never seen Jesse before that morning, and perhaps his strong response to the child was a result of his latent desire to be a father, or because of his great anger at Jesse's having been so badly misused. Whatever the reason, he was very taken with the boy.

Noticing Kyle in the doorway, Jesse at once got up and came over to him, holding out the book.

With a strange sense of déjà vu, Kyle asked, "You'd like me to read to you, would you?"

Head tilted far back to look up at him, the boy nodded eagerly, firming up his grip on the bear.

Kyle took the boy in from head to toe: the dark hair and pale skin; the heat of his gaze and the slight flush to his cheeks; the long-sleeved yellow rugby shirt, blue jeans, and brand-new, impossibly small sneakers, one with laces undone. He was an arrestingly intense little fellow. "All right," Kyle said with a smile. "Come on, then, Monkey."

Jesse continued to gaze up at him. After a moment's hesitation (Was he overstepping? Would Kyra mind?), Kyle scooped him up—surprised at how almost weightless the boy seemed—and carried him toward the stairs, slightly unnerved by the ongoing intensity of Jesse's gaze. Thinking to make him laugh, Kyle scrunched up his face and emitted a playful bark. At once the child shrank, his eyes clouding with fear.

"I'm just playing with you, Monkey," Kyle whispered, mentally kicking himself. Holding the boy a little closer to his chest, he started down the stairs. "I didn't mean to frighten you, dear one. I'm ever so sorry."

Jesse released a long, slow sigh, but continued to watch Kyle's face closely.

"I'm sorry," Kyle whispered a second time, stunned to learn just how fragile the boy was, in every way. He was going to have to tread very carefully. The games, the animal noises and funny faces that other children found so amusing weren't going to go over well with a small boy whose past encounters with adults had brought him primarily pain. "We'll have a nice long read and forget that Uncle Kyle just behaved like a dolt. Okay?"

A small, reserved nod; the eyes were somewhat shuttered now, less trusting.

"You think I'm an idiot, and you're absolutely right," Kyle said. "You're in very good company, though. Any number of people think I'm an idiot."

At this, one tiny finger tapped the tip of Kyle's nose, causing him to smile.

"So you forgive me, do you?"

His eyes relenting, Jesse nodded.

When Kyra came down a short time later to make a cup of tea, she found the pair ensconced in an armchair in the living room—Kyle reading aloud from *Stuart Little;* Jesse nestled contentedly in the crook of her brother's arm, eyes half-closed, thumb in his mouth.

Kyle glanced over and smiled.

Jesse didn't notice her, too engrossed in the story.

Kyra stood listening for a moment or two, as lulled by her brother's mellifluous voice as Jesse obviously was. And as she watched and listened, suddenly hers and Kyle's embattled childhood history no longer tainted her view. Their time at the pond was having some sort of delayed effect upon her so that she was all at once able to see him as someone real, with sensitivity and a full compliment of feelings. It shocked her to realize that ancient run-ins and disagreements had colored her image of her brother in distorted hues; decades-old antipathy had prevented her from seeing that he had long-since grown beyond the posturing and pretensions and petty cruelties of his youth. He'd evolved into a man of good humor and honesty, and she'd failed, until today, to know or appreciate him. Shameful, she thought, to be so judgmental, so tied up in the past.

Going to the kitchen, she stood looking out the window at the lengthening afternoon shadows, noting that the foliage was at its deepest, richest, height-of-summer green. In the weeks to come, the color would gradually begin to alter as the season ebbed and the leaves died in one sustained, brazen flourish. She seemed to find metaphors for death everywhere, and thought once again of how a casual good-bye had turned out to be forever. *Have a good trip. I'll phone you when I get in. I love you. I love you, too. Good-bye, good-bye.*

While the tea was steeping, she sat at the table with one arm wrapped around her midriff, lost to random recollections, her husband's absence nearly intolerable. If he'd left two minutes earlier or later, he'd still be alive; they'd be together, making plans for family outings with Jesse—trips to the zoo, to children's plays, to Disney films. A complete family, not two damaged, very separate individuals clumsily attempting to make contact.

At last, she got up to pour the tea into two mugs and a two-handled plastic cup for Jesse, who had made it known (to the amazement of Roddy and Gage, who'd been under the impression that only grown-ups drank the horrible stuff) that he had developed an immediate fondness for hot tea.

Interestingly, Jesse stayed close to Kyle for the remainder of the afternoon and evening, declining invitations to play, ultimately situating himself next to Kyle at dinner. And as if he'd always done it, Kyle reached over to cut Jesse's food and instructed him in an undertone on how to manage his knife and fork. Jesse copied Kyle's every gesture faithfully, a perfect little mimic, and by the end of the meal was handling the utensils with ease. Then, later, Jesse made it clear he wanted Kyle to come along when it was time for his bath.

Refusing to focus on the condition of Jesse's body, Kyle told foolish jokes and limericks he remembered from childhood as Kyra got the quietly amused boy bathed and then into bed. Jesse reached for his copy of *Stuart Little* and, after bestowing a look of apology on Kyra, gave the book to Kyle.

Gladdened by the rapport the two had established, Kyra said, "I'll leave you to get on with it." She caressed Jesse's cheek, then gave her brother's arm a gentle squeeze as she left.

That night she slept in the shirt of Gary's she'd retrieved from the laundry hamper before leaving the apartment the day of the funeral. His scent still lingered in the fibers but it seemed to be fading, and she decided she'd have to store the rest of his laundry in a sealed plastic bag to preserve its essence.

When Kyle and Beth were leaving the next morning (Beth had a fashion shoot scheduled that evening), Kyra embraced the younger woman, feeling a stab of pity for her. It was like holding a soft cotton bag crammed with an assortment of sticks and a pair of water-filled balloons. None the less, Kyra put some energy into the effort. Yes, Beth was thick as mud and oblivious of everyone's feelings but her own, but her life was about to take an unexpectedly nasty turn and Kyra, of late, had acquired an intimate knowledge of just how harrowing that could be.

Beth was completely thrown by this display and verbally stumbled about, trying to come up with something to say. Rescuing her, Kyra said, "Thank you for coming. Safe trip home, Beth," and released her, relieved to put some distance between herself and an essentially failed gesture.

Jesse came scrambling down the stairs, witnessed the exchange of good-byes, and ran to attach himself to Kyle's knees, breaking into soundless tears. Kyra moved to go to him but, holding up a hand to stop her, Kyle said, "Excuse us a moment, please." He lifted Jesse into his arms and carried him a short distance away to stand talking to him for several minutes, blotting Jesse's face with his handkerchief. Kyra watched from the front porch, so absorbed that she started when Glenna's hand closed around hers.

"This is a new and different side of Kyle," Glenna murmured. "One day some lucky child will have a lovely father."

"Yes," Kyra said neutrally, hurt by the irony of the observation, and wondering if life was ever fair or if it was sheer vanity to hope that it might be.

Beth waited impatiently in the station wagon with Cliff. Roddy and Gage sat on the tree stump, maintaining their distance as if out of deference to Jesse's unhappiness.

Finally Beth leaned out the car window and called, "Kyle, we'll miss our *train!*"

"There's plenty of time," Cliff said quietly, his eyes, too, on Kyle and Jesse. Everyone heard the unmistakable irritation in Cliff's voice, and they were all pleased to have the irredeemably insensitive creature put, however tamely, in her place.

At last, Kyle brought Jesse back to the porch and set him on his feet, saying, "We'll be seeing each other again very soon. Kyra will be bringing you to London in a week or two and you'll get to meet your new grandparents. You'll like them, Jess. Granny's ever so silly and knows tons more funny stories than I do. And Grandpa *seems* scary but he's quite silly, too, once you get to know him." He smiled encouragingly and said, "It won't be long before you'll be seeing everyone. All right, Monkey?"

Jesse nodded, his face working. Kyle bent to kiss the boy on each cheek, then straightened and turned away. Jesse stood clutching the porch railing with both hands, as if for support, his eyes glossy with tears, his lower lip caught between his teeth.

Kyra came down the steps to walk her brother to the car. "You've been so good with Jesse. I wish you weren't leaving," she said, embracing him. "We haven't had nearly enough time together."

"I'll ring you in a day or two, see how you are and fill you in on the progress of the divorce wars."

"Don't forget to do that. I mean it, Kyle."

"I know you do, and I feel the same way." Kyle looked past her to where Jesse was standing on the top step, watching them. His tiny body looked poised for flight, as if at a signal from Kyle, he'd come racing over to go off with him. "I've developed an enormous fondness for that boy. He's so...There's something about him...."

Beth leaned across the front seat and pressed her hand flat on the horn. The sudden blare startled everyone.

Kyle turned and shouted, *"Stop that bloody racket at once!"* Beth instantly withdrew her hand and sat back, dumbfounded. "I

will be so goddamned *glad* to see the back of her, I can't *tell* you."
A kiss on Kyra's cheek, another hug, and he said, "We'll talk soon.
Take good care, Kyra. I love you, you know." Then he hurried to
climb into the rear of the car, where he apologized to Cliff for keeping him waiting before turning to Beth to say, "You want to be
bloody-minded, do it in private. Did you not *see* I was talking to
Jesse? Did you not *see* he was upset? You are the most hopelessly
self-absorbed creature who ever *lived.*" With that, he turned to
wave good-bye and blow a kiss in Jesse's direction as the station
wagon began to move down the driveway.

Jesse watched forlornly from the front steps until the car was
long out of sight. Then, with a deep sigh that seemed to shake his
entire body, he trudged, head down, into the house. When Kyra
went to look for him, she found him curled up on the floor in the
farthest corner of the closet, his face buried in his teddy bear. Re-
spectfully, she left quietly.

The next few days were taken up with arranging the documentation
that would enable Jesse to be issued the passport he was eligible to
have as a minor child in the custody of a legal guardian, and Kyra
looked after the three boys while Glenna was at work with Cliff.

After Jesse's return visit to Renny Hogan—who administered
several booster shots, said the various bruises and burns were heal-
ing nicely, and presented Jesse with a handful of sugar-free can-
dies—Kyra took the boys to storytelling hour at the library on
Friday afternoon, and then to Baskin-Robbins for ice cream. In the
midst of wiping clean their sticky hands and smeared faces she
looked at each child in turn, taken by how individual, how complete they were. Everything they would be was predetermined
within them, all of it set by genetic maps and markers. And she tried
to imagine what the littlest boy, the silent one with haunted gypsy
eyes and a rare gift for making himself understood without words,
might become. Something unique, she thought. And, for the first
time since Gary's death, she experienced a moment of pure happiness at the realization that she would be there to see it.

Sunday evening as they were finishing dinner, Catharine called.
Glenna was on the phone with her for almost forty minutes. When
she finally hung up, her expression was fraught.

"Oh, no," Cliff said. "What now?"

"She's drunk and hysterical. Henry's gone. He announced this morning he was leaving, and packed a bag while she begged and pleaded. He told her he'd make arrangements to get the rest of his things and then he went. She sat down to wait, convinced he was just making some sort of statement. But of course he wasn't. He's finally had enough. I think I should go to her. I'm afraid she'll do something stupid."

"Where's Luz?" he asked.

"It's her day off. I've really got to go, Cliff. She's raving, out of her head."

"Yup, you do," he agreed wearily. "But somebody ought to go with you."

"You go, Cliff," Kyra said. "I'll stay and look after the boys."

"I've got a better idea," Cliff countered. "The two of you go, and I'll stay with the boys. I'm no good with your mother, Glenna. I always wind up wanting to throttle her, she makes me so mad."

"Will you come, Keer?" Glenna asked. "I know it's a lot to ask..."

"No, of course I will."

When Kyra explained to Jesse that she'd be away for the night, he at once got upset, his brow furrowing, chin quivering. The week had seen too many departures.

Her explanation didn't make a dent on him. "Look, Jesse," she said, deciding to talk to him as she would to another adult. "I'll tell you the truth. Glenna's mother drinks too much sometimes. Do you know what I'm talking about?"

She had his complete attention now. He didn't look quite so upset as he indicated he understood.

"When she drinks too much she does crazy things, and Glenna's afraid she'll hurt herself. So we're going to look after her to make sure she doesn't do anything crazy. If it wasn't important, I wouldn't leave you. But it's for one night, no longer. And I'll be back tomorrow afternoon, I promise. And you remember I told you I always keep my promises?"

Jesse nodded.

"Okay, good. Shall I tell Cliff you'd prefer not to have a bath this evening?"

One slow nod.

"I'll tell him. Thank you for understanding, Jesse. You're a good boy." She held his hand to her lips, a gesture that bewildered but did not displease him, then hurried to get her bag with the slightly coppery, play-soiled, boy-smell of him tingling in her nostrils.

"I *knew* this was coming," Glenna said in the car. "I'm frankly amazed Henry's stayed as long as he has. He's been very good to us, you know, Keer, gave me and Cliff the down payment for the house, even set up trust funds for Roddy and Gage. The thing is, he's a simple soul, really. All he's ever wanted is an attractive, undemanding companion, a bit of peace and quiet, trips to someplace exotic now and then. But Mummy's driven him mad with the endless entertaining, the endless cosmetic surgery, and her sundry and endless bloody *needs*. She has got to be the *neediest* woman who ever lived."

"Where's Dillon?" Kyra asked.

"On Long Island for the weekend with friends. He's due home soon, and I hate the idea of him trying to cope with her alone. I just hope to God he doesn't get there before we do."

"Don't be too hard on your mother, Glen. She is what she is."

"You've never had to live with her. You can't imagine what a daily diet of her can be like. I thought as she got older there might be a little less drama. But, no, there's actually more. Please, please let us get there before Dill."

They did, but barely, finding Catharine passed out naked on the bathroom floor as Dillon called from the front door, announcing he was home.

"Damn, damn, goddamn!" Glenna swore, frantic.

"Go talk to him! I'll see to your mother."

Glenna continued to stand in the bathroom doorway, staring in at her unconscious mother.

"Go *on*, Glen!" Kyra took her cousin by the shoulders and turned her around. "Unless you want Dillon to see his mother this way."

Paling at the idea, Glenna rushed off.

Kyra was strong, but her aunt was a dead weight, impossible to lift. The air in the master suite was gelid, and Catharine's flesh was a mottled purple-white, very cold to the touch; it was also fragrantly oversoft, like perfumed, well-ripened Brie. Anxious to get her aunt into bed before Dillon came looking for her, Kyra spread a bath sheet on the floor, turned Catharine onto her back atop the towel, and managed to drag her to the bedroom. There, with Catharine propped against the side of the bed, Kyra grabbed the nightgown from under the many hand-embroidered pillows and struggled to get her aunt into it. It was like trying to dress a large rubber doll filled with thousands of lead pellets.

Finally, sweating in the chilly room, she locked her arms around Catharine's waist, hoisted her onto the high antique four-poster bed and got her under the bedclothes. Satisfied, she turned to go, then stopped and turned back. Fearing Catharine might aspirate in her sleep, Kyra shifted her onto her stomach and turned her head to one side. That done, she stood catching her breath, hearing Glenna and Dillon coming down the hall.

"Don't snow me, Glen," Dillon was saying. "You and Kyra wouldn't be here if something wasn't going on." He marched into the room, stopped halfway to the bed, looking first at his mother and then at Kyra.

He was fair, like Glenna, but had blue eyes, not brown like hers, that were of a rare, almost royal, blue. His complexion had the same olive caste as his father's, and from his mother he'd inherited a pointed chin and the straight patrician nose she'd had surgically altered to its detriment. Tanned and glowing from the weekend's sun, he looked the epitome of handsome, healthy youth.

"Is she drunk?" he asked bluntly, knowing Kyra would tell the truth. He trusted her as he did few others. Even though she was twenty years older—old enough, in fact, to be his mother (and there had been many times in his childhood when he'd secretly wished that she was), she had never talked down to him. He dearly appreciated that, since his own mother—even now—had an infuriating tendency to start using baby talk on him at unpredictable, usually embarrassingly public moments.

"I'm afraid so, love," Kyra answered.

"Why don't I make some tea," Glenna said, "and we'll talk."

Dillon took a slow look around. "Dad left, didn't he?" His jaw tightened as his eyes went back to his mother. "He packed up and left, and she went nuts, right?"

"Let's talk in the kitchen, please," Glenna begged.

Grudgingly, he allowed his half sister to lead him away.

"Go ahead," Kyra said, "I'll be along in a moment."

Upset and angry, Dillon went with Glenna, asking, "Why the hell will you never tell me what's going on? I'm not a child, you know. I don't *need* protecting."

Kyra didn't hear Glenna's answer. She returned to the bathroom to gather up Catharine's clothes, pausing to drop the silk undergarments into the basket beside the tub. Uncle Henry wouldn't be sitting on the throne anymore with his wife's soiled knickers in plain view. Having finally made his move, Kyra didn't think that he'd ever return.

The rest of the clothes over her arm, she went to the dressing room, opened the built-in closet doors and had to stop for a moment, gazing—bowled over every time—at the contents. Her aunt's suits, skirts, trousers and sweaters were exclusively in shades of black, gray or brown, and to go with any outfit there were at least two dozen different styles of white silk designer shirts. Everything was hung in groups, broken down into subsections by color: an amazing amalgamation of Luz's organizational skills and Catharine's obsessive nature.

Before joining the others in the kitchen Kyra studied her sleeping aunt, listening to her stertorous breathing. Catharine must have had an enormous amount to drink or she'd been self-medicating again, or both. It was so dangerous, Kyra thought, touching her aunt's cool, taut cheek. If she wasn't careful, one of these days she might accidentally do herself in. But perhaps that was what Catharine secretly wanted. Perhaps she'd been trying for years to become a suicide without actively making the decision but simply by repeatedly tempting fate.

Kyra adjusted the bedclothes, turned the thermostat up to seventy-four, switched off the lights and went out.

CHAPTER 10

"I can't believe he didn't leave some kind of message for me," a distressed Dillon was saying when Kyra arrived in the kitchen.

"I'm sure he'll be in touch," Glenna said placatingly. "I expect he left on the spur of the moment."

"Don't patronize me, please. This was no spur-of-the-moment thing. It's been coming for years and everybody's known it but Mom. She didn't *want* to know. She *never* wants to know!"

"You're right. It has been a long time coming." Glenna's tone was resigned as she got the teapot from the cupboard. "I wasn't patronizing you."

"Okay. Maybe I'm overreacting. But hell!" Fists jammed into his pockets, Dillon started pacing back and forth across the starkly white, ultramodern kitchen that, unlike the rest of the apartment, was devoid of any warmth or charm—probably because Catharine didn't cook and spent very little time here.

Kyra got cups and saucers, set them on the counter and went to the refrigerator for milk.

Dillon looked over at Kyra, saying apologetically, "Another Blaine family drama is the last thing you need after what you've been through."

"I'm sorry about this, Dillon."

"You know what? In a way I am, too; but in another way I'm not. It's kind of a relief. I've been expecting it. I just wish—"

The telephone rang and he pounced on it. Sagging with relief, he said, "Dad, am I glad you called! Are you okay?... Good, that's good.... No, I don't, not really. I just got back from the island. Glenna and Keer are here, and Mom's in bed, out cold."

"I was hoping Henry would call him," Glenna whispered to

Kyra. "Dill hates being alone with Mummy when she's on a bend-
er. It scares him, and that makes him angry, because he thinks he's
too old to get scared. As if age has anything to do with it. Luz is
really the only one who can handle Mummy when she's drinking
or drugging."

"Perhaps you should phone Luz," Kyra suggested, "let her know
the situation so she doesn't come into this cold tomorrow morning."

"Good idea." Glenna paused for a few seconds, thinking, then
said, "I'm going to clean out the medicine cabinet, get rid of her
pills." She got a paper bag from the utility cupboard, saying,
"Won't be a minute."

Kyra took over making the tea while Glenna hurried to the master bathroom.

Dillon was saying, "I *do* understand, Dad. But I have to be here
for six more weeks. It'll be horrendous.... No, I know that.... No,
I understand. I do. I mean, I hate to sound selfish, but is it fair to
me? I've got my job at Abercrombie; I've got stuff to organize for
college. I can't hang out here and baby-sit Mom.... No, I know that.
But it *is* my responsibility in a way.... Yes... Yes... Okay... Sure I
know where that is. What time?... Okay. I'll see you then....
What?... No, it's okay, Dad. I honestly do understand.... I'm just
relieved you called. Love you, too. 'Bye." He hung up and leaned
against the wall. "What a goddamned mess!"

"Certainly is," Kyra said.

"To tell the truth, I'm on Dad's side. All the things she's done, supposedly to keep him interested, are the things that've driven him away.
It's like she never believed she was good enough for him in the first
place, so she started making 'improvements'—that's what she calls
them, for chrissake—so she'd be able to keep him. *Improvements.* As
if butchering your face so you come out looking like some kind of
science experiment is an improvement. She's out of her fucking *tree!*"

"It's sad, Dillon."

"Yeah, that, too. I mean, when I think of the mother I used to
have, it's like thinking of some other person who wasn't anything
like this one. I was so proud of her because she was more fun and
more beautiful than any of my friends' mothers."

"Yes, she was," Kyra agreed.

"I don't remember her drinking or taking pills. When did all this
start? Or was I just too young to notice?"

"I think it's been so gradual that none of us noticed until it began getting obvious."

"I know I come off like some kind of spoiled brat saying it, but I don't want to have to deal with her if she's going to stay bombed night and day. She starts clinging, breathing her boozy breath all over me, and saying all this heavy shit about how much she *loves* me and *depends* on me. I hate that, Keer. I don't know what to say or do, so I get mad and kind of push her away, and then I wind up down on myself for feeling that way and not being able to handle the situation."

"I'm sure it must be very difficult."

"Are you being sarcastic?"

"You know me better than that, Dillon," she reminded him. "No, I'd hate it, too. And, ideally, you shouldn't have to deal with it. I suppose it would be best if she were in some sort of program."

Dillon barked out an atypically rancorous laugh. "First you'd have to get her to admit she had a problem. Good luck with that one! Nothing wrong with Mom that an *improvement* or some Valium and vodka won't fix." Calming down, he said, "Well, at least I know Dad's okay. We're meeting for dinner tomorrow to talk things over."

"That's good. I doubt he expects you to cope alone."

"That's pretty much what he said. But short of committing her somewhere, I don't think he has a clue what to do. And neither do I, that's for sure."

Glenna came back, the paper bag bulging with her mother's pill collection, and looked around for somewhere to put it.

"What's that, Glen?" Dillon asked as Kyra poured the tea.

"Mummy's pills."

"Right on! Toss 'em down the garbage chute."

"Perfect!" Moving purposefully, Glenna went to do that.

Kyra thought of Kyle on his way back to London to start divorce proceedings. Henry would likely start them now, as well. And Gary was dead, gone forever. One way and another, the family was in the process of disintegrating, with lost or abandoned partners everywhere.

"Are you okay, Keer?" Dillon asked, his hand on her arm.

She found a smile for him and said, "Sorry. Yes, I'm fine. My mind tends to wander lately."

"Hardly surprising, considering."

"It's been a rough couple of weeks."

"I'll bet! It's such a shame about Gary. I *loved* that man. The basketball games we went to, letting me be ball boy for the airline softball games, you two taking me out to dinner..." His eyes filled and he broke off, throwing his arms around Kyra to give her a fierce hug.

"Gary loved *you*," she whispered as they separated and Dillon slumped into a chair.

Returning, Glenna said, "Why doesn't anyone warn us we'll grow up and have to take care of our parents? I thought one grew up, detached, so to speak, and went off to live one's own life, while the parents got on with theirs."

"That might work if you had a set of parents who were both grown up," Dillon said. "Whatever you want to say about my dad, at least he's not helpless. At least he doesn't need a personal attendant to make sure he doesn't overdose or rearrange his face."

"Henry's been very long-suffering," Glenna said. "No one's criticizing him. But we do have the problem of what to do with Mummy."

"Why do *we* have to do anything? Seriously! Six more weeks and I'm gone. She's going to have to sink or swim by herself. That's what Dad says and I agree. You're not responsible for her, and neither am I."

"I can't just turn my back on her!" Glenna argued. "And if her own children aren't responsible for her, who is?"

"Dillon has a point," Kyra interceded. "Wrong or right, she has to make her own decisions."

"And if she decides to drink and drug herself to death, I can sit back with a clear conscience?" Glenna challenged angrily.

"In a way, yes," Kyra said. "You can't live her life for her because you believe you'd do a better job of it. All you can do is show you care."

"Keer's absolutely right," Dillon said with energy. "With Mom, though, if you show you care, she kind of...*swarms* you. Out of the blue she's all over you, with these big meaningful hugs and 'I love you, I love you,' over and over, until you want to *shove* her away, get her the hell *off*. And you end up wishing you'd played it cool, the way Luz does."

"Luz can be cool because she's not related," Glenna said.

"Lucky her!" Dillon shot back. "Now is one of those times when I wish *I* wasn't."

"That's cruel." Glenna was shocked by his vehemence.

"Maybe. But you haven't lived here in a long long time, Glen. You have *no idea* what it's been like."

"I had fifteen years of it before you came along, Dillon. Please, let's not turn this into a pissing contest."

"Sorry," he said, then fell silent and sat staring unhappily at his tea. After a minute or so, he asked, "Are you guys spending the night?"

"We are," Kyra answered.

"Okay, good. D'you mind if I crash now? I'm kind of wiped and I have to be up early for work."

"No, go ahead," Glenna said.

"Okay. See you in the morning." He bent to kiss Glenna's cheek. "I'm sorry for coming on so strong, but I've reached my limit with this scene."

"I know you have, Dill. So have I. But we'll sort something out."

"Nothing I'd like better." He turned to kiss Kyra. "Thanks for being here," he told them both. "Sorry if I came on too strong. 'Night."

After he'd gone, Glenna said, "I'm going to phone Luz and then Cliff. I'll ask after Jesse for you. Won't be long."

It was disconcerting to be once again in the Early American guest room with its blue-white ceiling and antique needlework samplers. It seemed somehow far longer than two weeks since Gary's death. And while Kyra no longer checked her wristwatch every few minutes, expecting a call from Paris, she did keep thinking she'd be seeing him soon. Her heart would lift in anticipation before she remembered, and then it would sink again. Time was a very strange concept, something elastic that could contract and cause entire days to vanish, or it could expand so that a single hour seemed interminable.

Switching off the light, she lay for a time with her hand closed tightly around Gary's insignia, listening to the street sounds drifting upward from the avenue and watching the shadow play of lights on the ceiling. Jesse would be asleep now, a tiny dark form on the closet floor, curled around a greasy teddy bear. She wanted to be with him, not here in this embattled household.

In the middle of the night she got up to go to the bathroom, and on her way back to bed heard what sounded like the soft mewling of an infant. She tracked the sound to the master suite, where Catharine lay sobbing into her pillow. Kyra stood poised on the threshold for several seconds, thinking, "Even the self-deluded feel pain." It was a line from a play her mother had appeared in years ago, and it had an application here. Perhaps Catharine was half mad because she'd never managed to find the means of giving voice to her tumultuous emotions, or because she'd failed to comprehend the emotions themselves.

Kyra went to sit on the side of the bed, gathered her aunt into her arms and tried to comfort her, stroking her and murmuring the ritualistic phrases: "Shh. It'll be all right. Everything will be all right." As she did, she wondered why one said such stupid things when the reality was that nothing would be all right. No matter how great or minor the cause of the misery, it could not be undone. Still, she kept right on whispering the stock lines, unable to think of anything else to say.

The sharp odor of alcohol was seeping from Catharine's pores. And, as Dillon had pointed out, she did cling. But Kyra didn't mind. She was neither eighteen nor this woman's child and, if anything, Kyra derived a certain comfort from the process of attempting to quell pain that had undoubtedly been a lifetime in the making. Just then pain—regardless of its origins—was something she grasped in an entirely new and personal way. And she also understood suddenly why so many people had sought to touch her at Gary's funeral: because on occasions when words were inadequate, touch became the only legitimate means of communication. The words were inconsequential; the touch was everything.

"What will I *do?* How will I live without him? I can't *live* without him." Catharine repeated her fears over and over. Kyra tried not to be annoyed by her aunt's blind self-centeredness. Catharine's primary focus was, and always would be, herself. Just like Beth. They were supposed adults who in reality, and for causes undetermined, would remain children forever. Kyra listened as, almost childlike in size and in her dependency, Catharine trembled and wept on Kyra's breast, and gradually quieted. Why, Kyra wondered, was she so tolerant of her aunt and of Glenna and Dillon, yet so intolerant of her own family? What was it about families that so often set you on the defensive, leaving you unable to sympathize with those closest to you?

"So sorry," Catharine whispered eventually. "What must you think of me?"

"It doesn't matter what anyone thinks. It's what you think that's important."

"What *I* think doesn't matter to anyone!" Catharine cried.

"Of course it does," Kyra disagreed.

"You couldn't be more wrong!" Catharine declared bitterly, with no trace of her odd, affected accent, and pulled away from Kyra to reach for her cigarettes on the bedside table. She lit one—the flame from the lighter casting brief eerie shadows over her shiny, damp features—and drew so hard on it that her cheeks went hollow with the effort. Then, one arm folded under her breasts, she sat with her head turned aside as if to avoid having to see her niece, and smoked intently, eyes slitted against the smoke. "Did you have lovers before you married Gary?" she asked, eyes still averted.

"I had a lot of them, actually," Kyra admitted.

"I envy you that. I've only made love with my two husbands. I think that was probably a mistake."

"Why?"

"Because now I'm at a great disadvantage. The world and the rules have changed beyond recognition and I have no idea how to navigate out there." The hand with the cigarette made a gesture in the direction of the windows.

"You don't need to worry about that."

"Oh, but I do, if I'm to be all alone. I don't have the same—*gifts* I had when I met Henry."

"Gifts?"

"I'm no longer young or beautiful. I really don't know what I'll do. I've never lived alone. I can't bear the idea of it. How does one go about meeting people nowadays?"

"You've got friends. You won't be alone."

"I will be alone," Catharine said with finality. "I suppose I've always known it would come to this."

"You'll be alone only if that's what you want. You have choices, you know."

"Choices!" Catharine exclaimed disgustedly. "I have *never* had choices!"

Kyra hoped she'd elaborate, reveal herself at long last. But Catharine took a final drag on the cigarette, then crushed it out. "I

must bathe," she said abruptly, and slipped out of the bed to stand
very close to Kyra. "I do apologize for disturbing you at such an
hour," she said, her quasi-British inflection returning. It was as if,
for a minute or two, she'd been real, accessible. Now the usual
Catharine was back, as remote and peculiarly formal as ever. She
placed a shockingly cold hand on Kyra's arm. "So kind of you to
listen to my raving, but you mustn't take it seriously. Do, please,
go back to bed now."

She turned and went wafting ghostlike across the room. Pulling
her nightgown off over her head, she let it fall to the floor, then
moved into the bathroom. The light went on and Kyra was presented with a view of her aunt's pale, not unattractive nakedness
before the door quietly closed.

Realizing she'd been holding her breath, Kyra exhaled heavily.
She stood looking at the closed bathroom door for several seconds,
then, hearing the water go on in the shower, she returned to the
guest room.

CHAPTER 11

Dark and aristocratic, somewhere between forty and fifty, Luz had been running the Blaine household for twelve years. She handled Catharine with a certain long-suffering indulgence, as if she were dealing with a wilful but not very bright adolescent, usually regarding the woman with equal measures of amusement and pity. But every once in a while, as she stood and listened to her employer blathering away, Luz smiled, as if she were actually fond of Catharine. Perhaps she was merely entertained by her. It was difficult to tell.

In the opinion of everyone but Catharine, Luz could never have been properly remunerated for the multiplicity of services she'd rendered over the years; services which, in addition to keeping the place spotless and providing two meals a day, ranged from almost single-handedly caring for Dillon from shortly after his birth until he started school, to grocery shopping, and to nursing Catharine in the aftermath of her surgeries. In the course of a given week Luz put in an average of three or four extra unpaid hours, inevitably because Catharine had forgotten something that entailed the housekeeper's going out at the last minute to fetch it, or staying on to fix it, or cook it, or mend it.

Kyra suspected that Luz had stayed so long with the family out of an abiding love for Dillon and a great respect for Henry, whom she treated with a calm deference, more attuned to his moods and needs than his own wife. Now, with Henry gone and Dillon about to leave for college, Glenna and Kyra wondered if Luz wouldn't also soon be departing.

When the housekeeper arrived at eight-thirty on Monday morning, Luz asked, with warmth in her expressive eyes, "How does it go for you, Kyra?"

"It's beginning to get a little better," Kyra answered honestly.

"How are the children, Luz?"

The housekeeper smiled and was at once younger and (from Glenna's viewpoint) less forbidding. "Oh, very good. Rosalina will be a senior in college this year, Tomas is a junior, and Louisa will teach the second grade."

"That's wonderful. You must be so proud of them."

Luz was about to say something more when Catharine came sailing in, looking miraculously fresh and well-rested in brown linen slacks and one of her white silk shirts.

"Ah, the coffee's been made. Lovely. Good morning, girls. And Luz, how was your weekend? I do hope someone's remembered to wake Dillon. Can't have him late for work. Not the way to make a good impression, you know."

"Mummy, he left twenty minutes ago." Glenna shook her head, marveling over her mother's notion that no one and nothing functioned effectively unless she personally had some input. The reality was that Catharine had little to no control of anything, except perhaps her daughter's capacity for guilt.

Flustered, Catharine stopped and touched a hand to the back of her neck, her lips moving as if testing a variety of words to see which ones might best be spoken. "Oh! Splendid. Have a good weekend, did you, Luz?" she asked again.

"Very nice, Mrs. Blaine," Luz answered, taking everything in. "And yours, it went well?"

"Hmmn. I thought we'd change the linens today," Catharine said, eyes gone vague as if reading from a list visible only to her. "And I suppose it's time we laundered the bed skirts."

"We did them last week, Mrs. Blaine." With the merest hint of a sigh, Luz crossed the room, took an apron from the utility closet and tied it on.

Befuddled, Catharine watched her, then emitted a brief shrill laugh. "Good God! That's right, we did. Starting to forget things in my old age. How frightful!" Again she touched an uncertain hand to her neck.

"Mummy, why don't you sit down? I'll make you some toast, or an egg. You really should eat something." *Soak up some of the residual alcohol,* Glenna thought angrily. *Put something into your body besides booze and chemicals.*

"No, darling, thank you. Not hungry, and too much to do. You and Kyra will want to be on your way." Her bloodshot eyes settled on Kyra for a long moment, and then, with sudden brightness, she announced, "Luz, Kyra's finally been given a child, a little boy. Isn't that *super?*"

Luz looked over at Kyra. "Finally, after so long. This is good. How old he is?"

"Three and a half."

"It's good, but a boy, I think, is not so easy as a girl. Too much energy. Small boys, they run, they shout; all the time they make the machine noises." She smiled again.

Kyra was about to agree, but Catharine jumped on this instantly. "Rubbish! What an absurd thing to say!" she declared with disdain, now leveling her jittery gaze at the housekeeper. "Dillon was far easier than Glenna. I can't think *why* you'd say something so ridiculous."

"I happen to agree with Luz," Glenna said, regarding her mother with apprehension. All the signs indicated Catharine was hanging on by her fingernails, and though it was obvious she wanted her and Kyra to clear out, Glenna was in no hurry to go home only to be called back in a few hours' time. She'd been this route too many times. The desperate, begging phone calls placed a terrible strain on her marriage, and she wished she had the wherewithal to ignore these hysterical summonses. She also wished she could stop her mother from venting her anger on Luz—something she did with hateful regularity.

Choosing not to respond to her employer's remarks, Luz poured herself half a cup of coffee, and drank some, glancing across at Catharine, who was now backed up against the counter, looking trapped and a little panicky. The atmosphere in the room was charged with static like a radio tuned to the dead air between two strong signals. Luz quickly finished the coffee, left her cup in the sink, got the vacuum cleaner from the utility closet, and went off to begin her chores.

Glenna excused herself and followed after the housekeeper.

Still leaning against the counter but marginally less tense now, Catharine got a cigarette lit and took a hard drag on it.

Kyra poured some coffee and carried it over, aware of the tremor in her aunt's hands as she accepted the cup. "You should talk to Luz, Aunt Catharine, explain what's happened."

"She and I will talk later," Catharine said, avoiding looking directly at Kyra.

Realizing her aunt was embarrassed about her middle-of-the-night confessions, Kyra gave up attempting to converse and sat down again. Frustrated by Catharine's lifelong refusal to face things squarely, her sympathy for the woman draining away, Kyra was all at once anxious to get out of the flawlessly decorated, essentially soulless apartment, and back to Jesse. Jesse was real; Jesse had needs she could attempt to meet. Catharine couldn't admit to her fears in daylight, let alone acknowledge that she needed help. And she was, as ever, so offhand and rude to Luz that Kyra wanted to shake her, and shout, "Don't be so bloody stupid! You *need* this woman. She's the only one who'll put up with you." But Kyra kept silent, thinking of how Gary had always found Catharine hilarious and pathetic. He'd laughed at her more outrageous remarks with such unfettered glee that Catharine had come to believe she possessed a previously unappreciated sense of humor. There'd be no one around now even to listen to her, let alone laugh, which was, indeed, pathetic.

Catharine chain-smoked and drank her coffee, poured herself more, while Kyra sat studying her until Glenna returned ten minutes later. At once Kyra stood up and pointedly looked at her watch, saying, "We should be on our way, Glen."

Glenna looked at her cousin, then at her mother, who gave her a quick glittery smile. "Yes, I suppose we should," Glenna said, bothered by that smile. The minute she and Kyra were out the door, her mother would tear the place apart looking for her pills. When she didn't find them, she'd start phoning the several pharmacies she frequented, ordering refills to be delivered, or to be picked up by Luz. The loss of her stash would, in the end, prove to be no more to Catharine than a short-term inconvenience. Pointless, Glenna thought. Another bloody wasted gesture.

Giving mother and daughter some privacy, Kyra went to the guest room to get her bag. She really needed to get away from her aunt. As Cliff had said, the temptation to throttle Catharine could be powerful, and Kyra felt the seeds sprouting inside her. It was, she recognized, a variation on the way Dillon claimed to feel: a set of emotions that left one undermined, guilty and chagrined. Again, Kyra had to wonder how Henry had managed to live with Catharine for so many years. Perhaps he had a mistress, someone he went to for the conversation and companionship his wife couldn't offer. Kyra sincerely hoped that he did.

Roddy and Gage came running the instant they saw the car pull into the driveway, but Jesse stayed by the swing set, watching and pretending not to. When Kyra went over to him, he wouldn't look at her. He lay on his belly across the seat of the swing, head hanging down, knees drawn up, and swayed gently back and forth.

"Would you like me to give you a proper ride, Jesse?" she asked, reminded by his actions of the way children's feelings lay right at the surface, with none of the protective layers that got acquired with time and served to conceal, ever more effectively, their true reactions. It made her remember how, whenever her mother used to return from filming on location, or from performing abroad, Kyra wouldn't go running to her the way Kyle did. Instead, sure her mother had forgotten her, she'd stand at a distance, watching, waiting for a signal. It must have hurt her mother in the same way Jesse's reluctance now hurt her. Yet it had never before occurred to her that parents and children were equal participants in the painful rites of passage.

"Shall I give you a ride?" she asked a second time.

Jesse shrugged, avoiding her eyes just as Catharine had earlier. She waited, and after a moment or two he righted himself on the seat, tiny, dimpled hands fastening to the ropes in readiness.

She gave the swing a small push, saying, "I know you're angry with me, Jesse, but I did promise you I'd be back. Sometimes grown-ups have to do things we don't like. This was one of those times. I didn't want to leave you, but I had to. You were all right with Cliff and the boys, weren't you?"

He nodded, then let his head drop back, closing his eyes to savor the sensation of flying as she pushed harder; the swing gained momentum, and he went higher and higher.

"Please try to be patient with me, Jess. I've never been anyone's mother, and this is as new to me as it is to you." When he still failed to respond, she said, "I've got to go in and make a few telephone calls. Do you mind? Or would you prefer me to stay?"

Another shrug.

"Sometimes," she said slowly, "children don't realize that adults are just large children. Our feelings can get hurt, too."

He looked over his shoulder at her, surprised.

"So am I forgiven?" she asked.

Facing forward again, he nodded.

"Good. Thank you."

Roddy and Gage were galloping over, making the whooping noises and doing the shouting that—as Luz had pointed out— seemed to accompany practically everything they did. Kyra gave the swing one last good push that sent Jesse soaring, and he emitted a spontaneous trill of laughter that took her completely off guard. It pierced her so pleasurably that she was moved nearly to tears, and as she headed toward the house she knew she'd been absolutely right to take him. It had only been a matter of days, but they'd opened a channel of communication and he was already able to laugh aloud.

That night she reached for *Stuart Little* and started chapter five but stopped when Jesse shook his head.

"Did Cliff read it to you last night?" she asked.

He indicated yes, so she went on to the next chapter and read about Stuart putting on his sailor suit before heading for Fifth Avenue. Jesse lay back holding his ratty bear and listened intently as Stuart managed to board an uptown bus. Halfway through the chapter Jesse's eyes were closing but he struggled to stay awake to the end. Then he turned onto his side, curling inward around the bear, and she wished him good-night, stroking his head before tiptoeing out.

"Last night, I went up to check on the boys and nearly had heart failure when I found Jesse's bed empty," Cliff said over coffee in the kitchen a short time later.

"Oh, hell! I didn't think to warn you," Kyra said.

"You mean he always sleeps in the closet?"

"So far, he has done. It didn't even occur to me to mention it. I am very sorry, Cliff."

"I didn't know what to think," he said. "You know? Whether it was a one-time thing, a reaction to your being away, or what. Anyway, he seemed okay so I left him there. Otherwise, everything was fine. He got himself ready for bed and was sitting waiting for me with his book when I finished with Roddy and Gage. I read him a chapter and when I left he seemed to be out like a light. Then I go to check and he's gone. Complete heart failure," he repeated, this time with a grin.

"I can't *believe* I forgot to tell you that he travels at night."

"No problem, Keer. He's a great kid, easy as pie."

They could hear Glenna's voice rising in the living room where she was on the telephone with her mother.

"That goddamned woman's going to drive Glenna crazy," he said, his jaw tightening. "There is no way I'll let her go back to the city tonight. Enough is enough. Catharine's going to have to learn to deal with her own problems, once and for all."

"I doubt she knows how. I think she's been living for years in a mental novel she writes as she goes along. She certainly doesn't live in the same world as the rest of us."

"That's for damned sure. And if she doesn't start pulling herself together PDQ, Luz'll quit and then Catharine'll really be up shit creek without a paddle."

"Poor Dillon's a nervous wreck about being there alone with her."

"Can you *blame* him? She can't do a damned thing for herself, except spend money. She can't balance her checkbook, so she's constantly overdrawn, then she goes into a tailspin when the bank manager calls to tell her. When it comes to Christmas or birthdays she's the most generous person I've ever known, but day to day she's totally indifferent to the people around her."

"It's true," Kyra said, thinking of the previous Christmas when her aunt had taken her and Gary out to lunch at a wonderful Italian restaurant, then given them a decorative bag containing two pounds of exquisite Belgian chocolates, half a dozen classical cassettes, and a paperweight of Baccarat crystal. A few days later, this same woman refused to give Dillon a twenty-dollar advance on his allowance to pay for a book he wanted to buy at Brentano's. While Catharine was laying down the law about frittering money away, Glenna took a cab down to the store, got the book and was back before Catharine had finished lecturing her son, who, by then, was doing the *Times* crossword puzzle and paying no attention to her.

"Glenna's going to have to start saying no, and I have no idea how you'll get her to do that, Cliff. Catharine's always known exactly how to get Glenna to do what she wants."

"Believe me," he said determinedly. "My wife is going to *start* saying no. We've got two kids and a law practice. She can't be rushing into the city every time her lunatic mother calls with yet another drama. It upsets all of us, especially the boys. They don't like Catharine. They're actually afraid of her."

"Really? That's sad."

"In a way. But you know what, Keer? Secretly, I'm tickled they don't like her. It kind of validates my own feelings about the woman. Kids *know* who's for real and who's not."

"They do, don't they," Kyra agreed.

"Damned right! We're not raising any stupid kids around here, and that goes for Jesse, too. That boy's something else, Kyra. No kidding. Talking to him isn't like talking to a little kid. I look into those eyes and there's a fully fledged intelligence looking back at me. You know? It's a little unnerving until you get used to it."

"I know."

That night the sight of Jesse's empty bed was more than Kyra could bear. She put on her nightgown, got a pillow and a blanket, then crept into the closet to settle on the floor beside Jesse. She didn't think she would, but she fell asleep almost at once and was awakened by the sounds being made by Jesse in the throes of a nightmare. In the spill of light from the room, she watched the child struggle—fists clenched at his chest, shoulders shifting from side to side, torso writhing, face twisted—while noises of protest and terror came from deep in his throat.

It was frightful. She wanted to comfort him but was afraid to do the wrong thing. Relying purely on instinct, she carefully drew him to her so that his head rested in the bend of her arm and his body was sheltered in the lee of hers. Then, as she waited, watching, her warmth and proximity penetrating past the boundaries of his sleep, the rhythm of his dreaming altered, and gradually his sleep-panic subsided.

Somehow, she thought, the hulking new widow and the diminutive battered boy were managing to move beyond their separate sorrows to make a tentative connection. Adjusting the blanket over him, relishing the slight weight of his head on her arm, she listened for a few moments to the now barely audible flow of his breathing, then, satisfied, she slid back into sleep.

CHAPTER 12

"Darling, are you all right? Why haven't I heard from you?" Octavia sounded worried and hurt. "I've left a number of messages with your service. Did you get them?"

"I did, and I'm sorry, Mother. I've been unbelievably busy, and I wasn't sure when you were actually getting home."

"I thought I'd told you. But never mind." Typically, her mother came directly to the point. "Kyle told me you've been given a child at last."

"At last," Kyra echoed.

"What extraordinary timing!" her mother declared.

"It is, isn't it?"

"I'm sure he'll be a great comfort and joy to you," Octavia said, then emitted a melodious laugh. "Oh, dear. I'm sounding lamentably like a Christmas card. But it's *such* good news. Kyle went on and on about the boy, claims he's an adorable tike—but with problems."

"He's had a rough time, but he's very special. I think you'll like him."

"Of *course* I'll like him. Why on earth wouldn't I? *Are* you all right, Kyra? Tell me the truth."

Reluctant always to confide in her mother for fear of finding out, once and for all, that the one person with the greatest capacity either to console or destroy her was no more than the sum total of her press clippings, Kyra hedged. "I've had almost no time to myself."

"*Talk to me,* for God's sake!"

"When I do have a moment to myself," Kyra confessed in a rush, praying she wouldn't regret this, "I think of Gary and feel as if I'm drowning. Or, suddenly, an entire day's gone by and I'm guilt-stricken because I *forgot* to think of him. Nights are the hardest."

"They always are. The hours of dark go on and on and on."

"Endlessly," Kyra agreed, relieved to learn—yet again—that her mother was capable of great understanding. "But I'm getting through it day by day."

"That's how it has to be," Octavia said. "If you start trying to think beyond the next day everything seems impossible."

"How did the shoot go?" Kyra asked, needing to change the subject. The wound was still too raw; the temptation to give in to tears too close to the surface, and she was as self-conscious about emotional displays with members of the family as she was about displays in general. Being British, she thought with grim humor, could be hazardous to one's mental health.

Picking up on her daughter's cue, Octavia switched tracks effortlessly, saying, "In the end, poor Charles threw out the script and had everyone extemporizing like mad; turned it into a bloody luau. I really am getting too old for such nonsense. He'd have done better to stick with the script. It, at least, had a degree of logic." She laughed.

Kyra smiled. She'd had one or two "luaus" of her own—the family term for when a film had no feasible ending, or the director decided at the last moment he didn't like what was written, and so he had the cast go dancing off across a lawn, or shot them backlit against a sunset, something he hoped would be viewed as symbolic. It was a gambit that rarely succeeded. Audiences were left bewildered, and critics usually savaged the end product.

"I don't know why I'm laughing," Octavia said. "It was hellish and I'm just grateful the damned thing's finished. With any luck, it'll never be released; I'll never have to attend the premiere or go on a publicity junket, pretending I think it's the best film ever made." A hint of alarm crisping the edges of her voice, she asked, "You are still planning to come home, aren't you? I want to see you."

"I want to see you, too, if you don't mind my bringing Jesse along."

"Kyra, why on God's green earth would I *mind?* He's my only grandchild. Obviously, you're still in a state of shock, not thinking clearly. Is it possible you've taken on too much?"

"I don't think so, but it's difficult being back here." Kyra glanced around her small kitchen. "Jesse's been a bit blue since we arrived yesterday. He misses Roddy and Gage and he's not at all sure of me. Neither am I, for that matter. Plus, I've been trying to get my nerve up to do something about Gary's things."

"It can wait. Everything needn't be done at once. How are you for money?"

"Fine, fine. Glen's helping to sort out the estate."

"That's good of her. How are she and Dillon coping with Catharine?"

"Dill's counting the days until he can leave for college. And poor Glen's frazzled from driving back and forth to the city because she's had yet another hysterical call. Cliff's ready to have Auntie Cath committed. He's even drawn up the papers. Of course Glenna won't sign, and they're fighting about it. It's a horror show."

"I love my sister, but she truly is barking mad. Tell Glenna she's got to let Catharine handle her own problems."

"We've *all* tried to tell her that, but Catharine plays on Glenna's guilt."

"Of course she does. She's a guilt virtuoso. But it would be a terrible mistake for Glenna to allow Catharine to come between her and Cliff. He's a sweet-natured man, but there's only so much he'll take."

"I agree. But Catharine presses the buttons and Glenna comes running."

"Perhaps I'll call my sister, have a word. I won't have her breaking up a good marriage."

"It may help. You're the only person Catharine listens to."

"Consider it done. So, now, when will I be seeing you and Jesse?"

"I thought next week. Would that be good for you?"

"Very good. Perfect, in fact."

"I'll ring you when I've booked the tickets."

"Good. I'm longing to see you, Kyra."

"And I you."

The call ended, Kyra put down the receiver and broke into tears, wishing she could see her mother there and then. Such powerfully contradictory feelings; strands of love and mistrust hopelessly tangled in her brain. She was brought back by a small hand patting her arm, and she looked up to find Jesse regarding her cautiously. He pulled his hand away as if expecting to be punished, and his action brought her yet more insight into the immense responsibility of parenthood. She was going to have to remember that she now had a permanent resident audience who was affected by every last thing she said and did.

Fishing a tissue from her pocket, she blotted her eyes. She'd have liked to take him in her arms, but she'd learned to exercise restraint. Embraces confused Jesse, sent his breathing haywire and his small body rigid. "It's okay, Jess," she said. "I'm just feeling a bit sad."

He indicated he wanted to know why.

"Everyone feels blue now and then. It's not important. Would you like your juice now?"

He shook his head, his questioning eyes holding hers determinedly.

"Are you hungry?"

Another shake of his head.

"I promise you nothing's wrong."

His eyes bore into hers.

Giving in to his insistence just as she had to her mother's, she sighed and lifted him onto her knee, saying, "I had a wonderful, wonderful friend, Jesse, someone I loved with all my heart. There was an accident and it took him away forever. Now when I think of him, I miss him—the same way you've been missing Roddy and Gage since we got here—and it makes me sad."

Satisfied with this explanation, he gazed at her for several seconds, then offered her another consoling pat on the arm before climbing down from her knee. Opening the refrigerator, he got the tumbler of juice he hadn't finished at lunch and stood by the counter to drink it, holding the glass with both hands while eyeing her thoughtfully over the rim.

She sat looking back at him, thinking of comfort and joy, and knowing that her mother was right. She had, through the years, been right about many, many things. So why did Kyra go on doubting her mother's authenticity as a person?

Mainly it was because so much of what Kyra knew (and could quote from memory) about her parents came from the scrapbooks that had accumulated during her life. The custom-made, leather-bound, embossed volumes contained clippings and programs, even pages from scripts with either her mother's notes penciled in the margins or her father's directorial comments scrawled in black ink between the lines and running down the sides.

Her parents were people who almost never explained themselves and spoke only anecdotally of the past. Kyra's interest in the family history had long been thwarted by her family's preoccupation with work and with the present tense. It was as if her mother and father had disowned their pasts, which early on contributed to Kyra's sense that they and Kyle were—like Aunt Catharine—writing their lives as they went along, creating an ongoing work of fiction.

What Kyra had gleaned (but hadn't necessarily believed) from her repeated reading of those scrapbooks was that Octavia Bell had always been a gifted mimic; possessed of innate poise and a singularly rich speaking voice, she'd begun actively planning an acting career at the age of ten.

By the time she was twelve, Octavia was attending dance and elocution classes, reading everything on theater she could find. She was in love with the theater, obsessed with it; every aspect of production, from directing to lighting to set dressing, was of interest to her. She was determined to learn how to create the magic that so captured her from the moment she'd first set foot inside a theater at the age of eight, when her mother had taken her to see a Christmas pageant.

She left home in 1932 at the age of eighteen to attend theater school in London. She was, according to an interview in the London *Times* in 1937, "...arresting rather than beautiful, with a strong, prominent nose balanced by an assertive chin. She has startlingly luminous green eyes, a fine fair complexion, and a full expressive mouth." At five foot eight, she was considered very tall for stage work, but her height and the shapely maturity of her figure gave her what she believed was an advantage, namely that she could go after meatier character roles rather than the usually vapid parts written for ingenues.

Mature beyond her years and exceedingly disciplined, she was a standout at the Academy and was offered several professional roles immediately after appearing as Portia in an uneven and somewhat stilted presentation of *Julius Caesar* midway through her first year at the school. "She chose not to accept any of the offers, preferring to complete her training so that," according to a lengthy interview published in 1972 in the *New York Times,* "when she did set foot on the professional stage she would be fully prepared."

The *Times* article went on to say, "Diligent and determined, with an acute gift of concentration, she won most of the major prizes at the end of her second year, and only two weeks after leaving the Academy went into rehearsal for a supporting role in a new

West End drama. She received better notices than did the play it-self, which ran for only twenty-four performances. But with her agent's guidance and her own intelligent instinct for a good script, there quickly followed a better role in a better play, then another and another, until, by the age of twenty-three, her name alone could fill a theater. Her ascent to stardom was, by everyone's meas-ure but her own, meteoric."

"That sort of thing could happen in those days," Octavia said in a *Tatler* interview in 1947. "I was fortunate to be in the right place at the right time. And I was never afraid to tackle difficult roles. I wanted the parts other actresses turned down because they didn't want to risk damaging their images. I've never had an image to pro-tect. What mattered to me was the character, and what I could bring to it. The more unpleasant the better, because difficult people are far more interesting than nice ones."

By twenty-four she was married to Richard Latimer, the ac-claimed young director of her first ill-fated West End show, and the mother of twins. She stayed home to nurse the babies for six months before signing on to star in her first film, *A Letter From Home.* She disliked the experience—"Far too much hurry-up-and-wait to suit me, I'm afraid," she told an interviewer from the *Evening Standard* in 1939. "But I have to confess I was pleasantly surprised by the end result. I really do think it's a very good film."

The critics thought so, too. It was one of the last features to be widely distributed before the start of the war, and she received uni-versally glowing notices as well as a flurry of offers from Holly-wood. She declined them, choosing to act exclusively on the stage during the war years. She also did volunteer work with the Red Cross and traveled throughout Britain to entertain at army bases, while Richard directed war films that were, despite their high pro-paganda levels, very effective. Both partners won numerous awards between 1939 and 1945. And Richard, too, turned down wildly lu-crative offers from Hollywood.

Kyra and Kyle were ensconced for the duration of the war in a damp and drafty Midlands cottage with the nanny, and saw their parents only infrequently. "It was a very difficult time for our fam-ily—as, indeed, it was for everyone," Octavia later claimed in a piece published in 1951 in *Queen.* "I missed my children terribly but there was no question of keeping them in London. It was far too dangerous. It's funny, though, how worried I was about their well-being, yet how little thought I gave to my own. I was appearing on stage eight times a week from August through October 1940. The performances were regularly interrupted by the sirens, and everyone would hurry to the shelter. But once the all-clear sounded, we returned to our respective places and continued on 'til the final curtain. There was an extraordinary collaborative feeling between the cast and the audiences, as if we could, through sheer determination and goodwill, find an hour or two of pleasurable distraction in the midst of that ongoing horror. I've never experienced anything quite so uplifting as the nights we spent on stage during the bleakest hours of the war."

While it was becoming increasingly obvious to their friends and to their two young children that Richard and Octavia were beginning to disagree about all manner of things, finding co-habitation less than compelling, they were—always had been and always would be—in complete agreement when it came to their careers. Both were driven by an overwhelming desire to give their absolute best, and they were hugely successful, much admired and sought after—Octavia because she was such an utter original who introduced new levels of passion and subtlety into stage acting; and Richard because he, too, was one of a kind and produced seamless, uncluttered films of extraordinary impact. No one had ever seen films quite like his, or performances like hers. They each set standards everyone else afterward tried to live up to. Their rewards were a knighthood for Richard in 1962 and two years later Octavia was made a Dame Commander of the Order of the British Empire.

If you read between the lines, it was possible to see that her mother and father were real people. Yet Kyra had struggled all her life to accept the truth of this. What, she wondered, was it going to take for her to capitulate to her love for them? And what was so terrible about loving two people who just happened to be famous?

Jesse had finished his juice but his eyes were still on her, as if he was somehow able to track the evolution of her mood.

With a smile, she said, "I feel happier now. Shall we go out and buy ourselves something completely silly that we don't need at all?"

He actually smiled back at her and nodded vigorously.

Jesse lay asleep with his bear on the carpeted floor of the aircraft beneath a blanket, his head on a small pillow. Kyra looked around the first-class cabin—empty except for one other passenger. It was that portion of the flight when the lights were lowered so that those who were able to sleep could do so for a few hours. She looked again at the singular, silent little boy who'd been given to her because a birth certificate named her as his grandparent. She could not fathom how that had happened but she absolutely didn't care. He was *her* child now. His presence in her life was changing her in ways she hadn't thought possible, and she loved every moment of it. She loved him so much that just the sight of him gave her pleasure.

Emerging into the arrivals area holding a groggy Jesse with one hand and pushing a luggage trolley with the other, Kyra saw a sign bearing her name held aloft by a uniformed chauffeur. She gratefully surrendered the trolley to the man, hoisted Jesse into her arms, and followed the driver to a secluded indoor parking area.

As they neared a gleaming black Rolls-Royce, the rear door opened, Octavia stepped out of the car, and Kyra felt the impact in the pit of her stomach. Hair silvery and cut becomingly short, bearing as erect and regal as ever, her mother wore a simple pale green cotton dress with white low-heeled sandals. She seemed to be growing more beautiful as she got older, and Kyra felt herself begin to thaw deep at her core, anticipating the true pleasure of her mother's company. No one could be as interesting and insightful as Octavia at her best. And no one, Kyra reminded herself, could be colder or more disdainful than Octavia at her worst. Happily, in the years since her parents' divorce, Kyra had rarely seen her mother at her worst.

Octavia hurried to offer an embrace that enclosed Kyra and Jesse both.

Kyra breathed in her mother's softness and the essential fragrance that was Octavia's alone—a rich custom-blended *chypre* modulated by hints of rose and freesia (a scent capable of hypnotizing the unsuspected)—murmuring, "You smell just like my mother."

It was Kyra's standard greeting and Octavia laughed silently—no more than an abrupt inhalation followed by an expulsion of air near Kyra's ear—then said, "I've missed you desperately, Kyra." Leaning away, Octavia studied her daughter, noting that Kyra's eyes had a new haunted aspect. And, typically, she was dressed down with a vengeance, in the hope of going unnoticed. As if that were ever likely to happen! A slight shake of her head and Octavia finally looked at the boy, immediately taken with him: an imp of a child with a fine heart-shaped face and the eyes of an old man; cautious, darkly liquid eyes that missed nothing and betrayed a wealth of emotions.

Jesse was squirming and Kyra set him down.

Her mother kissed her again, then bent to offer her hand to Jesse, saying, "I've been told you're very fond of having stories read to you. Shall I tell you something?"

Jesse nodded, visibly captivated. Children always adored Octavia on sight. And the sound of her voice, the way she addressed them, somehow elicited the very best they had to offer. Jesse was no exception. He gazed up at her unblinking, mouth slightly open, as if he'd never seen or heard anyone quite so fabulously alluring.

"I simply *adore* reading stories to little people," Octavia told him in a confiding tone. "And I've got tons of them to read to you. What do you think of that?"

Jesse smiled. For the first time since he'd come into Kyra's life he looked happy.

Octavia smiled back at him. "I'm Kyra's mother, your new granny, and I believe you and I are going to have a splendid time together. There are all sorts of wonderful things for us to see and do. And you like to see and do new things, don't you, Jesse?"

He nodded, eyes aglow.

Kyra's lungs were fluttering as if she'd been plunged into very cold water, and she was close to tears. Her mother was a whimsical sorceress; magic was her business.

"Just as I thought," Octavia declared. "We're going to be great friends, aren't we, my boy?"

Jesse kept nodding and smiling.

Straightening, Octavia turned and led a mesmerized Jesse by the hand to the limousine, saying, "Louise is preparing something of a breakfast feast. I do hope you're both hungry."

Throughout the ride into the city Kyra sat back, fascinated by the ease with which her mother won Jesse over. By the time they arrived at the house he was ensconced in Octavia's lap, thumb in his mouth, listening avidly as she spoke of the outings she had planned.

"And here we are at Granny's house," she said, as the Rolls-Royce pulled into the driveway. "Rather a big old heap, isn't it?"

Jesse nodded, peering through the window.

"It's a good house for playing hide and seek. Do you know how to play?"

A shake of his head.

"I'll teach you. It's great fun. I believe there are some surprises waiting for you, but I expect you'd rather have some breakfast first and a little lie-down, wouldn't you?"

In agreement with everything she had to say, Jesse went with her up the front walk. Then suddenly he stopped and looked back at Kyra, eyes clouding; clearly prepared to be castigated for daring to enjoy himself.

"Go with Granny, love," Kyra reassured him. "It's all right."

"This is Louise, Jesse." Octavia introduced the housekeeper who had obviously been watching for them and now opened the front door. "She takes care of Granny's big old heap."

"Takes care of big ol' Granny, too," Louise said, grinning at Jesse. "'Ello, pet," she said. "I've laid on a smashin' breakfast for you. 'Ope you're 'ungry."

He motioned that he was, and Louise gave him a pat on the head before leaning around to greet Kyra. "'Ello, luv! Lovely to see you. Good flight?"

"Very good, thank you, Louise. How are you?"

"Never better, luv."

While Octavia tipped the driver, with Jesse staying right by her side, Kyra went with Louise to the kitchen.

"Probably could do with a cuppa, couldn't you?"

"I'd adore one, thank you, Louise." Kyra stood by the large rear window to look out at the lush garden. Colors seemed more intense here than anywhere else; emotions did, too. The walls of this house were swollen with memories, and each room contained faint echoes of their voices. Every corner of the place revived all but forgotten scenes, but none more than the garden.

It was where her mother had always spent most of her free time—good weather or bad. If she wasn't planting, or weeding, or pruning the roses, she was seated on the chaise under the big umbrella, reading or learning lines. It was also where she did most of her entertaining. Kyra could remember so many parties, the grounds illuminated by paper lanterns and torches set at intervals along the paths and the borders of the flower beds, with lavish buffets set up under canopies and uniformed staff—usually out-of-work actors—offering trays of hors d'oeuvres and drinks.

Octavia cared more about the garden than the interior of the house, which she left fairly much to Louise's care. But the only other person allowed to do anything to the garden was Henry, who lived down the road and had started mowing the grass and trimming the tall hedges to earn pocket money as a boy thirty-eight years before. Now a successful businessman, married and the father of three, Henry lived in his boyhood home and in his spare time still tended to this garden as well as to his own. Henry was, Octavia had always insisted, a singularly gifted gardener. Green things flourished at his touch.

Turning from the window Kyra watched her mother and Jesse come into the kitchen. As at the airport, the sight of Octavia both eased and disquieted her. She cherished her mother, but had feared all her life that Octavia's declarations of love were merely well-delivered lines from some unpublished script. Yet looking at her now, Kyra had to ask herself why, even for a single moment, she'd ever doubted her mother's love. No one who didn't care deeply for her could have held her the way Octavia had at the airport, or looked at her with such undisguised affection the way Octavia looked at her now before once again enfolding her in her arms. *I'm the dishonest one in the family,* Kyra thought, ashamed. *It's never been the others; it's been me all along.*

CHAPTER 13

Octavia had always been able to gauge her daughter's state of mind by the manner in which she used her body. Until she was in her early twenties, Kyra had offered herself perfunctorily for stiff little hugs and hasty kisses, holding back as if fearful either of giving more than was required or of receiving less than was expected. When she fell in love with Gary, her hugs became pliant and she exuded the languorous warmth of a giving, satisfied woman. At the airport Octavia had felt a new yielding in Kyra that showed in the tenderness and duration of their embrace. She was displaying greater depth and receptiveness, and it was obvious that she and this child had come together at precisely the right time—a stroke of good fortune for them both.

Despite his obedience and his visible attachment to Kyra, Octavia saw a certain feral aspect to Jesse's gaze and to his energy. He was a child who might, depending on the circumstances, succumb to his darker side and run wild. There were bound to be times when that side would take over, sending him out of control, and she wondered how Kyra would handle matters when that happened. Still, Octavia found the child enchanting. He shone with intelligence; a quicksilver creature who bore the imprint of his past experiences as a shadow that descended from time to time over his eyes, and then, in an instant, it was gone and he capitulated to transitory joy.

Watching Jesse lift his cup with both hands to drink with obvious pleasure, Octavia said, "Your uncle Kyle also enjoyed a good cup of tea as a little boy. But Kyra preferred lemon squash." Seeing his unspoken question, she explained, "It's rather a boring lemon drink mixed with water."

"It's not boring, and I still like it," Kyra disagreed, enjoying her mother's interaction with Jesse, and trying to remember if Octavia had been as observant and as interested in her own children. With a guilty pang, Kyra realized that she probably had. But Octavia's celebrity had been an impediment to their intimacy. Kyra had been afraid to trust a mother who could, so very convincingly, become someone else. She'd seen it happen dozens of times. How was she to know which woman was the real one?

Jesse gave a dismissing shrug to show Octavia his lack of interest in boring drinks and offered a small apologetic smile to Kyra, then put his cup down carefully and began to eat with gusto, as if to satisfy both women as well as the housekeeper. Mother and daughter exchanged a smile across the table. There followed a comfortable silence while the three of them ate Louise's grilled tomatoes and mushrooms, gammon rashers, coddled eggs and fried bread. Then, sated, Jesse drooped, his eyes glazing over and his head slowly falling forward.

"I think perhaps it's time for your lie-down, Jesse. Don't you agree?" Octavia asked.

He looked at Kyra, who gestured that the matter was entirely in his hands, then he nodded to Octavia, who said, "Very sensible," and stood up, extending her hand. At once he scrambled down from his chair to take hold of it.

Delighted by Jesse's lovestruck response to her mother, Kyra followed the two of them upstairs.

"This was your uncle Kyle's room when he was a boy," Octavia explained, drawing the curtains closed. "Of course it's nothing like it was then. It's tidy, for one thing; clean, for another."

Kyra, busy removing Jesse's shoes, noticed him eyeing the closet door.

"He was a very naughty boy, was Kyle," Octavia went on. "And a grubby packrat, too. Hated to part with anything. So we'd find bits of food everywhere, and dirty clothes chucked under the bed, mountains of books and papers, toys. Has Kyra told you about that?"

Jesse shook his head and settled under the blanket with his bear.

"You doubt me, do you?" Charmed by his mute expressiveness, Octavia leaned in close to him, with a smile, saying, "You'll learn soon enough that Granny never misrepresents. Close your eyes and have a lovely sleep, my sweet. Later, I'll tell you some tales about naughty little Kyle, and we'll also see if we can't find those surprises for you. All right?"

He nodded and looked over at Kyra.

"I'll be nearby if you need me," Kyra assured him. On her way out she stopped to glance into the empty closet and left the door ajar.

"What was that bit of business with the cupboard door?" Octavia asked a short while later when they were seated side by side in the deeply cushioned garden chairs beneath the green-and-white-striped umbrella.

"I'm not honestly sure, but I suspect Jesse's been forced to sleep most of his life in a cupboard. At least that's where I find him every night, even though he starts out in bed."

"Kyle told me about the boy's being abused, but he didn't tell me that." Octavia frowned, shocked.

"He didn't know."

After a moment Octavia said, "You're very good with him."

Lifted by the praise, Kyra said, "I'm playing it strictly by ear, taking my cues from him for the most part."

"He's obviously grown very attached to you."

"You think so?"

"Yes, I do."

"I hope so. *I'm* very attached to him. The garden looks magnificent," Kyra observed.

"It's been a good year for the roses, not too wet."

A good year for the roses. It repeated in her head as she looked at her mother, thinking she looked considerably younger than her years, and without benefit of plastic surgery. Which led her to say, "You're not going to believe it, but Catharine's talking about having yet another face-lift. I think she thinks that might bring Henry back."

"Poor, silly thing. I'm sure it's a sickness." Octavia gave a slow shake of her head. "I could understand it, I suppose, if she'd had visible flaws to begin with. But she didn't. Cathy was a stunningly beautiful girl."

"But she didn't think so," Kyra guessed.

"No."

"Why?" Kyra asked. "What happened? Why is it none of you ever talk about your childhood, your parents? Most of what I know about Catharine and you and Dad I've learned through the years from interviews the two of you have given."

Testily, Octavia said, "I can't speak for your father or for

Catharine, but I would willingly have told you almost anything—
if you'd ever expressed any interest. Or perhaps," she qualified, "I
should say curiosity. You were such an intensely private child, and
somewhat judgmental. So often I felt I was failing with you, but
couldn't think how or why, and had no idea how to rectify matters."

"That's awful!" Kyra was distressed to think they had misperceived each other so drastically. "I *was* judgmental," she admitted.
"And not just somewhat. I thought you, Father and Kyle were a unit,
and I was excluded for some reason, didn't belong. Now I think perhaps it was about self-confidence. You three had it and I didn't."

"Poor Kyle's only ever pretended to be confident. Whatever energy didn't go into his work went into his sundry pretenses. Surely
you must have seen that for yourself by now. But how sad you
should have felt that way, Kyra. Perhaps I failed both of you."

"No, you didn't," Kyra argued, as upset as her mother. "We simply didn't communicate terribly well. It hadn't anything to do with
failing. Please don't think that." This was why it was so much safer
to maintain a careful distance, she thought disconsolately. It allowed one to avoid awkward situations, occasions when unruly
emotions got the upper hand.

"My whole *life* is about communication!" Octavia disagreed. "If
I haven't managed to communicate with my own children, I *have*
failed."

Could she truly mean that? Or was this just another dimension
to the performance? Immediately Kyra was overcome by shame
for thinking it. "Oh, look. I love you," she said, her voice unsteady.
"I always have. That's what matters, really. Don't you think?"

"Ultimately, yes, I do. You're very changed, Kyra."

"Perhaps I am. I'm seeing everything very differently since Gary
died. You didn't fail me," she insisted, wanting to erase whatever negative sentiments might exist between them. "I probably failed myself."

Octavia threaded the fingers of both hands through her hair,
then let her hands drop to her lap as her head fell back against the
seat. There was an awful parallel between her sister and her daughter—one trying to preserve her beauty by surgical means and in
the process destroying it, the other trying to erase her beauty with
compulsive eating but managing only to make herself more beautiful. "If we're being honest here, the truth is, Kyra, there were any
number of questions I didn't want you to ask, and I managed suc-

cessfully to transmit that message to you. You've always been far more sensitive to nuance than your brother. In any case, it's ancient history. Sometimes, you know, I simply can't believe I'm so old.

"I went along to the costume fittings for this last film and there was a moment when I was between outfits, standing in the workshop, quite nonchalant in my petticoat, thinking vain thoughts about what good shape I was in for a woman over sixty. Then I happened to see myself in the full-length mirror." She made a grim face. "Horrifying, when only a short time ago my body was my ally, a great natural asset I thought would stay perfect forever. But there I was confronting the indisputable evidence that only the mind, if we're fortunate, remains untouched by age. Needless to say, I've taken pains to avoid full-length mirrors since then." She laughed ruefully.

Kyra was shaking her head. "It's not true. I've been thinking you've never looked better."

"You can say that because you don't know yet what's been lost. The Fates willing and I'm still alive, we'll have this conversation again when *you're* sixty-two and *then* you'll understand."

"I've understood about mirrors since I was eleven."

Octavia reached over to curve one well-tended hand over her daughter's cheek. "My dearest girl, you've been *mistaken* about yourself since you were eleven. But I know better than to try to change your mind."

"Quite right. Tell me about your family."

With a sigh, her mother withdrew her hand, saying, "My mother was lovely, fair and willowy—a gentle, very fragile, soul. Anna Alicia Bell. I adored her. She was English, you know. Have I ever told you that?"

"No," Kyra answered quietly.

"Born in London and grew up here. The family moved to New York in 1908. My grandmother died two years later of what they called then the 'wasting sickness'—undoubtedly some form of cancer. Mother and her older brother, Andrew, took it badly, but my grandfather was decimated. Andrew had to leave university to step in at the age of nineteen and take over the family importing business. Eventually he persuaded his father back to work, and in the autumn of 1911 the two of them traveled to England on company business, leaving Mother at home with the staff. The following April, to celebrate the success of the trip, they booked passage home on the *Titanic*.

"I remember Mother telling me about it when I was a little girl, talking about how desperately she'd wanted to come home to England after her brother and father died. She made all the arrangements, but was so terrified of the prospect of drowning at sea that she couldn't bring herself to climb the gangplank. She tried again and again over the course of several years, but at the last moment couldn't ever board the ship. Finally, resigned, she accepted the proposal of an older man who'd been wooing her assiduously. By the time she was eighteen and pregnant she knew that Augustus Corde—" she spoke the name as if it had a vile taste "—had pursued her solely for her money. Luckily, my grandfather had drafted a will that allowed Corde no direct access. The income from the trust was generous, but any extras had to be obtained by petitioning the executors—none of whom had any fondness for my father. He was a vain, handsome and pretentious man—dangerous. By the time I was five or six his fabled charm was something I saw only when my parents entertained, which was less and less often. Mother had a few friends—young women she'd met while at school—but Father found ways to discourage them from visiting and, in time, she ended up effectively isolated.

"For seven years my mother and I inhabited our own private world, and we were very close. Then Catharine was born. Almost from birth my sister was gloriously oblivious to everything except Father, and he blatantly favored her, showing a strange, quite vulnerable, side to his nature. She was a remarkably beautiful child, and people were forever stopping on the street or in the park to smile at the sight of her. I was prepared to love her unreservedly, but Cathy seemed merely to tolerate me and Mother, while her eyes kept moving past us, hoping for the sight of Father.

"I did admire her skill at manipulating him. She knew instinctively how to get whatever she wanted from him. And his pride in her was boundless. He actually held her up to Mother and me as an example. This biddable, pretty toddler represented his ideal of female perfection. Laughable, really. Still, his preoccupation with Cathy allowed Mother and me some latitude—for a time. Then he went back to tormenting her. There were many occasions," she said softly, "when I was awakened by the sound of her sobs or her screams. The next morning Mother would say I'd had a nightmare. Everything was fine. There she was, all of a piece. Just a bad dream, she'd tell me. But I knew otherwise. I knew. I'd seen the blood-stained bedding, seen items in that bedroom whose significance I didn't comprehend until years and years later. And of course the staff knew. Everyone but Cathy knew."

Octavia paused a moment, examining a gallery of interior images. "In our last conversation my mother admitted that she shouldn't have stayed; she shouldn't have allowed Father to exert his ugly influence on Catharine. But just as she'd been afraid to climb the gangplank and return home, she'd been afraid for any number of reasons to leave her husband. She wanted me to know that she'd filed the necessary papers at our births: Catharine and I had British citizenship, and someday, if we wished to, the two of us could go home.

"That same night, while Father was out at his club and Cathy and I were asleep, Mother killed herself. She was thirty-three years old." Reaching into her pocket, Octavia brought out a handkerchief and blew her nose.

Kyra put a hand on her mother's arm but said nothing.

After a time, Octavia continued. "Following her father's example, Mother had had a will drawn leaving her entire estate to Cathy and me. But what she hadn't known was that Corde had already—illegally, of course—managed to appropriate, and lose, a fair amount of her money. He'd even managed to get a mortgage on the house as collateral against his so-called investments. Her death froze what was left of her assets.

"The house was sold to make good on Father's debts, and the interest on the remaining funds was used to pay the rent on the Fifth Avenue apartment the executors organized for us. Father never stopped complaining about the place—it wasn't grand enough to suit him—or about the fact that we no longer had five on staff but only the housekeeper, Mrs. Abbott, and the maid. The next four years were the longest of my life. I wasn't allowed to continue any of my private lessons, nor was I permitted to go anywhere unless I took Cathy with me.

"She cared as little for the situation as I did, primarily because she enjoyed being paraded about as Father's paragon of virtue. To her credit, she was never one to gloat. She simply accepted her status as the preferred child. I did try, so many times, to instill in her some sense of self-reliance, but she just didn't *get* it. She was too young. And besides, she couldn't see the point of being independent when she could get anything she wanted from her father.

"So—" Octavia sighed "—on my eighteenth birthday I gained access to my inheritance and within a week I was on a ship, headed here. I had qualms about leaving my sister behind but Corde would never have allowed me to take her. Cathy didn't want to leave in any case. And the truth is I was happy to be free of them both.

"So, I got away and Cathy stayed. As far as I'm aware she doesn't know to this day that Mother's death was a suicide. But that's beside the point. Something happened. One week I received a typically airy letter from my sister, telling about the boys she'd been dating and the super new clothes she'd bought. And the next week she wrote to say she'd booked passage and would be arriving in London in a month's time.

"Later, Mary Abbott, the housekeeper, wrote me that the atmosphere in the apartment had, overnight, turned very tense, with Cathy refusing to speak to Father and, against his wishes, staying away most nights at the homes of her girlfriends. Then, all at once she was packing to leave, and Father was alternately ranting at her and pleading with her to reconsider.

"What I think happened is that he somehow managed to get his hands on her trust fund. She's always been hopeless about money, but she isn't completely stupid. I imagine she had a run-in with the bank manager, who told her she was overdrawn, or something to that effect. And she would've been devastated to discover that the father she'd idolized had helped himself to her assets. Money's always been very important to Catharine and she had very little left by the time she got here. As well, she refused to speak of Father. What she did worry over, aloud and often, was her looks. Did I find her as pretty as she used to be? Were her breasts too small, or just right? Did I think she should bob her hair, or go on a diet? Her confidence was badly eroded. When we learned five or six years later that Corde had been murdered, Cathy said, 'Good. I'm glad. He deserved it. Now, if I want to, I'll be able to go home.'"

"*Murdered?*" Kyra shivered, feeling the hair rise on her arms.

"Stabbed repeatedly. Mary Abbott found his body when she returned to the apartment after her Thursday afternoon off. The killer was never found."

"My God!" Kyra exclaimed.

"But getting back to Cathy. The only explanation she could come up with for why Corde would have stolen from her was because she was no longer beautiful. That had to be why, otherwise he'd never have done it. Twisted, I grant you, but it set a precedent. Twice she married rather distant men, then kept an anxious eye on each, waiting to be betrayed. As fate would have it, *she* betrayed poor Clive because she was on a desperate quest for passion. All her life, she's had a somewhat cinematic concept of sex that culminates in a fade-out—women being acted upon, you know, not equal participants. The real thing was far too messy and clinical for her.

"We both had rather too much to drink one evening just before she left Clive, and the conversation turned to sex and her profound disappointment in it. She had no idea there was such a thing as foreplay or that love could be made in anything other than the missionary position. When I suggested she have a go at oral sex her face turned scarlet. She was scandalized, thought I was being obscene, trying to shock her, and refused to believe ordinary people engaged in such perversity. The implication being, of course, that we theatrical types were all depraved." Octavia rolled her eyes. "Now Henry's gone, and it stands to reason she'd believe it's because of her looks, not because she's sexually squeamish and has such a penchant for drama. She's constitutionally unable to see situations, or people, as they are. And her sexuality's never really been explored because both times she's set her cap for rather timid men, which is a pity and a waste because she's a tremendously sensual woman."

"She is, isn't she?" Kyra agreed, thinking of that closet filled with silks and cashmeres. "The night Henry left she asked me if I'd made love with other men before I married Gary. I told her I had and she said she'd only made love with her two husbands, which she thought had been a great mistake."

"In all likelihood she'll go off on one last desperate quest for passion before she gives up and spends the rest of her life blaming everyone but herself for her failure to find it."

"Weren't you frightened, coming to a strange country all alone?" Kyra asked.

"Not in the least. I was coming home—making the trip finally

for Anna Alicia. And I had two elderly great-aunts here, my grandfather's spinster sisters, Emily and Lucia." Octavia smiled fondly.
"They were a darling pair who lived out their lives in the family
home off Sloane Square. I stayed with them until I finished theater school, and it was a very happy time. Then I signed on to do
the play with your father, and the rest is history."

"What happened to your great-aunts?"

"They died within weeks of each other shortly after your father
and I were married. The proceeds from their estate paid for this
house and gave me a bit of a nest egg."

"I wish I'd known all this a long time ago," Kyra said, weariness suddenly descending heavily upon her.

"Why?"

Finding it increasingly difficult to maintain coherency, Kyra
said, "Because now that I have some idea of what shaped you and
Catharine I can see you more clearly." *You're more real to me,* she
added silently, thinking of a mother screaming in the dead of night
and a murdered father. Too Gothic not to be true.

Octavia saw Kyra's eyes losing their focus and said, "I think you
need a nap."

"I'm suddenly stupefied."

"Go along and have a rest. I'll come wake you in an hour or two."

Without warning, Kyra broke into tears but lacked the energy to
reach into her pocket for a tissue, so she sat and snuffled like a
child, finally wiping her face on her sleeve.

Octavia took hold of her hand, saying, "You lost a lovely man;
he was so good for you. It's a terrible loss—for all of us, really."

Kyra looked down the length of the garden. "With him, I wasn't
an obese freak. Now...now I'm not sure what I am."

"Now you're a mother," Octavia said. "You'll have precious
little time from now on to worry about your supposed freakish-
ness. You'll be far too busy chasing after that boy. And let me
ask you this. Do you think Kyle feels any more or less of a freak
than you do?"

"He told you?"

"He didn't have to tell me. Did he have to tell you?"

"No."

"Right, then. So the truth is that every last one of us feels like a
freak at some point. But that doesn't mean we are. It's about emo-

tion, or instinct, or bad luck temporarily getting the upper hand and making us feel ugly or abnormal. Both my children are talented and beautiful, with good hearts, good minds and, occasionally, faulty wiring." Releasing Kyra's hand, she said, "Now, go in and rest for a while. We'll talk more later."

After a quick look to see that Jesse was asleep on the floor of Kyle's closet, Kyra continued on to the room at the rear of the house that had always been hers. For a time, she looked out the window at her mother in the garden below, watching Octavia don her reading glasses and open a script. *A good year for the roses.* Her smile becoming a yawn, she turned from the window and walked over to the bed.

CHAPTER 14

Kyra was roused from the depths of sleep by a voice she knew intimately whispering, "Time to get up now, you." With the hum of jet engines still thrumming deep in her body, and fatigue fogging her brain, for a few moments she was tricked into believing the voice belonged to Gary. A few moments of soaring hope and happiness before the truth rudely grounded her.

Then, with an effort, she opened her eyes to see her brother grinning at her. "I've got orders from Dame Octavia to get you up."

Kyra offered him a drowsy smile. "Hello, love. How are you?"

"'Tis a far happier man I am now that Beth's hied off home to Mums and Daddy. I did offer to sign the flat over to her, but she wasn't interested. All she wanted was her clothes. Took two burly blokes a dozen or more trips to shift the lot—filled an entire lorry."

"You're exaggerating."

"Only slightly, I promise you."

Seeing the time, she sat up abruptly, asking, "Where's Jesse?"

"Not to worry. He's in the garden with Mum. I think you'll want to see what's going on."

"Why? What is it?"

"Come down and see. It's well worth the price of admission." He got up and started for the door, then turned back. "Perhaps," he said with atypical diffidence, "we'll have a chance to finish that conversation we started in Connecticut."

"I'd really like that."

"I was hoping you might. See you shortly," he said, and continued on his way.

Niggled by the irrational sense that she'd been negligent in failing to be there when Jesse woke up, she splashed cold water on her face, brushed her teeth, then hurried downstairs.

As she approached the umbrella, she heard indecipherable words spoken by a low, husky voice, then her mother's and Kyle's appreciative laughter. In her travel-wearied state, she couldn't quite recognize the voice and wondered if her mother had a guest. But no, she didn't. There, leaning against Octavia's knee, was Jesse— clad in a red long-sleeved rugby shirt with white collar, stiff new jeans and soft leather moccasins, all of which he'd chosen himself. He looked exotic, more gypsylike than ever; his color high, eyes alight. He was lending his voice to a handsome, furry hand puppet crafted into a most lifelike rabbit who was responding to some question Octavia had put to it.

Sensing her presence, Jesse whirled around and ran over to her, brimming with excitement as he moved the mouth of the rabbit to say, "Hiya, Kyra!"

Thunderstruck, for a few seconds all she could do was look first at the puppet, then at Jesse, and finally at her mother and brother who both seemed very pleased—with themselves and with what was happening. An inner buoyancy taking her over, she directed herself to the puppet, saying, "Hi. What's your name?"

"Name's Drick an' I'm a magic rabbit."

Her knees were wobbly, and so was her smile; she was caught halfway between a shout of laughter and an eruption of tears.

"Magic?" she asked in a voice that was also wobbly.

"Uh-hunh," responded the rabbit.

"Who gave you that interesting name?"

"He did." The puppet inclined its head toward Jesse.

"I see. And where have you come from, Drick?"

"Granny! She gived me to Jesse." The gleeful child had the rabbit point at Octavia.

"Well, Drick, I'm very happy to meet you," Kyra said.

"Very happy to meet you," replied the puppet, mimicking her accent with surprising accuracy.

"So, Monkey," Kyle asked, "are you and Drick hungry?"

Jesse made a show of whispering to the hand puppet, which then turned its head to Kyle and said, "We's hungry."

As Jesse went skipping off toward the house with his hand in Kyle's, Kyra hung back to wind an arm around her mother's waist, saying, "I want to fall down and howl like a wild animal. You are *so* clever. I'd never in a million years have thought of that. He's *talking.*"

"Children are usually responsive to puppets," Octavia said offhandedly.

"No, you're *clever;* you're *brilliant!*" Kyra declared. "And I can't thank you enough." She caught her mother in a sudden, crushing hug. "Thank you, *thank you.* You *are* Glinda. I've always secretly believed you were."

"That's adorable," Octavia said archly. "Glinda, indeed. Should I be flattered?"

"Absolutely. She was the good witch."

"I'd much have preferred Margaret Hamilton's role."

"You're perverse."

"True."

"Seriously, thank you."

"I'm just pleased it worked. I've got tons more things hidden about the house," Octavia said as Kyra released her and they continued hand in hand up the garden. "Little ones always love a treasure hunt. You and Kyle certainly did."

On hearing this, Kyra suddenly saw herself and Kyle searching through a series of small, cold rooms, looking for concealed treats, while their mother followed them, saying, "You're cold. Oh, you're getting warmer. Yes, you're much warmer." They'd played this game, she now recalled, every time Octavia had come to the cottage to visit them during the war. *Every time, for months on end.* If she could have forgotten something as important as the way her mother had turned each visit into a festive occasion, what else had she forgotten, what other truths might have been distorted? Was it possible she was as deluded in her own way as Aunt Catharine was in hers? A very scary notion.

"What?" Octavia asked.

"I was remembering the treasure hunts."

"Ah, yes." Octavia gave Kyra's hand a squeeze.

"You made every visit special. And now you're going to do the same thing for Jesse."

"I have been waiting a long, long time to play granny, my darling. I intend to revel in it, to bask in it; yea, verily, I *shall* swim in it. Auntie Mame *redux.*"

"Oh, God!" Kyra laughed. "You really mean it, don't you?"

"With every fiber of my being," Octavia said dryly.

Jesse reluctantly set Drick aside while he ate his lunch. The instant he was done, lining his knife and fork up across the plate as Kyra had taught him, he retrieved the puppet from beneath his chair, fit it over his hand and butted Drick's furry head against Kyle's arm.

"Steady on there, Drick," Kyle said, making a show of rubbing his arm. "You don't know your own strength."

Doubt at once reshaped Jesse's features. Irked with himself, Kyle smiled, saying, "Sorry, dear one. I was just fooling about," and the doubt disappeared.

"You gonna take us to see cricket, dear one?" Drick asked.

Kyra and Octavia exchanged amused looks.

"I did promise you that, didn't I?" Kyle said.

"Yah." Drick's head went up and down.

"A group of us will be playing on Sunday. Would you and your friend Jesse like to come along, if Kyra says it's okay?"

"Yah!" Jesse looked over at Kyra, who signaled her permission. "When's Sunday?"

"Today is Thursday," Octavia explained, immensely gratified by the boy's quick-wittedness. Kyra had got herself a very, very bright child. "Tomorrow is Friday. After that comes Saturday, then Sunday. Do you know how many days that is?"

Jesse shook his head, for a moment forgetting Drick.

Octavia held up her hand and counted off the days on her fingers, one, two, three. Jesse lifted his free hand and silently copied her, chubby fingers curling down into his palm. Then Drick came to life, complaining, "That's a long time."

"Not really," Kyra said. "Besides, you and Jesse will be so busy, you'll scarcely notice the time passing."

"What doin'?" Drick's face came close to Kyra's. Stupidly, painfully touched, she stroked the pink silk lining of the rabbit's ear.

"For one thing," Octavia said, "we're going to visit the biggest toy store in all of England. Would you enjoy that?" Jesse's head bobbed vigorously up and down. "Yes, I rather thought you would. Then, on Saturday afternoon we're going to see a play. Do you know what a play is?" Jesse shook his head, and Octavia explained. "It's a story with people acting out the parts of the characters on a stage. This play has singing and dancing, as well."

Jesse's eyes widened, and Drick declared, "We *like* stories!"

"I know, and so do I," Octavia said approvingly. "We're also going to go to a concert to hear some wonderful music, and we'll eat in a restaurant; *and* we'll take a boat ride on the river to visit a fantastic castle."

Jesse's mouth was now agape, his eyes enormous.

"You've laid on a full schedule," Kyra observed.

"I certainly have. So I thought next weekend we'd drive down to visit a friend in Cornwall and relax at the seaside for a few days."

"You lot are going to have a splendid time," Kyle said. "I think I'm jealous."

All Jesse could do was keep on nodding.

"What friend?" Kyra asked.

"You remember Kenneth, don't you?"

"The one who's a duke or a lord?"

"He's a baronet, actually."

"Mum's great romance," Kyle teased. "The *paparazzi* hang about all the important venues just waiting for a chance to get a few shots of the two of them."

"Don't be hateful," Kyra admonished him.

"It's the truth, actually," Kyle told her. "Isn't it, Mum?"

"We've had our fair share of press, but we're old news now, so they leave us alone for the most part. At any rate, it's more an intimate friendship these days," Octavia said blithely. "We're past the truly hot and heavy part of it."

"Really? How far past?" Kyra asked, impressed by her mother's candor.

"At least five years," her mother replied. "Now it's whenever our moods coincide which, all things considered, is fairly often."

Kyra laughed aloud. "Aren't you wicked!" she said admiringly. "But I don't think you ever told me you two were involved."

"Kenneth and I have been together so long I suppose I just assumed everyone knew." Turning her attention back to Jesse, Octavia said, "Shall we walk up the road to the shops and buy some sweets while Kyle and Kyra have a visit?"

"Sweets?" Drick asked.

"Candy," Kyra translated.

Drick said, *"Yah!"* Jesse slid down off his chair and scooted around the table to stand beside Octavia, ready to leave.

She chucked him under the chin and said, "Give Granny five minutes to get herself organized, then we'll go. Do you need to visit the loo, Jesse?"

"What's 'at?" asked Drick.

"The toilet."

"Oh! Nope. Don't gotta go. You gonna visit the loo?" The puppet craned its head to look at her.

Octavia burst into merry laughter. "Yah, Drick," she said in perfect imitation. "I'm gonna visit."

"Keer, why don't you come home?"

"What do you mean? I *am* home."

"Don't be obtuse. I mean for good."

"Kyle, I don't know if I want to do that."

"You like the idea," he said. "I can tell."

"I don't know if I do or not."

He folded his arms behind his head and extended his legs, crossing them at the ankles. "Once your adoption of Jesse is finalized, you can apply for British citizenship for him. If you're both here and a job out of town comes up, there'll always be one of us around to take care of him while you're away."

"You're going too fast," she protested.

"No, you're just a little frightened. You've never liked change. Even when we were kids the slightest shift in routine threw you off."

"You make it sound like a character defect. And I'm not sure that's true."

"It is true, you know. Remember when Rose retired and Mum hired Louise? It was a good year before you'd even *look* at Louise, a year before you'd let her clean your room when you were home for visits. I could cite other examples, but I won't. All I'm saying is I realize I've suggested rather a massive undertaking, and you're not unreasonably rattled by it."

"Yes, I am." What he'd said about Louise was true. Perhaps she did dislike change. She was so tired it was hard to think clearly.

"It's a sensible idea, though. If you sell the New York apartment, you'll likely realize a good profit, and even after taxes, what you net should allow you and Jesse to get set up in a decent house or flat here."

"Why are you doing this?" she asked, feeling unfairly pressured.

"Because I like the idea of having the two of you nearby, of being able to see you and talk to you regularly. So does Mum. Because I've accepted the sad fact that I'll never have kids of my own, and I'm smitten with Jesse. And because, finally, I think in your heart of hearts you *want* to come back. No matter how long you live over there, it's never going to be home—not the way this is." He lowered one hand to make a sweeping gesture that took in the house, the city and, by inference, the entire country. "Put the apartment on the market, take the money, and come home, Kyra. I'll be happy. Mum will be happy. You and Jess will be happy. Even dear old lugubrious Dad probably will be, too. Everyone wins."

His optimism was contagious, and she could feel her enthusiasm beginning to build. "I would like to be nearer to all of you, but I'm reluctant to make any hasty moves right now, Kyle. The best I can do is to promise I'll give the idea serious consideration."

"That's all I ask. And Jesse would benefit from some positive male input, you know."

"You see that as your designated role, do you?"

"Sure. Why not? I'll teach him to appreciate cricket, among other things."

She smiled. "Something no boy should grow up without."

"Too bloody right."

"Is it really going so easily with Beth?"

"Relatively," he said. "She asked for a ludicrous amount of alimony, but she'll settle for considerably less."

"How much less?" she asked.

"About seventy-five percent—a couple of hundred a month. It's not as if she doesn't have an income. When she works, she makes ten times what I do, for God's sake. But it'll be worth every penny to be rid of her. I've already arranged to have the flat painted, ordered a new bed."

"A new bed?"

"It's symbolic."

"Fair enough. And work?"

"I've got the film in September, and there's the possibility of a telly six-parter."

"So you're not worried."

"I'm always worried. I'm just not *very* worried. What about a cuppa?"

"Good idea. I'm really dehydrated from the flight." Kyra looked over at the house. "Where do you suppose they've got to?"

"Surely you remember that buying sweets is a time-consuming business for little kids. Jess has probably never experienced anything remotely like those jars in the tobacconist's. And knowing Mother, she's undoubtedly showing him off to all and sundry. She's been waiting forever to play Granny, you know."

"So she says. But I didn't know. I'm beginning to think I've been living with a sack over my head or something. I mean, I must have known about Kenneth but I can't remember ever hearing her talk about the two of them as an item."

"I think you have been covering your ears on some metaphoric level. But I took it to mean that Mum and Dad and I weren't your favorite people."

It was, she knew, the impression she'd always given. And suddenly it was important to correct the record. "The truth is the exact opposite. I adore the three of you," she confessed, with the sense that she'd embarked upon something very dangerous. "But I felt like one of the fans, if that makes any sense; one of those people queueing up outside the theater, waiting to talk to Mother; one of those moonstruck girls who're forever asking you for autographs. I didn't feel *related* to the three of you. I was only incidentally, accidentally, a family member."

"This is just like our conversation at the pond," he said. "We're finally talking truths to each other, and I'm shocked by the things we're admitting. It's dreadful to hear you say that, Kyra. Truly dreadful. Especially since I've always admired you enormously."

"Why, for heaven's sake?"

"Because you're so unimpressed by the things that impress most people. As well, you're gifted yet so practical, such a realist."

"Oh, Kyle, I'm an immense, quivering mess of doubts and insecurities. Only very short, very thin people could ever be impressed by me."

He stared at her for a moment then yelped with laughter.

"It's true," she said as he mopped his eyes on his sleeve. "I'm the least impressive person who ever lived."

"Never!" he disagreed.

"Well, certainly the least impressive one in this family."

"Absolute crap! I won't listen to this. You're so wrong it's painful. Listen, Kyra," he said, taking hold of her hand. "We're four fairly fucked-up people, each in our own ways. But we've also got redeeming qualities, and I know you know that. Your nasty view of yourself notwithstanding, you probably see this family more clearly than anyone else ever could. Please sell up and come back. As you said a week or so ago, we've made a connection at long last. I'd like to maintain it, make sure it grows."

"Yes," she said, "so would I."

"Let's go put on the kettle." He got up and stood waiting for her. "I won't keep pushing it," he said, looping his arm through hers as they started toward the rear door. "But please know that we'd all be very happy to have you home."

Kyle was plugging in the electric kettle when the front door opened and Octavia sang out, "Here we are!"

Kyra turned to see Jesse come racing down the hall, Drick on one hand, a bag of sweets in the other. She and her mother simultaneously called out, "Don't run, Jesse!" But it was already too late. He'd arrived at the kitchen, and the smooth-soled moccasins sent him sliding on the polished linoleum. His feet flew out behind him, he fell belly-down, and went skimming over the floor. The sweets and puppet falling from his hands, his momentum carried him forward at such a speed that he was unable to stop himself from colliding, headfirst, with the heavy base of the kitchen table. The whole incident lasted no longer than five or six seconds.

There was a terrible moment of frozen silence after the audible crack of his head meeting the table base. Then, trying to right himself, his arms lifted toward Kyra. She scooped him up, seeing the swelling already starting on his forehead. In a voice gone breathless with fright, she said to Kyle, *"Get some ice!"* and carried Jesse to the living room where she sat on the sofa with him cradled to her breast. "It'll be all right," she crooned, stroking him, as the swelling continued at an alarming rate, and Jesse wept soundlessly, his face red and hot. After the fact, she was so scared she felt as if she might faint—sweat breaking out around her hairline and brackish fluid filling her mouth. He might have suffered a concussion, or worse. That horrible sound of his head hitting the base! She kept swallowing, dizzy. "It's all right, all right," she kept on saying. "Just a bump on the head, Jess. You'll be fine."

Kyle came running in with a tea towel filled with ice cubes and Kyra shifted Jesse to one side to hold the makeshift icepack to his head. He howled in pain and tried to push it away, but she said, "You've got to let me do this. It'll make you feel better, Jess, I promise. Please, be still now. I know it hurts, but close your eyes and be still."

His chest heaving, he made one last attempt to push the icepack away, then surrendered.

"There we go. What a good boy! That feels better, doesn't it?"

Jesse made no attempt to respond, but he stopped fighting and lay heavily against her.

Watching fearfully, Kyle turned to Octavia asking, "Shall I ring the doctor?"

"That's Kyra's decision," Octavia said quietly.

"I don't think so. We'll stay as we are for now," Kyra said, battling her nausea. "We'll be fine, won't we, Jess?"

Jesse lay unmoving inside the circle of her arm, still sobbing but gradually calming, the ice serving as a sedative.

"We'll be in the kitchen if you need anything," Octavia said, taking Kyle by the arm, impressed by the level of concern he was demonstrating—both for his sister and for the boy—and impressed, too, by the way Kyra was handling the matter.

Kyra closed her eyes as Jesse's breathing steadied. She'd never felt such fear, and kept seeing, over and over, Jesse's excited face as he came running down the hall toward the kitchen. Then that ride he'd taken on his belly; his head colliding with the table base; the dreadful sound.

The nausea was passing but her stomach hurt, and she thought it safest to keep her eyes shut. He was so tiny, so easily hurt. A tear leaked down her cheek as her arm tightened around him. Such a special little boy, so intuitive and funny and clever. *Mine to protect, mine to console.* "You'll be fine, love. I promise," she whispered, rocking him gently.

Some time later, Octavia tiptoed to the doorway to check on them. She studied them for a time before returning outdoors to the garden, where she said, "I do believe you're right, Kyle," and bent to pluck an offending weed from the border of one of the beds. Upright once more, she stood gazing thoughtfully at the house. "She will come home."

PART TWO
1985–1986

CHAPTER 15

Kyra was in what she termed the "honeymoon phase" of the costume design for a big-budget period film, set in the late nineteenth century, which was to be shot at Elstree and on location in the Midlands. She was excited about the project, having worked twice before for the director, James Elway. The film they'd done four years earlier had received seven American Academy Award nominations. It had won three: for best director, best actor and best original screenplay. As a result of her own nomination for costume design, she'd since been greatly in demand, and her fees had gone up proportionately.

Having read the script and signed on, she'd gone along to a creative meeting with Elway, the producers, the production manager, the production designer, the art director and two of the money men. She'd worked twice before with Lucia MacIver, the production designer, who, unlike the majority of men dominating that field, actually knew as much about costuming as she did about construction. For Kyra, that meant realistic staff and time allowances in her budget. It also meant it was unlikely she'd be taken off the film because one of the stars made a strong pitch for his or her favorite designer. And with Elway directing there was little possibility of the director, producer and stars each wanting something or someone different. Because what Elway said at the outset was precisely what he meant, he never changed personnel once he'd embarked upon a project.

So Kyra was now happily engaged in the research, making sketches, scouring costume rental houses, searching for fabrics, hiring shoemakers to create the period footwear, and getting her favorite cutter organized with a workroom and a team of a dozen cutters and seamstresses for the creation and/or rental of some one hundred and seventy costumes. There would, inevitably, be some last-minute casting, which would result in a burst of frantic activity to get the latecomers measured, fitted and dressed in time for their calls.

And once shooting started, right up until the film was wrapped, Kyra would have to be present on the set to make sure everyone looked right, that the costumes fit and moved properly. She would oversee her assistant and a crew that included a wardrobe mistress, an assistant in charge of the set, and sundry other assistants who would take charge of the costumes, moving them in and out of dressing rooms, and seeing that they were kept clean.

But that was weeks off. For the present she was doing the sketches, her favorite part of any job, when she allowed her imagination to embellish upon the research, designing garments that fit the characters and the principal actors who would portray them. Later on, the frenzy would set in when she tried, and invariably failed, to stay within the budget; when Lucia MacIver vetoed half the Polaroid shots of the completed costumes or insisted on tedious, sometimes unneeded, alterations; when something that worked perfectly on the dress form didn't work at all on the actual actor and had to be recut; when she had to juggle her schedule with the cast's rehearsal schedule in order to get them in for fittings; when the materials failed to show up on time and the measurements were somehow off, which meant the costumes didn't hang correctly; when the head cutter—her single most important co-worker—being overworked and frazzled, needed to be taken out for an evening and wined and dined and generally cosseted; or when additional materials were required and it was impossible to get hold of the too-busy people whose approval she had to have in order to make the purchases.

By the end of this twelve-week shoot, she'd be exasperated, exhausted and vowing never again to do another film. But for the present, well in advance of the first day of principal photography (but not so far in advance that she'd lose her energy), seated at the drawing board in the afternoon quiet of her studio, with the sun streaming through the window and a Mozart piano concerto on the portable stereo, she was content.

Often a piece of fabric would inspire a design, and at that moment the inspiration for one gown was a bolt of extravagantly rich egg-yolk yellow brocade she'd happened upon in a stall in Petticoat

Lane. She was just adding a wash of color to the sketch so she could put it aside and organize tea before Jesse got home from school.

Since coming home to London and buying the West Kensington house almost nine years before, Kyra had learned a great deal about Jesse—in particular, that, more than most children, he needed definite routines and timetables. This became clear about six months after they'd moved back, when she got delayed at a costume rental house and was late collecting him from the widowed neighbor who baby-sat him several days a week.

When she finally got to Mrs. Plummer's house almost an hour late, a scowling Jesse was sitting on the floor by the front door, wearing his coat, hat and boots, with Drick on one hand and a mitten on the other. Kyra apologized to Mrs. Plummer and to Jesse, but he refused even to look at her. Jumping to his feet, he got the door open, marched through it and stomped off up the pavement in the icy rain, chin out-thrust, elbows swinging, like a miniature soldier on maneuvers. When they arrived home, he stormed up the stairs and deposited Drick on the floor outside the door before racing into his room. In a frenzy, he began tossing books and toys about, sweeping things from the shelves and windowsills. When every surface had been cleared, he dragged the linens off the bed, tossed them to the floor and jumped up and down on them until they were a muddied mess. He then flew around the perimeter of the room, pounding the walls with his fists and kicking the furniture—like a deranged wind-up toy, she'd thought, watching from the doorway. Finally, exhausted, his outrage dissipated, he'd sat down on the floor, his back against the bed frame, arms tightly crossed, chin almost touching his chest.

She'd waited until his breathing slowed and the flush had left his face, then asked, "May I come sit beside you, Jess?"

His response had been a shrug, his head remaining lowered.

Settled beside him, she'd asked reasonably, "Even though it's the time I usually get to Mrs. Plummer's, did I promise to collect you there at precisely three-thirty today?"

No answer.

"I *didn't* promise you that, Jess, because as I've explained to you several times before, in my work things often don't go according to schedule. So I can't say for certain I'll be anywhere at a specific time. I didn't make you a *promise* that I'd get to Mrs. Plummer's at three-thirty, did I?"

An angry shake of his head.

"I told you I always keep my promises and I have so far, haven't I?"

A long pause, then a reluctant nod.

"I'm very sorry I was late fetching you today, Jess. Did you get scared and think I wasn't coming back?"

Several quick nods; his eyes began to fill.

"Ah, Jess. You mustn't ever be scared about that, because I wouldn't leave you. You've got to believe it, because that *is* a promise. I like you so much, Monkey, and I wouldn't *want* to leave you. Being with you makes me happy." She risked putting an arm around his shoulders, and he slumped against her. "But if something ever were to happen to me and I couldn't come fetch you, Kyle or Granny and Grandpa would take care of you, because being with you makes *them* happy, too. You'll always have a family, so you mustn't be afraid. We're not going to go off and leave you. You have my word on that. Okay?"

A rueful nod.

"Come here, Jess." She'd lifted him onto her lap. "Quite the demolition job you've done," she'd observed, feeling the tension leave his small, hard body.

He'd looked around at the mess, actually seeing it at last, and began to cry in wretched, gulping sobs.

"Oh, it's not that bad, Jess. No real damage that I can see, nothing broken. Tell you what," she'd said, reaching into her pocket for a tissue to dry his face. "Let's go down and have our tea, then we'll clear this up together, put fresh sheets on your bed. Okay?"

A remorseful nod, okay. He still looked miserable.

"Listen, Jess. We all do foolish things when we get scared. When I was young and got scared, I ate too much. That's how I got to be so fat."

He looked up at her with interest and some doubt.

"Honestly," she told him. "Scared people tell lies, or they break things; they hurt themselves or other people. It's only human. We all try not to get scared, but sometimes we just do. And when we do, because we don't want other people to know how scared we are, we do things that are wrong. Understand?"

He'd nodded slowly, and she'd almost been able to see the comprehension pulling itself together at the back of his eyes.

In time, as his trust in her slowly grew, he gave in less and less often to destructive fits of rage, and she dealt with each as she had with the first, waiting it out until he crumpled with exhaustion and allowed himself to be comforted. But everything with Jesse took time and she had to learn to be patient.

He had slept under his bed for the first fifteen months because his room had a built-in wardrobe rather than a closet and there simply wasn't space enough in it for him. When he had nightmares and woke up screaming, Kyra would grab a blanket and pillow and go lie on the floor next to where he lay—beneath the bed and hidden by the bedskirt—holding his outstretched hand until he was able to go back to sleep. And then, one night, just after his fifth birthday, he'd awakened screaming and Kyra had hurried in to find him—not on the floor but actually in the bed. Lying down beside him, she drew him close and held him until he was calm. Every night thereafter he slept in the bed. And soon after that he forgot himself one day and began speaking without Drick. Within a few months Drick was consigned to a shelf in the bedroom.

Gradually the spasms of anger and the nightmares ebbed so that by the time Jesse was seven he'd settled into what appeared to be a genuine placidity. He was an easygoing and generous boy with a lively sense of humor. And she thought that her willingness to accept him on his own terms helped him come to grips with the anguish and terror (never far from the surface) that were the legacy of his early life. She accepted, for one thing, his refusal to wear any garment with short sleeves because he didn't want people to see the clusters of scars on his arms. For another, she accepted his declared need to have a lock on his bedroom door, and was genuinely moved when he made a small ceremony one afternoon of presenting her with a key. She accepted his periodic spells of deep melancholy when he'd spend an entire weekend in his room with the door locked, most often (he later confided) doing no more than listening to music and staring out the window, in the clutches of an enervating sadness he couldn't seem to fight off. During these spells, she left food on a tray outside the door and went about her business, confident he would emerge in time, having managed to grope his way through the murk of his interior landscape.

She accepted his fear of the dark and left night-lights burning throughout the house; she even carried several with her when they traveled together. She accepted the fact that he ground his teeth in his sleep; that his nightmares were sometimes so frightful that he wet the bed; that he could spontaneously burst into song or into tears. Dealing matter-of-factly, she taught him how to use the washer and spin dryer so he wouldn't have to present her with the evidence of his accidents. She sang along with him, or thought of Gary and allowed herself the luxury of tears. She accepted Jesse entirely, looking upon his shows of emotion as a form of permission he gave her to air her own. After a lifetime spent politely burying her true feelings, she was able, through Jesse, to let them surface. She and this boy became, ultimately, a team; two people who respected each other and had revealed themselves to each other in every aspect.

Jesse was an orderly child who needed rules, who liked to live within a structured environment, and who actually took pleasure in keeping his room tidy. When his possessions were neatly in place, his creativity seemed to flourish, and he'd spend hours writing one-act plays, or short stories, or long funny letters to Roddy and Gage. Kyra admired his sense of neatness and order, for it was not a tendency they shared. Jesse often, with a kind of amused tolerance, referred to her ground floor studio as "the storeroom."

It was not an inaccurate description. It was impossible to walk in a straight line from one point in the room to another. Her drawing board was an island surrounded by a sea of vaguely organized clutter: a hill of fabric swatches; a jumble of buttons, bindings and ribbons; an overflowing trunk containing hats and shoes and gloves; haphazard stacks of reference books; clippings from magazines and newspapers; and a variety of boxes filled with everything from sequins to embroidery flosses. The large room was clean but chaotic, with several dress forms in a group in one corner; an entire wall of shelves filled with books piled every which way; painting and drawing supplies stored in bins; photographs and sketches push-pinned to a big cork bulletin board, in some places overlapping; half a dozen thriving pot plants battled for ascendancy in a corner by the wide window overlooking the rear garden, and an antique refectory table accommodated the current project's completed sketches and fabric samples as well as her old portable typewriter.

Jesse's room reflected his love of reading, of music and of word puzzles: anagrams, crosswords and acrostics. His toys and games were tidily arranged on two wide shelves, his ever-expanding collection of books on half a dozen others; his stereo system was contained in a corner cabinet unit; and the computer and printer he'd bought with money earned from his first film work were arranged on an L-shaped desk. He was, in his compulsive tidiness, very like Kyra's father, and she thought that was, at least in part, why the two of them got along so well.

Richard Latimer had come to meet his new grandson one afternoon in the early winter of 1976 and was so taken with the boy that he'd begun visiting on a regular basis every week after that. Having seen her father only sporadically since her parents had divorced in 1950, Kyra was glad of an opportunity to get to know the tall red-headed Scotsman through his dealings with Jesse. Her father demonstrated a patience and humor she couldn't recall him ever displaying with her and Kyle, as well as an impressive comprehension of and fascination with modern technology. It was Richard who helped Jesse shop for his computer, and he and the boy could spend hours trying to configure a problematical piece of software, or playing some game involving space ships and galactic wars. Twice a month Jesse spent the weekend with Richard at the house in Stratford, or at his Chelsea flat. But Jesse spent most of his free time with Octavia, from the outset absolutely devoted to her.

Kyra found it interesting that neither of her parents begrudged the other the time each spent with the boy. Now and then the three of them and Kyle even went on outings together—to the theater or a concert. The family had, in a very real fashion, reintegrated because of Jesse.

In 1980, having difficulty casting a supporting but pivotal role in a film scheduled to begin principal photography in less than two weeks, her father had telephoned Kyra to ask if Jesse might be permitted to test for the part. "I can't find the right boy and I think your lad could do it. Will you put it to him, Kyra?"

"Of course I will," she'd agreed. "But the final decision is Jesse's."

When told, Jesse asked, "What would I have to do?"

"You'll stand in front of the camera and say some lines. But I should warn you, Jess, that if you get the job, it'll be very tedious. Sometimes it takes two to three hours for the crew to set up for a scene, and during that time you have to sit about waiting."

"Would I get paid while I sat about waiting?"

With a laugh, she said, "Very definitely."

"Then I think I'd like to try," he decided.

So Kyra helped him learn his lines, and two days later took him along to the studio where she sat on the sidelines to watch.

Jesse responded readily to his grandfather's off-camera directions, turning this way and that, changing from happy, to sad, to angry, upon request, and came away with the part. He did a total of nine days' work on the film, and in the often lengthy periods between setups he entertained the two other, younger children in the cast with Drick, or by telling them amusingly detailed, highly convoluted stories he made up on the spot.

When, afterward, Kyra asked if he'd enjoyed his acting experience, Jesse said, "It was all right, but I still think I'll be a writer. In a story things can be just the way I want them to be." He was eight years old. The good reviews his performance generated didn't mean very much to him, although he did keep the clippings in an envelope in his desk.

Unlike other boys who wanted to be astronauts or superheroes, Jesse had announced to Kyra at the age of six that he had decided to be a writer. After that first film, he declined his grandfather's offer to pay his way at a well-respected theater school for children, saying, "Thank you very much, Grandpa, but I don't think I'll become an actor, so I'd prefer to continue on where I am. I like it there and I'd miss my friends if I went to another school."

Subsequently, if a part was offered that didn't interfere with school, or with plans of his own or Kyra's, and if (most importantly) Jesse liked the script (and he was incredibly astute and very critical), he accepted. After his second film job, he went along to Kyra's bank on Kensington High Street to open a savings account, and from then on put most of his earnings into it.

Now and then Kyra asked herself why she hadn't told her family the truth about how Jesse had come to her. Initially, explaining had required more energy than she'd possessed, and then, as the years passed, there seemed to be no point. Her mother and father took well to their roles as grandparents, and it would only have muddied the waters for no good purpose had she attempted to explain about Jennifer Cullen. So she just never bothered.

* * *

The wash was drying on the costume sketch, the teapot was warming, and Kyra had just laid the table when Jesse arrived home. The tiny New York waif had evolved into a handsome, twelve-year-old English schoolboy who came in lugging his satchel of books, saying, "Hi! What's for tea?"

"The usual rubbish. How was your day, Monkey?" she asked, noticing that the delicate flesh beneath his eyes looked slightly bruised. Lately he'd been lacking his usual energy and she thought it might be a good idea to take him to the surgery for a checkup.

"Masses of homework, but otherwise fine. How was yours?"

"Unspecial. Feeling all right, Jess?"

"I'm all right," he answered offhandedly. "I'll chuck the uniform and be right down."

A short time later, as she was pouring the tea and he was helping himself to a slice of pound cake, he said soberly, "I have something to tell you."

"Hmmn. What's that?"

"Well..." He stopped, appearing discomfited.

"Is something the matter, Jess? You haven't been quite yourself lately."

Meeting her eyes, he chewed on his lower lip for a few seconds, then said, "I am a bit tired. But that's because I've been staying up late the past few weeks."

"You're having trouble sleeping again?"

"No. The thing is..." He hesitated, then all in a rush, blurted, "I've written a book."

"You have?" Kyra was flabbergasted, and tremendously relieved. This explained his fatigued state.

"Would you read it and tell me what you think?"

"Of course. I'd love to. But Jess, how fantastic! Your first book. You really are going to be a writer."

"It's not very long, only ninety-two pages," he said doubtfully.

"Ninety-two is a lot. In script terms, that's an hour and a half, you know."

"Depending on how much dialogue there is. If you like, I'll give it to you after tea." He broke off a corner of the cake slice and sat holding it between thumb and forefinger. "You've got to promise to tell me the truth, Kyra. If you think it's bosh, I want you to say so. If I'm no good at writing, I ought to know now and not waste my time."

"I'll be honest, I promise. But even if it needs work, Jess, it's a great accomplishment."

"We'll see," he said cautiously, and at last popped the piece of pound cake into his mouth.

CHAPTER 16

Joshua Goode and the Blackfriars Warehouse Saucepan Lids was set in turn-of-the-century London. It featured twelve-year-old Joshua, a Cockney orphan, the undersized leader of a ragtag group of a dozen lost, abandoned and/or orphaned "saucepan lids"—rhyming slang for kids—ranging in age from five to fourteen, residing in a small, derelict warehouse near Blackfriars Bridge. The children survived primarily by entertaining travelers outside Charing Cross Station during the day and theatergoers in the Strand in the evenings.

When not rehearsing, the group worked at fixing up the warehouse, furnishing it—and themselves—with castoffs they collected from as far afield as Knightsbridge and Chelsea. The older children had late-night jobs cleaning several nearby pubs and restaurants, and were paid in small sums of cash, substantial amounts of leftover food, and buckets of coal (used to fuel the warehouse stove)—an arrangement satisfactory to all concerned.

The older children kept an eye on the younger ones, and everybody had assigned chores. LaLoyd, at fourteen years and fifteen stone, was the Official Protector whose size alone stopped outsiders from preying upon members of the group. He also served as general peacekeeper. Red-headed, north country I-Lean, at thirteen the oldest of the girls, supervised the meals and the laundry, while Desmond and Cyril, the ten-year-old, black-haired, blue-eyed Irish twins, had charge of the jerry-built but effective bathroom and loo. Clive and Lu-Cee, both eight-year-olds from Aberdeen who had run away together to escape raging, drunken fathers, were in charge of trash disposal. Bill-E, Androo and Lionel, ages seven, six and six respectively, who had been found by Joshua and LaLoyd wandering, left and lost, in three different railway stations (Euston,

Paddington and Victoria), were the warehouse cleaning crew; and the two five-year-olds, Flora (who had been found, alone and terrified, one afternoon some months before, wandering through the crowds on Oxford Street) and Kate (discovered two years earlier by Clive and Lu-Cee huddled in a doorway in Fleet Street), did whatever light odd jobs were assigned to them by the others.

As it happened, each of the members had a particular talent. LaLoyd sang in a pleasing baritone and, despite his bulk, could do a very nice step dance. Desmond and Cyril, the twins, were both true sopranos, as was I-Lean, and all had an instinctive flair for three-part harmony. Bill-E, Androo and Lionel were splendid tumblers and acrobats; LaLoyd had taught Flora and Kate some simple dance steps which they performed with winsome grace; Clive played the spoons with an unerring sense of rhythm, and Lu-Cee, without instruction from anyone, had learned to produce quite lovely sounds from a tiny violin I-Lean had found in a dustbin outside Waterloo Station. Joshua, who could sing, dance and extemporize to suit any occasion, was artistic director, and served as compère for their public performances.

While performing near the Adelphi theater one evening, where there was to be a gala opening of a new show, a grand carriage drew in to the curb and a footman hurried to open the door for the most beloved member of the royal family, the Tall Princess. Pausing to watch the children perform, the Tall Princess was charmed by what she saw, and when the troupe had finished their turn she beckoned Joshua over to ask him about the group and how they had come to be.

In his typically forthright fashion, Joshua introduced each of the members—the girls blushed and curtsied, the flustered boys bowed—and then went on to explain, as best he could, their origins.

"We're a family, we are, Your Majesty. We tyke care of each uver and the basins of gravy—them's the babies, Your Royal Highness—an' we don't ask nobody for nuffink. We all of us work 'ard for our sugar an' 'oney. We're independent, see, Your Regal Loftiness, and proud of it, if I may say so."

Touched, the Tall Princess thought for a moment, then asked if the group might be free to provide the entertainment for the young Prince Alexander's forthcoming birthday party.

"We'd be dead 'onored, we would, Your Majestic Pinnacle. Just you tell us when and where, and we'll be there."

Amused and delighted by young Joshua's manner and speech, she gave him the details, said she looked forward to seeing the entire group of "saucepan lids" again soon, then turned to lead her mightily bemused entourage (a group who never failed to be surprised by the Princess's displays of interest in the oddest sorts of people) into the theater.

A fortnight later, they were such a success at the Prince's party that all the royal and semiroyal mums in attendance began clamoring to have the warehouse kids entertain at their little ones' birthday "festicles"—as Joshua called them.

In no time at all, the warehouse children were able to give up their cleaning jobs and devote themselves full-time to making new costumes and to rehearsing and performing. Things were going very well, indeed.

Then, one afternoon a dour pair from an ominous-sounding organization called Social Services came round to the warehouse, bent on taking everyone under fourteen into care. Luckily, only LaLoyd was there at the time and he was able to get rid of them once they had seen for themselves that he was alone.

"We'll be back," they threatened upon departing.

Returning home some time later, Joshua knew from the expression on LaLoyd's chevy chase that something was amiss.

"What's 'appened, me old china plate?" he asked.

Very worried, LaLoyd explained about the pickle-faced pair who had made it clear they intended to round up the saucepan lids and ferry them off to some frightful workhouse.

"Uh-oh!" Joshua exclaimed, now worried, too. "I don't care for this dewelopment one little bit."

That evening the older children discussed what to do while the younger children sat listening and made a valiant effort not to cry.

"We dinna want to go into care!" Clive and Lu-Cee wailed. "We'll go back to Aberdeen before we go into care."

"None of us wants to, pets," said gentle I-Lean. "We've all had enough 'care' to last a lifetime, and that's the God's honest. But what shall we do?" she asked, turning to Joshua. "If we've no notion of when they might come back, we've no way to protect ourselves. They could come any time," she said with dread. "Even in the dead of night, when we're all sleeping."

"Not to worry," he assured the group. "I've got an idea. It may come to nought, but it's worth a try." He would go at once to Kensington and try to elicit the help of the Tall Princess. "She's special, i'n't she? If anyone can 'elp, it's 'er. Now, you little ones, off you go to Uncle Ned. And I-Lean, if you will, my dear, save me a bit of that Lilley & Skinner for when I return."

He was summarily dismissed from the front door of the palace, and was no luckier at the servants' entrance. Finally, when the guard's back was turned, Joshua climbed the wall, darted across the lawn, scooted through a pair of open French windows, and found himself in the dining hall where the Tall Princess and her family were at dinner.

"I'm ever so sorry to come in fru the burnt cinder," Joshua apologized, nervously clutching his hat in both hands. "But me and the saucepan lids, we've got a spot of bovver, your Elevated Eminence. I've come in the 'ope you might see your way clear to 'elpin' us, out of the goodness of your gooseberry tart."

Prince Engeldrick, the Tall Princess's consort, was all for having Joshua summarily arrested and prosecuted for trespass, and was about to ring for the guards, but young Alexander and the Tall Princess hurried to Joshua's defense, telling how they had come to know him. Then Engeldrick apologized, and Joshua was invited to sit down.

"Would you care for something to eat, Master Goode?" asked the Princess, indicating the lavishly spread table with a delicate gesture of her hand.

"No, fank you very kindly, Your Towering Sovereignty," Joshua replied, although in truth he was ravenous after the long walk, and would be hungrier still by the time he got back to Blackfriars. But he didn't believe it was his place to break bread with royalty, nor did he wish to waste any time. He got right to the point, explaining in a rush about the visit from the pinched pair of do-gooders from Social Services and their threat that everyone except LaLoyd would be taken into care. The group would be split up forever, if someone didn't intervene on their behalf.

"Even if we're not blood-related, we're a real family, see," he elaborated. "And them people might fink they was doin' the right fing by sendin' us in twelve diff'rent d'rections, but we're 'appy together and we wouldn't never be 'appy bein' separated. There's some of flesh 'n' blood isn't as close as what we are to one anuver."

"Of course not," the Tall Princess commiserated. "I quite understand and I'm honored that you came to tell me, Master Goode; that you would place your trust in me. You have my word that I shall make every endeavour upon your behalf to find a solution to this problem."

"You're the tallest of the tall, your Dynastic Colossus, the most majestic of majesties. I fank you most 'umbly." He made a low bow, thanked the Tall Princess a final time, begged the pardon of Prince Engeldrick and his son, then left by way of the French windows.

After two anxious days and nights of waiting, when the children were fearful of leaving the warehouse and equally fearful of remaining inside it, a footman came to the warehouse with a letter for Joshua. It said that the Tall Princess had spoken of the group's plight to the Queen, who had, in sympathy, signed a decree stating that the twelve children were to become the Official Waifs and Strays of the Court, under the wardship of the Tall Princess.

And so the children were allowed to remain together in a grace-and-favor house granted them by the Crown. They continued to perform but also were given daily lessons by a court-appointed tutor, and in time other orphaned, abandoned and/or lost children came to take up residence. Joshua became, at fourteen, the youngest person ever to be presented at court, and was, in due course, made a Knight of the Royal Victorian Order.

Kyra got to the end of the manuscript and sat for several moments with her hand flat on the last page, in tears. Jesse's understanding of family dynamics, his kindness and humor, and his talent were enormous. She remembered, all at once, the party she'd held for his sixth birthday and his amazed and joyous expression as he'd played games with his friends, and, later, his radiant smile at their cheers and applause when he'd blown out the candles on the cake. His first party, first friends; his first experience of sharing an occasion.

"It's no bloody good, is it?" Jesse asked from the doorway. "I knew it."

"No, no, it's wonderful, Jess." She fished in her pocket for a tissue and mopped her face.

"Why are you crying, then?" he asked suspiciously.

"I don't really know. I suppose because I'm so surprised, and so proud of you."

"Surprised?" He remained in the doorway, his expression doubtful.

"Bad choice of word. I expected it to be good but it's far more than that." Reading his expression, she asked, "Aren't you happy with it?"

"I was while I was writing it, but once it was finished I completely lost all sense of it. I read it over and it seemed juvenile and embarrassing."

"It's neither of those things."

"I can't really be objective, can I?" he asked, coming into the room to sit down opposite her at the kitchen table. "It's not the same thing as, say, your designing a costume. I mean, you can look at your sketch and see it's right, it's appropriate. But writing's not like that. You get everything down on paper and then, when you read it, you can't imagine what you could've been thinking of because it's just so *bad*. It's *nothing like* what you set out to say."

"I suspect objectivity's something you'll get to eventually, a confidence in your ability to say what you want to say in the way that you want to say it. But this is good, Jess. I'm staggered by just *how* good it is."

"Tell me what you like about it," he invited eagerly, looking down at the stack of computer-printed pages as if he now could scarcely believe he'd filled them.

"Well, it's wonderfully funny, but very touching, too. The characters are original and lovable, especially Joshua. You've done your homework on the era; everything's most authentic. And you make some very pointed social observations. It's whimsical and altogether charming. It's a lovely book and you should feel very proud of yourself."

"Is it good enough to be published, do you think?"

"I'd say so. God knows, I've worked on scripts that were nowhere near as intelligent and well thought out as this."

"Would it be all right if I asked Sir Kenneth to read it? After all, he is a publisher and he'd know if it's really any good."

"Why not bring it along on Sunday and get Granny's opinion? She's an informed reader, far more so than I. Plus she's bound to know what would interest the man."

"I'll do that, then."

"You look awfully tired, Jess. Perhaps an early night would be a good idea."

"Okay." He leaned over to pick up the manuscript, asking, "You honestly, truly like it, Kyra? You wouldn't encourage me merely to be kind, would you?"

"I'd never misrepresent my feelings about something that's so important to you, Jess. It's a hugely entertaining book, and I especially loved the Cockney rhyming slang."

"It was a lot of fun to write," he admitted, all trace of doubt gone. "I laughed so hard, sometimes I was afraid I'd wake you."

Smoothing his hair, she said, "You're definitely going to have a career as a writer, Jess."

"It's all I really want," he said soberly. "Everything is material, something to remember; something I might want to use one day."

"I know that, love. I know how it feels."

His dark eyes fixed on her with intense interest. "Did you think you'd be a painter, Kyra?"

"I thought about it, but I knew early on I wasn't good enough. It's the difference between us, Jess. You *are* good enough."

Getting up, he gave her a rare spontaneous hug, saying, "Thank you for reading it and for telling me the truth."

"Thank you for letting me be the first to read it. I'm honored."

"You're the tallest of the tall, your Dynastic Colossus, the most majestic of majesties. I fank you most 'umbly." After bowing low, he grinned at her, then went off to his room.

The three inside the living room could hear Octavia laughing out in the garden and exchanged a look.

"I'd say she likes it, Jess," Kyra observed.

"Sounds as if she does," Jesse said nervously.

"Do I get to read it next?" Kyle asked.

"If you like." Jesse looked over at his uncle who was stretched out on the sofa reading a film script. "Is that any good, Uncle Kyle?"

"Total crap," Kyle declared. "Gratuitous violence every four pages, paper-thin characters, females with massive breasts and tiny brains, and a strong, silent hero with an arsenal of deadly weapons. Awful stuff."

"Why are you reading it then?"

"Optimism. I want to believe it'll get better. Of course it won't, and I'll turn it down, even though they're offering me a small fortune to play the lead. A shame, really. Perhaps you should write a script for me, Monkey."

"I bet I could," Jesse said.

"I don't doubt it." Letting the script drop to the carpet, Kyle got up and walked over to stand surveying the Scrabble board.

"He's trounced me as usual, and I'm stuck with seven vowels," Kyra said, glancing at the time, as nervous as Jesse about her mother's reaction to the book.

Kyle walked around behind her, looked at her tiles and said, "I'd concede if I were you."

Kyra studied the board one last time, then told Jesse, "You win again, love. Mum's the only one around here who's any real competition for you." Outside in the garden Octavia laughed again.

"She's having a jolly old time out there," Kyle observed. "I can't *wait* to read this. I don't suppose there's a part in it I could play?"

"Afraid not," Jesse said, clearing the tiles from the board. "Care for a game, Uncle Kyle?"

"No, thanks. I don't take defeat well. Anyone for a cuppa?"

"I'll go put on the kettle," Jesse volunteered.

"Let Louise do it," Kyle advised quietly. "She loves fussing over the lot of us."

"Right. I'll go ask her to do it." Jesse got up and went off to the kitchen.

Kyle was about to say something to his sister when they heard Octavia in the kitchen, exclaiming, "Who's a clever, clever boy? Come here and let Granny give you a great big hug!"

The twins got to the kitchen in time to see their mother throw her arms around Jesse, declaring, "It's such fun, Jess; simply a delicious book! I'll ring Kenneth at once. I know he'll want to see it."

Spooning tea leaves into the pot, Louise was chuckling softly and shaking her head.

"You think so?" Jesse asked softly, a look on his face as if he was suffering the effects of seismic tremors beneath his feet.

"In fact I'll take it round to his office tomorrow myself." Octavia placed both hands on his shoulders and gazed into his eyes, saying, "What will you do next, I wonder?"

"Perhaps I'll write a film script." Jesse smiled over at Kyle, then at Octavia. "With parts for you and Uncle Kyle, of course. Kyra will do the costumes, and Grandpa will direct."

"Perfect!" Kyle said. "Could you start right away, please? I'm desperate for a decent role."

"Out of my kitchen, you lot!" Louise ordered. "Can't 'ear me-self fink wiff this box o' toys."

"Noise," Jesse translated. "I plan to have an acknowledgment to Louise in the book, you know. She helped me with it, didn't you, Louise?"

"I dunno 'bout that." Louise's tone was dismissive but her face was rosy with pleasure. "Go on now, scoot. Tea's underway."

Lifting the manuscript from the table, Kyle said, "I'll read this now, if I may."

"I'd like your opinion, actually," Jesse said, going with him to the living room. "It's important to have as much feedback as possible."

Taking hold of her daughter's hand as they followed, Octavia said, "It's so well written I think people are going to have a hard time believing someone so young is actually the author. He's frighteningly talented."

"Why frightening?"

"He may be too young to handle the success that's going to come his way."

"I disagree," Kyra said. "I think Jesse could handle *anything*. It's the rest of us who may have difficulty handling it."

"Perhaps," Octavia allowed. "We'll find out soon enough. But, my *God*, he's gifted!"

CHAPTER 17

On a Sunday afternoon three weeks later, after a midday meal during which Octavia wore a singularly pleased expression, as if she were privy to some delectable secret she longed to share but couldn't, she, Kyra and Jesse were savoring the late spring sunshine in the garden when Louise poked her head out the kitchen window. "'E's 'ere!" she called momentously, then withdrew to open the front door.

"Who's here?" Jesse and Kyra asked.

"Just Kenneth," Octavia said offhandedly, running a hand through her hair as her pleased expression transformed itself into a rather sly smile.

Kyra studied her mother, thinking that the older she got the more attractive she became, actually looking better at seventy-one than women years younger. She'd been inundated with offers in the past few years, and had her pick of roles, for which her agent happily negotiated immense fees. Her only disappointment, she'd confided to Kyra, was Kyle's failure to commit himself to a permanent relationship. He'd been introduced by their father to Damien Haverford, an impossibly attractive, no-nonsense forty-five-year-old one-time lighting designer who now owned a small exclusive hotel in Stratford. Their involvement had so far lasted a good while longer than any of his previous affiliations. And perhaps that was because they rarely managed to spend more than a few weeks at a time together, or because, having lost his former lover to cancer four years earlier, Damien was as reluctant as Kyle to commit himself. But Octavia was becoming more optimistic since, after nearly three years, Kyle was still as interested in the man as he had been at the outset. One day soon he might actually settle into the relationship and stop denying his feelings.

But how likely was it that Kyle would ever take such a step? Kyra wondered, as her mother's longtime lover stepped out through the rear door, raised a hand to shield his eyes from the sun, and smiling, said, "Hello, my dears. So sorry to be late. Frightful traffic right the way from St. Ives."

Sir Kenneth Carter-Dobbs was a formidable presence. Tall, solidly built and silver-haired, he had deep-set hazel eyes, a brushy mustache beneath a great beak of a nose, a wide mouth made for laughter, and a squared chin that countered the prominence of his nose. His aura was one of simmering intelligence and energy, and his bearing, due to early years spent at a rigorously disciplined Scottish boarding school, was decidedly military. As always he was impeccably dressed—in cavalry twill trousers, Harris tweed jacket, sea-island cotton shirt and figured silk tie, with highly polished, custom-made wing-tip shoes. He was altogether a powerfully attractive man.

Octavia rose to greet him, and Kyra watched their affectionate exchange with an unsettling stab of envy. As she herself kissed the man's smooth cheek in greeting, and breathed in his sandalwood aftershave, she realized just how long it had been since Gary's death, how long since she'd accepted daily displays of male affection as a matter of course. A bit rattled, she found a smile and hid behind it as Jesse gave the man an enthusiastic handshake that was warmly returned.

"It's actually you I've come to see," Kenneth told him, with a gesture inviting Jesse to come sit at his side.

This visit was about the manuscript, Kyra realized, wondering how she could have been so dense not to have figured that out sooner. She looked from her mother to Kenneth, then back to her mother as Jesse responded to something Kenneth had said. Pay attention, Kyra told herself. But for a moment events seemed to be happening at a distance, and she was barely an adequate spectator, so suddenly preoccupied had she become with the thought that Gary's death had, in many ways, put an end to her life, too. Jesse had provided her with an alternate focus, and she'd gladly devoted herself to his care and well-being, politely discouraging the daylight advances of the men who'd shown any interest in her. But, God, she missed the sound of her husband's voice; the feel of him beside her in the night; the support and companionship that were the fundamentals of a marriage.

Quite a number of times over the years, when away on location, she'd gone to bed with someone after several glasses of wine for courage—a stills photographer, a head grip, a first A.D. These were occasions when she'd undressed in darkness, closed her eyes, and for an hour or so relished the heft of a male body bearing down insistently upon hers. In the sober light of morning she'd felt guilty and faintly ashamed, yet restored. She'd then gone back to work, her mind carefully closed to thoughts of how—like a vampire—she'd used the hours of the night to refresh her flagging energies.

Louise came across the lawn, all brisk efficiency, with a squat crystal glass centered on a small, doily-covered tray. "There you go, Sir Kenneth," she said, setting the glass on the table next to him. "Weak single malt with water in a short glass, just the way you like it."

"Splendid, Louise. Thank you."

"You're welcome, I'm sure, Sir Kenneth." Puffed up with pride, the housekeeper bustled off back to the kitchen.

"There you go, Sir Kenniff," Jesse repeated softly to himself. "Weak single malt wiv wotta, just the way you loike it."

Kenneth turned to him and said, "All the key people at Beauchamp-Dobbs have read your manuscript, Jesse. And it's received unanimous kudos."

"They liked it?"

"Tremendously."

"Does that mean you might want to publish it?"

"It means we definitely want to publish it."

Kyra could scarcely breathe, and Jesse was temporarily speechless.

"First off," Kenneth continued, "you really should have an agent. I've made a list of good people." He took this from his pocket and passed it over. "I suggest you interview at least five of them. When you've decided which one suits best, we'll enter into negotiations. The general consensus is that we should release *Joshua* as an adult title. Everyone had a jolly good laugh reading it, and the feeling is it will do well in the adult market, although of course children are bound to enjoy it, too, as evidenced by the fact that two of our key people took copies home to try out on their children. It went down very well, indeed."

"You're going to publish my book?" Eyes wide, Jesse seemed almost to be vibrating with excitement.

"That is our aim, yes. It's witty, imaginative and very well written. Of course it needs editing and a bit of rewriting here and there, but nothing significant. Our biggest asset, in terms of selling this book, Jess, is your age. There simply aren't vast numbers of authors not yet thirteen. The expectation is that we'll get enormous play in the media, which means you'd be expected to do a round of personal appearances. How would that sit with you?"

"I wouldn't mind," Jesse replied. "I've had some interviews for my film work, so I'd know what to expect."

"Our publicist is keen on the project. She presented some of her promotion ideas at our editorial meeting this past Friday, and I must say they're first-rate. And, of course, we'd like to discuss cover concepts with you, get your input."

Jesse gazed at the man for several long moments, then jumped up, exclaiming, "I'm going to be a published *author!*" Turning, he ran over to wind his arms around Kyra's neck, holding on tightly. "They're going to publish my book," he whispered. "It's actually going to happen. I'm a real *writer.*"

"I'm so happy for you, Monkey," she whispered back. "It's fantastic."

Straightening, he declared, "It's just the way I always imagined it would be!"

He whirled around in a giddy circle before flying toward Octavia, who raised a hand in warning, saying, "If you leap on me the way you did Kyra you'll break my poor old bones. Go gently, my precious."

Taking heed, he squeezed onto the chaise to hug her, saying, "It's all your doing and I'm so grateful, Granny. I'll never forget what you've done for me, *never.*" Then, some uncertainty wedging its way into his mind, he sat up and turned to Sir Kenneth. "You wouldn't do this just as a favor to my grandmother, would you, sir?"

"There is a lot I would do for your grandmother, Jesse," the man said, "but I would not go so far as to invest company funds in a book without merit. I do have a board of directors to answer to, you know. No, the company and I want this book because it's an entertaining piece of work with huge earning potential. We all stand to make a good deal of money from this venture."

"Oh! That's all right, then." Jesse got up and went over to offer the man his hand. "Thank you so much, Sir Kenneth. I'll do my very best for you."

"I have no doubt of that," Kenneth said with a broad smile.

Dazed and elated, Kyra had to wonder yet again what mysterious force had been in play when some unknown woman had put down a name other than her own as the mother of Jennifer Cullen; and in doing that, set in motion the events that ultimately brought Jesse (and her) to this juncture.

"Perhaps you should tell Louise your good news," Octavia suggested to the boy. "You did say she was a great help, didn't you?"

"She was. I'll go tell her right now!" He went running off to the house.

"It's so good of you, Sir Kenneth," Kyra said, more than a little convinced that, regardless of the man's claim to the contrary, the book might not have met with quite so enthusiastic a reception had it been written by someone other than Octavia's grandson.

"Not at all," he said, at last taking a swallow of his Scotch. "Your lad's going to make everyone involved a potful of bees and honey with his charming little Captain Cook."

There was a moment of silence while the two women translated the rhyming slang. Then they all laughed.

"Is something wrong, Kyra?" her mother asked as the two of them laid the table for dinner. Jesse and Kenneth were out in the garden discussing his manuscript.

"No. Why?"

"You seem distracted."

"Do I?" Kyra hedged.

Octavia read the reluctance on her daughter's features and asked, "What is it?" as she reached to lift a wisp of hair away from Kyra's eye. "Please don't play dumb. It doesn't suit you."

"I'm a bit worried about Jess," Kyra admitted.

"Surely not about Beauchamp-Dobbs taking on his book?"

"No, no. I couldn't be happier about that. Jess has been so tired lately. He insists it's because of all the late nights he put into finishing the manuscript. But it's been well over a month since then and he's still listless. Did you notice he's not eating with anything like his usual appetite, and that he only perked up when Sir Kenneth arrived?"

"I did notice."

"It's probably nothing," Kyra said in an unsuccessful attempt to convince both of them.

"There's more, isn't there?"

"Well, he's been very moody the past little while."

"He's an adolescent," Octavia reminded her. "It's a moody stage. Overheating testosterone, fulminating nonspecific desires. Sweet little boys become sex-obsessed, hairy little thugs."

Kyra laughed. "I know all that." Dropping her voice, she confided, "What really worries me is that he's stopped growing. He's still able to wear things he wore two and three years ago."

"Some children do have late growth spurts," Octavia said, feeling a sudden cold stab of fear.

"I know that, too." Kyra looked over at the window. "Undoubtedly I'm being an alarmist."

"Not your style. You've been extraordinarily unflappable where Jesse's concerned. No, if you're worried, then there's cause to be. Why not have a visit to the doctor, satisfy yourself there's nothing wrong, that Jess is simply going through very normal changes."

"That's what I'll do. Sorry to be such a bore."

"Don't be silly. Raising a child alone is no easy thing."

"Jesse's been no trouble, really."

"You've been lucky, and perhaps your luck's at an end. Adolescence can be hell for all concerned. Kyle was impossible, completely driven by raging hormones, able to think of nothing but sex."

"I don't remember that."

"You were rather preoccupied with your own problems at the time," Octavia said drolly.

"What problems?" Not that she didn't remember vividly, but Kyra was curious to know what her mother recalled of that time.

Octavia said, "Alienation, for one; your entire physical appearance for another. For a few years I dreaded having the pair of you home during the school holidays. When you weren't sniping viciously at each other, Kyle was locked in his room masturbating, and you sat about the house all hunched over, making detailed sketches of tiny perfect females, or pretending to read but actually listening in on your father's and my conversations, consumed with loathing for the entire family."

"How do you know that was what Kyle was doing?" she asked. "And I didn't loathe anyone!"

"Perhaps not," Octavia said. "But you positively radiated contempt for us, Kyra. I know it was an unhappy time for you, but you managed to make your father and me every bit as unhappy as you were."

"I'm sorry," Kyra said, filled with retroactive guilt. "That never occurred to me."

"I'm well aware of that!" her mother snapped. "I've never understood why children imagine their parents are impervious to the often hateful things they convey—the sneers, the rolling eyes, the exaggerated sighs. I'm sure you've been under the impression all these years that I was completely unaffected by your behavior."

"I wouldn't go that far...."

"No, because it simply never occurred to you that I could *be* affected."

To her great dismay, Kyra saw that her mother's eyes had a glaze of angry tears. "That's only partly true," she said. "But I am sorry. I certainly know better now. I'm affected by every last thing Jesse says and does."

"Of course you are. And as for my knowing what your brother was up to," Octavia said blithely, sailing right past her brief upset, "well that's simple enough. Kyle had the unfortunate habit of humming furiously while he was engaged in his frequent forays into self-gratification. One merely had to pause in the hallway and listen for a few moments to know precisely what he was doing." She shook her head in amusement. "Mercifully, after a few years matters improved. Kyle managed to lose his virginity, and you appeared to come to terms, if not with yourself, at least with us. I certainly wouldn't have brought the two of you over to New York that summer you were sixteen if both of you hadn't matured considerably. You do remember that summer, don't you?" Octavia asked, standing by the sideboard with her arms folded beneath her breasts.

"Vividly. It wasn't the family I was loathing, it was me."

"I know. But why, Kyra? Explain that to me."

"It's very complicated."

"You blamed us for your unhappiness, didn't you?"

"No. I've never blamed anyone else for my problems. The faults were all mine. I admit I wanted you and father to be something other than what you were. I didn't understand that what you were wasn't something that *could* be changed. I know that now, but I couldn't get my mind around it then. I wanted you to be *real* but I couldn't find a way to make that happen."

"*Real?* Of course we were real!" Octavia glared at her for a second or two, then, relenting, said, "Oh, I see. We were engaged in some sort of never-ending performance. Is that how you perceived us?"

"Yes," Kyra admitted softly. "That's precisely how I saw you."

Octavia now turned to look out the window, thinking. "It's inevitable, I suppose," she said at last. "Parents always think their children are going to be different; their children won't go through the terrible-two stage and turn into little chimps, getting into everything. And actors think their children will recognize that the acting only happens outside the home. A mistake, obviously. It's vanity, really. We're a vain bunch."

"It doesn't matter anymore," Kyra said. "I've always loved you and valued your insights, particularly where Jess is concerned."

"Thank you." Octavia turned from the window. "You're right, of course. It doesn't matter anymore."

"What matters right now is Jess, and how quickly he's changing."

"Did you think he was going to remain a sweet, rather eccentric little boy forever, Kyra?"

"As simple-minded as it sounds, that is what I thought."

"Well, darling, I hate to tell you, but the changes are only just beginning, and he'll get considerably worse before he begins to get better. In the meantime, take him for a checkup, put your mind at rest."

"I will. I'll do that."

"Mothers worry, Kyra, even when their children are grown and living thousands of miles away. It's what we do. I've long suspected it's genetic. Men get the sexual preoccupation gene and women get the constant worry one."

Kyra laughed and put her arms around her mother, saying, "Please don't get angry with the child I used to be. I adore you, and I feel so stupid and helpless when you get upset about things neither one of us can change."

Her mother sighed, then said, "You're right. I can't think where that came from."

"It came from my having been such a horror as a child. I'd like to think I'm well past that now."

"You are—long past, thank God," Octavia said, taking hold of

Kyra's hand and beginning, almost absently, to caress it. "Oh, I meant to tell you earlier. Catharine rang the other evening. She's coming to visit."

"When?"

"She was her usual dithery self, said she'd be arriving sometime next month, but not when or how long she intended to stay. All I know is she's coming on the Concorde and has booked into the Westbury."

"Funny, I had a long letter from Glenna a week or so ago and she didn't mention it."

"Perhaps she didn't know," Octavia said. "Cathy always was scattered, but since the divorce she's been hopeless. She undoubtedly decided on the spur of the moment and intended to tell Glenna, but never got around to it. But since she entertained the *thought* of telling her, that, to her mind was as good as the deed. She asked after you and Jesse, hopes to see you both."

"I don't know how we'll manage it. I have to be in Cheltenham by June fifteenth for the start of principal photography, and Jess will be staying with his friend Robert until school breaks. Then he comes to join me."

"Well," Octavia said, thinking aloud, "Kyle's due back from Prague in another ten days. I suppose he might be willing to come along in your stead, provided he hasn't already made plans with Damien. We'll have to play it by ear. She's had yet another round of surgery, by the way. She went on and on about cheek and chin implants, ear lifts, cortisone injections, liposuction; repositioning this, that and the other. Horrifying." She gave herself a shake and finally turned back to Kyra and again caressed Kyra's hand. "She told me about an encounter she had a few weeks ago with a professor or somesuch she'd met at a benefit. She was instantly besotted because he paid her some attention and they ended up back at her apartment, ostensibly for coffee and brandy but really for sex—at least, reading between the lines, that's what she was hoping for.

"Cathy, of course, being the complete *naive* that she is, invited said professorial type into her boudoir. And there, ensconced side by side, fully dressed, on her bed, he launched into a series of questions about her cosmetic surgery—which, naturally, she answered in full and gory detail. Then, after a bit of mild foreplay which resulted in her bared breasts being on display, he studied them for quite some time before asking if she'd had those cosmetically altered, as well. Shocked, she insisted that they were precisely as God had created them—which happens to be the truth. Cathy's surgical arena is limited exclusively to the area above her shoulders. But said fellow didn't believe her and, shortly thereafter, he departed. She was disappointed but philosophical, imagining they'd have a future together. Now she's wondering why he hasn't been in touch. Silly bloody woman," she said sadly. "Silly bloody world."

"Poor Auntie Cath," Kyra said, all too able to visualize the scene.

"Indeed. Take Jesse for a checkup," Octavia said. "You'll both feel better for it." She gave Kyra's hand a pat before releasing it, and headed for the kitchen, calling out, "Louise, I do hope you haven't left the sprouts on too long. You know I loathe them when they're overcooked."

Kyra looked out again at the garden where Jesse—too small and too pale—was paying close attention to what Sir Kenneth was saying. Something was wrong with Jesse, and her mother sensed it, too. It was why they'd had that little tiff. Octavia always turned combative when she was frightened. For a short time, Kyra's instinctive defensiveness in the face of her mother's anger had blinded her to the patterns of her mother's behavior. But Octavia was acutely aware of Jesse, of his moods, his attitudes, his manner. And now Kyra was very afraid; so much so that it felt as if ice water had suddenly been flushed through her bowels.

CHAPTER 18

"It may be something or it could be nothing, but I'd recommend that Jesse see a kidney specialist."

The receiver was suddenly slippery in Kyra's palm, her mouth dry as she asked, "Why?"

"The blood and urine test results aren't quite what they should be. I don't want to alarm you, but Jesse appears to be showing signs of some sort of kidney disorder."

"What signs?" she asked, gripped by dread. She'd been right to be afraid; something was indeed wrong.

"Well, aside from those things you yourself noticed—the fatigue, the loss of appetite and his slow growth rate—the tests indicated elevated levels of creatinine and blood urea."

"What are they?"

"In the simplest terms, creatinine is a nitrogen-containing compound, and urea is a waste product, both of which are normally eliminated from the body by the kidneys. As I say, it could be something minor, but I'd like Jesse to see a specialist for more specific testing."

"But what do you think the problem might be?"

"I'm not qualified to tell you that, Kyra. All I can say is that these elevated levels indicate a problem of some sort, and warrant further testing. There's a very good renal physician at St. Helen's I would recommend."

"Yes, all right."

She noted the doctor's name and number, said good-bye and hung up, half of her wanting to believe it was nothing serious, the other half convinced Jess had a fatal illness. She wiped her hands on her skirt, then picked up the receiver and dialed the number Dr. Kennedy had given her.

"It's very short notice, but if you could make it," she was told by the pleasant-sounding woman on the other end, "we've had a cancellation and could fit Jesse in tomorrow morning at nine forty-five. Otherwise I'm afraid Dr. Rule's next opening isn't until June twenty-sixth."

Kyra was due to be in Cheltenham by then, so while she felt unprepared in every way for this turn of events, she had to accept. "We can make it tomorrow morning," she said, her mouth even dryer now.

"Very good. Now, if I could get a bit of information."

The appointment booked, Kyra went in search of her medical dictionary, and looked up *creatinine*. (A normal metabolic waste, excreted in the urine, primarily by filtration; the clearance rate and the serum level are widely used as an index of kidney function. *c. clearance* rate at which the kidney removes endogenous or exogenous creatinine from the blood plasma.)

Next she found a definition for blood urea, which was as Dr. Kennedy had described. The second line of the definition, however, made her feel faint. *As kidneys fail the concentration of blood urea increases.*

Telling herself not to panic, she looked up kidney, and studied the several detailed drawings, then read the text: *kidney.* One of two bean-shaped organs, approximately four and one-half inches long, located in the posterior part of the abdomen, behind the peritoneum, on either side of the spine.

Beneath this listing were a dozen additional definitions covering everything from *a* for artificial kidney to *w* for wandering kidney. Having no wish to learn what a wandering kidney might be, she returned the dictionary to the shelf, telling herself not to go leaping to conclusions. Dr. Kennedy had said it could well be a minor problem. There was nothing to be accomplished by anticipating the worst. Still, she couldn't help feeling that the worst was precisely what she and Jesse were about to encounter.

"But *why* do I have to see a specialist?"

"Because Dr. Kennedy thinks you should have more tests—special ones he's not equipped to do. It may be nothing more than an infection, something quite simple."

"If it's something simple why can't he give me medicine instead of sending me to another doctor? I don't understand."

"Neither do I," Kyra said. "But we have no choice, Jess. I can't ignore Dr. Kennedy's advice. And, be truthful, you'd like to feel better, wouldn't you?"

"I feel perfectly fine," he argued.

Kyra was intrigued by how unattractive Jesse looked right then, with his eyes narrowed, nostrils flaring and mouth thinly down-turned. She knew he was (like her mother) masking his fear with anger, and she sympathized. She was, after all, masking her own with surface calm. There were responses that simply couldn't be shown to a child who lacked the ability to comprehend them, so, despite fear, or frustration, or any number of other negative feelings, one had to make an effort at concealment.

"Look, love," she said quietly. "We'll go along in the morning to see Dr. Rule. He'll ask you some questions, arrange for some tests, and if the results show there's nothing seriously wrong, that'll be the end of it, and we'll all be satisfied."

"Dr. Kennedy's a silly old fool!" Jesse exploded. "He's useless! I don't know why you're *listening* to anything he has to say. How do we even know his idiotic tests are right? I'm *not* going to see another doctor! There's no reason why I should. Nothing's wrong with me! I'm *fine!* I will *not* go!" He stood tensed, waiting to see how she'd respond to this outburst.

"Jess, come sit with me for a moment." She kept control, refusing to be provoked. He seldom made displays of temper these days, but when he did she couldn't help but remember the grubby three-year-old, repeatedly kicking the wall of the elevator with a tiny sneaker-shod foot.

"I don't *want* to sit down. Why the bloody hell *should* I?" Patches of color had tinted his cheeks; the rims of his ears were bright red.

"Because I'd like to talk to you."

"I don't *want* to *talk.* There's nothing to talk *about.* I *told* you I didn't want to see bloody Kennedy in the *first* place but you wouldn't *listen.* You *never* bloody listen! It drives me *wild!*"

"Jesse, sit down, please," she said a little more firmly.

Scowling, he perched on the far end of the sofa, arms folded stubbornly across his uniformed chest, refusing to look at her.

Knowing he'd shrug off any physical contact at this delicate stage in the negotiations (and, indeed, that was precisely what was taking place and they both knew it), she held back, saying, "The fact is you haven't been yourself for the past few months. You're not sleeping well and you're dragging during the day. You're off your food, and when you do eat you usually get an upset stomach. You've lost weight and you've got dark circles under your eyes. These things aren't normal, Jess, and I think we'd both feel better if we find out what's wrong."

"I *told* you! I feel *perfectly fine!*" He pounded the sofa arm with his fist to emphasize his words. "There's not a *bloody* thing wrong with me!"

"So you say. Nevertheless, I'm concerned, and so is Dr. Kennedy. Would you humor me, please, and come along tomorrow to see the specialist?"

"No!" he insisted, still avoiding her eyes.

"I know you think I'm every bit as useless and stupid as Dr. Kennedy, but I don't believe you, Jess. I don't think you do feel well, and I couldn't possibly go off on location with a clear conscience, knowing I'd failed in my responsibility to you."

"Why is it *your* failure if I don't want to see some bloody specialist?" At last he looked at her.

"Because I'm the adult, the parent, and it's up to me to make the decisions until you're old enough to make your own."

"Bollocks! I make decisions every day."

"Of course you do, and the older you get, the more you'll make. But this is different. Please don't make a battle of it. I'm not trying to force you to do anything that isn't in your best interest. I'd never do that, and you know it's the truth."

"I know," he relented, letting his hands fall to his lap and lacing his fingers together.

"Do you remember when I brought you to England for the first time and we stayed at Granny's house?"

He nodded.

"And do you remember the day we arrived, when Granny gave you Drick?"

He nodded again, a slight smile forming.

"And later that afternoon she took you up the road to buy sweets. Do you remember that?"

"I think so. I'm not sure." His face was uncreasing, the handsome boy returning.

"When the two of you got back, you came running to the kitchen to show me your bag of sweets. You fell on the slippery lino and went flying, gave yourself a terrible thump on the head."

"I don't remember that."

"I do. I'll never forget it. An awful knob started swelling up on your forehead. The first thing you did was hold out your arms, wanting me to pick you up."

He smiled and shook his head, as if embarrassed for the silly baby he'd been back then.

"It probably sounds insignificant, but it was a pivotal moment for me. It was when I knew for certain that things would work out for the two of us. Because when you were hurt, it was me you looked to for comfort. You trusted me to take care of you."

He gazed at her for several seconds, then abandoned his resistance altogether and leaned into her. She put an arm around him and drew him close. "I accepted full responsibility for you then, and I can't stop being responsible now because something's happened that you don't like. Good times or bad, I love you, Jess. I always will."

"I know you do," he murmured.

"Then, please, let's not fight any more about this. We have an appointment tomorrow morning. Let's go along, see the specialist, and do whatever we must to keep you well."

"It means there's something seriously wrong with me, doesn't it?" he asked anxiously.

"It may be not be serious at all. But we can't ignore it."

"I suppose not," he said, subdued finally.

"You'll have a few tests, then go to stay with Robert as planned until the end of term. I know how much you've been looking forward to that."

"He and I always have a good time."

"And you will this time, too."

"But what if it's something serious?"

"Let's not anticipate. We'll take things as they come. Okay?"

"Yes, okay." He was quiet for a time, then said, "I didn't mean what I said about Dr. Kennedy."

"I know you didn't."

"And I don't think you're useless and stupid."

"I don't think you are, either."

At this he laughed, and, heartened, she said, "Fancy a pizza?"

"Yes, please."

"Right. Run up and change out of your uniform, and we'll go to Pizza Paradise."

He went off to his room, and she sat and waited for him, wearied from the exchange but thankful that it had been relatively easy to bring him around.

Dr. Rule was a small, slim man in his late forties, with cool blue eyes, a harried air and a directness that, to Kyra, seemed rather too practiced for her liking.

"You'll spend a good deal more time taking tests than you will with me," he said after he'd completed his physical examination of Jesse. "Once I've seen the test results, we'll have a better idea of how we're to proceed. We'll retest your blood and urine," he told Jesse. "We'll also do something called GFR—the glomerular filtration rate—which will give us a good indication of how well your kidneys are functioning. It involves a twenty-four-hour collection of your urine, with a blood test to be taken at one point during that period. I realize it's an inconvenience, even embarrassing, but this test will indicate the amount of creatinine that has cleared. You see, when one's kidneys are failing, excessive creatinine accumulates in the kidneys. So the rate at which it's eliminated gives a very good assessment of the GFR."

He smiled mechanically and said, "Everyone agrees it's a terrific nuisance, because you've got to collect all your urine for those twenty-four hours. That means you'll have to carry the bottle with you everywhere you go. What I suggest to my male patients is putting a safety-pin through the top of your fly zipper so you're reminded that the collection is in progress."

Jesse laughed disbelievingly, and Dr. Rule's smile gained a few degrees in warmth. "I know. It sounds absurd. But you'll find that the pin does work. So now. Once we've had an opportunity to study the urine collected for creatinine clearance, as well as for an estimation of protein loss, and for calcium or sodium excretion, we'll have a decent idea what we're dealing with."

Kyra glanced over to see that Jesse seemed to be taking this well.

"We'll draw a few quarts of your blood before you leave here today, and you'll be given the bottle you're to use for collecting the urine."

"Quarts?" Jesse looked horrified.

"I'm sure it'll seem like it, but I'm teasing. We'll just take a few tubes. Any questions, either of you?"

"Does this mean my kidneys are failing?" Jesse asked bluntly.

"Not necessarily. We won't know that until we've had the test results. And even then, more tests may be needed before we have a definitive answer."

"What other tests?" Jesse asked.

"X rays, possibly ultrasound, or even a CAT scan. But for now we'll begin with the blood tests and the twenty-four-hour collection. My nurse will give you an instruction sheet and a booklet that explains some of the terms I've used this morning. Along with the dreaded bottle, of course."

In the car on the way home Jesse said, "I'm not taking any bloody bottle to school. So don't ask me to, because I absolutely won't do it!"

"I won't ask you to. I'll ring the head and explain—"

"I don't want you to tell him about any of this!" Jesse cut her off. "The whole school will know and rag me. I'm not having it! This is my business, nobody else's."

"Fair enough, I'll say there's a family problem and you'll be off school for a day."

"In fact," Jesse continued, as if she hadn't spoken, "I don't want you to tell anyone—not Granny, or Grandpa, or Kyle—not anyone."

"As you wish, Jesse."

"That's what I wish," he said flatly, gingerly touching the inside of his elbow where an Elastoplast strip covered the puncture site. Jaw clenched, he turned to look out the car window, remaining silent throughout the rest of the drive home. Upon arriving, claiming he had some studying to do, he went up to his room. A few minutes later, Kyra heard a Beethoven symphony start up, stately and solemn. She had no doubt that Jesse was sitting by the window.

Deciding it was best to leave him be, Kyra went to the studio to try to work. She couldn't. She sat and stared blankly at the window, preoccupied equally with dread and guilt. For the first time she had made Jesse a promise she had no intention of keeping. She intended to tell the family every last detail of what was happening as soon as the test results came in. She'd have to tell them. If she didn't, she'd go completely to pieces.

CHAPTER 19

"I'll ring you this evening at Robert's."

"Okay."

"And you have the number where you can reach me?"

"I have it." Jesse was anxious to be on his way, turning every few seconds to look at the boys heading into the school.

She knew he didn't want to be seen being dropped off like a five-year-old, and for a few seconds she missed his dependency. But as her mother had pointed out, adolescence was a tricky phase. That, coupled with the present uncertainty, was stealing the spontaneity and honesty from their relationship. It was sad, and the worst part was knowing there was nothing she could do to stop it happening. Forcing a smile, she said, "All right, Monkey. Off you go."

He turned and forced a smile of his own. "'Bye, Keer. Luck with the shoot."

"Thank you. I'm going to need it. I love you, Jess. See you soon."

"Me, too, you." Getting out, he opened the rear door for his suitcase, then ducked down to waggle his fingers at her before moving off to join the stream of uniformed boys on their way into the school. She watched until he was out of sight, then put the car in gear and pulled away.

The fast route would have been the M4 west to the northbound M5, connecting with the A40 to Cheltenham. But traffic on the major motorways was always heavy, with most vehicles moving at an unnerving average of eighty miles an hour. She preferred scenery to speed and had decided the previous night to pick up the A40 in London, stay with it through Oxford, and on into the Cotswolds to her destination.

The day was fine, sunny and warm, and she drove with the window open, trying to concentrate on the traffic. No matter what she'd been doing lately, her concern for Jesse lay very close to the surface. It was an effort to focus on her work, or the meal she was preparing, or, just now, her driving. Yet, somehow, despite her preoccupation, all the costumes had been created, or hired, in time. And now, although she felt as if she were in some way neglecting Jesse by going off, she was looking forward to the break. Jesse obviously was, too. They needed time apart.

Over the years she had come to the conclusion that raising a child as a single person was, in many ways, like marriage. There were occasions when she and Jesse abandoned any pretense of civility and displayed the worst of themselves. It was the result of living so close to another person, regardless of age. Proximity created friction, and the lines got blurred so that she was sometimes the needy or despondent child, and he the tolerant, understanding parent. It was shameful to find herself inflicting one of her darker moods on Jesse. Yet, oddly, he responded well at those times, displaying a forgiving comprehension that only deepened her shame and had her apologizing for days after the fact, while he assured her magnanimously that it didn't matter. He seemed stronger and wiser in the aftermath of her sporadic forays into bad behavior—as if her having revealed weaknesses served to put them on a more equal footing.

For his part, he could, without warning, sink into a sullen silence and wait first for her to notice, and then for her to attempt to determine the possible cause. The remedy invariably came in their finding something to laugh about. Usually, Jesse would begin imitating her when she was in a snit—exaggerating her tendency to stoop and her often sweeping hand gestures. It never failed to make her laugh. And when his mood turned foul, she'd reach for the nearest drawing block and pencil to dash off cartoons of an angry, scowling Jesse with storm clouds hovering over his head and lightning bolts shooting out of his ears, or a human-size Drick admonishing a Jesse puppet worn on its paw.

She and Jesse used their talents—his at mimicry, hers at quick sketches—to assist their communication. Yet in the few weeks since she'd taken him to Dr. Kennedy's surgery for a checkup they'd been unable to bridge the gap between them that seemed to be widening hourly, daily. Their fear had erected barriers neither of them knew how to circumvent. She'd tried to reassure him, but he'd been as polite as a stranger on a bus, insisting he wasn't afraid, thank you very much. She couldn't argue that he was; that she could see it in all he said and did. That would only have placed additional distance between them. He couldn't admit to his fear because he was almost thirteen and at a point when being afraid—of anything—was considered unforgivably childish.

Emotionally, he had set off along the tortuous road to manhood. But to date, the only physical manifestation was evident in his voice which, always husky, was becoming gradually deeper. Otherwise, he looked much younger than he was. The hair on his arms and legs was the downy stuff of childhood, and his face still had an appealing little boy's smooth softness. He had the classic look of an eight- or nine-year-old choirboy, with his large dark eyes, fine features and creamy complexion. And it was painfully obvious that he was bothered by his failure to change physically, to grow. Unfortunately, though, this topic had been added to the lengthening list of subjects not open to discussion. It alarmed Kyra to realize that the stresses of only a few weeks had caused the previously comfortable terrain between them to become strewn with any number of potentially explosive obstacles. Her feeling was that once the test results were in, they'd pull together, join forces again. Uncertainty was working against them now, and they needed, oddly enough, the conclusiveness of a diagnosis in order to know how to proceed.

She stopped in Oxford and took a walk along Broad Street through the city center, charmed by the architecture and the pale golden caste to the stone of the buildings. As on previous visits, she was captured by the beauty of a city that had existed for more than a thousand years. London was older, but too much of its core beauty had been lost in the postwar years, razed and replaced by hideous modern constructions. Oxford, though, was essentially unchanged and it seemed to cast a benevolent spell over visitors. An illusion perhaps, but the tourists here seemed less rowdy, more respectful than those shoving their way through the streets and public buildings in London.

She bought a sandwich and ate it as she walked, wishing she had the time to stop and tour the Ashmolean with its peerless collections of artifacts, and of Michaelangelo drawings. But she had to satisfy herself with strolling down Beaumont Street past the outside of the museum before heading back to the car.

As she unlocked the driver's door, she wished (again) that Dr. Rule would phone with the damned diagnosis so she could talk to her mother, and had to ask herself, suddenly, why she'd instituted an artificial deadline that prohibited it. She needed to talk to the one person who had always accepted Kyra just as she was; the one person Kyra sought out when life turned ugly, or incomprehensible; the one who could make sense of what Kyra failed to grasp. Her mother had always done those things for her—even during the years when Kyra had harbored such awful ambivalence about the family and such loathing for herself. God, but she longed to hear her mother's voice! Those adage-coiners had it all wrong, Kyra thought. Misery didn't love company. *Fear* loved company. Misery demanded solitude. Or maybe that was merely her old instinct asserting itself, that voice that told her to hide when things went sour.

Tightening her grip on the steering wheel, she traveled past Burford, into the Cotswolds. Absorbing the beauty of the rolling hills, she plummeted into sadness. She told herself she was overreacting; things would be fine. The tests would indicate some minor problem that could be easily remedied by medication. Jesse would start on a prescription and then, when school let out, he'd come up to join her. They'd spend her free time during the final weeks on location touring the countryside, visiting her father in Stratford, and seeing Kyle when he returned from Prague and came up to visit Damien. She told herself all sorts of things, but she couldn't shake the sadness, the fear like stomach acid that kept rising into her throat.

The film's female star—beautiful, talented and thick as a plank—had, during a break in shooting the very first setup, behaved as if she were wearing jeans and a T-shirt, not a custom-made period gown that required careful handling at all times. While waiting to be called, the feckless creature had plonked herself into a chair without bothering to lift her skirts, and had managed not only to separate the close-fitting bodice from the skirt but also to tear the delicate fabric.

Gillian Forsyth, the wardrobe mistress, had refrained from attempting to repair the gown, insisting it would have to wait, either for one of the more experienced seamstresses to come from town, or for Kyra to arrive. In the meantime, advised of the situation, the ever-practical Elway had gone ahead, shooting with the actress positioned at a slight angle so the damage to the gown wouldn't show on camera.

Arriving at the location just as the grips were organizing the next setup, Kyra saw Gillian begin picking her way over the cable-strewn ground toward her. Her expression funereal, the woman carried the gown in her arms like some exotic, mortally wounded creature.

As she waited, Kyra's eye was caught by a petite, fresh-faced young woman of nineteen or twenty who was eccentrically dressed in four or five layers of clothing—an outsize man's white dress shirt with a blue satin waistcoat over it, a long white leather jerkin over that, and a paisley shawl topping the lot. She had cropped cotton-candy pink hair, large blue eyes framed by thick mascaraed eye-lashes, and the dainty features of an old-fashioned porcelain doll. Several cameras were slung around her neck like heavy outlandish ornaments. Upon catching sight of Kyra, she lifted one of the cameras, aimed it and took several quick shots. Even from fifty or so yards distant, Kyra could hear the motorized advance of the film.

"Who is that?" Kyra asked, puzzled as to why her picture was being taken.

Looking over her shoulder, Gillian said, "Oh, that's Annie, the stills photographer. Weird get-ups, but an absolute poppet. Funny thing—" her eyes remained for a long moment on the girl "—I don't know what it is, but there's something about her. If I had to pick who I'd trust in an emergency among this lot, I'd pick Annie." Another moment, she shook her head, took a deep breath and, holding out the gown so Kyra could see the damage, said in a furious undertone, "*Look* at this! The silly bitch paid no mind at all. The silk's well and truly rent, and, naturally, there's been no one free to see to it. Everybody's tied up with last-minute alterations, and even if they weren't, I wasn't about to let just anyone at this. I'd like to *kill* the cow!"

Keenly aware of the pink-haired woman snapping away at them, Kyra studied the raveled silk. "I'll have to remove the skirt entirely," she thought aloud, "cut out the tear, make a seam and see if I can't cheat enough fabric round to the back to hide it. Why is she shooting us?"

Again Gillian looked over her shoulder. "Couldn't say, but I know she'd like to meet you. She's been asking when you'd be arriving. Would you mind, Kyra? As I said, she's a sweetheart, not a mean bone in her body."

"All right," Kyra agreed, curious.

Gillian signaled and, cradling the cameras with both hands, the photographer came hurrying over, smiling widely. "You're Kyra, right? I'm Annie Cooper. I've been wanting to meet you." The smile holding, she offered Kyra a solid handshake. "I'm a big fan of your work," she said energetically. "My favorite is the wardrobe in the second film you did with Elway. You should've had the Academy Award for those costumes. But you got the British one, right?"

"Yes, I did," Kyra said, taken with the girl's outspoken enthusiasm.

"Yeh, but you should've had the American one, too. *Fantastic* costumes, those were. I never in my *life* saw stuff like that. Hand-painted chiffon, layers of silk in graded colors. And the hats—like little kids' dreams, they were. Even the shoes. I remember this one shot where we saw the heroine's feet and she had on pink silk shoes with curved heels and tiny patterns of beads. I wanted those shoes more than anything, ever." Annie laughed, a sweet contagious sound.

"Did you?" Kyra smiled, relishing the metaphor. *Little kids' dreams.* "I hung on to them for some reason. They're stored in my studio, but I couldn't tell you where."

"Fantastic! That makes me really happy. I hated the idea they just got chucked after the shoot. Look," Annie said, "I know you just got here and there's stuff you've got to do, but I wanted to say hi."

"I'm glad you did. I like your outfit. Very imaginative."

Annie looked down at herself, then back at Kyra, her smile radiant. "Yeh, it's good, i'n't it? I was hoping maybe we could have a drink or something one evening, talk, you know."

"I'd like that," Kyra said, deciding she agreed with Gillian. There was a combination of intelligence and vulnerability in Annie's gaze that was both appealing and touching. "Give me a day to settle in, then we'll do it."

"Great. See you, then." To the wardrobe woman she said, "Sorry to interrupt, Gill." Then, once more cradling the cameras with both hands, she started back toward where the crew was setting up.

"What a delightful girl!" Kyra said.

"She's a treat, doesn't get in anybody's way, and the word is she's brilliant. I don't doubt it. You know?"

"I think I do. Well, I'd better get on this," Kyra said. "Where's the wardrobe van?"

"Back over there." Gillian gestured with her head.

"Right. Thanks for not letting anyone else at this."

Gillian snorted. "As if I would." Smiling belatedly, she said, "Good to see you, Keer."

"You, too. We'll get caught up later. Okay?"

Kyra turned and started back to the car to get her gear, thinking how typical this was. She'd only just arrived and already there was a crisis. Half the time on a shoot, there was more drama off camera than on. *Little kids' dreams,* she thought, and smiled.

By the time she'd had a quick chat on the telephone with Jesse and unpacked her bags it was well after seven. Having had a few cups of tea but no food since the sandwich in Oxford, she was light-headed from hunger.

The upper echelon members of the production, which included herself, were staying in the hotel in town, while the technical crew were in accommodations closer to the location. Pausing in the entry of the dining room, she saw James Elway was alone in the far corner. He looked up from the script on which he was penning notes and signaled her to come join him.

"You haven't eaten, have you?" he asked, half standing until she'd seated herself.

"No, actually, and I'm starving."

"I've only just ordered," he said, handing her his menu as the waitress came over.

"I'd like a steak, medium, and whatever comes with it," Kyra told the young woman without bothering to consult the menu.

"Some salad to begin?"

"Lovely. With vinaigrette, please."

"Care to share a bottle of Bordeaux?" Elway asked.

"Yes, definitely."

"And a bottle of water, I think. Fizzy or still, Kyra?"

"Still, please, Jimmy."

The waitress took the menu and went off to put in the order.

Elway said, "Excuse me a minute," and finished making notes in tidy printing that ran down the side of the page, along the bottom and over onto the back. Then he removed his reading glasses, closed the leather-bound shooting script and tossed it onto the empty chair next to him. "Sorry. I wanted to get that down before I forgot. So." He studied her intently for several seconds, then said, "It would appear you've survived the day."

She nodded and said, "It would appear we both have." She'd liked this man since their first meeting nearly twenty years before. She'd been hearing about him for a year or two before they actually met, and knew he'd attended film school in Los Angeles, and had worked there, first as an assistant editor, then as a postproduction supervisor, and finally as a unit director. He'd returned to England, signing on as first A.D. for her father at roughly the same time Kyra was designing the costumes for a play that eventually moved to the West End and firmly established her reputation.

Within eighteen months of his working with her father, Elway directed his first feature. He also edited the dailies, then went on to do the rough cut, the fine cut and, at last, the work print. Next he did the mix. When the answer print came back from the lab, he screened and rescreened it, examining it with the technicians for light grading, color balance and sundry other details. When the corrections were made, he finally approved a print from which release prints were prepared. Later, after the film's immensely successful release, when asked why he'd done so much of the work himself, he had said it was a matter of curiosity.

That didn't quite answer the question, but two things subsequently became common knowledge about the man: that he was driven primarily by curiosity, and that he hated being interviewed. But what was apparent from the first film was his incomparable vision. He had to understand fully whatever took his interest— whether it was how to create the coherent flow of a film by painstakingly patching together lengths of footage at an editing bench, or how certain lighting effects were achieved. And once he understood, he felt compelled to have a go. To that end, he was invariably involved in every aspect of production on his films. Nothing was left to chance, no detail went unnoticed, which was why he insisted on a minimum of a month's rehearsals with his hand-picked cast before shooting a single frame.

With every intention beforehand of entrusting tasks to the very fine people he hired in each area of production, he inevitably fell victim to his now legendary curiosity and ended up appearing unannounced, say, in makeup to stand in a corner watching and making quiet suggestions; or he positioned himself on the set while the gaffer and his crew placed the lights to the cinematographer's and Elway's satisfaction. And he alone edited each film.

Kyra had always found him attractive, thinking he looked more like an academic than a film director, usually clad in winter in corduroy trousers bagged at the knee, black roll-neck pullover, beige suede jacket, and a pair of well-worn desert boots. His summer attire was much the same, except that the trousers were cotton, and a T-shirt replaced the pullover. Tall and lanky, with light brown hair that was always falling into his eyes, he had an abstracted air, and was forever looking for his reading glasses. It fell to Ginny, his long-time personal assistant, to keep track of his glasses, as well as doing on-the-spot research, handling his personal correspondence, and overseeing—usually by telephone—Elway's staff in London which consisted of a full-time researcher, Ginny's own assistant, a receptionist and two office juniors.

Looking at Kyra, Elway thought of the famous black-and-white Cecil Beaton portrait of Octavia done in 1935. In an artfully draped, bias cut, satin evening dress that emphasized her height and accentuated her slim waist and ample breasts, she'd stood on an empty stage, one hand at her throat, the other at her side. Gazing directly into the camera, fair hair swept back from her face, eyes gleaming and full lips slightly parted, she'd been positively breathtaking.

He could remember every detail of the portrait which he'd seen for the first time at seventeen; he'd been impressed by the subtle lighting, by the meticulous clarity of the print, and by the intelligence and power Octavia had exuded. He'd thought then that it was no wonder she'd been such a success. And some dozen years later (very early in his own career) he'd developed a sudden ache in his belly during scene five of the first act of Latimer's famous West End production of *Macbeth,* when—in an incomparable portrayal of Lady Macbeth—Octavia had worked herself into a frenzy of purpose, her long, shapely hands suddenly clutching at her breasts as she'd delivered her lines in that deep, stirring voice. A woman then in her late forties, she had seemed to him the essence of female potency and sexuality. And now he was sitting opposite Octavia's daughter, who was, he realized, the same age her mother had been in that unrivaled production, and who had the same lucent green eyes. For a second time, a female in the Latimer family was responsible for a sudden ache in his belly. He'd never before reacted to Kyra this way, and had no idea why he was reacting so strongly to her now.

"How is everyone?" he asked, riveted by the sight of her. "What's your mother doing? And Kyle?"

"Kyle's on his way back from Prague."

"Oh? So he did Volkov's film, after all?"

"He did. And mother's just signed to do the new Hughes picture."

"I know the script. That's a lovely bit of casting. Shrewd of old Hughes. Octavia will be brilliant. And your father's well, is he?"

"Very. He says he wants to do one last film before he retires, but so far he's been unable to find a property he likes."

"I can't imagine Richard retiring."

"Nor can I."

"And how is your boy, Kyra? I'd like to use him one of these days. I've got a script in development with a part he'd be very right for."

The waitress returned just then with the water and the wine, saving Kyra from answering. Aside from preferring to keep her private life completely separate from her professional one, talking about Jesse would only have revived her apprehension. Instead, once the beverages had been poured, she asked about the script in development.

"Oh, it's very interesting," Elway said, eyes brightening. "Adaptation of a novel I optioned a while back. We're on the third draft, and getting close to a good script."

"Are you writing it yourself?" she asked.

"Actually, I am," he replied a bit sheepishly. "Thought I'd try my hand."

"I'm sure it'll be very good."

He rubbed his chin and said, "It's considerably more difficult than I imagined it would be."

"That wouldn't stop you."

He smiled and said, "No, you're right. It wouldn't. Of course I've had to set it aside until after this one's completed, but I plan to make it my next project." Leaning chin in hand, still smiling at her, he said, "This is pleasant, isn't it?"

"Yes." She found him very appealing. Had he been anyone else she'd have had a few drinks and gone to bed with him. But he wasn't just anyone, and she needed to keep her wits about her.

He kept gazing at her, his eyes radiating approval. Rather than turning her self-conscious, it had the rare effect of making her feel sexually and physically acceptable. *Delusional.* Her defenses seemed to be in tatters, and she wondered if they'd been drastically weakened by her fears for Jesse. For the last nine years the men she'd touched had been no more than nighttime shades, ghostly apparitions who got left behind with the arrival of daylight. She really didn't want this man to become another of them. Merely thinking about his attractiveness was dangerous in her present weakened state. She was overly susceptible, but couldn't think how to mend her damaged armor.

"Ah! Here are our salads!" He sat back and lifted his wineglass, tilted his head to one side and studied her with pleasure as the waitress set down their salads and a bread basket. "Cheers, Kyra." He touched his glass to hers.

"Cheers, Jimmy," she echoed, not allowing her eyes to remain connected to his for a moment longer than necessary. The voice in her head had started whispering urgent warnings about the countless negative repercussions of climbing into bed with this man.

CHAPTER 20

Halfway through the meal, after looking around the now near-empty dining room as if doing a quick count of its occupants, he said airily, "People will probably be talking about us by tomorrow."

"Oh, I doubt it," she said, wondering why, if the possibility bothered him, he'd asked her to join him. Men were so quirky, so seldom easy to read.

"Do you? Why?"

She took her time answering. "No one," she said at last, "would think your interest in me could be anything but professional."

"Now, why do you say that?" He leaned chin on hand, observing her as if her reasoning was of profound interest to him.

"Because, for one thing, I'm forty-seven years old. That fact alone makes me an unlikely candidate for your romantic interest. I promise you everyone who's seen us together thinks we're discussing the costumes. You needn't give it another thought."

"Okay," he said equably. "I won't."

Giving in to her own curiosity, she asked him about the breakup of his marriage. "What happened, Jimmy? I've always wondered. It seemed such an idyllic relationship."

"*Seemed,*" he said, pouring more water for them both. "But it wasn't. We met at university and got married two years later. I thought," he confessed with a self-mocking smile, "I was frightfully adult and mature. And she was under the misguided impression she was marrying someone who would, ultimately, be content with a detached three-bedroom, two children, two cars, and annual holidays on the continent."

"And what impression were you under?"

"That she'd grow, nurture her talent."

"Which was what?"

"Evidently for remaining unchanged from cradle to grave," he said, keeping a straight face.

She burst out laughing. "You make it sound positively criminal. Surely there are worse things."

"There are. But when I found myself forced to apologize for having to go off for months at a time to do the work I'd always wanted to do; to apologize for preferring to live in the city rather than the suburbs; and to apologize for having friends who were eccentric and gifted, and tended to get a bit rowdy when in their cups, we agreed we'd be best apart. It was an amicable split, surprisingly enough. I'd expected warfare, but I think she wanted it over quickly so she could net someone more suited to her needs while she was still reasonably young. And she did, fast. She is now happily ensconced in Sevenoaks, with a banker husband and a young son."

"How long were you married?"

"Thirteen years. Forever." He now poured more wine into each of their glasses. "What about you, Kyra?"

"What about me?"

"Your husband. What sort of chap was he?"

"Gary was uncomplicated and kind," she said. "We were together for just over ten years. Then, one afternoon, he stopped in midtown Manhattan to go to the bank and was killed by a runaway taxi." Her mouth stayed open, but for a few moments no more words emerged. She was feeling the shock of it again; her torso tensed as the pain clutched at her insides. But it passed quickly, and she thought there was probably some scientific theory that governed pain in relationship to time; some ratio that reduced the impact in direct proportion to the amount of time gone by. Perhaps in another five years the pain would be nothing more than a brief twinge.

"I would think it's the suddenness of something like that that's so hard to bear," he said. "I mean, old age, illness, one has an opportunity to prepare for the inevitable. But how does one prepare for a runaway taxi?"

"One doesn't." She remembered clearly having this very thought at the time, and found it strange to hear him giving it voice.

"Precisely. You know," he said with a frown, "when I hear something like that, I can't help thinking I haven't experienced much. My best and worst moments have all been inside my head. To be honest, in terms of life experience, I'm much as I was at eleven, with the same enthusiasms and single-mindedness. Sometimes I feel unequipped to deal with anything that isn't scripted. Sorry. I was digressing. Are you over it now?"

"I'm not really sure," she answered, wondering if he actually believed what he'd just said, or if he was trying to be humble. "Of course, if Jesse hadn't come along my life might have been very different. But he did, and...and he and I simply got on with it."

"You were pregnant when your husband died?"

"No, no. Jesse's adopted."

He speared a tomato wedge but made no attempt to eat it. "Does it help at all, or make any difference, if I say I'm sorry about what happened to your husband?"

"How can you be sorry about someone you never knew?"

"But I know you. It *happened* to *you*."

"Yes, but..."

"It's very sad for you, especially if you've failed to move forward from that point."

"I didn't say that." He was being a semanticist, and it was starting to give her a headache.

"Yes, you did. Well, what you said is you're not sure, which is tantamount, in some respects, to stasis." He saw by a darkening of her eyes that he'd overstepped, and at once said, "I didn't mean to come over all analytical. I have a tendency to view everything as cinematic, with a certain, almost clinical, detachment. And, of course, your life is not a film, and I have no right to be detached about something that has nothing to do with me. I apologize."

"It's all right," she said, willing him to change the subject. She wasn't in the mood to play word games.

"No, it isn't. You needn't be civilized. Feel free to hurl epithets, launch into full verbal abuse. I'll take my punishment like a man."

Amused, she shook her head.

"It wasn't that funny," he said, unable to fathom her response.

"Oh, it was, really. I've never hurled an epithet in my life. That's one of my failings, I suppose. I lack righteous indignation. But people like me tend not to feel they have a right to indignation, righteous or otherwise."

"People like you?" He was frowning again.

"Fat people, curiosities."

"You're neither fat nor a curiosity."

"Of course I am. Don't you think I own a mirror?"

"No, I don't think you do. You're quite wrong. It's staggering, how wrong you are. I can't believe you're actually serious."

For a few seconds, studying the agitation he was displaying— evidently on her behalf, but probably on his own because his judgment was being called into account—she had to wonder if some monstrous trick hadn't once upon a time been played on her, and that, in reality, she was not, in fact, immense. But, no. All she had to do was place a hand on her thigh, feeling its meaty bulk beneath the fabric of her dress, and she knew there'd been no trick. Caught between amusement and upset, she said succinctly, "I am an oversize misfit," and gave him a forced smile. "I made myself this way intentionally, as a means of self-preservation."

"Meaning?"

"My parents and Kyle were good-looking, but they were performers, always in the limelight, and they just didn't seem real to me."

"Not because they were attractive, surely."

"No, because they were performers." She wasn't saying what she meant, but couldn't think how to phrase it. "Look, I grew up part of a famous family. People approached me because they were curious about my family, not because they wanted to know me. They were looking for access, I suppose, or some means of self-aggrandizement by association. It was about my mother and father and brother, *the performers,* not about me." She thought she sounded incoherent, nutty. Why had she started this?

"You were suspicious of performers?"

"On one level, very. I never felt that I was actually a member of the family because I wasn't drawn to the things that were most important to them."

"And that's why you chose not to be a performer, too."

"Chose?" She gave a scoffing laugh. "It was never an issue, Jimmy. I mean, *really.* Can you *imagine* someone my size on a stage, or in a film? My shadow alone would've hidden the rest of the cast. The idea's ludicrous."

"It isn't at all," he said, bothered. "Do you remember the first time we met?"

"Yes, I do, distinctly."

As if having failed to hear her, he sailed on. "You came on the set at Elstree one morning, maybe twenty years ago. I had no idea who you were, but my immediate reaction was to wonder what film you were in and what genius had cast you."

She shook her head again, thinking of *Rashomon,* and the differing viewpoints of the same event. There wasn't any occasion involving more than one person that wasn't subject to more than one interpretation. And now she was being given Jimmy's version of a meeting she was certain they remembered in entirely different ways, for entirely different reasons.

"Your father introduced us," he went on, "and I thought it a pity you weren't an actress because you were one of the most unusual and startling women I'd ever encountered."

"I can well imagine." She was finding it hard not to break out into wild laughter; she had an image of herself, mouth agape as sound erupted from her throat and helpless tears of mirth leaked down her cheeks. She could almost feel the hilarity lodged, like a brick, in the middle of her chest. Life, she thought, was sometimes too bloody ridiculous. Why hadn't she just ordered a meal from room service? She could've been eating happily right now while watching some mindless show on TV.

"I doubt you can," he continued. "At best we only *think* we know what someone else is thinking. Occasionally we're right, but most of the time we couldn't be further off track. We *can't* know what anyone else is thinking. It's the part of life that could send me mad, if I let it, because I'd really like to know what other people are thinking. But anyway," he said impatiently, pushing the hair out of his eyes. "When we worked together a few years back, during the initial creative meeting I sat there wondering how I could have forgotten the contrast between your unassuming manner and your quite startling ferocity when it came to defending your work, your ideas. I had to wonder why you stuck so determinedly to the shadows.

"Now here we are again, and I'm beginning to understand your *modus vivendi*. And it's not just about your family or your looks, Kyra. Not at all." At last he popped the tomato wedge into his mouth, ate it, then said, "Your outward manner belies your inner anger, and I like the dichotomy. It's very intriguing."

"Look, Jimmy," she said, suddenly tired of their verbal fencing, of their talking all around the subject. "If this is in aid of getting

me into bed, you needn't bother with the flattery. All you've got
to do is ask."

Caught out and chagrined, without a clue how to respond to such
blatancy, he threw back his head and laughed.

Thinking his reaction proved she'd been right about his motives,
she ate some more of her overcooked Black Angus steak. This was,
she was convinced, no more than a variation on an old theme: a
glass or two of wine, some fairly meaningless chat as preamble,
and then grappling on a bed in a darkened room. Why couldn't he
come right out and ask her? Why was the truth always so much
more difficult than offhand prevarications? Probably because it left
one completely unprotected, and this was a man who'd just admitted to being no more than a child. So the coin of the realm in
this instance was tangential dialogue that glanced off the corners
of the actual subject—his sexual interest in her—without ever
landing squarely on it. It was fatiguing in the extreme.

"In some ways," he said, capitulating to a degree, "I find you
even more appealing now. You have a wonderful...*ripeness.*"

"You're being kind," she accused, thinking ripeness was a rather
nice synonym for fat.

"Not my sort of thing. Don't have time for it." He went at the
remainder of his meal with an almost frenzied appetite. Between
mouthfuls, he paused, thinking, then said, "Gratuitous kindness is
contempt in polite clothing."

She stared at him, caught off guard. "That's true, you know," she
said slowly. "That really is true."

"Of course it is," he said.

"You're very insightful when you want to be, aren't you?"

"I haven't gone and hurt your feelings, have I?" he asked, lowering his knife and fork.

"No," she said, not actually sure how she felt. All she knew for
certain was that they were going to end up in bed together, and she
couldn't think of any way to prevent its happening. She wasn't even
sure if she wanted to.

He walked with her to her room. She got the door open, stepped
inside and turned, thinking she'd made it safely to neutral territory;
nothing was going to happen. But then, visibly intending to kiss
her cheek, Jimmy's intentions got tangled. His gesture evolved into

a hectic embrace that culminated in Kyra finding herself pressed up against the open door, engaged in a fervid kiss.

Very aware that she had almost nothing on under her loose cotton sundress, she was nevertheless grateful that something so flimsy could, even temporarily, be a protective barrier. Reluctantly putting an end to the kiss, she placed both hands flat on his chest and pushed at him, saying, "This is a mistake, Jimmy. It's a truly bad idea."

He stared at her for several seconds, then backed off a bit, his hands settling on her hips. "Sorry," he murmured, his eyes simmering with intent.

"Don't be," she said, weak in the knees and trying to control her breathing. It would have been easy to send him away if she hadn't found him quite so appealing. "I'm flattered by your interest."

Still staring at her, as if, once again, he hadn't heard her, his eyes shifting from her eyes to her mouth, he said, "You are *so* beautiful, Kyra."

"Oh, please," she said, glancing up and down the hallway, fearful someone would come along and see them, and then the gossip would travel through the cast and crew like a virus. "I'm sick to death of hearing it."

"You don't have to believe me," he said earnestly, "but it's true."

"Oh, I know it's true, Jimmy. It's just that being beautiful has always been more of an impediment than an asset."

He nodded but she could tell he wasn't listening. When men decided they wanted something or someone, they never listened. They just went marching headlong after what they wanted, deaf to reason. But her own reason was diminishing. It had been a long time since she'd made love with a man she cared about even minimally. And this particular man wasn't going to be deterred by mere words. They bounced right off him; pointless to bother trying. The voice in her head was insisting, *It's a mistake, a terrible mistake.* But a second voice piped up, saying, *How terrible could it be? Why not go ahead, if it's what you want? The worst that could happen is that some people you don't especially care about will make you the topic of conversation for a few days.* Finally, she turned down the volume, shutting out both voices, and surrendered because it was easier than continuing to fight. And because she'd always found it hard to say no once someone put his hands on her.

She'd been right about the man: His famous curiosity made him an outstandingly inventive lover. And it had been a very long time since she'd allowed herself to be touched in such an exposed fashion. It was like unzipping one's skin and offering up raw nerve endings, denuded tissues; it was like placing one's bare hands in the fire and finding a ferocious satisfaction along with the searing pain. This encounter was all the more dangerous because her emotions had come into play. She actually liked James Elway, with his sometime auditory impairment and his boyish bursts of appreciation and of self-revelation. She liked the feel of him inside and out, and his enthusiasm for the act itself. It was, finally, impossible to resist someone who derived so much unadorned satisfaction from the active exchange of caresses, from having free access to her body. She gave herself like a cliff-diver, soaring breathless through space before plunging deep beneath the surface of sensation.

Near one in the morning, when he'd gone back to his own room, she lay in the dark, utterly sated, blinking at the knife edge of light showing between the curtains. In the lull before sleep, the nagging inner voice turned its volume back up. There were, it warned, formidable risks inherent in allowing herself to care, the primary one being the probability of loss, of hurt. But then, closing her eyes, she heard him whispering again—*You're so soft...your skin, God, your skin! The feel of you, the feel*—and her body responded with one last, lazy contraction as she slid away into the darkness.

Kyra sat down in one of the director's chairs near the set and accepted the paper cup of coffee Annie had volunteered to get her from the catering van.

"It's pretty foul," said Annie. "Afraid the best you can say is it's hot."

Kyra took a sip of the thick, slightly bitter liquid and looked at the gel-spiked, improbably pink hair, then into Annie Cooper's very clear, very blue eyes, jarred to see that, like Jesse's, they had an aged quality. "How old are you, Annie?" she asked.

"Twenty-five. I don't look it, I know." Annie tasted the coffee, made a face and set the cup on the ground. "That's well beyond foul," she said, reaching to take Kyra's cup from her. "Don't drink it. I'll fetch us some tea. It couldn't be as bad as this."

"Don't bother." Kyra stayed her with a hand on her thin arm.

"You sure?"

"Very," Kyra said, for a moment watching Jimmy and the cine-matographer talking, their heads close.

"I know it seems a bit of a cheek, my pushing to be introduced the way I did," Annie said, following Kyra's gaze. "But I really admire the lot of you—your mom, your dad, your brother and you."

"We're quite the family," Kyra said, wondering if the agitation she felt was the onset of lovesickness or a variation on her usual self-hatred.

"What's the matter?" Annie asked.

Kyra turned to look at her, recalling what Gillian had said about Annie's being the one person here that she'd trust, and discovering she felt the same way. It had to do with Annie's eyes and with her untarnished aura, as if it would be completely beyond her to harbor ulterior motives. "Nothing," Kyra said finally, deciding that she needed to hear herself say what she was thinking. Putting words to her jumbled emotions might bring them into line. "Everything."

Annie smiled knowingly. "One of those days, eh?"

"One of those," Kyra agreed, more and more taken with this young woman who, today, was wearing a white T-shirt and white leggings, with a high-waisted pastel-striped pinafore over top, her small bare feet in white clogs. She looked scarcely older than Jesse, yet seemed wisely level-headed and without pretensions, without any sort of agenda. "I'm trying to decide," Kyra confided, "if I've done something exceedingly stupid."

"Oh, dear. You think you have, don't you?"

Kyra looked at her with increasing interest, finding this a valuable opportunity to be candid with a relative stranger who was splendidly receptive, whose perception seemed particularly keen. "Perhaps yes, perhaps no. Probably yes. Half the time today I've felt a bit sick, certain I've done the wrongest possible thing. The rest of the time I've been feeling very hard done by because I shouldn't even have to be thinking about it. I've got a lot on my plate right now, and what does any of it matter in the larger scheme of things. You know?"

Those clear blue eyes gazed directly into Kyra's, and Kyra wondered anxiously for a moment if she wasn't compounding last night's mistake by discussing it, however obliquely, with someone she knew not at all. But no. Annie Cooper was trustworthy; it was in those unflinching, so-sane eyes.

"No specifics," Annie said softly. "But did you do what I *think* you did with the someone I *think* you did it with?"

Kyra couldn't help laughing. "Yes, I did. *My God!* Why am I telling you this?" Her face was burning.

"Because you know I'm not going to repeat it, and because you can see I'm not out to harm you," Annie said reasonably. "I'm one of the least harmful people you'll ever meet. And I don't believe we meet people accidentally. Do you?"

"How do you mean that?" Kyra asked.

"I believe there's a reason for every single person we meet in our lives. Sometimes, it takes a while to figure out what the reason is. But there always is one. So now, are you mad at him or at yourself for doing that thing you shouldn't've done but went ahead and did anyway and probably enjoyed more than you should've?"

Kyra stared at her for a moment, then they both laughed like giddy schoolgirls.

"You're wicked," Kyra accused, mopping her eyes.

"Nah. I just say the things nobody else dares to. So, which is it?"

"I don't know that, either," Kyra said, sobering. "Anger's so difficult to attribute with any accuracy. I think we get it all muddled up with the other things that usually go along with it—resentment, loneliness, self-consciousness, alienation."

"Yeh," said Annie, equally sober now. "I know what *that's* like. You're very truthful. I am, too. It can get you in a ton of trouble."

"Yes, it can."

"I reckon people've been going on your whole life about how beautiful you are. Right?"

"Uh-hunh."

"And you hate it, right?"

"Passionately."

Assessingly, Annie said, "You do have absolutely perfect features. It's why I was shooting you yesterday. For me, though, what makes you beautiful is your nature. The kindness shines right off you. But the wankers're forever coming on to you cuz they reckon you can't be all that bright if you're so beautiful. But once in a while you think, What the hell, maybe this one's not too terrible, and you give in, cuz you can't do without it altogether or you'll go mental. Which is what's happened now. Right?"

"Right. You're very good. And very outspoken."

"Yeh. I don't see the sense in playing games with people," Annie said matter-of-factly. "It don't get you nothing in the long run 'cept a lot of bother. It's best to tell the truth and just get on with it. He's a smashing director, isn't he?" she said, looking over at the set where Elway and the head gaffer were now in discussion.

"He's very gifted." Kyra tried to keep her tone neutral.

"Listen," Annie said, placing a small, soft hand on Kyra's wrist. "Don't worry. I'm not stupid and I'm no opportunist. You don't know me yet, but you'll find I'm a good friend. I get the feeling you could use one about now. So, if you find yourself needing to talk, I'll be around to listen. And they'd have to kill me to get me to repeat a word you said. Okay?"

Touched, Kyra said, "I may take you up on that."

"I mean it. You've got things you want to get off your chest, I can listen without playing judge and jury."

"Thank you, Annie."

"I'd best be gettin' over there now. They're ready to start. See you later, eh?"

Cradling the cameras hung about her neck, Annie started off toward the set, a most unlikely oracle. Kyra sat a minute longer, watching the spritelike young woman pick her way daintily over the countless cables. It was one of the oddest exchanges she'd ever had in her life, yet she felt much better for it.

CHAPTER 21

Traditionally directors viewed the rushes—the roughly assembled print of scenes shot the previous day—at the end of the day's shooting, together with the producer, the D.O.P., the production designer, and any other directly affected crew members, in order to ascertain primarily that no retakes were necessary. The rushes were shown untrimmed and in order of shooting, and, as a matter of course, this daily print was later used by the editor—in this case, Elway—as part of his work print in assembling the film.

Elway was in the habit of viewing the rushes a second time alone. Then he dined late, usually on his own, and studied the shooting script, making any last-minute notes to himself while he ate.

Because there was inevitably some sort of work to be done on at least a few costumes at the end of a day's shooting before she, too, viewed the rushes, then checked in by phone with Jesse, Kyra was also usually late getting to the dining room and most often ate alone, with a book for company. But on those evenings when they happened to arrive more or less at the same time, James immediately invited Kyra to join him. And, following the meal (as if some tacit agreement had been reached), they would go to her room. On those evenings when they ate separately, Jimmy came knocking at her door at nine-thirty or ten and, minutes later, they were on the bed, feasting on each other's flesh.

Kyra was in perpetual heat and she was worried. Jimmy was hollowing out a niche for himself in her affections. He seemed unconcerned about word of their alliance getting to the media, and, beyond returning to his own room to sleep, he made no effort she could see to conceal his actions. She couldn't help thinking that he either believed himself to be of no interest to the world outside, or that he just didn't care. If he didn't care, that had to mean that either he was becoming seriously attached to her, or that his involvement was so casual (she never refused his attentions, did she?) that it simply didn't warrant any undue attention on his part.

So now, on top of her ever-present concern for Jesse, was a layer of confusion about just what was going on with Elway. Was this a typical on-location affair, when both parties understood at the outset that it would last only as long as the shoot? Or was this something more? For her, it felt like something more. But perhaps that was wishful thinking.

After nightly lovemaking and their fourth dinner together in just over a week, when Jimmy automatically walked with her to her room, she decided she simply couldn't get into bed with him again until she'd clarified the situation.

"Let's sit down," she said, switching on the lights and then turning to study the surprise that overtook his features in the form of a flustered smile. "You and I need to talk, Jimmy."

"Oh, right," he said, and lowered himself into one of the room's two small upholstered chairs. He looked anything but comfortable, putting her in mind of Ichabod Crane so that she wanted to laugh at the sight of him—all jutting elbows and knees. "What's up?" he asked, insouciant, folding his arms across his chest.

Her anger flared at the question—so abrupt, so flip, as if her concerns were inconsequential.

Perched on the end of the bed, she asked, "What're we doing, Jimmy? Is this something or nothing? I'd like to know."

He leaned back in the chair, braced his elbows on its sloping arms, and contemplated her for a time before saying, "I've been asking myself why I didn't make an effort to get to know you better the last time we worked together."

"Oh?"

"I like you. I like your sense of humor, your intelligence. I even like your self-consciousness." He had a weakness for unorthodox women like Kyra—drawn to their fears and passions, their enticing vulnerability. In this instance, he was also drawn to the fact that she was a Latimer. The family was, after all, theatrical royalty. No matter what he accomplished, he would never be in their league— unless he became a part of the family. Something to consider, he mused, although he'd never been that cold-blooded or that pre-meditated in his life. No. The fact was that he found this woman positively irresistible in every way.

"I see," she said, coolly.

"I didn't intend to come across as uncaring," he said, seeing that he wasn't making any headway. "I do like you, Kyra. Very much. I thought it was mutual."

"You've assumed it is."

"Well, but...I mean...We're together every night...."

"That's just sex, Jimmy."

"But at dinner...we talk..." He tried and failed to find a new position for his arms, gave up, and returned them to the arms of the chair.

"Not about what we're doing in here every night."

"No, that's true. I thought it was understood, that we're—involved."

"We are, to some extent," she confirmed. Perhaps, she thought, sorry for him because he was so plainly discomfited and for herself because she wasn't enjoying this, they were no more than a pair of outsize children, with their joys and fears intact but hidden beneath a veneer of worldliness. They had the vo-cabulary and the money to facilitate their independent, seem-ingly adult lives; but, pretense aside, it appeared to distill down to a matter of two misfits (albeit socially acceptable ones) try-ing to connect.

"I like you, too, Jimmy," she said. "But the thing is, if they haven't already noticed, people soon will. Then the press will start hounding us—you more than me. If this is just a casual affair, how will you feel about that? Have you even thought about it?"

He knew she was right, but his newfound appetite for her was insatiable. Making love to her was an unparalleled experience for him; entering her fragrant voluptuous embrace was like a dream of drowning, panic and peace combining; just the sound of her voice (so like her mother's) was an enticement. "I don't care if peo-ple know," he said, like a reckless teenager. "Do *you?*"

"Actually, I do—for any number of reasons."

"You shouldn't. What does it matter?" He extended his legs, then drew them back up again. He was wretchedly uncomfortable.

"It matters. I can't be casual about the press and I'm frankly shocked if you mean what you just said."

"Would you rather I went back to my room?" he asked, unsure what she wanted him to say or do, and the too-small chair was driving him to distraction.

"No," she said, frustrated. Was he emotionally retarded? What was she doing with this man?

"What then?" He appeared bewildered, even threatened.

"I simply want to know where I stand, Jimmy."

"Well, where do *I* stand?" he countered.

"I care about you," she admitted.

"And I care about you. We're getting to know each other. Isn't this how it's done?"

She stared at him, feeling all at once too old for this. It was more rewarding to talk to Jesse and his friends. They seemed to have a better grip on reality than this man did. They were certainly more in touch with their feelings. "Let's give it a rest for tonight," she said. "I'm awfully tired."

"Sure, if that's what you'd like," he said, hoisting himself out of the chair.

At the door, he paused and said, "I do care about you, Kyra. I'm just not very good at talking about these things."

"It's all right, Jimmy. I understand."

He kissed her good-night and she stood in the doorway, watching until he disappeared around the corner. Then she shut the door, wishing she hadn't tried to talk to him. It had been a depressingly futile exercise.

The next morning she awakened to the sound of rain being thrown against the window. One look at the low, heavy sky and the wind-whipped trees told her it would be a down day. The grips would be on standby in case the weather cleared. And for her it would be an opportunity to examine the costumes, make sure they were clean and in good repair.

She was crossing the lobby after a solitary breakfast when the receptionist spotted her and said, "Oh, Miss Latimer. I've just taken a message for you."

The message read: Please call Dr. Rule's office at once.

Nervous, she hurried upstairs. In her room, she stood and dialed the number, one hand gripping the receiver, the other fastened to the rim of the desk.

Dr. Rule wished to speak to her personally. Would she hold on for a moment, please? Knees threatening to buckle, she had to sit down.

"I'm afraid the results are not encouraging," Dr. Rule said without preamble. "Jesse is in kidney failure. I want him to come in right away for more tests to see if we can't determine the possible cause."

"What does it mean?" Kyra asked, mouth dry.

"The tests indicate his kidneys are doing roughly only twelve percent of their job. There may well be a treatable underlying cause. If there isn't, we'll have to discuss the possibilities of dialysis or transplant. But let's not get ahead of ourselves. We'll arrange for an ultrasound and X rays and hope to get some definitive answers."

After advising her to bring Jesse in as soon as possible, he turned Kyra over to his receptionist to book an appointment. That done, she hung up and sat very still, arms crossed tightly, cold hands tucked into her armpits. *Kidney failure. Dialysis or transplant.* Closing her eyes, she relived the horror of her first sight of Jesse's tiny battered body, the massive bruise low on his back. Had that long-ago kick damaged Jesse's kidneys? She was furiously certain it had.

Kidney failure. Without some form of medical intervention, Jesse would die. She reached again for the telephone and got through to Susan Forrest, his friend Robert's mother, to say, "Will you please tell Jesse that I'm on my way home and I'll ring him as soon as I arrive?"

"Okay. Is everything all right, Kyra?"

"I can't discuss it now, Susan. I'll explain later." Kyra hung up and began packing. In less than half an hour her bags were waiting by the door as she did a final check of the room. Then she got back on the telephone to tell reception that she'd be leaving. Next she left a message at the motel for her assistant Mary and then, on impulse, asked to speak to Annie.

Annie said, "Hey, hi! Let's get together. Nothing's going to be shot today."

"I have to go back to London, Annie. I just wanted to let you know."

"What's happened?" she asked, picking up on Kyra's agitation.

"It's about Jesse. I really can't talk now."

"Why don't you give me your number so I can ring you later, make sure you're okay."

Kyra deliberated for a moment, saw no harm in the request, and gave it to her.

Annie said, "Be careful driving. And Kyra? Whatever it is, you'll handle it. So don't get in a flap. Okay?"

"Thanks, Annie."

Finally, Kyra dialed Jimmy's suite.

He answered himself, and she said, "I've got to go back to London at once. May I come talk to you for a minute?"

"Come on up," he said, and put down the receiver.

He was waiting in the doorway and asked, "What's going on?"

She paused, irked by his manner. Ignore it, she told herself. Think of him as a large, inept child. "Jesse's not well." *Kidney failure.* The words racketed noisily around the interior of her skull like marbles in a glass bowl. "He has to have more tests, so I'm going home."

"Oh, too bad. I hope it's nothing serious."

"Me, too. Look, between them, Mary and Gillian will take over for me on the set. They can handle everything. But if a problem does arise, I'll be just a phone call away."

"Don't worry about it." He put a hand on her arm. "Be sure to let me know how it goes with Jesse."

"I will. I am sorry to go flying off this way...." What they'd had for the past week and a half had been no more than a glorified location fling. She felt like a fool and couldn't wait to get out of there. "I really should get going." She turned and started for the door.

He caught hold of her arm, and she turned back, urgency surrounding her, he thought, like a radiant aura. "Call me."

"Yes, all right." *Call me.* What the hell did that signify? The man had no interpersonal skills. She'd been mad to go against her instincts, mad to think there'd been anything meaningful between them.

Still holding her arm, he opened the door, wanting to slow her down. She was going at a pace that wasn't healthy. "Please be careful."

"I will be." She looked down at his hand on her arm, finding this display more fraternal than loving. As she watched, his hand opened, releasing her. The gesture struck her as profoundly final and, in a way, she was relieved. No more fretting and analyzing; no more berating herself.

Then his arms went around her and he kissed her very caringly. A surprise. She put her hands on his face and kissed him again, thinking she'd been wrong; they'd made a connection, after all; he did have feelings for her. Like suddenly refracted light, previously hidden colors were revealed in something she'd feared was strictly monochromatic.

She pulled away, wanting to say something significant, but unable to utter a single word. Wishing she could stay, that they could turn off the lights and get into bed together one more time, to hide from the world and its atrocious tricks for an hour or two, she took a step away. Then, she turned and ran down the corridor.

"Don't forget to ring me!" he called after her.

She didn't dare look back. Every time she thought he was saying one thing, he was saying another. His skills were probably okay; he was just behaving like a typical man. Her skills, though, were questionable. Or maybe she'd lost them altogether somewhere along the way. Up, then down; up then down, then up again; a dizzying, stupid ride.

Throughout the drive she'd been planning to go directly home, but upon exiting the Ring Road she found herself headed for the Forrest house, instead, desperate to see Jesse.

"It's half day, but the boys haven't come back yet," Susan Forrest said. "Come in and have a cup of tea while you wait."

"Do you know where they went?" Kyra asked, settling at the table in the spacious modern kitchen while Susan plugged in the kettle.

"Actually, I don't." Susan leaned against the counter and reached for the cigarette burning in an ashtray. "They've been late getting home several times this past week. I have no idea what they're up to, but I do know they've been out on serious business." She smiled, took a final drag, and put out the cigarette.

"Serious?" Frazzled from the long drive, Kyra couldn't make sense of what the woman was saying.

"Wherever they've been, they wore their uniforms, even polished their shoes."

"That's odd." Usually, the boys started taking off their school clothes as they came through the front door.

"I'll say. And what's odder still, this is the fifth afternoon they've done it since Jess has been here." Opening the cupboard for the teapot, she laughed and said, "If I didn't know better, I'd swear the two of them had part-time jobs in some brokerage in the City."

Kyra dredged up a smile. She liked this woman.

"Sober as judges, the pair of them," Susan went on, warming the pot before spooning in loose tea. "Not a word about where they've been or what they've been doing. All very mysterious. It's adorable, really." She glanced at the wall clock. "They're usually back before five. Are you okay?" she asked.

"I'm just tired. The drive was a horror show."

"I can imagine." Susan glanced over at the rain-splashed window. "Have you eaten, luv? I've got some Cheshire and a fresh loaf."

Kyra was about to refuse automatically but realized she was hungry. "I'd like some actually, thank you."

Susan went about setting slices of bread and cheese on a plate, and Kyra watched, taken, always, by the woman's grace. At five foot four, she was exactly the size Kyra had always longed to be. With high cheekbones, artfully made up, large brown eyes, and a wide mouth, Susan was lovely. She had on white jeans and a yellow T-shirt; her dark blond hair was in a topknot, a few loose strands trailing down the back of her neck. She had the small lithe body, disproportionately long limbs, unpretty feet and very erect carriage of the dancer she'd once been. A principal soloist with the Royal Ballet at twenty (after twelve years of excruciatingly hard work), she'd been well on her way to becoming a prima ballerina when a lift in rehearsal went wrong. Her partner dropped her, she landed badly, tearing her Achilles tendon, and that put paid to her career. After the tendon healed, she took a job as receptionist in the head office of a multinational corporation where she met Stephen Forrest. They married within a year, and Robert was born a year later. She was happy being a wife and mother and didn't at all miss the ballet. Or so she claimed. Kyra wondered, though, about the size of her secret cache of sorrow. Hints of it came through now and then. But in the main Susan Forrest did seem happy.

Robert had inherited his mother's grace and good looks, and his father's height and heft. The same age as Jesse, he was the tallest boy in the form and, arguably, the best-looking—with his mother's wide mouth and clean-cut features set in an oval face. He looked more like sixteen than almost thirteen, and shared most of Jesse's interests—in books and computers and music. The two had met on Jesse's first day of term six years earlier and had been fast friends ever since. The two women had shared countless cups of tea in each other's kitchens, and attended a lot of school events together. They'd been friends these past six years in the way unique to mothers of schoolmates—interested and warm, but at a slight distance.

Susan poured milk into each cup, then added the tea, stealing glances at Kyra. Finally, she asked, "Are you sure there's nothing wrong, luv?"

She was unpretentious, charming and practical, and Kyra longed to unburden herself. But she couldn't, not before she'd told Jesse about the test results. "Just in need of a good night's sleep," she said, helping herself to the bread and cheese.

"How's the film going?" Susan asked, sitting sideways in her chair, one arm draped fluidly along its back.

"So far, very well," Kyra answered, between bites.

"Good. I'm glad." Never one to push, Susan allowed a silence to fall as her gaze drifted to the window. She watched the rain sheet across the window, while Kyra ate mechanically, trying not to think of how desolate and bereft of purpose her life would be without Jesse.

The boys came running in in their dripping raincoats and wet shoes.

"I saw the car outside. What's happened?" Jesse asked Kyra. "Is everyone all right? Why have you come back?"

"Kindly hang up your wet coats, and remove all offending foot gear, gentlemen," Susan said.

"Sorry," chorused both boys, scooting back to the front hall as the mothers exchanged a smile.

Moments later, Robert and Jesse seated themselves at the table, at once eyeing the bread and cheese.

"Yes, you may have some," Susan said. "I'll make a fresh pot of tea."

"Where have you been, Jess?" Kyra asked.

"I've been interviewing agents," he explained proudly. "As Sir Kenneth suggested, I rang and made appointments, sent copies of the manuscript to each of the people on the list. Robert and I have been seeing them. Today was the last appointment and the one I liked best. I've agreed to let her represent me. She's going to ring you to explain the agency terms and have you sign for me."

"Amazing," Kyra said, impressed by his initiative.

"And here we were," Susan said, "wondering if the pair of you had taken jobs in the City."

At this the boys looked at each other, then laughed buoyantly.

"Nice one, Mum," Robert said, giving her a thumbs-up.

"You haven't said why you've come back," Jesse said to Kyra.

"I'm afraid you're going to have to cut this visit short and come home."

"Nothing wrong with Granny and Grandpa, is there?"

"They're both well, so far as I know," Kyra assured him.

"Then why must I come home?"

"I'll explain later, Jess."

"No, I want to know *now*. Robert and I have *plans*."

"I'm sorry, but you'll have to postpone them."

"Why?" He was quickly growing belligerent.

"It's to do with the tests."

Confused, Robert looked from Kyra to his mother then at Jesse. "What tests, Jess? Are you sick?"

Angry now, keeping his eyes on Kyra, Jesse said, "No, I am *not!* They're just stupid bloody tests that don't mean a damned thing."

"Jess," Kyra admonished quietly.

"Sorry, but I want to know *why* I have to come home."

"Dr. Rule wants you to have more tests."

"No!" Jesse jumped up, nearly overturning over his chair. "I won't!" Face red and twisted, fists clenched, he glared at Kyra.

"Robert, let's give Jesse and Kyra some privacy," Susan said, and led her reluctant son off to the living room.

After they'd gone, Kyra said, "Jess, I know you're upset. So am I. But we're not going to argue about this. We have no choice in the matter."

"Why not?" he asked plaintively.

"Because your kidneys are failing. Dr. Rule has to do more tests to try to find out why."

Jesse went pale. Staring at her now with a fearful expression she hadn't seen in a very long time, he moved closer. She reached out and held him, thinking that if fear had substance, she was touching it. Jesse's body seemed to be vibrating at a low level and his breathing had turned quick and shallow. In the ensuing lull, she heard the kettle come to a boil and turn itself off.

"Am I going to die?" he asked in a husky whisper, a clinging little boy again, his cheek hot against hers.

"No!" she whispered back. "You are *not!*"

"But if my kidneys don't work, I will."

"There are bound to be alternatives, treatments. We'll find out what the options are." Easing back, she took hold of his small, cold hands.

He was shaking his head, ready to begin arguing again, and she said, "Let's discuss this at home, Jess. Would you go collect your things, please?"

"Okay." The fight draining from him, he trudged out of the kitchen, sighing.

A minute or so later, Susan returned. "Robert's gone up to help Jess pack. Is there anything I can do?"

"Thank you, but I don't think so."

"It's serious, isn't it?"

Kyra nodded. "His kidneys are failing."

Susan put a hand to her throat. "I don't know what to say. This is terrible."

"Yes, it is," Kyra agreed. "It is truly terrible."

In her turned-out, rolling, dancer's gait Susan walked over to the counter and lit a cigarette as Kyra sank back into her chair. "We all love Jess dearly, you know," Susan said, then took a long hard drag. "This is so dreadful," she said tremulously. "I'm going to come unglued."

"Don't you dare," Kyra warned. "It's up to us to stay glued."

Startled, Susan laughed. "You're so unflappable," she said. "You could run the world, if they'd let you."

"I can't even run my own idiotic life," Kyra countered. "Half the time these days I don't know what people are trying to say to me, what anything *means*. You don't want to go confusing size with adequacy, Susie."

Susan stared at her for a moment, then laughed again, loudly. "You dolt," she said fondly, then took another drag on her cigarette. "Size with adequacy," she repeated, shaking her head.

A few minutes later the boys reappeared. Jesse hung back in the doorway as Robert approached Kyra.

"Would it be all right if I come with Jess when he has his tests?"

"Oh, Robert, I don't think..." Susan began.

"Jess, is that what you'd like?" Kyra asked him.

"Yes, please."

"Then I have no objection," Kyra said.

"Are you quite sure?" Susan asked. "You've got a full plate as it is."

"I want to be with Jess," Robert told his mother. "Please say yes, Mummy. He'd come, if it were me. Wouldn't you, Jess?"

Jesse nodded several times—regressing minute by minute. Soon he'd be wearing Drick again, speaking through the puppet. Kyra wanted to weep.

"Please, Mummy?" Robert begged. *"Please?"*

"All right," Susan gave in. "We'd better pack you a bag."

"I've already done it," Robert said. "We're ready to go." He moved to stand beside his friend, draping a protective arm around Jesse's shoulders.

Fairly undone by the display, Kyra got to her feet saying, "Let's be off, then." Extending her hand to Susan, she said, "Thanks for everything, Susie."

"Keep me posted, please." Susan clasped Kyra's hand with both her own, going up on tiptoe to kiss Kyra's cheek, then said, "Robert, come say good-bye to me."

The sky was dark, the rain still pouring down. Kyra put the car in gear and reversed out of the driveway.

"Don't forget to ring your father later!" Susan called from the doorway.

"I won't!" Robert called back, then rolled up his window as they set off.

CHAPTER 22

"It's Kyra. I'm sorry it's so late. But you did ask me to call."

"I was beginning to wonder if you would," Elway said. "So how is Jesse?"

Giving him points for having asked about Jesse straight off, she told him what Dr. Rule had said. "They want to do more tests, and luckily his friend Robert's going to be with him, so he's not quite as scared as he was initially."

"Well, that's good," he said. "And how are you?"

"Tired, anxious. The boys have finally gone to bed and I'm waiting for Mother to phone. I'm dreading having to tell her."

"Worrying's a complete waste of energy, you know. It doesn't solve anything."

"That's true, but I'm afraid. I can't help it." The instant the words left her mouth she wished she hadn't admitted to her fear. The last thing she wanted was to come across sounding needy.

"You've got to try not to be," he said. "As I said, it doesn't help."

Platitudes. This was awful! Why had he asked her to phone him? He didn't appear to want to hear about her feelings, and she was back to wondering what, if anything, they meant to each other. Rather than concern for Jesse, it was this uncertain relationship that was the real drain on her energy. This he-loves-me-he-loves-me-not nonsense was for the young, for those with futures spreading off into infinity, not for a woman nearing fifty who had a sick child.

"Easier said than done," she said, striving for a lighter note.

"Make an effort, for Jesse's sake and your own. Now, keep me posted, okay?"

"If you like." There, she thought. Give him the option of backing away through a now-open door.

"I would like you to. I've been missing you, Kyra," he said hesitantly, as if the admission cost him dearly. "It seems days since you left." A pause, then, with a complete change of tone, he said briskly, "Well, take care. We'll talk again soon," and hung up.

She hadn't expected so abrupt an ending and put the receiver down slowly. She was a mess, her reactions all askew. She was going to have to make a decision about Jimmy, either to allocate the time he seemed to need or to remove herself as graciously as possible. Jesse had to be her first priority now.

She paced the length of the downstairs hallway from the kitchen to the front door, thinking that if Jesse died she'd be a double amputee, legless, rooted in place. He couldn't die; that couldn't happen.

Back and forth she went, trying to frame positive scenarios but coming up only with negatives.

When the telephone rang just before ten, she snatched up the receiver.

"Hiya, it's Annie. How's it going?"

"Annie, hi. I'm not great." What a relief to be able to reply honestly, without having to worry about the sort of reception she might get! Gillian was right: Annie was completely trustworthy. She was also very caring.

"What's going on, Keer?" She used the family nickname and Kyra felt a burst of fondness for this young woman. "What's wrong with Jesse?"

"It's kidney failure," Kyra said, sagging into a chair.

"Bloody hell! I'm ever so sorry. What's going to happen?"

"He's got to have more tests, to see if they can find the cause."

"You must be going mad. I wish I could help; wish I wasn't stuck here for another week and a half before we shift down to Elstree."

"It's sweet of you to say that, Annie."

"It's not *sweet.* You need your friends at a time like this. I'm only being practical. How's Jesse taking it?" she asked, as if she'd always known him, a boy she'd never even seen.

"He's very scared. So am I."

"Well, *naturally.* Who *wouldn't* be? I go mental if I get a paper cut. And your boy's sick. I'm surprised you're not frothing at the mouth. I would be. Look, soon's I get back, I'll come see you. And I'll help any way I can, so don't be shy about asking, no matter what it is. My Gran always said if you don't ask, you don't get. And that's true."

"I'll look forward to seeing you when you get back. You're very thoughtful, Annie. I appreciate that right now more than you could know."

"Listen, even if we've only just met, I care about you, and about Jesse, too. I'll ring again tomorrow, see how you're doing. Okay?"

"Okay. And thanks again. You've given me a lift."

"Take care, Keer. Go have a long soak and a big drink, and try not to think the worst. Okay? 'Bye."

When the phone rang again ten minutes later, it was Octavia. Not bothering with a hello, she said, "My demented sister arrived today without a *word* of warning beyond that vague letter weeks back. I had to cancel dinner and *Aida* with Kenneth to spend three *excruciating* hours with her. She's managed to make herself positively *grotesque*, Kyra, with a face as empty as a *blancmange*."

Kyra erupted into laughter.

Crustily, Octavia said, "I am *not* joking. On the one hand, I couldn't bear to look at her. On the other, I couldn't stop. It was fascinating, on a par with a traffic accident. The skin is stretched so tight over her sharp little nose and those ludicrous, bulging cheek implants that she looks oriental. And so much flesh has been removed from around her eyes that she seems constantly surprised, and when she smiles—which, mercifully, is not often—there are rows of horizontal pleats either side of her *huge* collagen-inflated lips. I swear to you, she looks as if she's wearing a lumpy condom over her head!"

Kyra was laughing so hard she was bent double.

The instant Kyra's laughter began to ebb, Octavia, with ever-impeccable timing, continued. "I think all the years of drinking and drugs have rotted what little brain matter she once had. She nattered on and on and *on*. Infuriating drivel about how Roddy and Gage have evolved into teenaged thugs. Glenna's a fool who's contributing to their delinquency because Gage has a girlfriend, and Glenna bought them contraceptives, which, in Cathy's view, is depraved behavior. Cliff is useless—always has been, always will be. And Dillon never comes to see her because his father has poisoned his mind against her. Of course, the fact that Dillon's teaching in Boston has nothing to do with it. *God!*" Octavia groaned. "It was the most *horrendous* evening. On the plus side, everyone was so busy staring at her that no one noticed me, which meant no quick call to alert the *paparazzi*. Thank God! Can you imagine photos in the papers? And the cutline: 'Octavia Bell dines with living medical experiment.'"

This set Kyra off again, laughing so explosively she was afraid she might wake the boys, but unable to stop for a good minute or more.

Finally, Octavia took a deep breath, and said, "Thank you for letting me get that off my chest, darling. You're a wonderful audience. Now, tell me what you're doing home. I thought you had another ten days on location. I wish *I* did. The thought of spending more time with Cathy makes me want to emigrate to Tonga. Please promise me you'll do duty with her one evening. Take her somewhere dark—the theater or a film—and let me have a few hours to recover."

"I'd like to, but I don't know what my time's going to be like. The thing is, I've got some bad news."

"What?" Octavia asked, instantly alert.

Kyra repeated what Dr. Rule had told her.

"Is he sure?" her mother asked sharply.

"He's sure."

There was a silence. Octavia started to say something, her voice cracked, and she stopped.

"I'm sorry," Kyra apologized. "I shouldn't have put it quite so baldly."

"You know I prefer to take liquor and bad news undiluted. But why the hell did you let me prattle on about Cathy?"

"Jess made me promise not to tell anyone, and I had to honor that. But that was before we had the test results."

"I understand. How is he handling it?"

"He thinks he's going to die."

"Poor Jess. He must be so frightened. And you must be, too."

"I couldn't bear to lose him." Kyra at last said out loud what had been on her mind the entire day. "I couldn't—"

"You are *not* to think that way!" Octavia cut her off.

"I'd be a fool if I didn't entertain the possibilities," Kyra defended herself.

"I suppose it's impossible not to," Octavia allowed. "But you mustn't dwell on the darker possibilities. When is he having these tests?"

"Tomorrow." Kyra fished in her pocket for a tissue. Finding none, she wiped her face with the back of her hand.

"Would he like me to be there?"

"Given that you're not supposed to know, it wouldn't be a good idea. And Robert's the one Jesse needs right now. There's something else I want to tell you," Kyra said, surprising herself.

"God, *what?*"

"I've been having an affair with Jimmy Elway."

"Is it over?"

"I honestly don't know. He's giving very mixed signals."

"Do you want it to be over?"

"I don't know that, either."

"Are you in love with him?"

"It's possible."

"You'll think I'm cruel, but for your sake I hope you're not. Someone very wise, or perhaps a victim of experience, once said never marry an actor. More accurately, the adage should be never marry a director, especially an *auteur.* Be careful, darling. I'd hate to see you get hurt the way I did."

"What did happen to you and Dad?"

"I adored your father, Kyra. He was the love of my life. I wouldn't have *looked* at another man, and I believed he felt the same way. But when he gave me gonorrhea, I discovered I'd been wrong."

"My God! That's appalling!"

"To say the least. He was abject, but it's impossible to repair a breach of those proportions. He claimed it meant nothing and I believed that. Directors seem singularly unable to resist temptation. We might even have been able to get past it, if he'd had the wits to protect himself. But he never gave it a thought; just had his brief fling, then came home and made me sterile."

Kyra felt as if someone had just driven a fist into her belly. "No," she whispered.

"A sordid ending to something that was wonderful for as long as it lasted. Sometimes, you know," she said softly, sadly, "I dream we're still together and it's as if we never parted. We're together and nothing ugly has touched us." She drew a heavy breath, then said, "You should try to get some sleep now, Kyra. You must be exhausted."

"Thank you for telling me. It answers questions I've had for a long, long time."

"You only had to ask, Kyra."

"We both know I'm not forthcoming at the best of times."

"True, but you're improving."

"Really, I'm so sorry."

"It's ancient history, darling, long-since forgiven."

"You still love him," Kyra said, realizing suddenly it was the truth.

"We'll always love each other, Kyra. But he's never been able to forgive himself, and my ability to trust him died. A marriage can't survive under the weight of two burdens that size. So now—" she sighed "—go along to bed. And forget what I said about baby-sitting Cathy. I'll draft Kyle into duty when he gets back, and have him bring Damien along. Despite her raging homophobia, she's too dense to be anything but flattered by the company of two handsome men."

"I love you so much, Mum. More than I could ever say."

"I know you do. And I love you, Kyra. More than you'd ever believe. Please try very hard not to panic."

A half hour later, Kyra lay in the dark of her bedroom, remembering an outing she and Octavia had had just before her tenth birthday. They'd been in a madly expensive shop on Upper Bond Street, and she'd been watching her mother in conversation with the manageress, when it came to her with a sudden jolt that her mother was someone quite alarmingly unknown to her, with so many private thoughts and feelings that Kyra might never truly know her, no matter how long and hard she tried. She'd seen her mother in so many different ways—projected hugely on a screen at the cinema; elaborately painted and costumed on a stage; without makeup, in her robe, at the breakfast table; on her knees in the garden, her face shadowed by a broad-brimmed hat as she tended her roses; expensively gowned and coifed, exquisitely made up, on her way to some important event—that she was never sure which one was her real mother. But what Kyra recognized that long ago day was that the anguished interior twisting she felt whenever she was with her mother was the effect of the immense love she had for her. And at that moment in the shop on Bond Street, Kyra had wanted to say:

I love you more than anyone or anything. I always will. I love the look of you, the sound of your voice, the way you feel and smell. I love you so much it's hard to breathe sometimes because the caring takes up all the room inside of me. No one could ever mean more to me than you do.

But what, she'd then wondered with alarm, if her mother didn't feel the same way about her? What if this incredibly changeable person had variable sets of emotions to go with the altered styles of dress and makeup in each of her different guises? It was too frightening to contemplate. So it was safer to hold back the loving words and sentiments accumulating year after year inside her, like hard nacreous layers deposited on the inner surface of a mollusk's shell. Someday, when she could be sure she had a firm fix on her mother's identity, Kyra would confess to her how she felt.

Now, thirty-odd years later, Kyra had yet to make that confession. Instead, at moments, she said, I love you, and hoped that the declaration—so overused by so many—conveyed some measure of the true scope and depth of her caring. Because with the passage of time, the love just went on accumulating, the layers growing thicker and deeper.

The technician, a rotund, rosy-cheeked woman, readily agreed to allow Robert to be with Jesse while the X rays were taken.

"Planning to go into medicine, are you, dearie?" she asked him.

"I don't think so. I came to keep Jess company. But I am interested in what's going to be done. We both are, aren't we, Jess?"

Jesse nodded, and it was plain to Kyra that his fear was undiminished. He was still a little boy, and so, despite his size, was Robert—a pair of stalwart children, each trying to be brave for the sake of the other.

"We're going to do an IVU, that's an intravenous urogram. It can take as long as three or four hours, I'm afraid," the smiling woman explained. "Dye will be injected into a vein in Jesse's arm." She lifted one of his arms, as if to illustrate, then kept firm hold of his hand. "You may feel rather flushed as the dye's injected, but you're not to worry. That's perfectly normal and it'll pass. Soon after the injection, we'll take the first set of X rays. Two hours later, we'll take another set. And, finally, after your bladder has emptied, we'll do one last set. The X rays will show us what's going on as the dye moves through the different parts of your urinary system. Understand now, the IVU will show how things are flowing but not how effectively your kidneys are doing their job. It'll show the shape and size of the organs and indicate any obstructions."

The ultrasound, she further explained to her attentive audience, took very little time, was absolutely painless and would produce a picture of what was going on inside the kidney; it would also show whether any cysts or tumors were present. Jesse was growing progressively paler and clung to the woman's hand.

"If the doctor decides it's warranted," she went on, "we'll also do a CAT scan—that's computerized axial tomography. Quite the mouthful, isn't it? But like the ultrasound, it's quick and painless. Pictures of your kidneys will appear on a screen, and they're developed like X rays. Each picture will be examined microscopically for any sign of damage or lesions. A lesion is a wound or an injury. Aside from some minor discomfort, you'll be quite comfortable, Jesse, and your mum will be able to see you between tests. So now, that's the end of my boring little lecture.

"If no one's got any questions—" she smiled at Jesse "—we'll let Mum go along to the waiting room and we three will get down to business. All right?"

"All right," the boys said in unison.

Knowing he'd be mortified if she kissed him, Kyra gave Jesse's arm a gentle squeeze. "I'll be just along the corridor," she told him. "See you soon."

She watched the boys go off after the technician, her eyes filling at the sight of Robert reaching to take hold of Jesse's hand just before the door swung closed, cutting them off from her view.

CHAPTER 23

Dr. Rule kept them waiting for almost twenty minutes, which intensified their nervousness and made Kyra angry. Why did doctors always keep people waiting, with never an explanation or apology? She wished someone would at least explain the delay. Jesse was suffering. His breathing audibly labored, he was staring fixedly at the doctor's desk, his hands gripping the arms of the chair. She moved to stroke his cheek but he shrank from her touch. That hurt, but she understood. Hadn't she as a child so often treated her mother in the same way? She had feigned detachment in order to protect herself from being rejected. In his fear of suffering physical pain, Jesse was retreating inside himself. To respond to her affectionate display would be to set aside his armor, and he couldn't do that. The fears of children could attain such immense proportions that they blocked out almost everything else.

At last the doctor came briskly in, a large folder of X rays in hand. Setting these on the desk, he slid into his chair, saying, "My apologies for keeping you waiting. I wanted to have another look at the test results before we talked."

Kyra's anger somewhat reduced by this explanation, she gave the doctor a thin smile. Jesse didn't move. His eyes merely shifted to fasten on the man.

"I'm sorry to say the tests confirm that Jesse is in end-stage renal failure. What the tests don't show is why, which is not unusual. In at least twenty-five percent of cases we fail to find a cause. In any event, it has little bearing on the treatment." Settling back in his chair, he embarked upon what sounded like a set speech he'd given many, many times before. There was a dry, impersonal aspect to his delivery, and she thought her father would never have been satisfied with such a performance. But this was no time to be thinking tangentially. She had to listen closely to what they were being told. Jesse, she saw, was now staring unblinking at the doctor, his mouth slightly open.

"All the functions of every cell and tissue of one's body are affected in ESRF," the man said in that arid lecturer's voice. "But what is of most concern, because Jesse is still very young, is the possibility of bone disease as a result of reduced levels of active vitamin D, and because, to put it in the simplest terms possible, when the kidneys cannot excrete acid normally, it's mopped up by the bones, which lose calcium in exchange for the acid. At his age, Jesse's bones are still growing but they're getting insufficient calcium, which is why his growth isn't what it should be. He's also at risk of calcification of the tissues around the joints, which can be extremely painful.

"If the ESRF is not addressed, and very soon, there are a number of further symptoms Jesse will encounter—increasing fatigue, anemia, a darkening of his skin pigment, excessive itching caused by uremia, possible nerve damage, digestive problems, fluid retention and so on. I'm painting a very bleak picture, I know, but you must understand how vital the kidneys are to one's health. We simply cannot live without them."

Kyra reached over and took hold of Jesse's hand. It was cold and damp as it clamped hard around hers. She was reassured by the gesture. He hadn't retreated altogether.

"My recommendation is that Jesse begin hemodialysis. An artificial kidney will do what his cannot do efficiently, which is to serve as a filter. Now—" he directed himself to Jesse "—in order to connect your bloodstream to a dialysis machine we have to gain vascular access, and there are three ways we can do that." He opened a drawer in the desk and brought out a small stack of line-drawing illustrations. He held one up. It showed the inside view of a hand and forearm, with arrows indicating two heavily drawn lines meant to be a vein and an artery. The illustration made Kyra's stomach contract and start to rise. She couldn't begin to imagine what effect it had on Jesse.

"I've found these to be helpful," the doctor told them. "This first drawing is of a fistula—a direct connection, under the skin, between an artery and a vein. Under local anesthetic, we sew a vein in the forearm to the artery that runs down toward the base of the thumb. Over a matter of months, the vein grows larger as a result of the increased amount of blood flowing through it. At that point, it's possible to put wide-bore needles through the skin into the fistula vein to carry blood to and from the machine each time dialysis is needed. The biggest problem the majority of patients have with the fistula is a buzzing or vibration in the area where the vein and artery have been joined. Eventually, though, this does subside. It's more a minor inconvenience than a genuinely serious problem."

Jesse's breathing had become heavier, his hand wetter. Kyra wanted to pick him up out of the chair and run away with him. This was the stuff of nightmares.

Placing the first illustration on the bottom of the stack, Dr. Rule held up the next, which was every bit as starkly awful as the first. "The second option is a catheter, which, as you can see, is usually positioned either in the vein beneath the collarbone, or the one on the outer side of the neck. Once in place, the catheter is quite comfortable, and the great advantage of this option is that it can be used immediately after insertion. The drawbacks are that it's a bit difficult to conceal, and it does restrict bathing, swimming, and so forth."

The final drawing struck Kyra as particularly gruesome, showing a side view of a lower leg and foot with what appeared to be a thin tube looping above and below the skin, with the bottom of the loop sitting exposed well above the surface and hanging down almost to the instep. How, she wondered, could these drawings conceivably be helpful to anyone except medical students?

"This is an illustration of a shunt," the doctor explained, "which is placed on the inside of the ankle. It's an artificial connection in two halves which can be separated for dialysis. The end attached to the artery is used to lead blood to the machine. Blood returns from the machine through the tube connected to the vein. The shunt does tend to get in the way of one's shoes. It can also separate accidentally, which might cause problems of clotting or infection. In my opinion, a catheter would be the best choice for Jesse, unless you prefer either of the other means of access." He placed the cards face-down on the desk and leaned back in his chair.

Jesse's breathing was now so loud, his fear so palpable, that Kyra was amazed at the doctor's failure to acknowledge it and to try to reassure him. But he didn't. Oblivious, he sailed right on.

"There are a number of different types of kidney machines but they all have the essential features in common: the lines, through which the blood and dialysate flow; the pump used to obtain a sufficiently high blood flow rate; and the bubble trap, which is a safety device to collect any air that might leak into the circuit. You may find your first sight of a machine rather daunting, but within a few weeks, you'll have learned how to sort out the system. I'll recommend several books for you both to read that go into greater detail on the procedures, and which give definitions for all the terminology."

Jesse was very pale; beads of perspiration had formed on his forehead and upper lip. His grip on Kyra's hand was so fierce that her fingers were starting to go numb. He looked as if he were on the verge of fainting. She had no idea what to do, how to stop what was happening.

"The kidneys," Dr. Rule told them, "produce a hormone called erythropoietin which stimulates the bone marrow to make red blood cells. As your condition worsens, Jesse, the kidneys gradually become scarred, the amount of the hormone secreted falls, and anemia results. To avoid this, you'll have to begin EPO therapy. Three times a week, at the end of dialysis, you'll have an injection of recombinant human erythropoietin which is a manufactured hormone identical to the one produced by healthy kidneys. In a few weeks—" the man now smiled "—you'll find you're less fatigued, your appetite will increase, and you'll feel far better in general. Now, let's talk about your home dialysis." He took a breath preparatory to continuing.

"*No!*" Jesse cried. "*I won't do it! I'd rather die!*" Jumping up, he turned wildly, and ran from the office.

Kyra rose and took several steps, ready to chase after him, then stopped, hearing Jesse go pounding off down the corridor. Best to leave him be for the moment, she decided. Turning, she watched the doctor calmly return the illustrations to his desk drawer. He then sat very still, waiting, hands folded together on the desk, as if he'd seen this scene played out countless times before and found its predictability boring.

"Isn't there some alternative treatment?" she asked from the doorway, aware of an odd fluttering in her neck as if her own veins were shrinking in sympathetic reaction to what she'd seen and heard.

"I hate to be blunt, but without dialysis and/or an eventual transplant, Jesse will die, Mrs. Latimer."

"*Miss* Latimer."

He ignored her correction. "Jesse's kidneys are functioning at slightly more than ten percent. Without dialysis, they will get progressively less and less functional, until they cease to function altogether."

"I can't believe those things you've described are our only options. There *has* to be something else we can do."

"Unfortunately, there is not. Jesse's frightened, understandably. No one is ever pleased at the prospect of dialysis. But once he begins..." Kyra was shaking her head, and, surprised at this interruption of sorts, he stopped speaking.

"He won't do it," she said.

"But of course he will. He must. His life is at stake here. As his parent, you'll have to make him understand."

"He already understands, Dr. Rule. You're the one who doesn't. You don't know Jesse; you couldn't possibly know what he's endured in his short life. He knows, better than you do, what's really at stake here. And he won't do it," she repeated.

The doctor looked scandalized. "If he doesn't agree to treatment, he will die."

"According to you, he'll die, anyway," she said. "I will make every effort to find an alternative course of treatment. But the choice, ultimately, is Jesse's." Approaching the desk, she offered her hand. "I appreciate your efforts."

"Miss Latimer—" he kept a tight grip on her hand, his expression affronted, his tone urgent and commanding "—consider your actions most carefully. Without prompt attention, Jesse will become a very sick boy in a very short time. There are *no* alternatives. And if you fail to provide this child with proper care, I have to warn you I may be obliged to take measures to ensure that you do."

Pulling her hand free, she said coldly, "I do not respond well to threats, or to your most offensive suggestion that I would in any way, *ever,* be negligent as a parent. You seem to think that anyone who dares to disagree with you is a criminal. Rather an arrogant stance, that." She paused a moment, her eyes narrowing as she drew a deep breath. "You're a prick, Dr. Rule; an insensitive, cold-blooded son of a bitch who shouldn't be allowed anywhere near children, because it's blatantly obvious that you don't like them. If you do *anything* to interfere with how my son and I choose to deal with his illness, I will make it my life's work to destroy you! And that, I assure you, is no idle threat." Then, dizzied by anger, she marched out of the office.

Jesse was nowhere to be found in the hospital. At a pay phone she telephoned Susan Forrest.

"No, he's not here," Susan told her. "Robert's been waiting to hear from him."

"Jess is extremely upset and may well be on his way to your house. If he does turn up, would you let me know, please, Susan? I should be home in about half an hour."

"Of course I will. Kyra, how did it go?"

"In a word, badly. The doctor delivered what might as well have been a medical school lecture on dialysis. When he began describing in graphic detail—complete with illustrations, no less— the various shunts and catheters that would get put into Jesse's body, Jess shouted he wasn't having any of it and ran off. I don't blame him. The doctor's an odious bastard."

"What a horror show! I know how squeamish Jess is. Look, luv, if he does come here, I'll let you know instantly. I feel so dreadful about all this, Kyra. If there is anything, *anything* we can do to help, just say the word."

"You're a sweet woman, Susie. Thank you," Kyra said thickly, and hung up.

Before leaving the hospital she tried her mother's number, but Louise said, "Your mum's gone up to the West End, luv, to see 'er agent and then 'er sister."

"If Jesse should come by, would you ask him please to ring me, Louise?"

"Righto, luv. Am I to send him home?"

"No, no. He can stay. I'd just like to talk to him."

Kyra hurried out to the car and started for home, trying not to lose her temper in the crush of traffic that moved only inches at a time. Their charlady, Irene, was heading up the road toward the bus stop on Kensington Church Street as Kyra signaled the turn into Gordon Place. Maybe Jesse would be sitting in the kitchen, with a cup of tea Irene had made for him before she left.

But the house was empty, tidy, freshly dusted, the air redolent of lemon oil and freesias in their prime. The message light on the answerphone was blinking. She pressed the play button. First was a call from her assistant Mary to let her know everything was under control on location; there were no serious problems with the costumes; and how was Jesse, she asked with concern.

Then Catharine, in garbled Bringlish, came on saying, "Kyra dee-ah, such diss-teressing new-ahs about, hum, little Jessay. I was, ahm, sooo looking foe-word to seeing yew, ah, both. But, erm, acourse I under-stoned. Yers, way-ell. I ahm, I spo-uck to Glenna ant the boys yes-tiddy ant they, ah, send their, hum, looove. Oh, ant Dillon said to tell yew, ah, he'll be in touch die-rectally. Now, be, ah, shew-er to...I, ahm, I'm at the Westbury for an-erther five day-uhs. Do puhl-ease ring me, ah, when yew, ah, get a chawnce. I'm, ah, ank-shuss to know if there's any, ah, new-as. So, erm, yes. Way-ell, good-bye foe now, ah, hrmn."

The third caller was Annie, saying, "Hiya. We're between setups, so I thought I'd check in. I hope you and Jesse are okay. Don't let this thing send you mental, Keer. Try to deal with stuff as it comes along. It doesn't turn into a mountain that way but just a bunch of little pebbles, like, that you can kick out of your way. So much for today's phone philosophy. Talk to you later. Big hug. 'Bye."

Next was her father, sounding harried. "Please phone me when you get a moment. I'm anxious to know the test results. And, Kyra, if you need money, or anything, let me know. I'm at the Stratford house." A pause, then her father said gruffly, "Love to you both," and rang off.

Following this came a cheery well-bred voice saying, "Juliet Ashburn here. I believe Jesse told you I'd be in touch, and here I am. I'd like to set up a date to meet and formalize our representing Jesse. We'd like to begin negotiations with Beauchamp-Dobbs, so I thought perhaps lunch early next week, possibly Tuesday if that would be good for you. Do let me know if you're free. Many thanks."

Kyra jotted down the woman's name and number as the final message played.

It was Kyle. "Keer, Damien and I got back from Heathrow an hour or so ago, and Jess was here at the flat waiting for us. He'd like to spend the night, and I said it would be all right with me but that we'd have to get your permission, so call me when you get in. Everything's under control. Please don't worry."

She reset the machine and sat down to have a brief, noisy cry. Then she blew her nose, washed her face and dialed her brother's number.

"The three of us are having a cuppa and a chat," Kyle said in a forced-sounding upbeat tone that told her Jesse was close by. "Hang on a second," he said, and asked Jesse, "Want to talk to Kyra?" She didn't hear a reply, but could picture Jesse shaking his head. Kyle came back on and said, "He says he can't talk now. Any problem with his spending the night?"

"He's still very upset, isn't he?"

"Yes," Kyle said in that same cheerful tone. "Hugely."

"Kyle, it was *awful*."

"So I hear."

"He told you. I was so worried, afraid he'd do something foolish."

"I can imagine."

"After that episode this morning, he needs to be with adult males he can trust. He made the perfect choice. So tell him he can stay as long as he likes. Just let me know when you plan to bring him home. Okay?"

"Absolutely. Monkey's sending you an air kiss."

"Love to all three of you. See you soon."

A cup of tea sounded ideal. She put the kettle on, then went to play her aunt's message again, laughing almost uncontrollably. Finally, she dialed Juliet Ashburn's number.

The woman came on the line, bubbling. "*Hello!* Good to hear from you. We're so excited about Jesse's book. It's brilliant."

"There's a bit of a problem," Kyra began.

"He hasn't changed his mind about our representing him, has he?"

"No, no. It's just that we have some family problems and I'm not sure when we might be able to make a lunch date. Could you possibly go ahead with the negotiations and meet with us at some point later on?"

"Well, I could, of course. But I do need you to sign the agency agreement on Jesse's behalf."

"I'll be glad to do that."

"What say I send it round by bike? Obviously the sooner it's signed, the sooner we can settle the contract with Beauchamp-Dobbs."

"Fine. I'll be in for the rest of the afternoon and evening."

"Okay. I'll get it to you right away. And if you don't mind, I'll have the courier wait so he can bring it back."

"I don't mind in the least."

"Sign all the copies and keep one for your records. And, look. When things settle down, I'd very much like to get together with you and Jess. He's a smashing kid and everyone here is mad for the book."

"We'll definitely make a date. It's just tricky at the moment."

"I quite understand. Lovely to talk to you."

While she drank her tea, Kyra tried to think how she might go about finding some alternative treatment for Jesse. She could begin by going to the nearest medical library to do some research, but that might take weeks and, according to Dr. Rule, time was at a premium.

There was only one person she knew who could set the wheels in motion and get the research done in a hurry. She hadn't spoken to Jimmy since their awkward conversation a few days earlier, but her feelings were no longer of consequence. She found the number of the hotel, and made the call.

He wasn't available, of course. She hadn't expected him to be. She left a message asking that he phone her as soon as possible, stressing to the hotel operator that it was urgent. Then she poured herself another cup of tea, and sat down to wait.

CHAPTER 24

Once the courier had come and gone with the agency agreement, the hours dragged by while she waited for Jimmy to get back to her. She made a quick call to let Susan Forrest know that Jesse was with Kyle. Then she washed and put away the tea things, all the while willing the telephone to ring. But when it did, just after nine, it was her father who, uncharacteristically overwrought, insisted on hearing even the minutest detail of what had gone on at the doctor's office.

Forty minutes later, the phone rang again. This time it was her mother, who also wanted to know precisely what had transpired during the visit to Dr. Rule.

As it got to be ten-thirty and then eleven, Kyra realized that Jimmy wasn't going to call. That possibility hadn't occurred to her. Now she was unnerved. Without help, how would she find an alternative course of treatment for Jesse? Aside from the library, she had no idea where to begin. Arms wrapped tightly around herself, she walked through the dark rooms of the house, resolute at one moment, incensed the next.

Why didn't he ring? By admitting in their last conversation that she was scared, she'd probably come across as too needy. But so what? Was she supposed to pretend to be unconcerned about what was happening to Jesse? Was she meant to put on some sort of performance in order to keep the man interested? She was incapable of that.

But how bad-mannered of him not to return her call! For all he knew, the message she'd left had to do with the film's costumes. There was no reason for him not to ring back, none. How dare he ignore her? The blood humming in her ears, escalating anger kept her marching back and forth the length of the hall.

Then, as if coming down from a sugar high, her energy was suddenly gone. She stopped to turn on the kitchen light and stood with her hand on the switch, feeling weariness seeping through her body like a fast-acting drug. She leaned in the doorway, catching a pleasant whiff of the Vim the charlady had used on the sink and countertops. Kyra blinked at the clean surfaces, then at the clock. Eleven twenty-eight. Everything inside her was slowing down, growing sluggish. She was starting to fall asleep right there in the doorway, her eyes losing their focus, eyelids drooping.

The ringing of the telephone startled her, so that she was shaky and uncoordinated as she reached to lift the receiver, mentally apologizing to Jimmy for all her harsh thoughts about him. He hadn't let her down, after all.

"Hiya. It's Annie. Is this too rude a time to be ringing?"

"No, no. It's all right. I've been waiting for a call, but it doesn't look as if it's going to happen."

"Oh, *please.* Tell me Elway's not hanging you up."

"What makes you say that?"

"You kidding me, Kyra?" Annie gave a short, sharp laugh. "Men, they run for the hills when you're not well or you need something. He's no different, puts his trousers on one leg at a time. Right?"

"Right," Kyra said, battling off the depression that accompanied this admission.

"Is there something you wanted his help with?" Annie asked incisively.

"Actually, there is."

"What exactly?"

Unable to think of any reason why she shouldn't, Kyra recited for a third time that evening the relevant details of Jesse's test results, winding down with, "I've got to find some other method of treatment, which means research."

"And you wanted Mr. Big to put those little drones in the London office to work on it for you. Right?"

"Right again."

"Listen, Keer, before you start catastrophizing, let me get in touch with a few mates."

"Catastrophizing?" She had to laugh.

"What would *you* call what you're doing?" Annie asked reasonably. "You're in a state cuz you're scared. You need help cuz you can't do it alone. Elway hasn't returned your call, so you're ready to fall off the edge. Do me a favor and don't fall just yet. I've got friends who do this sort of thing. I'll find someone who'll help."

"*Could* you?"

"I'm not just a pretty face attached to a pair o' tits, you know. I got connections. You want it, I can get it. Trust me."

"You're wonderful, Annie."

"Yeh, everybody says so." Annie chortled, *heh-heh-heh,* cartoonlike, making Kyra smile.

"I'd be so grateful. And, of course, I'll pay. The thing is, Annie, time's against us."

"You're coming through loud and clear. I'll get on the blower straight away, soon's we're done. Leave it to me. And a word of advice? You sound completely knackered. Get some sleep, and put this out of your mind for tonight. I'm on it; it'll get done. Okay?"

"Annie, you're an angel."

"Yeh!" Annie chortled again. "I am. Now stop fussing and go to bed! You'll be hearing from me soon."

Kyra turned off the lights and started upstairs, enumerating as she went the possible reasons why Jimmy hadn't returned her call. Annie was right: He was a goddamned coward. And Kyra would never forgive him for letting her down this way.

Kyle telephoned the next afternoon to say that Jesse wasn't quite ready yet to come home. "He'd like to spend the weekend with us, if that's all right with you."

"It's fine with me. How is he, Kyle?"

"Considerably calmer."

"Good. That's good."

"Actually, Damien thinks Jess and I should go back with him to Stratford. Dad's very anxious to see him, and a change of scene might help."

"Maybe it would. He'll need fresh clothes. I'll pack him a bag and you can come collect it on your way."

"Is this really okay with you, Keer? You're being awfully good about it."

"Kyle, I can scarcely force him to be here if he doesn't want to be."

"Don't get angry," he said. "I only want to be sure I'm not, with the best of intentions, usurping any of your rights."

She sighed and said, "Kyle, I would never think that of you. I know what Jess means to you, how much you love him. Just stop by on your way, and collect his bag, please."

When the bell rang an hour or so later, Kyra went to the door expecting to see her brother only to find Jesse waiting there.

"Hello, love. Why didn't you use your key?"

"I don't know. I just rang the bell without thinking." He gave her a bewildered little smile, then straightened his shoulders, took a deep breath, and said, "I wanted to say I'm sorry. I shouldn't have run off that way. And I should've telephoned you myself, instead of letting Uncle Kyle do it."

"I understand, Jess." She dropped down so that they were eye to eye, and took hold of his hands. "You wanted to be somewhere else for a while, to sort out your feelings. Had it been me, I'd probably have done the same thing. People need time apart. It doesn't mean they've stopped caring about each other."

"I was very scared."

"I know, love. So was I."

"But I meant what I said, Keer. I *would* rather die than have them put tubes in my neck or my foot, and hook me up to a machine to drain out all my blood." He shuddered and closed his eyes for a moment.

Enclosing him in her arms, she said, "Hush. You're not going to be hooked up to any machine and you're not going to die."

"Dr. Rule said I would, if I didn't agree to the dialysis."

"Dr. Rule's a pompous ass. Just because he only has two methods of treating a problem doesn't mean there aren't others. And we're going to find one that works for you."

"But what if we don't?" he asked soberly. "If I refuse treatment, will you respect my wishes?"

Ice water all at once rushing through her veins, she held him away so that she could see his eyes. "That's a tough question for me to answer, Jess."

"I know it is. But I need your answer. If I refuse, will you accept my decision?"

Seeing something resolute in his eyes, and knowing she couldn't suddenly begin making decisions for him when, all along, she'd encouraged him to make his own, she swallowed hard, then said, "Yes, Jess, I will. It's your life, not mine. I haven't the right to force you to do something you don't want to do." God! she thought. She had no legitimate reason, beyond the purely selfish one of desperately wanting him to stay alive, to fight him on it. All these years later, how could she renege on everything she'd ever told him and insist that this decision was one he wasn't qualified to make? She'd been laying the groundwork for this moment since the first day he'd come to her. She couldn't change the rules now because his feelings on the matter weren't the same as hers. But did a child have the right to make his own choice? Yes, she admitted. He did. Being an adult didn't equip you any more effectively to make a painful decision. She was obligated to acknowledge the depth of thought he'd put into this, and to accept his conclusions. "I will," she repeated.

He exhaled slowly, and said, "Good. I had to know how you'd feel."

"Just as *I* need to know how *you* feel—about all kinds of things. But let's go one step at a time, Jess. Let's not anticipate, please. What you're asking of me... It's painful and difficult because I love you so much."

"I know you do. But we've got to consider the possibilities, the eventualities. We've got to be *prepared*."

"We will be. And we'll deal with everything—in due course. We don't have to make any final decisions right this moment. I want you to go off and enjoy your weekend, read and relax, visit your grandfather, have some fun. Will you try to do that?"

He nodded, chewing on his lower lip. "I was awake most of the night, thinking about my options, and I know what my choice would be, Kyra," he said momentously, his gaze solid with intent.

"I understand," she said softly, stricken by the prospect of losing him, but powerless to change what had been set in effect a long, long time before.

"I think it's important for both of us to know what I'd want to do if worse comes to worst. And my mind is made up."

"Does that help?" she asked, astonished by what was being discussed, and feeling immense sorrow, like a well-remembered old school friend, sitting on the periphery of her emotions waiting to walk in and reestablish their acquaintanceship. She'd lost Gary; she could well lose Jess, too. How would she bear it?

"Actually, it does. I feel better, not so scared."

"Well, if you feel better, then I do, too," she lied, not really able to wrap her mind around the fact that this twelve-year-old was saying he'd choose to die rather than tolerate medical intervention.

Could he truly make a decision of this scope? she asked herself,
and at once had her answer. He not only could, he already had. He
never had been an even remotely ordinary child. "But I plan to do
anything I can to find some sort of therapy to keep you well. We're
not just going to sit back and resign ourselves to this. Now give me
a hug and off you go." God! She sounded exactly like her mother.

He hugged her tightly, and she breathed in his tangy young
boy's smell, profoundly aware that from this point on their every
exchange would be indelibly imprinted in her memory. Separating, she gave him his bag and walked with him to the car where
Kyle and Damien had diplomatically opted to wait.

As Jesse stowed his bag in the boot then climbed into the rear
of the Jaguar and belted himself in, Damien extended his hand to
Kyra through the open window, and she took hold of it, bending
to smile in at him.

Of medium height, brown-haired and blue-eyed, with the flat-
tened nose of a prizefighter, a lovely, dimpled smile, and a mellow
public school voice that was a startling contrast to his battered yet
attractive exterior, he said, "We'll take good care of him, Kyra."

"You always do. You're the best, Damien." She held his hand to
her cheek, then kissed the back of it before letting go.

"No, you are," he argued—his stock response in this now cus-
tomary exchange.

"And you," she accused her brother. "How is it you keep looking younger and younger?"

"Maybe I'm secretly addicted to cosmetic surgery, like dippy
Aunt Cath." He grinned at her, showing his teeth. "We stopped by
the Westbury to say hello on our way here. She's a truly terrifying
specimen these days. Her skin is stretched so thin it doesn't even
look like skin anymore."

Grimacing, Damien said, "It's like latex spread over a rural
road map."

"It looks," Jesse put in, "as if you could puncture it with a pin
and her head would deflate like a balloon."

They all laughed.

Kyra shook her head, saying, "She was so beautiful, once
upon a time."

"You'd never know it to see her now," Kyle said. "And she's less
comprehensible than ever."

"I, ah, erm, do soooo adowah Fortanums truff-ewels," Jesse declared in a flawless Catharine impression.

They all laughed again, then Kyra said, "Make sure your uncle behaves himself."

"Oh, I will," Jesse said, confident and back in control. They'd made a pact and he knew she would honor it, no matter what.

"We'll phone later, let you know we've arrived safely," Damien promised.

"Thank you." She ducked in through the window to kiss each man in turn. "Have a good time, the three of you," she said, stepping away.

"Take good care, my dearest," Damien said, and blew her a kiss.

"'Bye, Keer," Jesse called out the window as the car moved off down the road.

She waved until the dark green Jaguar turned the corner. Then she went back into the house, finding it too empty, too quiet. Furious with Jimmy, feeling lonely and scared, she went for her handbag. After making sure she had her reader's tickets, she set off to do some research at the British Library. If she had no luck there, next would come a trip to the old London Library in St. James's Square. If that failed, she'd start accessing medical libraries. Whatever it took.

Early Saturday morning, after a restless night spent imagining encounters with Elway where she told him, in numerous ways, what a total shit he was, how horribly he'd let her down, what a flawed and limited man he was, she was just about to make a pot of coffee when the doorbell rang. Wondering if it could possibly be Jimmy, she went to door, prepared to have her faith in the man restored. But there stood Annie, pink hair like cake frosting, saying, "Hiya. Thought I'd come cheer you up."

She was wearing a remarkably lurid oversize Hawaiian shirt, a pair of pale blue leggings, white sandals, and the inevitable camera suspended from her neck.

Kyra hugged the tiny woman, saying, "What a lovely surprise! Come in, come in. That's quite the shirt."

"Terrible, init? Mucky purples and blues, lizard green. It's so rotten, I absolutely love it."

"Come have some breakfast. Unless you're not hungry."

"I'm starving, actually. I got a lift down with one of the techies, so I've been up most of the night."

"Coffee?"

"Yes, please. Oh, what a smashing room!" Annie stood admiring the big sunny kitchen with its hunter-green walls and white trim. The room's centerpiece was a round blue table with four chairs, each painted in different primary colors that matched the dishes displayed on open shelves.

"If you like, I'll give you a tour of the house after breakfast."

"Yeh, I'd love it."

Kyra gave Annie coffee in a bright yellow Fiesta ware cup and saucer, set an orange sugar bowl and matching cream jug on the table, then went back to the stove. Annie stirred some of both into her cup, took a sip and sat back to watch Kyra, saying, "This place is just like you."

"Oh?"

"Yeh. It's warm and generous, lovely."

"You're overestimating my attributes."

"You should just say thank you, 'stead of putting yourself down all the time."

"I'll try to remember."

"Go on," Annie said. "Take the mickey. See if I care." She drank her coffee, contentedly looking on as Kyra broke eggs into a green mixing bowl, added milk, and then beat the mixture with a wire whisk. Her hair was loose and fell halfway down her back in a luxurious, fiery spill. Without thinking, Annie lifted the camera, adjusted the settings, and took several quick shots.

"Everything going well on the shoot?" Kyra asked without turning, for a moment recalling her dead-of-the-night imagined rants at Elway. The anger was close to the surface and, from moment to moment, all she could think of was shrilling at him on the telephone, letting her anger and hurt pour over him like a lava flow.

"Yeh. It's bang on schedule cuz the weather's been so good. Where's Jesse?" Annie looked down the hallway, as if expecting to see him.

"Kyle's taken him off for the weekend in Stratford."

"Nice. So how's the family taking the news?"

"Better than I thought they would, although, naturally, they're upset." She glanced over. "All right there, are you?"

"Great. Fantastic coffee."

"I buy the beans at the Algerian Coffee Store in Soho. I like strong coffee." She gave a low laugh. "That sounded like a bad TV advert."

"Nah. It's where I get mine, as well. Weak coffee's disgusting." Annie found it interesting that, given her exceptional creativeness in costume design, Kyra's own clothes were so plain and shapeless. Intended, of course, to conceal, instead they made her look even bigger than she was. But who was she to comment on something like that? Annie reminded herself.

For once in a rare while, the meal came together like clockwork with the toast done just as Kyra slipped the second omelet from the pan onto a heated plate already garnished with slices of a sunwarmed tomato that had spent two days ripening on the window ledge.

"This is t'rific," Annie said as Kyra brought the plates to the table.

"You got lucky, my girl. About the only thing I can cook is an omelet. And usually by the time I've made one, everything else is stone cold."

For a moment Annie was mesmerized—by the vivid colors, by the warmth of the kitchen and the smell of the food, and by the sight of Kyra's flawless features. Then, unable to help herself, she fired off two more shots.

"If you were anyone else, Annie Cooper, you'd be a bloodied pulp on the floor by now," Kyra said. "But I'm fond of you, so I'll let you live—*if* you'll *please* stop doing that."

"Sorry. Consider it stopped." With a sheepish grin, Annie put the camera down on one of the empty chairs.

"That's a good girl. Now eat your food before it gets cold."

"My friend Ian faxed me a couple of items he thinks might be up the right alley." Annie handed Kyra an envelope. "I read them and I agree that it's probably what you're after. Ian said to tell you if it is, he'll narrow the focus and get more specific. And, of course, he'll pass on to you whatever he finds. Got a fax machine?"

"No. Should I get one?"

"Nah. I'll tell him to send the stuff by bike."

"Is Ian a researcher?" Kyra asked, opening the envelope.

"Yes and no. He's a production assistant at the BBC, so he's got access to everything. Thing is, what he likes best is the challenge of a search."

"Lucky for me." Kyra quickly scanned the first article, written by an Italian doctor and published in something called *Kidney International*. She looked up, saying, "Would you have believed there were magazines devoted solely to individual organs?"

"Never," Annie answered. "Imagine subscribing to *Liver Local*, or *Regional Gallbladder*, or rushing up to the newsagent's to get the latest copy of *The Northern Spleen*."

With a laugh, Kyra continued reading. The final paragraph had been underlined. "We conclude that a moderate dietary restriction of protein and phosphorus is an acceptable and effective regimen for delaying progression of functional deterioration in early renal failure."

The second article, by a Swedish doctor, was also from *Kidney International*. The underlined text in this piece read "...available clinical data strongly suggest that progression of end-stage renal failure in man may be retarded or halted by a low-protein diet supplemented with essential amino acids or keto acids."

Excited, Kyra said, "Nutritional therapy. That makes such good sense. I *knew* there had to be an alternative! I'll track down one of these doctors and take Jesse to see him."

"Why not hold off until we get more information? Then let's try to find someone closer to home."

We. Her impulsive, lovable new friend had come through for her, while a man she'd slept with wouldn't even return her phone call. "Annie, it's wonderful of you to arrange this. I can't tell you how much I appreciate it."

"Quit that. If it helps Jesse, I'm glad. That's what matters. Hey, you promised to show me the rest of the house. Or have you changed your mind?"

"I haven't, but be warned. It's a bit of a mess."

"Yeh, I'll bet. I could see straight off what a filthy pig you are." Annie gave her cartoon laugh, *heh-heh-heh,* and again Kyra had to laugh with her. The girl's good humor was contagious.

"This is Jesse's, right?" Annie guessed, peering in at the biggest of the four bedrooms which was decorated in the same primary colors as the kitchen. "He's quite something, isn't he?" she said, taking in the books and games, the computer, the elaborate sound system, the many cassettes and CDs, and the marvelous Edward Steichen poster portrait of Fred Astaire in white tie and tails.

"Jess has written a book that's going to be published," Kyra said quietly, watching Annie reach up with a smile to touch one of Drick's ears.

"Yeh? Fantastic! The renaissance boy. I can't wait to meet him."

"He'll like you," Kyra said. Given how Jesse's interest was always sparked by quirky types, he'd probably go mad for Annie.

"I already like *him*," she said, reluctantly quitting her survey of the CDs to follow Kyra to her bedroom.

Done in Wedgwood blue and white, it was smaller than Jesse's and held little in the way of furniture. It was in fair disarray, with the duvet half off the bed, the dresser drawers standing open, and abandoned clothing draped over an old white-painted wicker armchair.

"It's a mess," Kyra said. "I told you."

"Nah. This is nothing. My friend Joan now, *she's* a real pig. Take-away wrappers strewn about, heaps of dirty knickers, floor so filthy you stick to it, cupboards crammed with stuff just tossed in any whichway. You, you're a goddess of domestic virtues, by comparison."

"A goddess, indeed," Kyra scoffed, leading the way back down to the large, uncluttered living room with its terra-cotta walls and white-painted trim. A fine Oriental carpet sat atop the bleached floorboards, and one entire wall was taken up with books. Either side of an exquisite antique white marble fireplace, two off-white sofas faced each other, heaped with pillows in a variety of fabrics and colors.

"Oh, fab!" Annie declared, taking a quick look at some of the book titles before going after Kyra through the dining room to her studio—an area so busy, and with so much to see that Annie didn't know what to look at first.

Kyra leaned in the doorway, watching as the dainty little female made her way around the room, pausing to pick up and examine whatever caught her eye. "Our char Irene won't touch this room," Kyra said. "She says it'd be too much like work, that it'd take the rest of her life to put it into any sort of order."

"Nah," Annie disagreed, touching a camel-hair brush to her cheek before returning it to the jar on the table. "Things are grouped by function. Fastenings of every sort over here, threads and fabric samples over here. Totally organized. You've just got to be able to recognize it."

"What must your place be like, if you can find order here?" Kyra wondered.

"Come see it," Annie invited, picking up a bundle of fabric swatches and studying it for a few seconds before returning it to its basket. "We could walk into the West End, stop at my place in Soho, have a meal. Or are you booked up today?"

"I have no plans."

"Come on, then, Keer. Take a break and hang out with me. You'll come see my place, then later we'll go to the karaoke bar. Eat chicken teriyaki, drink hot sake, get well pissed, then stand up and sing our hearts out. It'll be fun."

Kyra thought about it. She'd urged Jesse to go off and have fun. Shouldn't she follow her own advice? "Yes, okay," she said. "To be honest, I'd love to get out of here for a while. But no karaoke. I'm the one in the family who sings like a moaning dromedary."

"Yeh, right."

"I jest not. People have been known to offer me large sums of money not to sing."

"Go on!" Annie chortled away merrily.

"Would you mind waiting while I take a quick shower?"

"Tell you what. You go ahead and I'll get on the blower to Ian, get him going on more of the same."

After making her call, Annie went to have a better look at the photographs in the living room. One was of Kyle with his former wife, the gaunt fashion model who still turned up on covers all over the place and who Annie found dead boring with her huge pouty lips and vacuous expression. Next to it was a really old studio shot of Octavia and Richard, looking unposed and natural, each happily holding an infant twin. Beside this was a candid color eight-by-ten enlargement of a boy who had to be Jesse, at age five or six, rigged out in pirate gear, complete with tricorn hat bearing the skull-and-crossbones insignia. One hand on his hip, the other brandishing a sword, he was a cheeky cherub with a happy expression and wary, depthless eyes. Annie loved him on sight. Here was a kid with all kinds of history, and character to spare. He was also as singularly beautiful in his own right as Kyra was in hers. Annie couldn't wait to meet him.

Finally there was a black-and-white studio shot of Kyra and a handsome older bloke in some kind of uniform. Annie spent a good five minutes studying this picture and the happy faces of the pair before at last turning to admire the impressionistic watercolor of spring flowers in a clear glass jug.

"Is Jesse adopted?" Annie asked when Kyra appeared in the living room doorway.

"He is, as it happens."

"Yeh, I thought so. He doesn't look anything like you or... Is that your former husband in the photo?"

"Late husband," Kyra corrected her.

"Ah, what a pity. He looks like a t'rific guy, lovely smile, gentle eyes."

"He was."

"So Jesse's adopted. A right cheeky beggar, eh?" Annie said, taking another look at the pirate photo, at those deep, haunted eyes.

"He's that, all right."

"A beautiful kid, *beautiful*. Face like a naughty angel. And that's a brilliant watercolor," Annie said, smartly easing into less fraught territory.

"You think so? Thank you."

"Yours?"

Kyra nodded. "Several hundred years ago, when I was still at art school."

"I can't imagine being able to do something like that."

"I can't imagine doing what you do."

"Sure you could. What I do isn't art, not like painting."

"Of course it is," Kyra argued.

"Nah. Photography's a combo of luck, experience and darkroom manipulation. Can't compare that to, say, a geezer like Verdi. I mean, fancy walking about with your head full of music."

"You like opera, do you, Annie?"

"Some. I hate those breasty sopranos, come out 'n' sing with a throatful of phlegmies." She threw out her arms and burst into gargly warbling that, yet again, set Kyra to laughing. "Or the big-bellied, thick-thighed bearded blokes with the gluggy bass voices." An imaginary belly thrust forward, arms extended, she emitted a

throaty stream of hilarious mock Italian lyrics. "But," she went on
with a sense of timing as good as any Latimer's, "some of them
tenors and a few of those sopranos, they send me mental, they're
so great. 'Specially when they do Joe Green stuff like *Traviata,*
which is my all-time favorite. Or *Bohéme,* my second fave. Same
story, different language. Make me cry every time I hear 'em."

"You and Jess are going to hit it off," Kyra said. "He likes Joe
Green, too."

"Yeh, I noticed. So. Ready for your big day out?"

"I got fostered when I was three, and lived with Gran from the time
I was four. She wasn't my real gran, of course. She was a foster
mum who took in a ton of kids over the years. I was the last of the
lot. Neither of us had family, and she wanted someone to leave behind, to remember her, like, so she adopted me when I was six. We
got on great, me 'n' her."

"She sounds very special."

"She was. Nine years she's been gone, and I still miss her."

"It must've been difficult, being left on your own at sixteen."

"Nah, not really. Gran raised me to look out for meself. Sure, it
gets lonely sometimes, but I've got good mates. And Gran left me
the property in Old Compton Street. So it's not the end of the
world if I don't sell any photos for a week or two, or I don't get an
assignment. See, the ground floor used to be her caff; served up
breakfast and lunch there for near forty years. Everybody in Soho
knew her. Most of the old-timers are gone now, but I still know a
lot of the people. The caff and the first floor flat are let on long
leases, and the top two floors are mine. I've even got a little roof
garden. And, know what? It's probably safer in the middle of Soho
than anyplace else in London, cuz there's traffic day and night. I
love it. Fancy a sit-down?" Annie pointed out a vacant bench.

"Sure," Kyra said.

As she sat down, Annie noticed a couple lying locked in an active embrace on the grass directly opposite, some twenty feet away,
and said, "Now that's right enterprising."

"It certainly is. There was a time," Kyra said, "when I was mortified by public displays, of any sort. Now I simply find them interesting. And I actually tore a strip off Jesse's doctor this
week—something I wouldn't have *dreamed* of doing even a few

months ago. Strange, isn't it, how our attitudes change?" She looked up into the canopy of sunlit greenery, caught by the way the light seemed to skitter in and out, as if engaged in play with the fluttering leaves. The effect was hypnotic, making it hard to look away. As she studied the light play it occurred to her that after this weekend her life would be irreversibly altered—just as it had been when Gary died and Jesse was left in her care. This day out was a small island in the sea of time, a port of call this dear, eccentric young woman was providing for her. "Thank you for this, Annie," she said. "I really did need to get out of the house." Then, without warning, the anger with Jimmy and her fear for Jesse combined, flooding her senses. She wanted to weep, to rage, to do something drastic.

"If you don't talk about what's eating you," Annie said, "it'll only get worse. You'll probably go berserk with a machete and next thing anybody knows there'll be dead directors lying about everywhere."

Once again she succeeded in taking Kyra out of herself. Turning to look into Annie's very clear, very blue eyes, she smiled and said, "You're good for me."

"Yeh. And you're good for me, too. Bet that surprises you, eh? Tell me what's bothering you. Okay? Let's talk about true things for a while."

CHAPTER 25

Her eyes on the couple across the way, Kyra said, "I made myself fat at a young age so the girls at school would leave me alone."

"Did it work?"

She glanced over at Annie, whose eyes were also on the recumbent pair. "People don't get jealous of fatties. And they think we're impervious; we can absorb any amount of ridicule. Still, ridicule's preferable to jealousy, less savage in some ways." As she watched, the male of the pair across the way reached out to grab a nearby blanket and drag it over them. She lost her train of thought at seeing that beneath the blanket the couple had begun removing certain strategic items of clothing. A little shocked, she said, "My God, Annie! They're going to have it off right there in front of everybody."

"Maybe they're French."

Kyra laughed. "We probably shouldn't be watching."

"Why not? One of life's short features. Two reels of human interest. If they're going to do it in public, the public's got a right to watch."

"I suppose. They've got grit, I'll say that for them." The heat from the sun was penetrating Kyra's skull, spreading slowly downward. "Where was I?" she asked.

"Making yourself fat," Annie supplied. "And schoolgirl bitchettes."

"Bitchettes. I like that. Well, the other result of turning myself obese—" Kyra picked up the thread "—was a self-hatred that operated on a seemingly mathematical ratio. The fatter I got, the more I despised myself. The usually intentional but occasionally inadvertent cruelty of others was nothing compared to my self-loathing. And the kindness I sometimes encountered was impossible to bear, especially my mother's."

"How dare she see past your defenses and still love you when you were so unworthy? Right?"

"Bang on," Kyra said, beginning not to be surprised by Annie's insight. She consistently cut directly to the heart of an issue, bypassing the need for lengthy explanations.

"So now," Annie said, "we cut to a flash forward involving a few drinks and some crap chat, followed by bed in a room with the lights off."

"Am I such a cliché?" Kyra worried aloud.

"Nah. It's just that I've been there—plenty of times. You do a lot of that flash-forward stuff?"

"Before Gary, I did," Kyra admitted. "Since he died I've done it just enough to stay sane. Except for Jimmy; he constitutes a major deviation from routine. What about you?"

"Probably the same. Why are we so hard on ourselves?" Annie wondered. "You'd think the older we get, the kinder we'd be to our poor battered egos. But no. And have you noticed it's only us who do it? Men take whatever comes along as their due, never give it a thought."

Watching the rhythmic rise and fall of the blanket, Kyra said, "It doesn't matter what we've managed to accomplish. In the end, we're still tyrannized by our personal *bêtes noires*. They appear to be reaching a climax over there."

"Yeh. Glad it's not me. He's a bloody bunny."

A hoot of laughter escaped Kyra. "Maybe they've been saving up."

"All the more reason to make it last."

Beneath the blanket there was a final rush of movement, then stillness. "That didn't take long," Kyra said.

"Kids," Annie said disdainfully. "They've no idea. 'Course, neither do most grown men."

"That is true," Kyra agreed, continuing to watch the couple beneath the blanket, who were now obviously rearranging their clothing. "The majority think foreplay consists of removing their shoes."

Now Annie guffawed, clapping her hands. "Good one! You *are* wicked!"

"Only mildly. You know, I've been thinking over what you said about saying true things, and it occurs to me that it actually requires far less effort to tell the truth than it does to find inconsequential things to say."

"Wears you right out, trying to avoid the tricky subjects. You're

ready for a good long kip after one of those convos where nothing gets said but how hard you're working and isn't the weather
good or bad."

"Well, here's a piece of truth for what it's worth. I got involved
with Jimmy even though I knew it was a mistake. He behaved as
if the affair meant something to him; he said he didn't care if people talked about us. And I wanted to believe him. Maybe because
it's been a long time since Gary died and I wanted to see if I could
care again. But Jimmy's recitation of the things he liked about me,
his supposed concern, his claim to be missing me, it was nothing
but rubbish. Last night all I could think of was confronting him.
But that'll never happen. So the net result is I'm angrier with myself than I am with him. And that's so bloody *typical.* I can't even
keep my anger pointed in the right direction."

"Self-loathing," Annie said, and sighed. "Some of us're really
gifted at it."

"Not you, surely."

"You kidding, Kyra? I'm the champion of the world. I could
win prizes."

"But you're so..."

"What? Funny?"

"I was going to say sane."

"Yeh, I'm that. But there are times when I've got nothing but
contempt for Annie Cooper. I think all women fall into it at one
time or another. Still, you shouldn't hate yourself cuz you bonked
a guy and he let you down. It's rotten, but it's no surprise, is it?
Show a man an unguarded emotion and it scares the piss out of him.
Except for gays. They'll hold your hand and have a good cry with
you. But it's your girlfriends who'll come through for you in the
crunch. According to that famous Annie Cooper book, The Rules
Of Engagement, rule number one is: Never count on a guy you're
bonking to help out in a pinch."

"I'll have to buy that book. Why were you put into foster care?"

In answer, Annie lifted her ugly shirt to reveal a shiny, puckered
patchwork of scar tissue that covered her entire midriff.

Kyra gaped, able to think only of the pain that had to have accompanied such a massive injury.

Annie went on matter-of-factly, letting the shirt fall. "It goes
right down to my knees."

"Oh, Annie. I'm so *sorry.*"

Meeting Kyra's eyes, she gave a strangled laugh, and said, "If you go on that way, we'll both end up with the weeps. So do me a favor and don't, okay?"

"Okay," Kyra said, the image of that expanse of ruined flesh branded into her brain.

"One thing's for sure, you'll never catch me in a bikini."

"Well, that makes two of us who won't be surrounded by drooling *paparazzi* at the Cannes Film Festival," Kyra said dryly.

Annie gazed at her for a few seconds, then the two of them went into such peals of laughter that the couple across the way—now in the process of collecting their bits and pieces prior to leaving—looked over with disapproving expressions.

"WHAT?" Annie shouted at them. "IT'S OKAY TO BONK LIKE BUNNIES IN THE MIDDLE OF GREEN PARK IN BROAD DAYLIGHT BUT IT'S NOT OKAY TO LAUGH OUT LOUD? PISS RIGHT OFF, YOU PATHETIC TWITS, OR I'LL HAVE THE PEELERS ON YOU FOR PUBLIC BLOODY LEWDNESS!"

Disconcerted and, without a word, the hapless couple scurried off, the blanket trailing along the ground behind them as they went.

"Fools," Annie muttered, grinning.

"Oh, well done, Annie!" Kyra congratulated her. "You're wonderful."

"Yeh, well, I didn't give a toss about them having it off. But to give us filthy looks cuz we find something funny, that's not on."

"Absolutely not."

"One more thing we agree on."

"You got burned?" Kyra asked, automatically taking hold of Annie's hand.

"Yeh. I was two and a bit, sitting in my high chair, waiting to be fed when my mum chucked a potful of boiling water on me. A complete nutter, my mum. They put her away after that and a few months later she topped herself with a torn-up bedsheet. Nineteen years old, she was." Annie gave Kyra a sad, crooked smile.

"God! What about your father?"

"Identity unknown. The miracle is the poor crazy cow didn't kill me, cuz she was definitely trying. F'rinstance, my shoulder was dislocated and my arm got broken when I was four months old cuz I squirmed so much I went right off the table while she was changing my nappy. At eleven months I managed to fracture my own left leg and crack four ribs by trying to climb out of my cot. At fifteen months they had to put twenty stitches in my scalp and treat me for concussion cuz I was, by now, a famous wild child who threw herself down the stairs. 'Cept there wasn't no stairs. We lived in a ground floor council flat. It's a wonder anybody believed her stories, but they did. In between times, according to what Gran said the socials told her, there was other minor stuff, like a compressed larynx and bruises on the neck, a shattered eardrum and some broken baby teeth that had to be pulled. On and on, medical records for days."

Freeing her hand, she shifted to face Kyra, leaning an elbow on the back of the bench. "After five and a half months in hospital, I was taken to live with Gran. The good part is, I don't remember much of it. The bad part is, I'll never forget going back into surgery over and over, how scared I got each time she'd tell me I was gonna have to go again. I'd hide in the cupboard and wet myself, knowing how much it was going to hurt.

"It took a long, *long* time, but she taught me not to be scared of anything—'specially when I kept having to go back for more ops. Cuz the more I grew, see, the tighter the skin got, so the more grafts they had to do—right up 'til I was fifteen—so I could move about like a normal kid. Twelve ops in all. The two other important things Gran taught me were to speak my mind, and that it was okay to find things funny. And she was dead right about both. You gotta say what you think or you lie in bed at night and eat yourself up cuz you didn't. And you have to laugh, or the weight of the bullshit and lunacy will drive you neck-deep into the dirt. *You* gotta laugh, Kyra. Seriously, what do a few wasted bonks matter? Did you *really* think it was love? Be honest."

"No, I guess I didn't," Kyra answered. "Put in that light, I guess I've been angry over nothing but hurt pride. Jesse was a battered child, too."

"I reckoned he was. That pirate photo of him, he's got the eyes. There's photos of me as a kid, have that same look. And I volunteer at the shelter when I can, go spend time with the kids who haven't been placed yet. They've all got it. I heard or read somewhere once about the 'thousand-yard stare' that soldiers get after combat. That's what these kids have. It's this combo of rage and resignation, fear and hurt, hope and need all mixed together."

"It's hard to accept that people treat children that way."

"Yeh. But they do, Kyra. A lot. See, it's one of the hidden things. Like headaches, to give you a tame example. Nobody talks about them. Then, one day you mention you've got one and suddenly everybody's talking about their headaches. Or PMS, or depression. Granny-bashers, abusers of all stripes, people who hurt people— for whatever reason—they don't advertise. And neither do the ones getting hurt. Follow? There are these *things,* these *secrets* people're keeping; like partners almost."

"That's how you see it?"

"That's how it *is*. People hoarding their secrets like private bank accounts; things get added, things get taken away. I'm your mom and I bash you, what're you gonna do about it? It's got to be your fault, cuz she wouldn't've done it otherwise. So Mom takes something out of your account and adds it to hers. Son's fed up with old ma's whingeing all the time, so he gives her a kick. What's she gonna do about it? Tell the socials and next thing she knows she's drugged stupid and tied to a wheelchair in some nasty overcrowded shelter. So Son's made a withdrawal, and Ma's gotta let it happen. It's all about secrets and private issues. Like, for another example, how you look. It's the big issue of your life. Right? Everything you've done since—what was it, nine or ten?—has been because of that. That's been your secret bank account, withdrawals only. Right?"

"I suppose so."

"Sure it has," Annie insisted. "Somebody comes at you saying how beautiful you are, you're out the door, cuz it's not what you're about and if that's all somebody sees, then he's a waste, not worth your time. Another withdrawal from your account. The too-bad part is you're not going to find any kind of support group for your particular problem. Who's going to sympathize, and say, Poor Kyra, what a tough break you're too beautiful? Never gonna happen. And that's a pity, really, cuz I reckon it's as real and horrible a secret to you as my nutty mum and her legacy are to me."

"Do you still have nightmares?" Kyra asked, too embarrassed to acknowledge the truth of Annie's observations. Her "secret" was trivial when held up for comparison.

"Nah, not anymore. Does Jesse?"

"Now and then."

"Does he ever talk about the things that happened to him?"

"Never. I don't know how much he remembers, although I suspect it's quite a lot. I've always felt it would be wrong to ask if he didn't volunteer. I got the impression it was too shameful, too wrenching for him to talk about it; that he was afraid if I knew the details I'd care less for him. Do you think I was wrong?"

"Nah. Sounds dead sensible to me. But once I meet him, I'll know better. Sometimes it's easier to talk to someone who's been where you have. You don't need to explain yourself or give the horrible details you've been working so hard to forget. Why go dredging up stuff if you don't have to? We like to think we can put it out of our minds, but the truth is it never goes away. It's always there, makes us into the people we end up being."

"Perhaps he'll want to talk to you."

"Hey! *Everybody* wants to talk to me. I'm the local agony aunt. An answer for every question. That's me. But seriously, I get on well with kids like Jesse, cuz I know what scares them. They're the same things, see, that still scare me now and then when I least expect it. The stuff never goes away, Keer. It lives in the back of your head like a nest of spiders. We learn to deal with it, though. We do learn. So—" Annie changed the subject with a smile "—ready to see my place?"

Annie's flat consisted of a kitchen, living room and remodeled bathroom on one floor, with two good-sized bedrooms and a former box room that had been fitted up as a darkroom on the floor above. The living room was a treasure trove of reclaimed castoffs: sections of decorative masonry and molding salvaged from building sites had become bases for a pair of tables—one for dining, one holding magazines and a glass bowl filled with marbles. Wall hangings had been fashioned from pieces of old, worn oriental carpet by attaching them to painted wood dowels mounted on two pairs of cornices that had once graced the roof corners of a small bank. Antique bottles in a variety of colors and sizes were positioned on a windowsill so that sunlight could pass through them, casting multihued reflections on the wide, black-enameled floorboards.

On the wall opposite the hangings there were five expensively matted and framed fourteen-by-eighteen-inch portraits. The uncluttered black-and-white compositions made the breath catch in Kyra's throat, created a quivery excitement inside her.

Moving slowly from one to the next, she absorbed the textures and details of each shot. The first was of a fair-haired girl of thirteen or fourteen with the clear, placid features of a cloistered nun.

"That's my mate Joan, the total sloven I was telling you about, back when we were teenagers," Annie said.

"She looks like a nun."

"Yeh, it's what I thought when I took the shot. Goes to show how deceiving looks can be."

"How so?"

"Her mum put her on the game when she was twelve. Her mum was right there in the scrambled brains depot with mine. Worked full-time at Sainsbury's but it wasn't enough. She wanted extra money to buy a spin dryer. Then it was a new Hoover; after that she had to have a dishwasher, then a big Aga cooker. Turned her only kid out so she could have *appliances*. Joan's a good sort, though. Never once had a bad word to say about her mum, not even after the old loon croaked five years ago in the middle of haggling with a salesman over the price of a nice new telly."

"You're joking," Kyra said, half smiling.

"I am not. Can you *imagine?* I'd've given anything to be there. Anyway, Joan's a real friend, someone who'll come running if you need her. Lately all she talks about is packing it in; she's scared. There's too many sick freaks on the streets, out looking to hurt women."

"What would she do?"

"She wants to take a computer course, go legitimate, work in an office. But see, she's scared of what people will think of her, which is pretty ironical, considering. Joanie's surface is pure as snow. And you, better than most, know you can't always tell just by looking what a person's like."

"True, but it's scary, changing your life. Maybe she'll actually do it and surprise everyone, herself most of all."

"Yeh, it's what I'm hoping."

The next portrait was of a strong-featured woman in her late fifties or early sixties with a square assertive jaw and thick, side parted, short gray hair. Wisdom and good humor were evident in the woman's wide smile and laughing, wrinkle-bracketed eyes.

"That's my gran," Annie said, touching her fingertips to the glass. "Wasn't she lovely? Took this at her fifty-fifth birthday bash, when I was fifteen."

"Lovely," Kyra echoed, lingering to absorb fully the image of someone she'd have liked to know.

The third portrait was of a delicate black boy of seven or eight with a halo of wild curls, a smooth rounded forehead, immense eyes and a sweet, shy smile, revealing a gap between his front teeth. "Isn't he a poppet?" Annie said. "That's Andrew, my mate Ian's boy. I could eat that kid up with a spoon. And talk about comput- ers! Eight years old and Andrew's a genius with 'em. Ian's prob- ably got him helping with your search."

"He's heavenly," Kyra said, awestruck by the quality of the work.

Next was the close-up of a dark-haired, middle-aged man with a roughly sculpted face and warm, deep-set eyes, the hint of a smile. "That's Bill," Annie said, "Gran's gentleman friend. Took that one the same night I took Gran's. Ever such a nice bloke. He had the pub over the road. Died two years after Gran. I think it was from a broken heart. He wasn't never the same after Gran went."

"That's sad," Kyra said quietly.

"Yeh. They were best mates for twenty-seven years but couldn't be together cuz Bill had a sick wife—who's still around, I'll have you know. Sick, my aunt fanny, just determined to hang on to the man. The week after he died she sold the pub and a month later off she went to live in Spain. But Bill adored Gran; they saw each other every single day until she died."

The last was a self-portrait: Annie with long, glossy brown hair falling well below her shoulders. She had positioned herself be- tween two mirrors so that she was reflected over and over endlessly, both to the front and to the rear. "That one I did a couple of years ago. I call it *Annie to Infinity.* Took me *hours* to get it set up."

Turning to take a long look at her young friend, Kyra said, "You are remarkably talented. These are breathtaking."

Annie glowed. "Yeh? You think?"

Kyra turned again to the self-portrait, admiring the clarity and intelligence of the pellucid eyes, as well as the clever interpreta- tion of how one's past and future coexisted. "Yes, I do. And, *please,* don't try to tell me this isn't art. This is exactly the same as Joe Green walking around with his head full of music."

"Wow! Okay, I won't say anything." Annie grinned at her. "Jesse's going to need an author photo for his book. You think maybe he'd let me do it? I'd really like to. He's *such* a gorgeous kid."

"Ask him," Kyra said. "He probably will. You know, Annie, I feel very lucky to have met you."

"Hey! *I'm* the lucky one, getting to meet *you*. You're great to be with, Kyra. You never go judging people, you're never unkind, and you can be dead funny sometimes. The people we meet, it's always for a reason. It's like my self-portrait. There's always what we see and what we don't see, what's behind us and what's ahead. We're friends, you and me, and that's got two sides to it. I mean, maybe I've been missing my gran lately, feeling too much like an orphan. And here you are, saying my work is art, listening to my ideas and taking me seriously. Most people think I'm just another idiot punk with statement hair."

Kyra laughed. "Statement hair."

"Men think foreplay is removing their shoes?" Annie countered. "Fancy a cuppa?"

"I'd love one."

While Annie was off in the kitchen, Kyra took another, longer, look at each of the remarkable portraits.

Kyle had left a message letting her know everything was fine. "You're not to worry about a thing. I'll have Jess home by eight Sunday evening. If we're going to be late, I'll let you know. We're off to dinner now with Dad. I love you very, very much, by the way."

Her mother had also called. "It's after eleven, and I expected you to be in. Silly of me. Why should you be? Nothing important, darling. I just wanted to chat. Phone me when you've got a moment."

Next was Dillon phoning from Boston to say, "Mom called to give me the news. I'm so broken up to hear about Jess. Please keep me posted on how things go. And if I can help in any way, let me know. The whole family sends their love. I miss the two of you like crazy. Talk to you soon."

After that, Glenna was saying, "Ever since Mother phoned last night, I've been thinking about the afternoon that horrid girl brought Jess to the apartment. I didn't want you to take him but you wanted him. I was wrong, of course. You were absolutely right to take him. The two of you were meant to be together; you've been good for each other. Now this. I really don't know what to say. I keep remembering that next morning when we tried to get him into the tub...the condition he was in. And I can't help thinking that what's happening now has to do with what was done to him then. Do you think that, too, Keer? Sorry, I'm rambling. I just wanted to say I love you both—we all do—and if there's anything we can do for either of you, we'll do it. If you have a moment, please call me. We'll be thinking only good thoughts, hoping and praying everything comes right for Jess."

The last call was from a very sober-sounding Robert. "I know Jess is visiting his grandfather for the weekend, but I wanted to tell you I've talked it over with my mum and dad and if Jess has to have a transplant, I'd like to give him one of my kidneys. I know it's a serious op, but I'm not afraid. Jess would do it for me, if I was the one who was sick. And according to the books I've been reading, a person doesn't need two kidneys. So I'll give Jess one of mine, and then we'll each have one. Oh, my mum says will you ring her please when you get a chance. Right. That's everything I wanted to say. Thank you very much. 'Bye."

CHAPTER 26

Dr. Vita Kendall was a thick-set woman in her mid-fifties with abundant short black hair, a wide face with fans of laugh-lines at the corners of clear gray eyes, and an open, no-nonsense manner. She looked the gung-ho type schoolgirls years before used to call "jolly hockey sticks." Kyra was predisposed to like her.

Having reviewed Jesse's records prior to their arrival at her office, Dr. Kendall immediately put him at ease by getting up to give his hand a hearty shake, saying, "I expect you're fed up with the medical profession by now."

"I am a bit," Jesse said with a cautious smile.

"Well, I can't say I blame you. Before we three sit down to discuss your options I'd like to have a look at you, Jesse."

"Tests and needles?" he asked, wincing.

"None of that," she said. "Blood pressure, weight, height and some measurements—skin thickness, the circumference of your arm, and so forth."

"Oh! All right."

"Good lad. Won't be too long," she told Kyra, and took Jesse off into an adjacent examining room.

While she waited, Kyra suddenly wondered what they'd do if Dr. Kendall refused to take Jesse on. They had no backup plan. Agitated, she stood and began pacing, berating herself. Nothing in life was a given. She shouldn't have assumed that finding this doctor and getting an appointment was all that was needed. She sat down again, crossed her legs one way, then the other, got back up and resumed her pacing.

When the doctor brought him back some fifteen minutes later, Jesse actually seemed relaxed as he slid into one of the chairs in front of her desk.

"First, let me say that, according to the most recent tests, at roughly ten GFR, you still have some kidney function, Jesse, and your general health is not bad. But were I to take you on as a patient there is no guarantee we'd be able to maintain you at your current level."

"But the articles I read—" Kyra began.

Dr. Kendall held up a hand. "What you read pertained to *adult* patients, Miss Latimer. The dietary protein requirements for children are considerably higher as it's necessary for the growth of new tissue as well as for the maintenance of existing tissue. Nutritional therapy for children is extremely tricky because it has to accomplish two things. It has to retard the progression of the renal insufficiency while, at the same time, supporting growth. In other words, restricting your protein intake, Jesse, runs the risk of further slowing your growth rate, as well as any number of other serious attendant problems. My patients must follow their diets to the letter, which means working closely with the nutritionist, and coming in for regular assessment."

"I could do that," he said quickly. "I *want* to do it. Please couldn't we try?"

"It would be no simple thing—for either of you," Dr. Kendall warned. "It would involve a completely new eating pattern for you, Jesse, which entails changing how your mother cooks, and the strictest adherence by both of you to the new regime. The diet entails protein and phosphorus reduction, and requires your taking vitamin, calcium, mineral and keto acid supplements. You'd have to keep a record of every last thing you eat and drink, and that record would be monitored by our nutritionist, whom you'd see every six weeks. Then, depending on your growth rate, your adherence to the diet, and the resulting assessment, the diet could well require adjustment at three-to-six month intervals. And there's more.

"Usually I see patients at six-week intervals for a complete physical examination. In your case it would be four-week intervals. I'd be measuring your height, weight, triceps skinfold thickness and mid-arm muscle circumference. I would do periodic radiographs of your hands and wrists in order to assess your growth relative to your bone age. Along with that, we'd be analyzing everything from your blood urea nitrogen and creatinine, to urinary sodium, with a whole host of other factors."

"I'm willing to do all of it," Jesse interrupted.

"This wouldn't be for a few months or a few years, Jesse, but the *rest of your life,* with periodic modifications."

"You mean I wouldn't get better?"

"Jesse," she said gently, "no one can cure you. You've lost most of your kidney function and you will never regain it. *But.* It's possible, by eating foods low in protein and phosphorus, to reduce the amount of waste products accumulating in your blood, therefore making your kidneys work less hard. Keto acid supplements provide the essential amino acids the body needs but in a pure form that, again, doesn't overload the kidneys. And while the other supplements may be changed, the KAA will not. That is forever."

"Perfectly healthy people take vitamins every day," Jesse reasoned. "My granny does, for one. So does my best friend, Robert. This isn't so different."

Dr. Kendall leaned back in her chair, contemplating Jesse with growing interest. "Planning to take up the law, are you?" she teased. "You put up a good argument."

"I plan to be a writer," he told her.

"Actually," Kyra interjected, "his first book's about to be sold."

"Really? I'm very impressed. At twelve, my son was interested in cricket and little else. But he did love to debate a point, just as you do."

"I like cricket, too."

"What does your boy do now?" Kyra asked.

"He's a barrister." The doctor laughed. "And he's still keen on cricket."

"I'm willing to go on the diet, *and* take the supplements, *and* come here every four weeks," Jesse insisted. "Whatever's required. I can do it. I'm *very* disciplined."

"I have no doubt you are. But I want you to be very clear on what's involved, Jesse. Initially you'd find it a radical change, cutting back on animal foods—meat, fish, eggs, and dairy products—even eliminating some of them altogether."

"What's left?" he asked, thrown.

"Quite a lot, and I'll get to that in a moment. With damaged kidneys, some foods are not only unhealthy, they're potentially dangerous. So you wouldn't be able to give in to the temptation of a chocolate bar, or peanut butter, or fish and chips, pizza, even some types of bread."

"I'd have to become a vegetarian?" He looked over at Kyra, then back at the doctor.

"No. It's more a matter of changing old habits and acquiring new ones. Where most of my patients find it most difficult is eating at the homes of friends and relatives, or in restaurants. But once they've learned which foods they can and cannot eat, they manage quite well."

"Even if it won't cure me, would it keep me from getting worse?" he asked.

"I honestly can't say. Nutritional therapy is difficult for children, not impossible but close. It takes a special child, in very special circumstances. To be blunt, I haven't had much success with the few children I've treated, primarily because keeping track of one's protein intake is problematical for patients of any age, but it seems particularly difficult for children. As well, there's a risk of developing malnutrition, and of curtailing your growth."

"So I could follow all the rules and stay as I am now, even get worse?"

"Dr. Kendall did say the therapy was primarily for adults, Jess," Kyra said, sharing each up- and downswing he took.

"Would that mean I'd go through it all for *nothing?*"

"In essence, yes," Dr. Kendall said. "Look, Jesse. There's no question that transplant or dialysis would prolong your life. They do offer better long-term results. You see, the younger one is, the better chance one has of living longer with dialysis. Even so, only about fifty-eight percent of children up to age nineteen survive ten years on it. And the ten-year survival rate for the same age group with transplant—either from a dead donor or a blood relative—is approximately the same. A transplanted kidney will not last forever. How long one *does* last depends in part upon the type of kidney. The ideal comes from an identical twin, and very few patients are fortunate enough to have one. Next best is a close relative, and finally a cadaver. But quite often patients have to have two or three or, in some rare cases, four transplants. The point I'm making is, you'd have at worst ten years with these options; at best you might live to a ripe old age. Nutritional therapy might have little or no effect; it could even possibly make you worse, shorten what time you do have left. Are you quite sure you couldn't tolerate dialysis?"

At this Jesse squirmed in the chair, his hands tightly fastened to the armrests. "I couldn't," he said anxiously. "I really couldn't. Please won't you take me on?"

Dr. Kendall looked at him for several long beats, then at Kyra. "I can't promise results. Do you understand that?"

"Yes. Yes, I do," Jesse said. "But you're my only chance, Dr. Kendall. If you won't agree to treat me, Kyra and I will have to find someone else, someone who doesn't come as well recommended; someone I might not like. Because I can't do the dialysis and I won't have surgery. I can't. I honestly *can't.*" Near tears, he sat silently pleading with her to take him on.

Again the doctor looked hard and long into his eyes. Finally, she said, "Our chances of success are very slim."

"But it *is* a chance," he said urgently. "I want to take it."

"You'd have to follow the guidelines closely," she said. "With no cheating, because you'd only be cheating yourself."

"I understand, and I wouldn't cheat."

"As I've told you, it's an exceedingly difficult transition. The best we could hope for, if we manage to get the balance right, is that you'd begin to gain a little ground in terms of physical growth. There's simply no way to predict how much you might grow, Jesse. But, to be brutally candid, it may be not at all. On the plus side, there are no drugs involved that might affect your hormones, thereby further impeding your growth. Many of the ones given with transplant will. Prednisone, the most commonly used one, can have very serious side effects, and it suppresses growth in children. I would be derelict if I didn't warn the two of you that if this therapy isn't successful, it may well be too late for transplant or dialysis. Time is of the essence here, and I want you to make an informed decision, to know what's at risk."

"I want to do it," Jesse said firmly.

"Miss Latimer, anything you'd like to say?"

"If it's what Jesse wants, then he has my consent."

"Be very sure, Jesse," the doctor said. "There's a lot involved and there may be no road back."

"I want to do it!"

"I don't often meet someone your age who knows his own mind so clearly. But you seem to know your limits, Jesse, and I respect people—of any age—with a strong self-knowledge. So, let's just pop down the corridor and have you meet our nutritionist, Patricia."

* * *

Patricia's Liverpudlian accent captivated Jesse, who listened as closely to the way she shaped her words as he did to what she was actually saying.

"I'll be sending you home today with a whacking great load of paper," she told them with an apologetic smile. "And to begin with you'll hate me for the diet and the masses of reading: lists of the high-phosphorus foods you should avoid, and the substitutions. Also, based on your weight, Jesse, a recommended daily intake of calories, protein, sodium, potassium, calcium, phosphorus, vitamins, trace minerals and fluids. We recommend an intake of forty-seven calories per kilo of weight. Therefore, at six stone or just over thirty-eight kilos, your daily caloric intake should be roughly seventeen hundred and eighty calories. At ten grams per kilo, your intake of protein daily should be thirty-eight grams, and your phosphorus between six to eight hundred milligrams. I know Dr. Kendall has told you about the importance of protein in your diet. But I want to tell you a little more.

"You need protein to keep your body tissues in good health and to replace cells that are normally lost each day. Protein's used by almost every part of your body to help you grow, to build muscles and to repair tissues. Some of what you eat can't be used by the body and gets broken down to a waste product called urea. It's the kidney's job to filter the urea out of the blood and get rid of it in the urine."

"Avoiding excess protein helps decrease the workload of the kidneys," Jesse quoted from memory.

"That's right!" Patricia exclaimed, pleased. "And that slows the progressive loss of kidney function. Proteins are made from 'building blocks' called amino acids. Twelve of these can be made by the body but the other nine must come from the food you eat. For the body to make protein, all the amino acids must be present at the same time.

"The nine you can't make are called *essential* amino acids. Proteins that contain all the essential amino acids leave the least amount of urea after being digested. Now, there are two types of protein: high biological value, or *complete* protein that comes from animal sources, and low biological value, or *incomplete* protein that comes from vegetables and grain products. The animal proteins are used more readily by your body than the vegetable or grain proteins. In his new diet, seventy percent of Jesse's protein has to be high quality. So, when you do a grocery shop, Kyra, be sure to read packaging labels very carefully.

"Now the first page you've got gives the protein content of four food groups, and the amount of protein per serving. Obviously, it's not a complete list, but it covers basic items in the milk, meat, vegetable, and bread and cereal groups. As well, there's an additional listing of miscellaneous and free foods—items you can use to increase Jesse's calorie intake. Fruits and juices contain negligible amounts of protein and won't be restricted just now.

"Next you'll see that we've broken down the amounts of a serving into six different groups. You'll be referring to these pages often until you become accustomed to the diet. Jesse is to have high-quality protein foods at only two meals each day. He's not to have large servings or second helpings of high-quality protein foods. And choose snacks that don't contain it, either. On the last page there's a list of foods containing little or no protein that can be eaten as desired. Included in the package are the names and addresses of some specialty shops, but they're rather expensive and most of the children find they don't taste as good as home-cooked items."

"There's a lot to learn, isn't there?" Kyra said, cowed by the many lists and the thick packet of facts and instructions.

"Kyra doesn't really cook," Jesse explained to the woman. "She's not very domestic."

Patricia laughed, and Kyra said, "I'll suss it out. It can't be that hard to follow a recipe."

"Well, feel free to ring me if you have questions or problems, Kyra. You're bound to have some to begin with. Everybody does. And, Jesse, I give all my patients one big piece of advice. Don't let yourself get too tired, too discouraged, or too lonely. I'm here to help in any way I can, even if it's just to chat for a bit. So if you're feeling down or even just hungry, get in touch. Okay?"

"Yes, okay. Thank you very much, Patricia."

"Same goes for you, Kyra," she said with another smile. "Sometimes it's harder on the family than it is on the patients."

"This is definitely going to be a challenge," Kyra said at home later, as she and Jesse sat in the kitchen reviewing the food lists, the recipes and the general data.

"What will I do about lunch when term starts?"

"You'll have to take one with you."

"And if I go to Robert's, or to Uncle Kyle's, or Granny or Grandpa's, what do I do about my food?"

"You'll start bringing your own. No one's going to mind, Jess. I promise. But these lists are daunting, to say the least."

"There *are* a lot of do's and don'ts," he agreed, scanning his own copies of the sundry pages.

On the Foods to Avoid list were milk, drinks made with milk, custard, pudding, yogurt, ice cream, cheeses, cream soups, nuts and seeds, peanut butter, salmon, sardines, smelts, scallops, crab meat, fish eggs, carp, flounder, liver, organ meats, whole wheat, dark rye or pumpernickel breads, rolls, crackers, whole grain cereals, dried beans, peas and lentils, artichokes, cocoa, cola drinks, chocolate and beer.

The Better Choices list had nondairy creamers, custards and sorbets, clear soups, cream soups diluted with water, all other fish, all other meats, all other fruits and vegetables, noncola soft drinks, vanilla, strawberry, butterscotch flavored drinks or desserts.

The Free Foods were any fat as desired to increase calories (butter, margarine, oils, mayonnaise and salad dressing); coffee, tea, hard sweets, honey, jams, sugar, corn syrup, vinegar, spices, herbs, pepper, salt, cornstarch and nondairy creamer.

"I've never *heard* of some of these things," Jesse said after a few minutes. "I thought capers were small escapades, not food."

With a laugh, Kyra said, "They're pickled buds from a caper bush."

"Bush buds?" He wrinkled his nose. "I don't fancy those."

"Then I won't use them. We'd better go do some marketing. The cupboard's rather bare and most of what there is you can't eat."

"Are you bothered, Keer?" he asked with a small frown.

"Not at all. I expect in time we'll forget we ever ate Cadbury's fruit and nut bars, or ice cream cones with Flake bars."

"You're going to do the diet, too?" He was plainly surprised.

"Of course. It would hardly be kind of me to sit in front of you, eating something you couldn't have." Studying the list of specialty shops, she said, "The shop in World's End seems to be the closest, and the parking shouldn't be too bad. Let's try that one, shall we."

"You're going to need help," he said as they climbed into the car. "So I think I should start to do some of the cooking."

"If you're willing, I wouldn't say no. I'm not brilliant in the kitchen, as you pointed out to Patricia."

"Should I not have said what I did?" he asked, at once concerned that he'd hurt her feelings.

"It's only the truth, Jess. I'm not domestic, am I?"

"That's what you've always told me," he said, smiling with relief. "Besides, it's time I learned to do more than pour milk over cereal or make toast."

"It couldn't hurt. Thank you for offering," she said, as she put the car in gear and pulled away from the curb.

"It's only fair," he said. "You know, now that I can never have it again, I want pizza with pepperoni and extra cheese. And Louise's trifle."

"I know," she commiserated. "Eggplant parmesan and caesar salad."

"Mrs. Forrest's bread pudding with caramel sauce, Damien's French toast, Aunt Glenna's Yorkshire pudders. Patricia was right. I *will* hate her. I hate her already. But anything's better than what Dr. Rule wanted," he said. *"Anything."*

"I agree, Monkey," she said quietly.

CHAPTER 27

"Hiya. How'd it go?" Annie asked when she rang just after eight that evening.

"We had a long visit with Dr. Kendall, and after that a session with the nutritionist. Now we've cleared out everything Jess can't eat and stocked up on what he can, plus all sorts of supplements. We also bought some cookery books."

"Wow! You *have* been busy."

"I had no idea it would be quite so complicated. Everything is based on calories, according to his weight. And I've never been brilliant at maths."

"The two of you will figure it out," Annie said. "And once the shoot's over next week, I'll help."

"Annie, you've done so much already."

"I *want* to help. Don't you *get* it? It makes me feel useful."

"I'm grateful..."

Jesse came into the kitchen, raised eyebrows indicating he wanted to know who was on the telephone.

"It's Annie," Kyra told him.

"Can she come round? It's about time we met."

"Here." Kyra handed him the receiver. "Tell her that."

"Hi, Annie. I was wondering if you'd like to come round. I'm anxious to meet you." He listened for a few moments, then grinned, said, "Great! See you soon," and passed the receiver back to Kyra.

"Is it okay with you if I come round?" Annie asked.

"Absolutely. And I'll run you home later."

"Right. I'll be there in half an hour."

Jesse beat Kyra to the door, and from the kitchen doorway she saw him do something he'd never done before. He took one look at

Annie, said "Hi!" and then hugged her. "You're much younger than I thought you'd be. The hair's first-rate," he said happily as he walked with her to the kitchen.

"It's getting kind of old," Annie said. "I've been thinking I might add some blue and green."

"Oh, I wouldn't," Jesse said. "You'll look like a feather duster."

Annie laughed merrily and slung an arm about his shoulders, saying, "I knew I'd like you. You're funny, like your mum."

Jesse seemed taken slightly aback by this comment, as if Kyra's having a sense of humor was something he either hadn't noticed or had simply always taken for granted. "She can be funny, can't she?" he said, as if having been given an entirely new view of her.

"Some tea or coffee, Annie?" Kyra asked.

"Coffee, please. So," she said to Jess, settling with him at the table while Kyra put the kettle on, "what'd you think of Dr. Kendall? And tell me about the diet and what-have-you."

Jesse launched into a description of their interviews, providing snippets of detail about the doctor and Patricia—items of jewelry he'd noticed, the type of shoes Patricia had been wearing, the posters on the examining room wall—and Kyra found it astonishing that, even under the most stressful of circumstances, Jesse absorbed details about people and places. He had the true writer's limitless curiosity, coupled with the tendency to store away information for future reference.

Annie listened appreciatively, from time to time reaching out to give him a pat on the hand or arm, or to muss his hair. Jesse seemed to welcome these displays and his eyes glowed when he looked at her. Perhaps fifteen minutes later, when Robert telephoned, Jesse was plainly reluctant to take the call. But after assuring Annie he'd be back, he went galloping off up the stairs to speak to his friend in private.

"So," Annie said, "it looks as if things are gonna work out."

"I would like to think so," Kyra said cautiously. "But it would be foolish to pin all our hopes on this."

"Why? The research showed this therapy's been very successful."

"With *adults*. Dr. Kendall hasn't had much luck with children. In fact, she told Jess he'd have a better chance with dialysis or a transplant. Of course, he wouldn't hear of it. He begged her to take him on, and she could see how scared he was. I think she's accepted him as a patient out of sympathy, not because she believes this will work. But at least, unlike Dr. Rule, she's someone who likes children."

"You don't know that it won't work," Annie said.

"No," Kyra conceded. "And we'll follow the rules to the letter. But..." She shrugged.

"You can't go getting negative."

"No, I'm being realistic," Kyra said in a lowered voice. "I'm preparing myself for the inevitable."

"I hope you're wrong," Annie said, bothered.

"I hope I am, too. You'll never know how much. But given what I know about Jess's condition, I'd be crazy to think this'll be a miracle cure."

Annie sat silent, looking at her. Then she drank some of her coffee, as if needing to lubricate her throat. At last, she said, "I suppose you're right. Anyway, a few more days and my time'll be my own again. I'll be available for moral support and whatever else either of you needs. Okay?"

"I'm not even going to think about arguing with you."

"That's right." Annie gave her a smile. "You're learning."

The next morning Jesse was writing up the details of his breakfast. "Two thirds of a cup of cornflakes, that's three grams of protein," he said, making notes in a small book he'd bought especially for this purpose, "with strawberries, free food and a half cup of skim milk, which is four more grams of protein, for a total of seven grams. Why," he wondered, frowning, "is it taking so long for Beauchamp-Dobbs to make an offer on the book? Maybe they've changed their minds."

"Oh, I doubt that. It's only been two weeks, and if publishing's anything like the film business, it takes ages before decisions get made." Kyra got up to pour herself more coffee as the telephone rang. "A tenner says that's probably your agent."

"Never. It's only nine o'clock."

"Are you accepting the wager?" Kyra asked.

"No. Just pick it up, please."

"I hope I'm not calling too early," Juliet Ashburn said with what Kyra was beginning to think was a constantly high bubbling level of enthusiasm. "It's very good news and I was hoping to speak to Jesse."

Kyra said, "Of course. Just a moment." Covering the mouthpiece, she said, "I told you," and passed the receiver to him. "It's Juliet."

"Clever you," he said, making a face.

His side of the conversation consisted of a number of increasingly delighted exclamations. Then he said, "I'll have to ask. Hold on, please, Juliet." To Kyra he said excitedly, "They've offered thirty-five hundred, and she thinks she can get them up at least another five hundred, possibly even a thousand. Either way, she says the deal will be completed by midday today. When it is, she'll set up a lunch date with some of the key people from Beauchamp-Dobbs to celebrate, and she wants to know which days next week would be good for us."

"I'll go get my diary." Kyra hurried to the studio. Returning, she said, "Any day but Thursday. You've got a dental appointment that afternoon."

"Any day but Thursday," he told Juliet, listened, then said, "Right... Yes... Okay... Super... Thank you *so* much. Talk to you later, Juliet." He hung up wide-eyed. "She'll let us know which day. Kyra, it's *amazing!* They want to publish in November to capitalize on the Christmas market. Which means they're rushing the manuscript into production, so they need the rewrites as soon as I can get them done. When they've finished negotiating, my editor's going to ring to introduce herself and discuss the changes. *Thirty-five hundred pounds!* And she's sure they'll go *higher.*"

"It's wonderful, Monkey. Congratulations." She bent to kiss the top of his head.

"I can't *wait* to tell everybody," he said, his color high. "But I've got to keep the line free until Juliet rings back." His energy level so elevated he couldn't sit still, he said, "I think I'll go take a look at the manuscript so it'll be fresh in my mind when my editor calls. My *editor*," he repeated. *"My editor!"* He hugged her, then went flying upstairs.

Kyra spent the next hour copying out the half-dozen recipes she'd managed to find that met Jesse's stringent dietary requirements. He would soon get bored if she couldn't come up with meals he liked. Spending more money on books that yielded only two or three recipes was a ridiculous waste, so another trip to the library was in order. But first she had to prepare a few things in case Jess got hungry.

A large bowl of mixed fresh fruits and berries took no time at all. Then she got out the blender to make up the recipe she'd found for garden vegetable juice: ripe tomatoes, green pepper, cucumber, lemon juice, horseradish and a dash of Tabasco sauce.

When she went up to let him know she was going out, Jesse spoke without taking his eyes from the monitor. "Okay. I've got to be here for Juliet's call and then my editor's."

"I shouldn't be long, but if you fancy something to eat, I've left a bowl of fruit salad. And there's a jug of fresh vegetable juice in the refrigerator. Okay?"

"Okay," he replied absently as the telephone rang. *"That's for me!"* he cried, leaping up to run to the extension in her room. "I *really* need my own phone," he complained en route. "And a diary," he added.

She waited in the doorway, just in case. Jesse said hello, then, "Hi, Juliet," and cheerfully signaled to Kyra that she could go.

She waved good-bye. Back down in the kitchen she added "diary" and "extension" to her shopping list.

For the remainder of that week, now that the school term had ended, Jesse worked at the computer from early morning until late evening, breaking off only to ring his editor to discuss some change to the manuscript, or when Kyra insisted he take time off to eat. "You'll exhaust yourself, Jess, and that's not acceptable. Remember what Patricia told you."

Reluctantly, he'd enter the key command to save the most recent changes, and go with her to the kitchen to have a cup of tea with skim milk—"It just doesn't taste the same, but I'll learn to live with it"—and two biscuits—"Three grams of protein"—he noted in his book, desperate to get back to the computer and decidedly resentful of these regular interruptions. When at last he was free to go, he tore out of the kitchen like someone escaping from prison.

And while he worked on the manuscript, Kyra fielded what had become regular hang-up calls—one in the early morning, and one or two more late in the evening—and read and tested recipes. She had to purchase additional pots and pans, as well as a food processor. But she was actually enjoying herself. Shopping for ingredients; slicing, chopping and dicing; creating stock; seasoning a dish; taste-testing as she cooked, was satisfying in a way she wouldn't have thought possible. Her mind was free to roam and, while she performed the more mechanical aspects of food preparation, she had time to wonder, with a small spurt of anger, why she'd never heard from Elway.

She also thought about Jesse's obsessive attitude about his writing and his barely controlled exasperation at being interrupted. As well, she wondered why someone had decided to start pestering her with hang-up calls. Probably some kid playing about on the telephone who happened to dial her nonpublished number at random and decided, with typical kid-logic, to keep on with it. A prank, no doubt, but a nuisance.

The results of her culinary efforts were mixed. Jesse loved the lamb and vegetable curry with rice and mango chutney. "Takes me back to Injah," he said, patting his belly, then twirling the tips of an imaginary mustache. "The days of the raj. Fiery hot curry just the thing to combat the frightful heat. Makes one sweat, creating the illusion of coolness on the skin. Rugged country, you know, Injah."

The stuffed tomatoes with onions, mushrooms and bread crumbs, topped with Parmesan cheese did not go over well. He said, "They're smooshy, Keer—definitely not my favorite texture. Sorry. Only a four point two, with the Russian judge abstaining."

He gobbled up the skinless baked chicken breast and the new potatoes stuffed with low-fat cheese, minced parsley, chives, green onions, fresh dill and black pepper.

"Not smooshy?" she asked with a smile.

"Au contraire," he answered, sounding remarkably like Kyle at that age. *"Très délicieuse, ma chère."*

The strawberry pie with a cornflakes crust was a great success, as were the apple-raisin crisp, and the piña colada made with non-fat milk powder, coconut extract, ripe banana and pineapple juice concentrate.

He made a face at the spinach-orange salad with radishes and a dressing of vegetable oil, white wine vinegar, dried marjoram and nutmeg.

"Surely not smooshy?" she asked.

"No, merely revolting."

"Less than four point two?"

"Disqualified, I'm afraid. Better luck next time."

Wednesday evening when Annie came to dinner, the two women

watched as Jesse wolfed down the Mediterranean salad of white tuna, lettuce, tomatoes, onions, sweet pepper and mushrooms with a dressing of olive oil, red wine vinegar, crushed garlic, fresh basil and oregano.

"I don't think he likes it," Annie joked. "He's Hoovered the lot just to be polite."

"Ah, no. Lovely stuff. Very Côte d'Azur," he said, making a circle of his thumb and forefinger and holding it to his lips. "Reminds me of those delectable half-naked starlets at the film festival; those outdoor cafés with striped umbrellas, *café au lait,* and the distinctly pungent aroma of Gaulloises."

"Interested in half-naked starlets, are you?" Annie teased.

"But of course," he replied. "I live and breathe for them."

Annie slapped his hand. "You dirty boy!" she accused, then laughed at the ogling face he made, his tongue lolling.

Thursday's dinner of oriental salad with shredded chicken, lettuce, snow peas, onions, bean sprouts, carrots and water chestnuts, with a dressing of light sesame oil, rice wine vinegar, fresh ginger and sesame seeds was the outright winner of the week. "This I like very much, indeed," Jesse articulated in ripe, plummy tones. "Reminds me of the good old days when the lads and I dined at the club in Shanghai after a hard day's trading on the Bund."

Kyra laughed, glad to see him so energized, so happy.

By Friday morning, having spent the best part of every day either searching for recipes or cooking, she was looking forward to that afternoon when she'd drop Jesse off at the Forrest house for the weekend. Susan had assured her that fixing food for Jesse wouldn't be a problem, but Kyra went ahead and prepared a container of oriental salad with a jar of the dressing, as well as a sack of fresh fruit, and a tin of the gingersnaps Jesse so liked, made with low protein flour, reduced-calorie margarine, and a blend of ginger, cinnamon and cloves.

Kyra put the last of the pots and utensils into the dishwasher, then went to tell Jesse it was time to go.

"Five more minutes. Okay? I want to finish this one bit."

She stood watching as he typed quickly, stopped to read what he'd written, and smiled. Then he scrolled ahead, altered several words, shook his head, changed something, then nodded, satisfied. Knowing he'd keep on at it unless stopped, she interrupted again. "Jess, Robert's waiting for you."

"Coming," he said irritably, eyes fixed on the screen. "One more minute."

It took almost another half hour before she was able to get him to shut down the computer. Then he ran around the room, dragging things from the wardrobe and the chest of drawers and shoving them into his rucksack. He couldn't find his favorite T-shirt and while he searched for it, she phoned Susan Forrest to let her know they were running late.

By the time she dropped him off they were both anxious for some time apart.

Kyra gave Susan Forrest the bag of Jesse's food, saying, "It needs to go into the refrigerator."

"No problem," Susan said. "And Robert's managed to find a few treats for Jess. He spent a good hour reading packaging yesterday."

"That's very kind of you, Robert," Kyra told the boy, turning to have a last word with Jess. "Have fun, love, and please don't forget to take your supplements."

"I'm hardly likely to forget," he said, irritable again and plainly wanting to get away.

"And remember, no cheating."

"I *won't*, for God's sake! I'm not an idiot."

"Of course you're not. I know it's been rough, but you've been a very good sport about my experiments in the kitchen."

"So've you," he said, placated. "It can't have been easy, doing all that cooking."

"I haven't minded. Enjoy yourself, Monkey."

"You, too. And give my best to Annie. Tell her I'm waiting to be introduced to some half-naked starlets." He winked, comically lewd, then he and Robert went rushing off up the stairs.

"What an imp!" Susan observed with a shake of her head.

"I'll be back to collect him by four on Sunday."

"No rush. We'll be here."

Arriving home, Kyra fixed herself a cup of tea and sat at the table to drink it. No meals to prepare, no need to force Jesse away from the computer and deal with his resulting irascibility. At seven-thirty she was to meet Annie for dinner and she was quite ashamed of how much she was looking forward to food that wasn't on any list.

CHAPTER 28

In August, deciding she'd lose her mind if she spent all her time cooking and fretting over Jesse, Kyra signed on and started the preliminary sketches for a big-budget West End musical. When Jesse finished his rewrites, he began preparing dinner a few evenings a week. Making careful note of the ingredients and their caloric, protein and phosphorus values, he stir-fried lean beef or chicken with a variety of vegetables in the wok he'd bought, and served the stir-fry with Oriental noodles, or with different types of pasta. At cooking, as at so many other things, he excelled. Unafraid to experiment, casually daring, he produced consistently delicious concoctions.

But now that their positions were reversed and it was Kyra who had a deadline, it seemed as if Jesse got a malicious little kick out of interrupting her in the studio. "Dinner is served, Madame," he'd announce, and when she didn't come at once he would wait in the doorway, arms crossed over his chest, sighing impatiently, until she put aside her brush or pencil.

Initially, Kyra was amused. But her amusement didn't last beyond the first week. Still, she bore the interruptions without comment, thinking it wouldn't accomplish a thing if she rose to the bait he dangled so blatantly.

On the evenings when she cooked, Jesse went upstairs and sat down at the computer to work on his new book.

"I'm not ready to discuss it yet," he responded when she asked about it. "All I'll say is it's nothing like *Joshua*." Even Juliet and his editor, Liz, were being kept in the dark. "If I talk about it before everything's set in my mind," he explained, "it'll go flat and I'll lose interest."

Kyra understood and respected that. Designs came to her in the same way, fitting themselves together in her mind until they had attained cohesiveness and she could begin committing them to paper. What niggled her was his manner, the subtle and proliferating gibes about almost everything—her opinions, certain clothes she wore, the amount of coffee she consumed, even the way she made toast. It was demoralizing. She could feel him steadily pulling away from her, every day placing a bit more distance between them, and she didn't know how to make it stop. She doubted she could have described the experience to anyone with any accuracy and still have come across as credible or sympathetic. After all, she really had no grounds for complaint. He was a decent, well-behaved boy who just happened to be acting upon some private agenda that no doubt had its roots in his illness. But the situation made her think that this was how her mother had to have felt all those years ago when Kyra had become so critical of her. Did every child put every parent through this? Was this a classic rite of passage to which she was overreacting? Her common sense told her this was likely the case, and so she steadfastly refused to allow herself to display her annoyance.

By late October, after nearly three months of adhering faithfully to the diet, Jesse had gained only a few ounces of weight and hadn't grown any taller. And in November, as the date of the book launch drew near, he became more and more agitated and bad-tempered. Only telling Kyra after the fact, as if believing that she would have disapproved, he arranged to hire a dinner jacket for the launch and went shopping in the West End with Robert to buy a dress shirt, a pair of onyx cuff links, a black bow tie and new shoes. Then, two weeks before the party, he asked Kyra in a decidedly confrontational manner what she was planning to wear for the occasion.

"I won't embarrass you, Monkey," she told him with a smile.

"Of course you won't," he said restively. "I just wish you'd wear something flattering for a change, instead of your usual circus tents. This *is* a special occasion, you know. It's important that you look good. The media will be out in force at the launch. It's *important*," he repeated.

"I'll do my best to look good," she said, concealing her hurt.

"Thank you. I'd appreciate it. Oh, and there's something else I've been meaning to mention."

"What's that?" she asked, fascinated by his self-absorption.

"You've really got to stop calling me Monkey. It makes me sound such a child. I am thirteen now, you know."

"All right, Jess," she said crisply. "I'll make every effort to remember."

"I hope you're not going to be upset that I've said what I have," he said almost angrily.

"No, no. You're a teenager now, as you say. We can't have people thinking I'm unaware of that. No more Monkey. Have you thought to tell Kyle how you feel?"

"Actually no, but—" he checked the time "—that's a good point. I'll phone him right now," he said, and hurried upstairs.

"Have you had enough calories today, Jess?" she called after him.

"Yes, I've had enough bloody calories," he snapped. "I *know* how much I'm supposed to eat. I don't need you constantly reminding me."

"You have no call to be rude to Kyra," Kyle reprimanded him unexpectedly when, after an exchange of greetings, Jesse began complaining. "She's only concerned for your well-being."

"But I'm not an infant," Jesse defended himself. "I don't need to be reminded to eat, or be told to put on warm clothes, or that it's time for my bath."

"I would think you'd be glad she cares as much as she does. I don't think I need to remind you that not everyone's quite so fortunate." Kyle paused, debating the wisdom of saying more, then said, "Well, I expect you've got a lot to do, so you'd best get on with it."

"I was hoping you and Damien would come to dinner Thursday, Uncle Kyle," Jesse said, somewhat contritely.

"Sorry. Afraid we can't. We're taking your grandmother to the theater that evening."

"Oh. What are you seeing?" Jesse asked.

"Revival of *The Corn Is Green*. One of Granny's old chums is playing Miss Moffat." Kyle groaned, indicating what he thought both of the play and of the actress.

"Well, have a jolly time, old bean," Jesse offered.

"Do my best," Kyle said curtly. Then, deciding not to hold back, he said, "Frankly, Jess, I'm appalled by your attitude. If I were you, I'd be looking to make points with Kyra, not with me."

"Sorry, Uncle Kyle," Jesse said quietly.

"Don't waste the apology on me, my boy," Kyle said. Then, softening, he said, "Look, Monkey. I know this isn't easy for you. But it's not easy for Kyra, either. Everyone in the family, and that includes Damien and Annie, loves you and cares about your well-being. Are you planning to start attacking all of us, too, when we display our concern?"

"No, of course not."

"Then, let me give you a word of advice. Go downstairs and make your apology to the proper person. Mend your fences."

"But you don't understand—"

"Oh, I do, perfectly," Kyle cut him off. "But lashing out at the people who care most for you won't solve a damned thing. It'll only make matters worse."

"I'm not 'lashing out.' I simply want to be treated as if I've got a brain."

"Then *act* as if you do! You're out of line, Jess. And trying to pit me against Kyra is unworthy of you. Have you forgotten she's my *sister?*"

"No, but—"

"Jesse," Kyle said evenly, "I am not enjoying this conversation. Let's not pursue it. You've said what you wanted, and I've responded. It's up to you now how you choose to proceed. We'll talk again soon." Kyle hung up.

"Bloody hell!" Jess muttered, lowering the receiver. After a time, he sighed deeply, got up and locked his door, then put Richard Strauss's violin concerto on the CD player. Settling by the window, he sat staring blankly at the glass until Kyra came to fetch him for dinner.

Two days later when he was late getting home and Kyra asked where he'd been, Jesse erupted, instantly transmogrified into someone she didn't recognize.

"You don't need to know where I *am* every minute of the *day* and bloody *night!*" he raged. "I'm sick of having to go through a goddamned *inquisition* every time I walk through the bloody door."

"I expected you more than two hours ago, Jess," she said, maintaining a calm exterior. "I was concerned, that's all. There's no inquisition."

"I've come *home,* haven't I? I'm here, living and breathing. What were you so 'concerned' about?"

"It's past six. I expected you at four. Naturally, I was worried. Any parent would be."

"Weren't you ever *young?*" He stood glaring at her, hands on his hips, upper body pushed forward in her direction. "Didn't you *ever* stop out late with friends or do something on the spur of the moment?"

"Of course, I did," she said quietly, an ache in her throat. "We wouldn't be having this conversation if you'd just phoned to let me know you were going to be late."

"Why do you have to clock my comings and goings like some sort of jailer with only one prisoner? I'm not a baby, for God's sake. *When* is this going to *end?*"

"Probably never," she said, her tone remaining quiet. "I'll undoubtedly be fretting over your well-being in perpetuity."

"THERE'S NO NEED FOR YOU TO POLICE MY EVERY MOVE!" he shouted.

"Stop shouting, please."

With slightly less volume, he said, *"Do me a favor and keep your worries and concerns to yourself because you're driving me stark, staring mad!"* He stood waiting for her to respond, his hands curled into fists, his dark eyes molten.

When she failed to say anything further but merely stood staring at him, he marched off up the stairs. His door slammed. Silence. She sank into one of the kitchen chairs, hearing the echo of his envenomed words caroming off the walls and ceiling as she considered how to put the incident to one side and get back to work. Impossible. She just couldn't.

Wearied, she got up to plug in the kettle, recalling how Glenna liked to say that the making of tea was a fine British delaying tactic. It was that, and more. It was punctuation, comfort, routine; it was what you did when you didn't know what else to do. She got down the pot and the strong Indian leaf tea, and while she waited for the kettle to boil, she battled the temptation to ring Annie, or her mother, seeking consolation and advice. But she couldn't do that, either. Not only was it unfair to burden her mother and friends, it was also embarrassing. She ought to have learned by now how to play out her role as a mother. But this situation went beyond normal parenting requirements. Something had happened to send Jesse into such a state. And she intended to find out what, just as soon as she got one thing out of the way.

She went to the telephone, and when her mother answered, Kyra said, "Could you help me shop for something to wear to Jess's launch party?"

"But what about the dress you were planning to wear?"

"I've been given strict orders. Have you any free time the next day or two?"

Hearing hints of desperation in her daughter's voice, Octavia said, "Tomorrow. Let's have lunch, make an afternoon of it."

"Yes, let's," Kyra agreed gratefully. "I'd adore it. I'll come collect you at eleven-thirty, if that suits."

"It suits," Octavia said. "Everything all right, darling?"

"No, but I'll fill you in tomorrow."

Putting down the receiver, Kyra looked at the time. Seven-ten. It was a school night, and they hadn't had a meal. As well, she still had a lot of work to do. But, God, what she really wanted was to get out of the house and away from Jesse's casual cruelty, his inexplicable rage. Instead, leaving the kettle to turn itself off, she went up and knocked at Jesse's door. He took his time responding, which she knew was intended to bother her. And it did. When finally he called out "Come in," she opened the door and from the doorway said firmly, "We have to talk, Jess."

He was sitting by the window and glanced over, asking casually, as if nothing had happened, "What about?"

"Any number of things, but primarily about how you've been behaving for the past month or so, and in particular about that spectacular fit you just pitched."

His eyes narrowed, his chin lifted, and his back straightened; sure signs he was ready to defend himself by going on the offensive, and she moved quickly to avoid that. Crossing the room, she bent to hug him, saying, "Turn off the music and come downstairs. Talk to me."

Returning her hug, he went pliant and said, "I admit I was out of line. It's just that I'm nervous about the launch...and other things."

"I know you are." She kissed the top of his head. "So let's sit down and discuss the things that are putting you so on edge. Okay?"

"Yes, okay." He turned off the CD player, then allowed her to take his hand and lead him downstairs.

Settled side by side on the sofa, she said, "It's a terrible thing when you start finding your own child so dislikable that all you want is to get away from him. It's a dreadful feeling; makes me think I'm hard-hearted and uncharitable."

Shocked, he said, "You don't want to live with me anymore?"

"Of course I do. But, Jess, you've been so mean-spirited and rude lately. Perhaps you haven't meant to be, but it's made me feel rotten. And that scene before... We can't live like this. Obviously there's a reason why you're behaving as you are. If you tell me about it, we can try to fix it. But having a go at me at every possible opportunity isn't the answer. I'm far from perfect, but I am doing the best I can."

"I know that," he said huskily. "You always have done."

"Talk to me, Jess. I'm not your enemy or your jailer. But I can't help if I don't know what's troubling you."

He looked around the room. "It's hard," he said at last. "It isn't at all the way I'd thought it would be."

"What isn't?"

"It feels as if, if I admit what I'm thinking that'll somehow make it real."

"That's only superstition," she said gently. "Saying something out loud won't cause it to happen."

"But it's already happening."

"What is?"

"The diet, the supplements...they're not working." He stopped and gazed at her guiltily, as if he'd said something monstrous.

"True, you haven't made any great gains," she allowed.

"No, they're *not working*," he repeated more forcefully. "We both know it. And Dr. Kendall knows it, so does Patricia. Everyone knows."

"Has Dr. Kendall actually said that, Jess?"

"I keep thinking it's my fault somehow. I've got the wrong attitude, or I'm not making enough of an effort. But I'm doing everything I'm supposed to. So why didn't I gain any ground?"

"Have you talked to Dr. Kendall?" Kyra asked again, chilled by his use of the past tense.

"That's why I was late," he confessed. "I stopped by for my visit with Patricia but Dr. Kendall... She wants to see us both."

"Why didn't you tell me?" she asked, alarmed.

"I don't know. I suppose I thought if I didn't say anything, if I could just keep on as I have been, things would improve and I wouldn't have to tell you...any of it."

Drawing him close, she said, "You mustn't hold things in, keeping them to yourself. That only magnifies your fears, makes them seem worse than they are."

"I'm not going to get better," he said ominously. "I know that's what she's going to tell us. She was so serious today; she didn't smile or joke with me the way she usually does; she didn't even ask how the book was coming along. And she *always* asks about the book."

"If you're having second thoughts, it may not be too late for dialysis or a transplant."

"*No!* I'm not having second thoughts!"

"What then?"

"I'm angry," he said, sitting away from her. "I expected to have more time."

A cold drilling of fear in her belly, she said, "You've got time."

"Not enough," he declared flatly. "I don't even know why I've started another bloody book when I'm never going to be able to finish it."

"Then why *did* you start it?"

"I don't know. Perhaps to prove something."

"What?" she asked, helpless in the face of his fatalism.

"Bad choice of word," he said. "I'm challenging fate, I suppose. I think I thought that if I started a new book I wouldn't die."

"It's not about fate, Jess," she said, relying on reason to control her emotions. "It's about having a disease that you know could kill you, and wanting to do things—like starting a new book—to show that you're still in control."

"Yes," he agreed, surprised. "That's exactly what it is."

"But back in July, when we first got the diagnosis, you told me you'd decided what your choice would be. You were very firm about it."

"That hasn't changed, Keer. It's just that I thought I'd have *longer.*"

"You don't know that you won't, love." Were they actually quietly discussing his death? Was she really going to lose him? She was, yes. It was ending, and they both knew it. They just hadn't put it into words while there was the possibility, however slim, that the alternative therapy might succeed.

"I *do* know, though," he said, sagging back against the sofa. "I can tell—I can *feel* it. I'm so tired, all I want to do is sleep all the time. But I make myself get up and keep going. I make myself do the things that have to be done, as if just doing them will prove I'm all right."

"Come over here," she said, and shifted him easily onto her lap. He was still as small as he'd been at nine and ten, and as leery of his need to be physically comforted as he'd been at three. "Now that you're a teenager, you're probably mortified by this. But I miss our lovely cuddles."

"So do I," he confessed, settling in the crook of her arm. "I don't see what's so bloody great about being thirteen, you know. It's no different than twelve was." He was quiet for a few moments, then said, "I'm sorry I've been such a hateful misery-guts."

"It's okay, Jess. I understand. We'll make an appointment to see Dr. Kendall tomorrow."

"She's expecting us, actually. At eleven."

"But you weren't planning to tell me?"

"I was. All the way home I was working out what I wanted to say, but I came through the door, you wanted to know where I'd been, and I went mental, as Annie would say. I honestly didn't know I was going to carry on that way."

"It's okay, Jess. I really do understand."

"I wish *I* did. The odd thing is, I'm not at all scared."

"No?"

"No. I'm just so bloody *angry.* It's my own fault, though. I shouldn't have started a new book."

"You might surprise yourself and finish it."

He simply shook his head, and said, "No, I won't," then closed his eyes. "I've already thrown away the hard copy and put the computer file in the trash."

Realizing there was nothing else to say for the moment, she just held him. And in minutes he was asleep, his head heavy on her breast.

CHAPTER 29

For the third time in fifteen minutes Jesse was rapping on the bedroom door, calling, "We're going to be *late,* Kyra!"

"Almost ready," she called back.

"*Hurry,* please! Annie and I have been waiting *ages.*"

"Two minutes," Kyra said, looking in the mirror at herself in the long-sleeved, low-cut, unstructured full-length black crêpe de chine dress her mother had persuaded her to buy. Feeling most unlike herself, she picked up her evening bag and went to the door. Only the outrageously expensive, new low-heeled black suede shoes were genuinely comfortable.

She stepped into the living room doorway, and said, "All set. Sorry to keep you waiting."

Turning, Jesse and Annie exclaimed simultaneously.

"Is it too extreme, do you think?" she asked, looking down at what she thought was an almost indecent display of cleavage.

"No, it's super!" Eyes widened, Jesse appeared stunned. "You look *beautiful!*"

"Fantastically beautiful," Annie said. The dress was the single most flattering garment she'd ever seen Kyra wear. As well, rather than the usual braid, her hair was twisted into an elaborate knot at the nape of her neck; pearl studs were fastened to her ears, and she'd actually put on eye makeup, some blush and lipstick. The effect was staggering.

"Honestly?" Kyra asked. "It's not too much, is it?"

"Never. You're perfect. Shall we be off? Our young author's a tad anxious."

"Yes, could we go now, *please?* I'd really hate to be late for my own party," Jess said, already on his way to the door.

"Hang on, Jess. Where's your coat?"

"I don't need one. Let's just *go*."

"But it's cold..."

"I don't *need* one," he repeated, stepping outside and leaving the front door open behind him.

"He'll be fine," Annie said, holding Kyra's bag for her as she put on her coat. "Kids his age don't feel the cold the way we old folks do. You look gorgeous beyond words."

"So do you, Annie. I don't think I've ever seen you in a dress."

"Hardly anyone has. Is it okay, d'you think?" Annie looked down at the full-skirted dress of deep green fabric patterned in tiny flowers, with a bodice panel in velvet of a darker green, and long flowing sleeves. With it she wore a pair of handsome, flat-heeled, knee-high black leather boots, and a billowing black vintage cape lined in scarlet silk.

"It's charming, and you look magical. Why am I so nervous?" Kyra asked as she locked the front door. Jesse was waiting by the car, fairly dancing with impatience.

"Doesn't he look adorable in his hired gear?" Annie said.

"Utterly," Kyra agreed, hoping his energy was going to hold out. For the past week he'd been going to bed upon arriving home from school at midday. He'd get up for dinner, do his homework and then go back to bed. Annie had been staying with them for several days now, to lend a hand where needed.

"You nervous, Jess?" Annie asked, settling into the rear of the car.

"Horribly," he replied, then was silent throughout the ride from West Kensington to the Savoy, gazing fixedly out the window. As they pulled into the short road leading to the hotel, in a voice barely above a whisper, he said, "I think I'm going to sick up my tea."

He did look rather green about the mouth and nostrils, and Kyra said, "Try to hold on another minute or two if you can, love, until we can get you inside to the loo."

Annie saw him swallow hard, then clap a hand over his mouth, and said, "Kyra, I'll take Jess to the lav. We'll meet you inside." She jumped out, dragged Jesse from the car and ran hand in hand with him into the hotel.

Becoming increasingly concerned, Kyra waited in the lobby for close to twenty minutes before they reappeared. An arm around Jesse's shoulders, Annie was whispering something in Jesse's ear. Kyra watched them approach, touched by the unerring degree of solicitousness—neither too much nor too little—that Annie consistently showed Jesse. She'd been a true godsend the past few days, escorting Jesse to Dr. Kendall's offices for tests, running errands and keeping Jesse company while Kyra was working and he was too enervated to do anything more than watch television.

"Not to worry, Keer," Annie said. "We're right as rain now, aren't we? And we've had a nice look at the ladies' loo, as well. Pretty posh, eh, Jess?"

His color better, but still pale, Jesse nodded.

"Ready for the festicles?" Annie asked him with a smile.

"Ready. Thank you very much, Annie."

"You're very welcome, luv. Whenever you fancy another tour of the facilities, just let me know. All set?" She looked from Jesse to Kyra. "Right, then, team. Let's do it."

Allison Hughes, the Beauchamp-Dobbs senior publicist, had managed to generate so much advance interest in *Joshua Goode and the Blackfriars Warehouse Saucepan Lids* and its author—who just happened to be the youngest member of the renowned Bell-Latimer family—that the media representatives far outnumbered the invited guests, which was precisely what Allison had hoped for. The launch was going to get an enormous amount of publicity, and that would, in turn, sell a lot of books.

Upon arrival, each family member was swarmed by the uninvited freelance photographers (who'd been warned they would be forcibly removed if they failed to remain outside the doors of the River Room) and greeted by a cacophony of shouted questions. Each arrival in turn spoke for a few moments of his or her pride in Jesse and of how much they'd enjoyed his book; each politely but firmly declined to answer any personal questions and was at last allowed to enter and join the party.

Allison had hired a quartet of costumed buskers who energetically played and sang old favorites—everything from "Maybe It's Because I'm a Londoner" to "Knees Up, Mother Brown"—that created a cheery atmosphere and had people humming along, while waiters offered drinks and trays of canapés. The many invited photographers clicked away nonstop, the journalists pounced on the celebrity guests, and several cameramen took video footage for TV of the illustrious assembly. Stationed near the door with Juliet to meet people as they arrived, Jesse, aglow, greeted an instantly bedazzled Robert, proudly introducing him to Juliet and Liz, while Kyra led Susan and Stephen Forrest over to meet Annie and the family.

When the last of the latecomers had come hurrying in, Allison quieted the buskers, and Sir Kenneth stepped up to the microphone. "Good evening, everyone. Beauchamp-Dobbs welcomes you to a very special occasion. It is the first time in the company's long history that we have had the privilege of publishing a book by so young an author. But then, neither the book nor the author are in the least ordinary, as you'll discover for yourselves—as, indeed, I did—once you've met the author and read his delightful book. So without further ado, I am proud and honored to introduce to you Jesse Latimer."

Flushed, a Jesse who couldn't stop smiling moved from the sidelines, stood on tiptoe in front of the microphone, and said, "Hello. Sir Kenneth is a tad taller than I am, so I just need to do this." As appreciative laughter rippled through the room, Jesse spent a few moments lowering the microphone. The photographers clicked away, flashes flaring.

"I reckoned he'd be brilliant," Annie whispered to Kyra, taking hold of Kyra's hand. "He looks dead edible."

Admiring Jesse's exceptional aplomb, filled with loving admiration, Kyra watched him finish adjusting the microphone and then smile again at those assembled.

"Right," he said, in the low, very adult voice that invariably took people off guard because it was so unexpected emerging from the mouth of someone who looked no more than eight years old. "That's better. So, hello again and thank you all for being here this evening. This is unbelievable to me, really; just exactly as I've always imagined a book launch would be. I had actually written several pages to read to you, but then I reconsidered and decided it had rather too much of an Academy Award acceptance speech ring to it." More laughter, and he waited before continuing. "Instead I'd like to tell you about some of the people who made this event possible. First, Sir Kenneth. He read *Joshua* and thought it was worthy of being published. That was amazing enough, but he's also guided me every step of the way, and no one has to tell me how lucky I am. So thank you, Sir Kenneth. I'm more grateful than I could ever say. My editor, Liz Thorne, has been incredibly kind and patient, and has taught me a lot about the mechanics of writing. I thank you, Liz. My agent, Juliet, drives a hard bargain and knows fabulous places to have lunch. I'd like to thank you for introducing me to the Groucho Club." Laughter again, and again he waited. "Then there's Annie Cooper, the best photographer anywhere and my secret dreamgirl. Thank you, Annie, for the super back-of-the-book photo, and for making me laugh so hard I think I've got permanently damaged ribs.

"My friend Damien Haverford has always been honest and kind, even when I've come up with ideas that would've sent anyone else mental. He is one of the most generous people I know and I thank you for being so generous to me. My best friend, Robert Forrest, let me tell him the entire story of Joshua bit by bit over a period of several months, and he made really good suggestions. I modeled LaLoyd on him even though Robert sings like a bullfrog expiring from heat prostration. Thank you for being such a good sport and such a great friend, Robert.

"And now for my family. You probably don't know them. They're a shy, retiring bunch." This sent those assembled into hoots of laughter. "There's my grandfather, Sir Richard, who occasionally plays at being a traffic warden but mostly he helps me with computer problems. He's got a wicked way with a hard drive." Jesse smiled through another wave of laughter. "And there's my grandmother, Dame Octavia, who is a devoted rose grower but reluctantly makes public appearances here and there." He blew a kiss to Octavia who put out one elegant hand and snatched the blown kiss from the air. "Then, there's my Uncle Kyle who, at this very late date, has finally decided what he's going to be when he grows up. Turns out, it's a police officer on TV. I expect he'll look very good in uniform.

"Finally, there's my mum, Kyra, who's forever mucking about with scissors and bolts of fabric, and forcing people into all sorts of outrageous gear." He paused again, then said, "*Joshua* is for you, Keer. Words do sometimes fail me, so I just want to say that you always have been and always will be my tall princess." He paused one last time, then said, "And that's it. That's everything I wanted to say. Thank you, everyone. I hope you enjoy yourselves."

There was tumultuous applause as the buskers began to play energetically and waiters circulated through the room, their trays laden with copies of *Joshua*.

"That was t'rrific!" Annie said, squeezing Kyra's hand. "His dreamgirl. I'll give him what-for about that, the little devil."

Choked with pride, Kyra was watching as one person after another stopped Jesse on his way through the room to have a word. She heard Annie quietly say, "Uh-oh," and turned to see James Elway working his way through the crowd toward them, apparently oblivious of the pack of frenzied *paparazzi* falling over each other as they tracked his passage through the room, and of the startled journalists who caught sight of him and fell in with the group.

Astonished, Kyra stood frozen.

"Just don't kill him in front of this lot or you're sure to be convicted," Annie murmured. "Take him outside and top him in private." She began to slide her hand free but Kyra's fingers closed firmly around it, keeping Annie in place.

"Don't you move!" she whispered. "I need moral support."

"Righty-o," Annie said, curious to see what would happen.

Elway came directly up to Kyra and attempted to kiss her as at least thirty cameras flashed, and the blinding light to enhance half a dozen video cameras came on. "For God's sake," Kyra exclaimed, ducking back so that the kiss landed to one side of her mouth. "What are you doing here, Jimmy?" she asked in an undertone, trying to turn away from the snapping shutters.

"I was invited." He pulled an invitation halfway from his pocket to show her, then pushed it back. "I thought you..."

"I didn't invite you," she said, taken aback.

"Oh! I simply assumed..."

"Sorry, no. Jess probably put you on his guest list."

"Yes, perhaps he did. Hello, Annie. How are you?"

"Brilliant, thanks, Mr. Elway."

"Good, good. Look, Kyra, could we go somewhere to talk?"

Did he ever pay attention to what was going on around him? Kyra wondered. Was he actually unaware of the rowdy gang that was still busily shooting the two of them and shouting out questions even while they were being slowly herded toward the door by a number of uniformed hotel staff?

"A quiet corner's the best we'll get." Leaving Annie, she walked back to the rear of the room with Elway following. As far as possible from the nearest people (which was only a matter of a few feet), she stopped and asked, "What was it you wanted to talk about?"

"Well, I, um...I felt I owed you an explanation, perhaps an apology."

"Oh?"

"The thing is, I did intend to phone you, Kyra, when I got your message, but I imagined it was a personal matter and I just couldn't deal with that right then. We were falling behind schedule because of those few days of bad weather. I wasn't happy after the fact with a few of the earlier takes I'd approved, and we had to redo them. Then, when I realized how much time had gone by, I wasn't sure how I'd be received. I dialed your number a few days later, then put the phone down. The next morning, the same thing happened. And after a while, every time I finished dialing I'd find myself ringing off."

"The hang-ups," she said. "Every day for weeks, months now, and you couldn't manage even to say hello?"

"Evidently not," he said bashfully. "Appalling, isn't it? I'm quite ashamed. I don't know *why* I couldn't."

Folding her arms over her breasts, she took a long look at him. He was wearing his usual uniform of ancient pullover, baggy trousers and a tweed jacket somewhat the worse for wear. Incongruously, he had on a gleaming new Rolex wristwatch. A genius he might be, she thought, but an adult with any sense of occasion he was not. Recognizing this aroused her sympathy.

"Please don't make any more hang-up calls, Jimmy," she said gently. "It was maddening and I was seriously considering getting a new number, which would've been a dreadful inconvenience."

"No, sorry, I won't. I was actually pleased, you know, when the invitation arrived. I thought it would be an opportunity to clear the air, because I do care about you, Kyra. I have been thinking of you—often."

She shook her head. "You care about people when it's convenient to your schedule, Jimmy, when you can fit it in after the rushes, during dinner, for a few hours here and there, if nothing more pressing requires your attention."

"That's hardly fair. We *were* on a shoot," he reminded her.

"Yes, and what we had was a location fling."

"Then why did you ring, leaving that urgent message?" he asked.

"If you had bothered to phone me back, you might have learned why. All these months later, I can't recall what it was about," she lied smoothly, looking back over her shoulder, trying to spot Jesse. His energy was bound to be flagging and they'd agreed beforehand that they wouldn't stay too late. "Look," she said, turning back to him, "I've really got to get back to the party."

"Yes, of course," he said, completely at a loss.

Remembering what Annie had said that afternoon in Green Park, she could admit the truth of it to herself now. She hadn't *really* thought what she and this man had was love. She'd simply wanted to believe it was a possibility. "Look, I'm sorry if we've misunderstood each other, Jimmy. But we have cleared the air, so we'll put it behind us. Why not have a glass of wine and go say hello to the family? I'm sure they'd be pleased if you did."

With a slightly bewildered, yet grateful, air, he said, "Yes, all right. Thank you. I would like that."

"Good," she said, and, on impulse, gave him a quick kiss as a burst of light caught them.

"Oh, bloody hell!" she exclaimed, turning to see one of the more enterprising photographers grinning devilishly as he fired off several more shots while quickly backing away. "Lovely, my dears," he said, fending off one of the security personnel who'd come rushing over to roust the man. "Ta very much, Kyra, Jimmy. Now, now, no need to get stroppy, my old darling," he told the guard. "I'm going, aren't I? See? Here we go. These feet are moving right out the door."

Laughing, Kyra went in search of Jesse.

Once they'd shot enough film, most of the invited photographers and videographers departed. The journalists remained, keeping their eyes open for any newsworthy tidbits as they ate hot hors d'oeuvres in lieu of dinner, washing them down with what Kyra overheard a woman from the *Times* refer to as "superior plonk."

Kyra slipped away to the far side of the room and sat down to watch the action as she sipped a glass of red wine.

Jesse had gone from vomiting in the loo to offering ready smiles and quotable remarks to the press and television people. It was subtle, but she was all at once aware of something in his manner that strongly reminded her of Kyle at the same age.

"Our lad's quite the star turn this evening," Octavia observed, settling in the chair next to Kyra's.

Kyra leaned over to kiss her mother's cheek. "You are divine, mother of mine."

"A goddess among women." Octavia laughed, taking hold of her daughter's hand. "Who invited Jimmy?"

"Apparently Jess did."

"Are you bothered?"

"Surprisingly, no. In fact, I'd have to say I couldn't care less."

"Well, good. I'm delighted to hear it."

"Annie deserves the credit. She talked sense to me."

"She's a remarkably canny young woman," Octavia said. "Completely lovable."

"Jess obviously agrees with you."

Kyra turned to her mother. "Do you know what I've recently discovered? That children have no idea how their parents feel until they get to be parents themselves. Then we become mired in guilt for what we've put our parents through."

"Most children go through an obnoxious stage when their parents would gladly strangle them and be done with it. Life in prison would be preferable to the day-to-day hell of living with a hateful adolescent. But eventually it passes, the children become people it's possible to talk to, and the next thing one knows, all the unpleasantness has been forgotten. Are you mired in retrospective guilt, my precious?" Octavia asked with mock superciliousness.

"Only occasionally." Kyra laughed and took another sip of her wine.

"Good. I feel thoroughly rewarded. How is he doing?" she asked seriously.

"Not well," Kyra answered. "He's attending school only in the mornings now. And Annie's been taking the car to fetch him home. Another week or two, and he'll have to stop attending altogether."

"It's hard to believe," Octavia said. "He seems so well tonight. There's no possibility of his changing his mind about the treatments?"

"None whatsoever."

"No," Octavia said. "He'd be as compulsive in this as in everything else he does. I suppose all we can do is honor his choices."

"That's all," Kyra said.

Octavia sighed, then said, "We mustn't remain on the sidelines. Come along." She rose fluidly and wafted with inimitable grace toward where Sir Kenneth, Jesse and Annie stood laughing about something with Richard, Kyle and Damien. After a few seconds Kyra got up and followed.

CHAPTER 30

Late the next morning Kyra had just arrived home from a quick trip to the market when Kyle turned up at the door.

"Hello. This is a nice surprise," Kyra said.

"I thought I'd take a chance and drop round with this lot, see what sort of coverage the launch got," he said, indicating his armload of newspapers, "and have a visit with Jess when he gets back from school."

"I'm sure he'll be pleased. Some coffee?" Kyra asked as they filed inside.

"Please."

Kyle dropped the newspapers on the table and went to put a consoling arm around his sister's shoulders. "How are you doing?"

"I'm coping." She embraced him, drawing comfort simply from his presence. At last separating from him, she said, "Let me get the coffee going, then we'll talk."

While she ground the beans, he sorted through the papers, found the one he wanted, and laid it open on the table.

"I thought you should see this," he said, when she came to sit down.

What he wanted her to see was a large photograph of her and Elway on the front page of the entertainment section. The accompanying text was about filmdom's hottest new romance—the celebrated film director and the designer daughter of Octavia Bell and Richard Latimer. The launch party was mentioned only incidentally.

"Oh, hell!" she said. "I wonder if Jess has seen this."

"Probably. The kids at school are bound to have arrived with all the papers."

"The fellow who took that shot actually had the temerity to thank us before he was hustled off by one of the security people."

"That's okay, then. As long as he was polite," Kyle said mordantly. "It's rather a good photograph, though."

"I'll ring up and see if I can't order a dozen eight-by-ten glossies," she said, matching his trenchant tone. "It's completely misleading," she said, taking another look. The kiss she'd been in the act of giving Jimmy could easily be interpreted as representing significantly more than mere affection.

"Perhaps you should check your machine," Kyle suggested.

"God!" she said with a little shiver, and went to look.

The steadily flashing light indicated there were more than ten messages.

"Tape full?" he asked, one eyebrow lifted.

"Looks to be," she said, getting the cream and sugar.

"They'll be after you and Elway with a vengeance," he warned. "It wouldn't surprise me if this photo has already been sold to the wire services and winds up in newspapers around the world."

"I'll handle it, if and when." She brought two mugs to the table.

"Will Elway be as insouciant as you?"

"I have no idea. The man's impossible to predict. In the worst-case scenario, we'll each be hounded for a week or two, then they'll find someone more newsworthy and that'll be the end of it. What does bother me is that they all but ignored Jess and his book. Biscuit?"

"Yes, please. It was a super party and Jess was a wonder. I was so proud of him."

"So was I. It was very kind of Damien to make the trip down just for the occasion."

"Be serious, Kyra. He loves Jess almost as much as I do. He wouldn't have missed it. Plus, his coming saved Dad the bother of having to hire a car and driver. His eyesight's not good enough now for night driving. He'll soon have to give up daytime driving, too. He's an absolute menace on the road these days, along the lines of Mr. Magoo."

Kyra laughed.

"You may laugh, but you haven't driven with him lately. Anyway, I gave the two of them tea and toast at an ungodly hour and they were off back to Stratford by six-thirty this morning." He paused to yawn. "Not much of a visit," he complained, "but better than none."

"When do your rehearsals start?"

"The third of January. And what a schedule! It's like being in rep. Rehearse a week, shoot a week—on and on, until we've got thirteen episodes wrapped. I'm still not convinced this is the best career move I've ever made. But the scripts are bloody well-written, and my character's got some depth for a change. He's a bona fide one-off, quick-witted and clever, a widower with an eye for the ladies. Some great dialogue."

"You'll do brilliantly. And I will watch faithfully every week."

"Good to know I can count on at least one member of the viewing public. The thing is, since it's going to be such a heavy schedule, Damien and I thought we might spend ten days in Paris over Christmas and the New Year. Unless," he added meaningfully, "you think the timing's bad."

"No, you should go. You could do with a break."

"I'll wager you could, too."

"True, but it's out of the question." She studied the newspaper photograph again, unable to recognize herself. "It doesn't really look like me."

"Don't be a ninny! Of course it does. You looked smashing last night, and it actually is a very good pic. I only hope you're prepared for what's to come."

"You don't think you're rather overstating the case?"

"I do not," he said succinctly. "The zealous buggers will dog your footsteps relentlessly, morning, noon and night, until you're ready to kill the next one of the scruffy turds that steps into your path. What time will Jess be home? I want to see him, but I've got costume fittings in an hour."

She checked the time. "Fifteen minutes or so. Annie's gone to collect him."

"Jesse's dreamgirl." Kyle smiled. "She's a poppet, isn't she?"

"I don't know how I'd manage without her. I shouldn't have signed on for this show. It's massive, far too time-consuming."

"What's the alternative?" he asked. "You can't just hang about the house, hovering over Jess. It would drive both of you bonkers."

"That was my thinking. But the work's taking up most of my time. It'll be weeks yet before I'm done."

"Probably for the best, if you think about it," he said. "You need the distraction—take your mind off Jess for stretches of time."

She looked across the table at him, considering that. "You've become quite wise in your advancing years."

"No." He shook his head. "Nothing to do with wisdom. I need to have my mind taken off him for stretches of time, too. Because if I start thinking about what it'll be like without him..." His eyes all at once glistening, he fell silent and shook his head.

It turned out that Kyle was right—about everything. Kyra couldn't believe the fevered degree of interest the media displayed as a result of the photograph, and was initially flustered, then infuriated by the persistence of the people who started phoning that same afternoon, who came knocking at the door at all hours in the days following, and who went so far as to leap into their cars or onto their motorbikes to follow her when she left the house to do the marketing or to go to a production meeting. No matter where she was or what she might be doing, someone was inevitably lurking nearby, waiting to snap her picture or to start shouting questions at her: Were she and Elway planning to marry? How long had they been seeing each other? What did her son think of the affair? Could we come in, take some shots of the house, of her and Jesse together? No? How about in her studio, or the garden, or out here, then, on the pavement?

The other members of the family had been contending with this atrocious attention for most of their lives, and it spoke well for them that they hadn't been driven insane by it. For her part, she sought refuge in her work but had to keep the curtains drawn in the studio because one particularly intrepid photographer kept sneaking into the garden and hovering outside the window, popping up at intervals like a deranged jack-in-the-box.

Initially, Jesse was amused by the small crowd that took to pursuing her but that regrouped itself around him whenever he entered or left the house. They shouted their questions, asking how was *Joshua* doing, and was he working on his next book. What did he think of his mum's affair with Elway? He laughed them off and said nothing.

During the week following the launch party, before school broke up for the Christmas holidays, Allison arrived early each morning with a hire car and driver to escort Jesse to breakfast radio or television chat shows. After his appearances she'd drop him off at school, and would be there waiting at midday when he came out (still in his uniform because, Allison had patiently explained, it heightened his schoolboy appeal), to take him to more interviews. Sales of the book were brisk, and *Joshua* went back to press for a second printing just over a week after its initial shipment to the stores.

"I *wish* this would end," Kyra told Annie as they were waiting for Allison to deliver Jesse home. She peeked out the living room window at the group loitering in the street who were drinking coffee in large take-away cups and helping themselves to pastries from a box someone had placed on the bonnet of a parked car.

"Be glad you're not a rock star," Annie said. "The media *never* leave those lads alone. And think of it this way: Jess's book is bound to be a best seller with all the press you're both getting."

"Perhaps. But he's exhausted by the time Allison brings him home each day. I had a quiet word with her yesterday afternoon, explained about his health and asked her to ease off. She's promised to keep the information to herself and said there'll only be two more days of it. Jess'd be livid if he knew I'd said anything to her, but he can't continue at this pace. He's on the verge of collapse. Dr. Kendall rang this morning to go over his latest test results. They're not good."

"Look," Annie said. "If it'll help, I can stay on through the New Year. I'm not doing much of anything at the moment, although I actually got some bookings after Jess said what he did at the launch. But none of them're until after the first, so I'm free to lend a hand."

"I'd be so grateful, if you're sure you wouldn't mind, love."

"I don't mind. When're you gonna absorb that fact, Keer? Keeps my Geisha training from going to waste." She emitted her cartoon laugh and managed to get a smile out of Kyra. "Anyway, it'll be great not spending Christmas alone. So," she went on quickly, allowing no time for Kyra to comment, "are we still on for Sunday with your mum?"

"Definitely. There's only so much interference in my life I'm prepared to tolerate. Jess has been looking forward to it, and so have I. Fancy a coffee?" she asked. "I could do with a jolt."

"Yeh, great. Me, too."

They started along the hall to the kitchen just as the telephone rang. Kyra paused for a moment to listen, in case it was important. Hearing Elway's voice, she said, "I'll take this. Would you mind putting on the kettle?"

Annie grinned and said, "It's himself, Mister *Love.*"

With a smile, Kyra picked up the receiver.

"What the bloody hell have you been saying to the press?" Elway demanded.

"I'm fine, thank you, Jimmy. And how are you?" she said, instantly irked.

"Fit to be tied. They won't bloody leave me *alone!*"

"And that's *my* fault? Oh, I don't think so. Aren't you the man who said he didn't care what the media thought?"

"Well, I didn't at that point. But this is completely out of hand. Something's got to be fueling the fire."

"I see. And the something must be me. Let me ask you, Jimmy, did I force you to come to the launch?"

"No, but..."

"Did I in any way encourage you to make displays of affection at said launch?"

"Well, no, but..."

"Exactly! So why then were you in the midst of leaving a message just now, accusing me of feeding tidbits to that pack of hounds outside my door?"

"Oh!" Surprised, he said, "They're pestering you, too?"

"Can you honestly be this naive?" she wondered. "Did you really think you and you alone were the subject of their interest?"

"Well, I suppose I did," he said, considerably subdued.

"The first night we had dinner together back in July, you made the observation that you are as a man essentially as you were at the age of eleven. I thought at the time it was just so much charming hyperbole, but I'm beginning to understand that you were telling the truth."

"Of course I was," he said with indignance. "I never misrepresent."

"Nor do I," she said. "But you really are an eleven-year-old. Only a child would make endless hang-up calls because he couldn't think what to say. Only a child would ring up now, wanting to blame someone else for a situation he'd created. For the most part, grown-ups accept responsibility for their actions, and get on with things. You are *really* starting to piss me off, Jimmy!"

"Look, I'm sorry—"

"I'm sure you are. But I don't have the time or the energy to deal with your nonsense right now. Those people outside your door will give up soon and you'll be free to come and go as before. In the meantime, you're going to have to live with it, just as I have to."

"I've behaved like a complete prat with you from the outset, haven't I?" he said balefully.

"Rather," she said.

"I apologize, Kyra. I don't know why, but where you're concerned, I seem unable to cope. I never intend to behave badly toward you but I always manage to somehow. The awful part of it is, I do care very much about you. So, will you accept my apology, please?"

"I will. And will you do me a favor, Jimmy?"

"Absolutely."

"Please don't ring me again for a while. Things are very difficult right now, for reasons I can't explain. Let's talk again after the New Year, if you don't mind."

"Yes, all right. I *am* sorry, Kyra. Please don't think too badly of me."

"It's okay, Jimmy. Forget it." She put down the receiver, muttering, "Wanker!" which sent Annie into peals of laughter.

By the week before Christmas the last, most zealous of the media people had given up, and Kyra was again free to come and go without fear of being bothered.

The promotional stint completed and school out of the way, it meant Jesse could sleep for long periods of time, but he seemed none the less to be losing a little more ground each day. After preparing for it by spending most of the morning in bed, he and Robert spent the afternoon of the twenty-third shopping for gifts among the crush of people who'd come to the West End to see the shows and to admire the decorations on Regent Street. Jesse treated his friend to afternoon tea at the Ritz, during which he gave Robert a sporty Swatch wristwach along with the computer game he knew Robert had been wanting, and handed over the packages from Kyra that were to go under the tree at the Forrest home.

Arriving back in a taxi, with the help of the cheerful cabbie, he stowed a large number of gift-wrapped packages in the living room, then sat down in the kitchen to tell Kyra about their outing. "It was hard to move about, the crowds were so thick, but we had a good time. Robert ate a full cream tea and could easily have eaten a second. But you'll be pleased to know I was good and completely ignored the clotted cream and the smoked salmon sandwiches. Talk about tempting, but I didn't cheat—although I had to use my calculator to do the calorie count." He laughed tiredly.

"Good for you," she said. "It sounds as if the two of you had a fine time."

"I deserve the VC for sticking with the cucumber-and-watercress sandwiches. Oh! And guess what?" he said happily. "I got asked for my *autograph.* An elderly couple were at the next table with their grandson. He leaned over to say he'd seen me on the telly and that he'd put *Joshua* on his Christmas wish list. Robert thought it was a big giggle, wouldn't stop ribbing me about it afterward. Anyway, I got presents for everyone. A Burberry scarf and rain hat with matching umbrella for Louise. Think she'll like that?"

"I'm sure she will."

"Hand-dipped Belgian choccies, some embroidered handker-chiefs and a little antique paperweight for Granny. I went mad in N. Peal—got cashmere sweaters for Grandad, Damien and Uncle Kyle, and a shawl for Granny. A book on Le Corbusier and leather driving gloves for Damien, and Cartier wallets for Grandad and Uncle Kyle. Small things for everybody's stockings—notebooks and diaries from Smythson's, choccies and what-have-you. It was hard to know what to get for Annie. But in the end, I got her a silk scarf at Hermès and I found a gold locket at Asprey's that looked right."

"That's incredibly generous, Jess. I'm sure she'll be thrilled."

"I like her," he said with a shrug. "I had a gift box made up at Fortnum's for Robert's mum and dad, and sent it along home with him. All that's left to buy is some of Sir Kenneth's favorite single malt to go along with the other little things I got for him. I know Annie won't be back 'til late tonight 'cause of that last-minute job she picked up, so I need you to come with me to the off-license."

She checked the time and said, "If you're up to it, we could go now, get it out of the way."

"I'm up to it," he said, although he looked anything but.

On the walk home, carrying the round canister of Glenfiddich, Jesse said, "Unimaginative, isn't it? But I couldn't think of anything else to get him."

"No. It's perfect, and he'll be very pleased. You went a bit mad today, love."

"Meaning?" His eyes narrowed.

"Meaning you bought a lot of very expensive gifts."

"It's *my* money," he said defensively. "If I want to, why shouldn't I?"

"I'm not saying you shouldn't."

"It sounded as if you were."

"No, Jess. I was merely commenting on your generosity."

"You're generous, too," he said, still defensive. "I've seen the packages stacked all over the studio."

"I'm not criticizing you, love."

"Sounded as if you were," he muttered.

"No, I'm impressed. You put a lot of time and effort into it, and got fabulous things for everyone. What's the matter, Jess?" she asked, putting an arm around his shoulders. "You were in such a jolly mood when you got home. Now, suddenly, you seem very down."

"It's not as if I don't know how many gifts I bought and how much I spent, Keer. But these are parting gifts, really, and I wanted them to be special."

Absorbing this statement as if an icepick had been driven into her chest, she couldn't respond for a moment. Then she bent to kiss the top of his head and said, "They're *very* special and I know everyone will be flabbergasted."

"I'm just not sure about the driving gloves for Damien. They cost a packet but they're still only gloves. I don't think I'd be thrilled if someone gave me gloves. It seems so unimaginative. If I show you them when we get home, will you tell me what you think? Because I could go and get him something else, something better, nicer, tomorrow."

"I'll be happy to look at them. What say we have supper on trays in your room, and then afterward you can show me all the things you bought."

"Okay, but I'm not very hungry."

"A little something," she coaxed. "I've made some of that winter vegetable soup you like so much."

"All right, but just a little."

"That's my good boy," she said, locked onto the words *parting gifts*.

CHAPTER 31

In the late afternoon on Christmas day the telephone rang. Louise picked up in the kitchen and moments later came to the living room doorway where everyone was half asleep after an enormous meal and signaled to Kyra.

Reluctant to disturb the others, Kyra got up and went to the kitchen to take the call there.

"Hello, it's Allison Hughes. I am sorry if I'm interrupting—"

"No, it's all right, Allison. Is there a problem?"

"I'm afraid there might be. A friend of mine at the *Telegraph* rang a few minutes ago to say she thought I'd want to know that some American woman named Collins, I think—I didn't quite catch it, my friend was in a bit of a rush—is organizing a press conference for the day after tomorrow. Apparently she's claiming Jesse is *her* son and that you stole him from her."

For a moment or two the words made no sense. Then Kyra exclaimed, "My God!" Images of a pale, elfin girl with dark angry eyes and cropped brown hair came to mind; the girl wobbling off in platform shoes, and a grimy, desolated tot chasing wildly after her. "My God!" she repeated. "This can't be happening!"

"Obviously it's rubbish. But I thought you should know, so you could take action, get on to your solicitor, or something. The press conference is to be held at the Regent Palace, so I'm assuming she's booked in there. I am sorry to be the bearer of such bad news, today of all days."

"No, no. I appreciate your letting me know." She remembered Kyle's prediction that the photograph of her and Jimmy would travel around the world, and knew he'd been right. One way or another, Jennifer Cullen learned of her son's success, had got a whiff of money and come on the run.

Kyra hung up and stood with a hand pressed to her breast, heart racing and breathing shallow.

"You all right, luv?" Louise asked.

Kyra shook her head, trying to think.

Louise went back to the table near the window, picked up the morning's newspaper and, after casting another sidelong glance at Kyra, pretended to read.

Kyra moved to where she could see into the living room. Her mother and Kenneth were dozing in the companion wing chairs either side of the fireplace. Jesse lay curled up asleep on the sofa beneath his grandfather's sheltering arm. Only Annie was wide awake, and she looked over at Kyra with a questioning expression.

She was going to have to explain, Kyra thought. But what could she say? She looked at Annie, wondering if those documents Glenna had so hastily drawn up were actually legal and binding. Of course they were. The British courts had accepted them in granting her petition to adopt Jesse. Why was she working herself into such a state? The woman could say whatever she wanted, but Kyra had a piece of paper, signed and witnessed, proving that Jennifer had long ago surrendered any rights to Jesse.

Her eyes on Jesse, Kyra signaled to Annie, who set aside her book and hurried over. Anxious to keep this under wraps if at all possible, for everyone's sake, Kyra took Annie's hand and led her upstairs and down the hall to her old room, where she closed the door before sitting heavily on the side of the bed.

"What's happened?" Annie asked. "You've gone dead white."

"Allison—you know, the publicist from Beauchamp-Dobbs— just had word from a journalist friend that Jesse's mother has scheduled a press conference for the day after tomorrow. She's issued a preliminary statement saying I stole her son."

Annie's eyes went round. "His *mother?* Why would she say that? Is it true, Keer?"

"Jesse is *legally* mine," she said, a passionate quaver in her voice. "She was going to abandon him, turn him over to Children's Aid if I refused to take him. She didn't give a damn about him. She must have seen that bloody photograph of me and Jimmy, or read about Jess's book, his success."

"And now she's come, bent on some easy dosh."

"Probably," Kyra said, grappling with escalating anger, and fear, too. "She can give all the bloody press conferences she likes. But the fact is, she *has* no rights. She signed them away long since. The thing is, I don't want Jesse—or the family—upset right now."

"Have you got all the documentation?"

"Of course I do!"

"No need to be snappish," Annie said calmly. "I'm just asking."

"Sorry."

"You think she's come expecting to be paid to go away?" Annie asked.

"That's *exactly* why she's come," Kyra answered firmly. "She's never had any interest in Jess. If she had, she'd have been in touch long before now."

"Have you got copies of Jess's medical records at home?"

Kyra nodded. "Actually, I do. Why?"

"I'm trying to think like a greedy cow who's ready to hold a press conference without so much as a letter or a telephone call to the precious son who was supposedly *stolen* from her. And I'm trying to imagine what might send her packing before she's able to meet with the media. Whatever we decide to do, we've got to do it quickly, within the next few hours."

"You're right," Kyra said, her mind scrambling to concoct a viable scenario. "Strike a peremptory blow."

"There's a couple of ways we can handle this. But we've got to come up with some story to tell everyone." Annie looked at her wristwatch. "Okay. First off, see if Sir Kenneth wouldn't mind driving Jess home later, say by nine. That'll give us a few hours. Easiest thing is to say there's some cock-up with the costumes and you've got to get on it ASAP. I'm coming along to lend a hand."

Kyra said, "Right! Let's do it!"

At five-fifteen, following a quick stop at the house in West Kensington so Kyra could pick up some papers, she parked not far from the Regent Palace and turned to Annie. "Ready?"

"Ready, captain."

At the desk, they got the room number from the clerk who, after checking the slot, said, "Key's here, so she's in. Want me to ring up?"

"It's been ages since we've seen each other and I'd like to surprise her, if that's all right," Kyra said.

The clerk said, "No never mind to me, dearie," and went back to her paperwork.

In the elevator, Kyra said, "There's something you should know."

"What's that?" Annie asked, eyes on the floor indicator.

"This woman is under the impression that I'm her mother. My name's on her birth certificate."

"*Are* you her mum?" Annie asked.

Kyra shook her head. "No. I can't have children—a birth defect."

"Pity. I'm sorry, Keer. So how'd your name get on her birth certificate?"

"*That* is the big mystery."

The lift doors opened and they filed out.

"All set?" Kyra asked outside the room.

"All set, captain."

Kyra wouldn't have recognized the woman who opened the door. Jennifer Cullen hadn't aged well. She'd lived hard and it showed in the flat, coarsened planes of her face. She still wore black eye-liner on both her upper and lower lids, still favored short cropped hair, and still applied pale pink lipstick to her small, mean mouth. She was, if anything, even angrier than Kyra remembered, and had the skeptical eyes of a pawnbroker. Her expression was one of permanent wariness, ingrained distrust. Small and bone-thin, clad all in black—sweater, slacks and lace-up shoes—she looked at the two people in the hallway. "Oh, great!" she said sourly. "Mommy dearest. And who's this," she asked of Annie, "your latest lawyer?"

Kyra was transported back to the awful scene almost ten years earlier when Jesse had clung to this woman, refusing to let go, and she'd shoved the three-year-old away with such force that he'd staggered backward, almost falling. "How did you know I was here?" Jennifer now asked with undisguised leeriness.

"Think you can announce a press conference and we're not going to find out?" Annie said, walking right past Jennifer into the room. "You're a right nana."

"Yeah, don't wait to be asked or anything. Come right on in," Jennifer said belligerently. "Make yourself at home. Jesus," she said to Kyra, "you hang with the weirdest goddamned people."

"*I'm* weird?" Annie snorted. "And you're not, with a faceful of *Night of the Living Dead* makeup, and that sad black gear that went out of style maybe *thirty* years ago. Good one."

In a hurry to be done with this as quickly as possible, Kyra said, "You've come because you want Jesse back. Is that right?"

"Yeh, I want him back. He's my kid. Of *course* I want him back. I didn't give him to you for *life.*"

Kyra had abandoned their script, and Annie just stood watching, waiting for her next cue and thinking Jennifer Cullen had to be the stupidest woman who'd ever lived. But then again, she was smart enough to know there was money to be gained from the Lattimer connection. But to throw her kid away, then come thousands of miles in the hope of profiting from that kid ten years later was nothing short of evil.

"Fine!" Kyra said, opening her bag. She pulled out a sheaf of papers, saying, "Have him back! Come to the house tomorrow morning and get him. He'll be packed and ready to go. I'd suggest you make arrangements and get a hospital bed lined up for him, though, because he's dying."

"You're scamming me," Jennifer accused.

"Here are his medical records," Kyra said, thrusting them at her. "He'll be ready first thing in the morning."

Seeing an opportunity to return to the script, Annie jumped in, saying, "Unless you're ready to do the testing the day after tomorrow. The surgery could be scheduled twenty-four to forty-eight hours later—once the test results are back and your tissue type's been confirmed. And of course it will be, given you're his natural mother."

"Wait just a goddamn minute! Okay? *What* test, *what* surgery? What the *fuck* are you two *talking* about?"

"The transplant, of course," Annie said. "So you can give Jess one of your kidneys. 'Course, that'd mean your staying in London for six or eight weeks, but we'd pay your expenses. And you did come for money, after all, didn't you?"

Kyra could almost see the woman's mental machinery engaging; cogs and wheels, sprocket to sprocket, turning, turning. Jennifer didn't like what was happening, didn't like having no control of a completely unexpected situation. Annie really was a genius. She'd come up with this scenario in no time flat, and had even rehearsed it with Kyra during the drive to the hotel.

"Hold the goddamn phone a minute!" Jennifer was poised as if for flight.

It was working, Kyra thought, in awe of Annie's grit and imagination.

"You want money. Here's your way to get some," Annie said.

Boggled, Jennifer said, "Yeah, sure. When's this test thing supposed to be?"

"Day after tomorrow," Annie said. "We've written the details down for you," she went on, taking a piece of folded note paper from her pocket.

"What kind of expense money are we talking about?" Jennifer asked Kyra.

"All the medical expenses and the cost of your accommodations," Kyra answered.

"That's it? That's *all?*"

Kyra pretended to think for a few moments as she studied the naked greed in the young woman's eyes. For the right sum, Jennifer might actually decide to donate one of her kidneys. "We'd also reimburse you for your airline tickets."

"Ring us later and let us know what it's to be," Annie said. "Either we see you first thing in the morning when you come to fetch Jess, or we see you at the doctor's office the day after tomorrow."

"Sure, whatever." Jennifer flew to the door and got it open. "I'll let you know."

Once inside the elevator and safely out of earshot, Annie said, "That was tons of fun."

"Oh, tons," Kyra said. "Right up there at the top of my list, just below drinking liquid drain cleaner."

Annie let out a shriek of laughter. Kyra managed a smile.

"She's actually *thinking* about it," Annie said in wonderment. "What kind of creature *is* that?"

"Let's just get the hell out of here," Kyra said, as the elevator doors opened onto the lobby.

By the time they arrived back at the house, Kyra was depressed. "Until this is settled and I know she's actually gone..."

"What if she says she'll donate a kidney, Keer? What if she agrees?"

"It'll never happen," Kyra said flatly. "Let's have a drink."

"Good idea. I could do with one."

As she fixed two gin and tonics, Kyra said, "She doesn't *want* Jess. She never has. And even as greedy as she is, she's far too self-ish to consider giving anybody anything—especially not a body part. But maybe, with luck, she'll take some money and go away." She reached over to stroke Annie's cheek. "I couldn't have got through that without you, Annie. You know, you're so much a part of the family now my mother takes it as a given you'll come along to Sunday lunch. Jesse adores you—so do Dad and Kyle and Damien. We all do. Next to having Jess given to me by that odi-ous little wretch, you're the best thing that's happened in my life."

Deeply moved, Annie said, "Yeh, well, ditto, mate," and touched her glass to Kyra's.

They'd just finished breakfast at eight-fifteen the next morning and were drinking coffee over sections of the *Telegraph* when the door-bell rang.

"Expecting anyone?" Annie asked, automatically looking down the hallway toward the door.

Kyra answered, "No," but she knew who it was.

There on the doorstep stood Jennifer, scowling in the downpour.

"We need to talk," she said, bare-headed and wearing a thin cot-ton raincoat inadequate for the weather.

"Do we?"

"Look, could I come in? I'm getting very wet here, in case you haven't noticed."

"I've noticed. What is it you want to talk about?"

"I can't *believe* what a hard-ass you are. You're my mother, for chrissake. Couldn't you be a *little* nicer?"

"I am in no way related to you, thank God. You *are* Jesse's mother, however, and you were anything *but* nice to him in the time you had him."

"What the hell is that supposed to mean?"

"*Please*. You know exactly what I mean."

"So he got hit a couple of times. What's the big deal?"

"Are you crazy or just stupid?" Kyra said disgustedly. "Jess was severely beaten, and often. He was burned with cigarettes and God only knows what else was done to him."

"I *never* laid a hand on Jess."

"I'd say that sums up your entire contribution to his early life."

"Okay, so I'm not going to win any prizes for mother of the year. I still need to talk to you. Let me in, will you? It's freezing and I'm *drowning* out here."

"I'll give you five minutes," Kyra said, standing aside and allowing her to enter.

Jennifer muttered something under her breath as she stepped into the foyer.

"Take off your coat and come to the kitchen," Kyra said. "I'll give you some coffee."

"Thanks." She removed the raincoat to reveal the same outfit of black sweater and slacks she'd worn the day before.

On her feet and ready to move, Annie said, "I'll finish my coffee upstairs."

"No, stay. This won't take long. Sit down, Jennifer. What do you take in your coffee?"

"Regular," she said, her angry eyes on Annie. "So are you guys an item or something?"

"You've got a twisted mind," Annie said with disgust. "I've a mind to give you one right in the cakehole."

"Don't waste your energy, love." Stirring cream and sugar into a mug of coffee then placing it on the table, Kyra said to Jennifer, "You're down to less than four minutes. Say what you came to say."

"What if want my kid back?"

"Fine."

"Where is he, anyhow?" She looked around as if he might be hiding in one of the cupboards.

"He's upstairs asleep. If it's your intention to take him, I'll wake him and get him ready to go."

"I didn't say I was going to. I only said what if."

"Are you going to tell me why you're here, or am I meant to guess?"

"I'm thinking of heading home, but I'm kind of short on cash."

"Ah!" Kyra nodded.

"*Finally,* we get to what you're really after." Annie stared at the surly female, riveted by an egocentricity so complete that it seemed to have actual density, like some sort of force field. "Right out of a science fiction flick, you are."

"How would *you* know what I'm like?" Jennifer shot back. "You don't *know* me."

"That's right, I don't," Annie said. "Nor do I want to, you nasty piece of piss."

"God, you people are mean!" Jennifer drank some of the coffee, eyeing them both over the rim as she did. "Okay," she said, putting the cup down and holding it with both hands, as if for warmth. "I need money to get home. I figure it's the least you could do."

"When were you thinking of leaving?" Kyra asked.

Jennifer shrugged. "I don't know. Tomorrow evening maybe, if I can get on a flight."

"So you wouldn't stay long enough to test to see if you'd be a tissue match with Jess?" Kyra asked rhetorically.

Jennifer shrugged a second time.

"Charming," Kyra said. "How much do you need?"

"I don't know. Whatever it costs to get the hell out of this lousy country. You've got the worst goddamn weather I've ever *seen.*"

"Shall I go book a ticket for her?" Annie asked Kyra.

"No, thank you, Annie. I'll take care of it."

"I'll need some cash, too," Jennifer pushed on.

"Of course you will," Kyra said, barely concealing her anger.

"I can't pay the hotel bill. I don't even have enough money left to get to the airport."

"Anything else?" Kyra asked.

"Yeah." Jennifer smiled slyly. "Ten thousand pounds in cash to call off the press conference tomorrow."

"And if I refuse?" Kyra said, suddenly scared, imagining another media crowd storming the house.

"I'll go ahead and tell everyone how you stole my son."

"You *cow!*" Annie jumped up, her fists clenched.

"How much time do I have?" Kyra asked, a hand on Annie's arm bringing her back down onto her chair.

Jennifer checked the time. "Let's say by ten o'clock tonight."

"It's a *holiday,*" Annie protested. "How's anyone supposed to get that kind of cash on Boxing Day?"

"That's *your* problem," Jennifer said.

"Right!" Kyra said. "Your five minutes are up. Have you finished your coffee?"

Jennifer pushed the mug away. "I'm finished."

"Good, then I'll see you out."

"Wait a minute!"

"What?"

"Could I see Jess?"

Several seconds of stunned silence followed this request as the two other women stared at her.

Finally Annie said, "You have *got* to be joking."

"No I'm not. I'm his mother. Maybe he'd like to see me."

"Kyra's his mother," Annie corrected her. "You're just the cesspit the lucky lad climbed out of."

Rising, Kyra said, "I'll ask him."

"Yeah," Jennifer said, her slitted eyes on Annie, "you do that."

Upstairs, Kyra knocked at Jesse's door, then opened it to see that he was awake. The new synonym dictionary Sir Kenneth had given him lay face down across his lap.

"Who's here?" he asked.

Filled with apprehension, Kyra sat down on the side of the bed. "What's wrong?" he asked.

"Your mother's here," she said quietly. "She's asking to see you."

"My mother?"

"If you don't want to see her, that'll be the end of it. I'll send her packing."

"My *mother?* Why does she want to see me?"

"Jess, I honestly cannot fathom what makes this woman tick. But whether or not you see her has to be your decision."

"What do you think I should do?" he asked, looking frail and utterly bewildered.

"I can't answer that, love," she said gently. "This is about you, about what *you* want."

His eyes traveled slowly over the room. He wet his lips and at last looked again at Kyra. "I suppose I'll see her," he said. "I'm curious."

"I understand," she said, getting to her feet.

"Are you angry with me, Keer?" he asked anxiously.

"Of course not." She bent to kiss him, then straightened, saying, "I'll send her up."

Returning downstairs to see that Annie and Jennifer were still locked in visual combat, Kyra said, "He'll see you, but you're only to stay for a few minutes."

"Fine." Jennifer stood and started out of the room. "Oh," she said, turning back. "Where'm I going?"

"Just go upstairs. His door is open," Kyra said, dropping back into her chair.

"He actually agreed?" Annie whispered.

Kyra nodded, then closed her hands tightly around Annie's across the width of the table. In silence, they waited.

Within ten minutes, Jennifer reappeared in the kitchen. She looked considerably less cocky, even somewhat shaken. "Well," she said from the doorway, "the kid really is sick, that's for sure."

"What?" Annie said. "You thought we were fantabulizing?"

"What is your fucking *problem?*" Jennifer said tiredly.

"You!" Annie fired back. "You are *everybody's* fucking problem! You're a bloody nightmare with feet!"

"Cute. Fine. I'm out of here. What about my money?"

"You'll have it by this evening," Kyra said.

"I'd better!" Jennifer waved a warning finger in the air.

Kyra stared at the woman's chipped bright red nailpolish, thinking those gaudily painted but flawed fingernails said everything one needed to know about her.

Jennifer marched to the foyer to retrieve her raincoat. "Some fucking mother you turned out to be."

Kyra moved very close to Jennifer, towering over the woman, whispering, "I am *not* your mother, but even if I were I'd still find you loathsome." In a fury, she threw open the door and when Jennifer didn't move, Kyra gave her a push. "Cancel the press conference. You'll have your money by tonight. Now get out of here."

Jennifer laughed derisively. "You think you can push me around?"

"Yes, I do," Kyra said, and shut the door in Jennifer's face.

"Bloody hell," Annie said after a moment, sliding an arm around Kyra's waist. "What're you gonna do? Have you got that kind of dosh?"

Kyra shook her head. "Jess needs his breakfast and I've got to find ten thousand pounds in cash," she said breathlessly. "I cannot and will not go to my parents. My *God!* How am I going to *do* this?"

"You go see how Jess is while I get his breckers organized," Annie told her. "Then we'll put our heads together, see what we can come up with."

CHAPTER 32

"Why did you agree to pay her?" Annie asked as soon as Jesse had finished eating and gone back upstairs.

"Because I can't risk putting Jess through the after-effects if she goes to the media. And you know they'll run with the story, Annie. You *know* they will."

"Yeh, I do. But how do you know she won't try it on again at some point in the future?"

"With what?"

"Oh, next time she'd say you killed her kid. That'd be worth a few quid to old Murdoch's crew."

"God!" Kyra was horrified. She hadn't thought beyond the immediate present.

"She'd do it, too."

"She probably would," Kyra agreed.

"It's bloody blackmail!" Annie sat staring at the tabletop for a moment or two, then said, "Okay, so I'm thick, but why not ask your mum or dad for the money?"

"They don't know anything about Jennifer, for one thing. For another, they're already heartbroken over Jess. I *can't* go to them, Annie. I just can't. Besides, they don't have that kind of cash on hand any more than I do. No. There's only one person I know who could put his hands on this much money in a hurry, even on a holiday."

"Elway," Annie guessed.

Kyra nodded. "He always carries a lot of cash. And I've got no other options. Even if I could access my accounts, to get the money would entail a lot of transactions. It'd take days."

"And, of course, you don't *want* to ask him," Annie said.

"I categorically do not. But I will. There's no one else."

"It's a right bugger."

"To put it mildly. But if I can get rid of that woman, it'll be worth it." Feeling as if she'd taken a physical beating, Kyra went upstairs to check in on Jesse, who was back in bed, listening to music through his headphones. He hadn't yet said anything about his meeting with Jennifer, and Kyra was prepared to wait for him to open the subject for discussion. Until he did (or didn't) she was content to leave it alone.

"Okay, love?" she asked.

He lifted one side of the headphones and said, "I'm okay. Tired, that's all."

"Anything you need?"

He shook his head and went back to his music. She kissed him, then went to use the telephone in her bedroom.

Jimmy was actually at home, and picked up on the second ring.

"Hello," she said, surprised. "I thought you'd probably be off somewhere exotic like Barbados for the holidays."

"Kyra," he said happily. "What a treat to hear from you! And, sorry, but the very *idea* of a place like Barbados makes me shudder. It'd be chockablock with celebs, all playing at being unspeakably casual. No, thank you. I'm quite happy to stay here and wait for the holidays to go away."

"Well," she said, smiling automatically, "as long as you're happy. Look, Jimmy. Are you doing anything right now?" She glanced at the clock. It was almost ten.

"Not a thing. Why?"

"Could I come round and see you? We've got a bit of a situation and I need some help."

"Of course, of course," he said.

"I'd like to come straightaway, if I may."

"Okay. Let me give you directions."

Clad in his usual professorial gear (tan corduroy trousers bagged at the knees and a black V-necked sweater over a white shirt), he greeted her with a quick self-conscious hug before inviting her inside to a vast, all-but-empty living room with a pair of unadorned floor-to-ceiling windows overlooking the Thames. There was a black leather armchair and matching ottoman, with a small table beside it. The only other piece of furniture was a large-screen TV.

A VCR sat on the floor next to it, and all around were stacks of videocassettes. Precarious piles of books and magazines leaned against one wall; some had tumbled to the floor and slid across the bare wood.

"Come in, do," he said eagerly. "It's lovely to see you." Being with her was, on every occasion, like a gift of incredible magnitude. Why, why, *why,* had he behaved so badly, so childishly when he cared so much for her? Because, he all at once understood, that when he was at a distance from her, the possibility that the caring might be misplaced frightened him.

"Lovely to see you, too," she said. And it was true. There was something about his unfettered enthusiasm for her that lifted her spirits. "What a fantastic space, Jimmy!" she said. "But it could do with some furniture."

"No question," he said, and laughed. "It could, indeed. Care to see the rest?"

Curiosity overriding her sense of urgency, she said, "Actually, I would." What difference would a few more minutes make? This place and its barren condition spoke volumes about the man, revealed a depth of loneliness and isolation that touched her.

He showed her the large sterile kitchen that looked as if it had never been used. "I think I boiled water for tea once," he said. "But I may well have imagined that."

She smiled and took a good look at him, starting to remember the reasons why she'd found him so attractive only half a year ago, as he led her back through the echoing expanse of the living room. The first door beyond it opened on to a large, black-and-white-tiled bathroom that seemed to have everything in pairs: side-by-side sinks, toilet and bidet, tub and shower stall, twin medicine cabinets, and two cupboards.

Out into the hall and on to a room with absolutely nothing in it. "Don't know *what* this is," he said, "so I keep the door shut." The room next to that (also with its door shut) contained only awards: framed citations from every conceivable organization even remotely connected to the film industry placed haphazardly in stacks against the walls. And on the floor sat statuettes, his Academy Awards, plaques and trophies: a massive, jumbled collection of international accolades.

How interesting, she thought, that the awards seemed to mean so little to him. Evidently, all that mattered was the work itself. And she knew from firsthand experience just how very much it mattered. Her fondness for him was heightened by the fact that he kept that impressive accumulation of prizes so casually hidden from view. Whatever else he might be, Jimmy was not an ostentatious man.

The master bedroom was almost as big as the living room and it, too, had a pair of windows overlooking the river. There was a neatly made king-size bed, a bedside table, a desk between the windows, and a large chest of drawers on the far wall.

"How long have you lived here?" Kyra asked, thinking—just as she had on that miserably raw, wet day months ago when she'd had to hurry back from location—how good it would be to pull the curtains over the windows and lie down with Jimmy on that big, inviting bed; to indulge in pure sensation and shut out the world for a time.

"Ages," he said, leading the way back to the living room. "Six or seven years, at least."

"I don't suppose you've got a cache of priceless antiques in storage somewhere?"

"Don't I wish." With a frown, he took in the massive near-empty room.

"Some decorator would go wild in here," she said.

"An idea that appeals to me about as much as a trip to Barbados, which is why the place is as you see it. Please do sit down, Kyra," he invited, offering her the armchair and taking the ottoman for himself. "So," he said, "what's going on and how can I help?"

"Jimmy, we've got a desperate situation on our hands and you're the only person I know who could conceivably provide what we need, given the time constraints."

"Desperate?"

"Afraid so," she confirmed, looking away at the far corner of the room and wishing she didn't have to be here to beg this man for money. "Jesse's very ill," she said, her eyes coming back to him. "More than ill. He's dying." Twice in less than twenty-four hours she'd had to say aloud words that resounded like gunshots inside her skull and sent tremors through her very bones.

"Kyra, no!" Instinctively, he reached over to take hold of her hand. "I don't know what to say. Words fail, they truly do." He was shocked and upset, and gripped her hand tightly in both of his. "I am so..." At a complete loss, he could only shake his head in disbelief.

"There's more and it gets worse," she said grimly, then went on to tell him about Jennifer, all the while thinking, *Don't let me down, please don't let me down.*

He listened without interrupting until she finished. Then he gave her hand a squeeze, released it, and stood up, saying, "How much've I got here? Oh, that's stupid," he said impatiently. "Hang on a minute and I'll go look. There's Perrier in the kitchen, if you'd like some. Be right back."

Her relief was so immediate, the loss of fear so sudden that she couldn't move. She felt leaden, dozy, as if she could sleep for a week. Her head actually seemed to fall forward of its own accord and she gazed at her hands, intrigued by the size of them and how aged and ill-cared-for they were—unlike her mother's, which were always smooth and perfectly manicured. But then her mother's hands were part of the package and had to look good. Kyra's were the hands of an artisan, someone who mucked about with inks and watercolors, with pins and razor blades and long-bladed shears; hands that got nicked and jabbed and stained.

"I've got twenty-eight hundred pounds in cash," Jimmy said, returning with two thick wads of notes. "It's a start. And it'll involve a fair amount of to-ing and fro-ing, but I know how we can get most of the rest." He held the money out to her, and for several seconds she could do no more than stare at it.

Then she looked up at him and said, "We should probably get a bag or something to put it in."

"Oh, right! Yes," he said, and looked around as if deciding where a bag might likely be hiding.

Hoisting her leaden body out of the chair, she said, "Jimmy," and he stopped to look back at her. "Thank you for this. I can't begin to tell you—"

"Not necessary," he said. "I'm glad I'm able to help you out. I mean it, Kyra. I haven't behaved very brilliantly with you the past five or six months, so...I'm just glad to help. Okay?"

"Yes, okay."

"I think I've got a small hold-all that'll just do the job. Two minutes. Okay?"

"Yes, of course."

She walked over to the window to look out at the river view, blurred by the rain striking the glass in slanting needles. They'd give Jennifer the money; the heartless bitch would get on a plane and fly out of their lives. In six or seven hours, perhaps less, this horrific interlude would be over.

"Okay," Jimmy said, returning with a small Louis Vuitton satchel. Coming to stand beside her at the window, he said, "I've got at least a dozen bank accounts in sundry countries. And I've got bank cards for all of them. If we start now and go like the blazes, we should be able to withdraw perhaps another five thousand. Possibly more. The cards have different daily limits, but the American ones are good for a thousand dollars a day and I've got four of those."

Turning to look at him, she found herself unable to speak and just let her forehead come to rest on his shoulder. He stroked her hair, saying, "Not to worry, Keer. We'll get it sorted."

Heartened, she lifted her heavy head saying, "I'll drive, shall I?"

"And I'll navigate. Perfect."

"Why do you have so many accounts?" she asked as they were en route to the third bank—this one at the top of Tottenham Court Road.

"It's easier. No matter where I happen to be, I can always get cash. I don't have to fuss with traveler's checks, foreign drafts, that sort of thing."

"Makes sense, I suppose."

"It does, really," he assured her. "Of course, some of the accounts are in banks so obscure I wonder now and then if they'll still be there next time I'm in Portugal or Morocco or wherever. But the system hasn't failed me yet. Okay," he said, pointing. "Just ahead on the left. Lucky for us it's a holiday and there's no traffic to speak of."

"Very," she said, pulling in to the curb and watching as he climbed out of the car and sprinted across the pavement to the bank machine. A surprising vein of kindness and compassion ran through this man. It redeemed him completely. And she would, from this point on, forgive him anything.

Following a brief stop—at Jimmy's insistence—for lunch at a small restaurant on the Kings Road, Kyra phoned home to check in with Annie. Assured everything was all right, they returned to the car, and worked their way to each of the last three banks at which he had accounts. One was on Oxford Street near Selfridges, the next was at the Park Lane end of Piccadilly, and the final one was in the Haymarket.

After stuffing the last of the bank notes into the now-full Vuitton bag, Jimmy tallied up the bank slips. "We've got seven thousand, give or take. Not quite enough."

"It's going to have to be," she said tiredly. "I want you to know that I'm proud of you, Jimmy. You've been so good today—racing hither, thither and yon in the pissing bloody rain, raiding your bank accounts to help me and Jess. You've been kindness personified. And I will never, ever forget it. So." She took a deep breath and said, "Let's go give the bitch her money and be done with it." She leaned across to kiss him, then, with a smile, smoothed the hair back from his forehead. "You've got some fairly heroic instincts hidden beneath all the grotty gear."

"And you've got some fairly fabulous flesh hidden beneath all the outsize garments."

"I'll tell you something," she said. "If the timing weren't so awful, I'd like nothing better than to go back to that empty cavern you call home and make love to you."

"Could we do it when the timing improves?" he asked, with an impish smile.

"You may consider it as a positive eventuality." Putting the car into gear, she quoted, "'The rule is, jam tomorrow, and jam yesterday—but never jam today.'"

"'Soup of the evening, beautiful soup!'"

"Well done, our Jimmy!" She smiled over at him, then turned her attention back to the road as she sped along the deserted streets toward the Regent Palace.

"I'll wait in the car," Jimmy said diplomatically. "If you don't mind leaving me the keys, I'll get a newspaper and come right back."

On edge and determined to put an end to this ugly episode, Kyra walked through the lobby to the desk. The same clerk she'd dealt with the day before was on duty and, recognizing Kyra, said, "Afraid you've missed her, dearie."

"Pardon?"

"Your friend. She checked out, left for the airport about an hour ago."

"She *left?*" This was so unexpected, Kyra didn't know what to think.

"She may well have made her flight, though I'd be willing to wager she didn't. Even without the usual traffic, it'd be touch-and-go, what with a five o'clock departure." The woman patiently waited for Kyra to say something. When she didn't, the clerk turned away and busied herself with a stack of registration cards.

At last, Kyra said, "Thank you," and went went back through the lobby and out to the car.

"That was quick," Jimmy said, closing the newspaper.

"She wasn't there. She's checked out."

"She's *gone?*"

"Gone," Kyra repeated. "This doesn't feel right."

"No," Jimmy said. "It certainly doesn't. What do we do now?"

"I don't know. It makes no sense," she said, looking out through the rain-drenched window. After a moment, she held the Vuitton bag out to him. "I don't suppose we'll be needing the money now."

"Hang on to it. She may well yet turn up asking for it."

"I don't think so. The desk clerk said she was hurrying to make a flight. Why would she just give up and leave without getting what she came for? I have an awful feeling this isn't over yet."

"All the more reason to hold on to the bag for a day or two, in the event she does turn up wanting the money."

"Okay, maybe you're right." She reached back to drop the bag behind her seat, saying, "I'll run you back."

"I can just as easily get a taxi," he offered. "You're probably anxious to get back to Jesse."

"No, I'll take you home."

Placing a hand on her arm, he said, "Maybe she really has gone and it's over. Let's hope that's the case." She nodded and turned on the wipers. "Kyra, might I stop by to visit with Jess?" he asked.

Turning to look at him, she said, "I think he'd like that very much, Jimmy."

"Would tomorrow be all right?"

"I should think so. Ring me in the morning and we'll see."

Upon arriving home, Kyra dropped her handbag and the Vuitton satchel in the front hall and went straight upstairs. Hearing her,

Annie emerged from the living room and hurriedly followed, saying Kyra's name so quietly that Kyra didn't hear.

Kyra knocked at Jesse's door and then opened it to stop on the threshhold, thunderstruck. Jesse lay asleep in the arms of a naked girl who looked over, held a finger to her lips, then signaled she'd be right there and indicated Kyra should close the door.

Kyra did just that, backing away to stand in the hallway, trying to make sense of what she'd seen. "Come downstairs," Annie said, taking Kyra by the arm and pulling her toward the stairs.

"Did I just see what I think I did?" Kyra asked, looking up the stairs as she removed her coat in the front hall.

"That's my mate Joan. I would've explained, but you just went barreling up there. Come on. I'll make us a cuppa and we'll talk."

Flopping gracelessly into a chair in the kitchen, Kyra sighed and said, "You're going to tell me I've been blind to something terribly obvious."

"Yeh, a bit," Annie said from the counter where she was plugging in the kettle. "He's a thirteen-year-old *boy*, Keer, and he knows he's gonna die. We talk, him and me, and I thought it was right for him at least to know how a female *feels*. And Joan's not a slag, not in her heart. She wanted to do this, asked if she could. They've been together most of the day, cuddling mostly and talking about computers, of all bloody things. Don't be mad at any of us, Keer, please. We didn't mean any harm."

"I'm not mad. I just feel stupid."

"You can't think of everything," Annie said reasonably.

"Maybe not, but I should've realized..."

"So you didn't, and I did. Does it matter?"

"No. Not really."

"She's a good girl, is Joan."

"I'm sure she is."

"Oh! Your mum rang, so did Robert. He wanted to know would it be all right for him to come round tomorrow. I said you'd get back to him."

"Right. I will."

"And Dr. Kendall phoned to say she'll be visiting Jess here from now on, and if you've got any questions you're to ring her at home this evening. She left her number."

"Right," Kyra said again, overcome by that same dozy feeling she'd had that morning in Jimmy's flat. They were beginning the countdown now, she thought; numbering the days, hours, minutes Jesse had left. Wearily, she leaned her elbow on the table and rested her cheek on her upheld hand. She could easily have gone to sleep right there; her eyes were actually starting to close, as light footsteps pattered down the stairs and Joan came down the hallway.

Tall but daintily constructed, she gave the impression of being smaller than she actually was, but she still had the untainted aspect to her features that Annie had captured so effectively in the portrait. In jeans and a pale pink pullover, thick white socks, she was carrying her shoes. Her long light brown hair gleamed; she wore not a speck of makeup, and her blue-gray eyes were large and fearful. She looked young and wholesome; she looked indeed, as Annie had said, like a good girl. Approaching Kyra hesitantly, she offered her hand, saying, "I'm Joan. I expect you're well-peeved with me."

Kyra looked at her a moment longer, then stood up and closed the young woman into her arms. "I'm not in the least angry," she said, releasing her. "I'm sure you've made Jess very happy."

"Well—" Joan offered a shy but relieved smile "—let's just say he's asked if I'll come again."

"Tea's up," Annie announced.

"Oh, lovely," Joan said, sliding into a chair, "I could do with some."

Kyra sat back down and looked from Joan to Annie then back at Joan. "If it's what Jess wants, then you're to come whenever you like. How very kind you are," Kyra said, studying Joan's eyes. It had been a day replete with kindness, and with good luck, too. Jennifer was gone; perhaps she'd had a last-minute attack of conscience. Still, Kyra found that nearly impossible to believe. The other shoe had yet to fall.

"He's a lovely lad, i'n't he?" Joan said, her smile singularly sweet. "And I'd really like to come back 'n' see him. It's not like as if anything *important* happened, if you catch my meaning, what with him bein' so sick 'n' all. It's more about him wantin' something—personal, sort of. Today's been one of the nicest times I've ever had, to be honest. Like bein' a kid again myself and knowin' how it might've been, if things'd been different for me. You know?"

Kyra nodded, thinking how wise and sensible Annie was to have done this both for Jesse and for Joan. She'd given Jesse a measure of adulthood while at the same time returning to Joan some of her lost childhood. "I understand."

"You're ever so nice, you are. Annie said you were and it's true."

"I've got Jess's salad done for later," Annie said, "and I thought I'd make us a treat: Annie's famous eggs and chips. If you don't mind Joan staying for a bit."

Kyra laughed softly. "I don't mind. Look, I'd better go return those calls." She got up, saying, "You're welcome to stay the night, Joan. Otherwise, I'll run you home after dinner."

"Oh, I'd love to stay," Joan said eagerly. "It's a smashin' house, most beautiful place I've ever seen."

"Then you must stay. How long until the famous eggs and chips?"

Annie checked the time. "An hour?"

"Right. See you shortly," Kyra said, and headed upstairs to the telephone.

CHAPTER 33

"You're not upset, are you? About Joan, I mean?" Jesse asked later, when he was settled in his bed for the night.

"Not a bit," Kyra said, smoothing the hair back from his forehead. He was faintly flushed, his skin warm but not feverish. "She's a sweet girl."

"Isn't she *super!*" he said with a flash of his old exuberance. "And really bright, Keer. I've promised to teach her how to use the computer. She's very keen to learn."

"That's good of you, love."

"Not really. It's just something I know about and it's not all that difficult to teach someone the basics." His energy suddenly, visibly, drained away, as he asked, "What did you think of Jennifer?"

"Not much," she answered carefully. "What did *you* think?"

"She's pathetic," he said without inflection, his eyelids beginning to droop. "Completely pathetic."

"You sleep now," Kyra said softly, bending to kiss his cheek. "I'll see you in the morning."

"'Night, Keer," he murmured, shifting onto his side.

"'Night, Jess," she said, pausing to turn on the night light before leaving.

The other shoe dropped at seven-forty the next morning when the telephone rang. She knew at once from the shaky way Jimmy spoke that something was very wrong.

"Kyra," he said, "I popped out to pick up the morning paper...." He stopped and she could almost hear him trying to package his words, to assemble them in a fashion that might make them more palatable.

"She gave the press conference after all," Kyra guessed.

"No. She gave the *Sun* an exclusive. May I come round with the paper?"

"Please," she said leadenly, "I'd appreciate it." She hung up and went downstairs to make a pot of coffee.

Only moments later, Annie came running down the stairs in her night gear—men's boxer shorts, oversized T-shirt and thick socks—asking, "Who was that on the blower? What's happening?"

"Jimmy's on his way with the newspaper. It seems Jennifer gave the *Sun* an exclusive."

"Oh, bloody, bloody hell! What do we do?"

"Wait until we see the paper, then decide."

Joan appeared in the doorway behind Annie. "Is there trouble?" she asked.

"Yeh," Annie said furiously. "Big bloody trouble, from the sound of it."

"I'll go home," Joan said quietly, and Kyra was again struck by her sensitivity, by her deciding that her presence in the house might be damaging.

Kyra sighed and said, "You needn't. The worst that can happen's already happened. It might be better if you're both here, to keep Jess distracted."

"Right, then!" Annie said. "We'll take over in here, organize Jess's breckers while you go get dressed."

Kyra looked down at herself—the ancient worn-thin night-gown and shabby robe—and said, "Yes, thank you," and hurried upstairs. There might well be media people waiting when Jimmy arrived. If she opened the door in her nightclothes, she'd be plastered all over the afternoon editions below some highly suggestive headlines.

As she had a quick wash—water sent splashing everywhere by uncoordinated hands—and brushed her teeth, she imagined the possible headlines, and rage, pure and hurried as a downhill stream in flood, poured through her system, leaving her in a state of glacial coldness.

The doorbell went just as Annie handed her a mug of coffee and Annie said, "I'll go. You drink some of that."

Kyra stood in the middle of the kitchen, swallowing a mouthful of the hot, strong coffee as she watched Annie greet Jimmy and

take his coat before stepping aside so he could make his way purposefully toward Kyra.

Seeing his intent, she put the mug down on the table and accepted his embrace—heartfelt and funereal in its sorrowful intensity—then she silently broke away, saying, "Do sit down, Jimmy,"
and poured coffee for him before joining him at the table.

"I wish I didn't have to show it to you," he said sadly, running
a hand over his rain-damp hair before pushing the folded tabloid
across the tabletop to her as the telephone rang and Annie sang out
from the living room, "I'll pick up in here."

Dry-mouthed even after another swallow of coffee, Kyra extended a forefinger and flipped the paper open. God! It was even
worse than she'd feared.

The banner headline read BESTSELLING CHILD AUTHOR NEAR
DEATH. Below was a photo of Jesse behind the microphone at his book
launch; a beaming, happy Jesse looking so much younger than his
age.

She lifted her head to look across at Jimmy, who was watching
her every move with mournful eyes, then she went back to the
newspaper.

Jennifer was identified as the suffering birth mother, whose
quoted descriptions of how Jesse looked—tiny and lost in a sea of
printed bedding, terribly frail—were quoted extensively. The piece
was structured to make it seem as if Kyra were somehow responsible for the dire state of Jesse's health. "When I gave custody of
him to his grandmother I thought he'd be well looked after," Jennifer was quoted as saying. "They had the money to take care of
him at a point in my life when I didn't. All this time, I thought he
was in good hands. Then, I arrive to find my boy on death's
doorstep. If I'd known this would happen, I'd never have left him
with her."

Kyra read to the end, then laid the newspaper face down on the
table and drank the last of her coffee, aware of Jimmy's eyes on
her. But when she tried to speak, nothing emerged. She had to
clear her throat, pour herself more coffee, before she could begin
again. And, just as she was about to try to articulate her feelings,
Annie appeared in the doorway, saying, "It's Allison from
Beauchamp-Dobbs."

"Okay," Kyra said, and walked over to pick up the kitchen extension.

Allison said, "Word has it they paid five thousand for an exclusive but their legal people wouldn't let them use most of the original feature. So this is the watered-down version. I don't know how much of it is true, but I'm afraid the stampede's on and you're going to find crowds massing on your doorstep any moment now."

"Thanks for letting me know," Kyra said hoarsely.

"I'm so very sorry, Kyra. Jess doesn't deserve this. Neither do you. Is this creature really his mother?"

"Unfortunately, yes."

"It's beyond believing that a woman would do this to her own son. Look, I'll let you go. Give Jess my love, will you? I'm so mad and sad...." Allison's voice cracked.

"I will. Thank you for letting me know, Allison. Take care."

Allison choked out a good-bye and Kyra put the phone down, turning to see three pairs of eyes now waiting expectantly.

"We're to be subjected to a full-scale media bombardment," Kyra told them. "They're probably going to start arriving any minute now."

"Wonderful," Annie said glumly.

"Look, would the two of you mind keeping Jess company for a few minutes while Jimmy and I talk? Jess is bound to be wondering what's going on and I want to tell him, show him *that*." She pointed at the newspaper with a trembling finger.

"Does he have to see it?" Joan asked softly.

"I've never kept things from him. I can't start now."

"Oh!" Joan gazed at her wonderingly, as if the notion of a parent who confided in her child was comparable to a vision at Lourdes.

"This is my mate, Joan, Mr. Elway," Annie said, nudging Joan with her elbow.

"Hi." Joan stepped over to offer her hand to Jimmy and actually made a little curtsey. "Ever so pleased to meet you, sir. You make lovely films. I've seen them all."

With gentlemanly courtesy, Jimmy got to his feet, shook her hand and said, "Thank you very much. Good to meet you, Joan."

"Right. Off we go now," Annie said, taking her friend's arm and towing her away.

Jimmy stood for a second or two, watching them go down the hallway, then sat down again, saying, "What an extraordinary face!"

"She looks like a nun."

"*Exactly!* Extraordinary," he repeated, looking over his shoulder as if expecting Joan to be still in the doorway. Then, remembering what had prompted this visit, he said, "I should go, let you get on."

"They'll be out there," she warned. "You're in the thick of it now."

He shrugged. "I'll deal with it. But what about you?"

"I'll deal with it, too. It's just so bloody *unfair!*" she erupted. Her self-control was at a dangerously low level as she tried to think of what they might do to shield Jesse, to maintain a level of calm in the household so that his final days would be peaceful. But all she could picture was everyone—Robert, her family, Jimmy, Dr. Kendall—having to fight their way through the noisy throng blocking access to the door, shouting questions, shooting photos, doing everything short of actually touching anyone.

"Perhaps you could move Jess," Jimmy offered. "Take him somewhere quiet."

"How? They'd track us like a pack of bloodhounds. And it's not as if they don't know where every last one of us lives. There's no place we *could* go. And why should we have to? That's the part that drives me wild."

"They don't know where I live, Kyra."

"You don't actually believe that, do you, Jimmy?" she asked, wondering yet again about the degree of his naiveté.

"No, they really don't. It's long and complicated, but only a couple of people know about the flat."

"Even so. It's generous of you to offer, but this is Jess's home, he's comfortable here. I *won't* move him. It's his right to be left in peace in his own home."

"They're starting to arrive," Annie said from the front hall.

"You'd better go, Jimmy," Kyra said.

"I'll stay if I can help. And I would like to visit with Jess."

"Go now and ring me later. We'll arrange it."

"Whatever you think is best," he said, getting to his feet but plainly reluctant to leave.

"For now this is best. I've still got to talk to Jess, tell him." She put her arms around Jimmy and, as on the previous day, rested her head on his shoulder. His embrace, protective and solid, helped

calm the low-level tremors that had been shaking her since his telephone call. "You've changed, Jimmy," she said, lifting her head to
study him, wishing for one lunatic moment that she could seal the
house and keep everyone inside: a safe, caring little unit. Eventually the media people would leave, fed up with waiting for someone to emerge, and then...and then what? No matter what any of
them did, Jess would still die.

"I've had to," he said simply. "I want to keep your friendship."

"You've never lost it." She kissed him on the mouth, then said,
"Ring me later. We'll sort out a time for you to visit." Holding his
hand, she went with him to the front hall where Annie was waiting with his coat. "You might as well take this." Kyra picked up
the Vuitton satchel and handed it to him.

Looking fairly bereft, Jimmy got his coat on, took the satchel
and stood for a moment as if there were so many things he wanted
to say that he couldn't speak at all. At last, he turned away. Annie
said, "Good-bye, Mr. Elway," then quickly opened the door, and
he slipped through it. At once, voices outside were raised, bellowing questions at him as Jimmy marched to his car, got in and
sped off.

"What'll we do?" Annie asked as someone rang the doorbell,
then knocked on the door. "Piss off!" she muttered, waiting for
Kyra to answer.

"First things first. I've got to show Jesse the article, explain. If
you wouldn't mind, perhaps you could ring everyone, warn them
what to expect when they get here."

"Yeh. I'll do that."

"Where's Joan?" Kyra thought to ask.

"Gone home. Nipped over the rear fence, went through the
neighbor's garden into Pitt Street."

"She didn't have to do that."

"She thought she did. Joan's dead sensitive. She wouldn't want
anybody wondering who she was, why she was here. And you
know what that lot're like." She hooked a thumb over her shoulder, indicating the gathering media people outside. "They'd make
a point of finding out who she was."

"I suppose so, but still..." Joan's leaving made Kyra sad, and even
angrier. She wanted to lash out, strike back, but could only try to

choke down her upset like a lump of gristly meat that wanted to stick in her throat.

"She'll be back," Annie said, a hand on Kyra's arm. "Later, after dark, she'll come in through Pitt Street, climb the fence. It's arranged. She promised Jess."

"My God," Kyra whispered. "It's turned into a complete horror show. I wanted this to be..."

Enigmatically, Annie said, "Somebody'll think of something," and went along to Kyra's office to start phoning.

Kyra knocked at his door, then walked over to sit on the side of the bed. Jess was sitting up, supported by half a dozen pillows, with several books and the remote controls for his stereo system and small TV set close at hand.

"How do you feel?" she asked. He seemed to be shrinking hourly, daily; succumbing to a deepening lassitude that made it seem as if the slightest effort required monumental determination and energy.

"Just tired, as usual. What's going on, Keer? Why've the vultures gathered outside again?"

"It's about this," she said, giving him the newspaper.

His eyes stayed on her, searching for meanings.

"I'm sorry, Jess." Her mouth too dry, her body still in the grip of those continuing tremors, she watched him pick up the newspaper.

His brow furrowed at the sight of the headline, his mouth going tight, but he didn't say anything until he'd read the entire piece. Then, with a burst of angry energy, he threw the newspaper to the floor, exclaiming, "Why did she *do* this?"

"She got five thousand pounds for that piece of fiction."

"But I *gave* her what she wanted."

"What?" Without being aware of having moved, Kyra was suddenly on her feet.

"She uses heroin. Has done forever. She told me she wanted to go into a rehab program, get cleaned up. I felt sorry for her."

Shaking visibly now, fists clenched, she asked, "What exactly did you give her, Jess?"

"A check for two thousand, made out to cash."

Two thousand, made out to cash. Unable to stop herself, Kyra's head fell back, and a shriek of pure rage ripped from her throat.

Turning, she drove her fist into the wall, then erupted into loud sobbing as she bent forward over her instantly aching hand.

"Don't be angry with me!" Jesse begged in his grown-man voice, climbing out of bed and coming to wind his little-boy arms around her. "Please, Keer. I didn't mean to do anything wrong."

Annie came tearing up the stairs and stopped in the hall, staring in, heart drumming as she tried to make sense of the scene.

Trying but failing to regain control, all Kyra could do was hold him tightly, crying noisily—as if she were the child—her entire body shaking, until she suddenly saw how badly she was frightening him. Still unable to utter anything coherent, she carried him back to the bed where he continued to cling to her, pleading. "*Please* say you're not angry! *Please!*"

"Not with you," she managed to tell him finally. "God!" she cried, working to contain the fury that still had her in physical spasms. "That evil, *evil* bitch! Not you, Jess. *Not you.*" Wiping her face on her sleeve, aware of the spreading pain in her hand, she eased him back into his nest of pillows. "God, *God!* I want to *kill* her!"

His eyes round as the pieces slotted together for him, he now got angry again. Too weak to give vent to it, he pulled several tissues from the box on the bedside table and gave them to Kyra. "I should've known better," he fumed. "I should've known. You promise you're not angry with me?"

Stepping into the room, Annie said, "Known what? What's happened, Jess?"

"I gave Jennifer a check for two thousand pounds."

"That *cow!*" Kyra's extraordinary behavior making sense now, Annie was furious. "The filthy cow!"

Belatedly hearing what Jess had told her, Kyra said, "Heroin?"

"Forever," he repeated.

Upon hearing this, Annie quietly slipped away.

Taking his hand, Kyra said, "I promise I'm not angry with you. It's just that...I love you, Jess. I *love* you, and she came here and *used* you, took advantage of you, and I want to kill her for that, just the way I wanted to kill her when Glenna and I tried to give you a bath that morning after she left you. Do you remember?"

"I remember," he said solemnly.

"Seeing what'd been done to you...I'd have killed her then. I want to kill her now. No one has the right to do to *anyone* the things she's done to you. But she shows up here and takes money from you. It's unbelievable!"

He sank deeper into the pillows and Kyra stretched out at his side, drawing him closer to her.

"It was only a matter of curiosity, my agreeing to see her," he explained. "I wondered if she'd changed at all. But she hadn't, not a bit. She was simply older. And when she asked me for some money, I thought it was worth it just to be rid of her." He turned his head and looked at the newspaper on the floor. "She sold me again," he said almost inaudibly, then, with a sigh, directed his eyes to the window. "The only decent thing she ever did was giving me to you. And she only did that because her boyfriend, Mario, was livid when he found out she was using heroin and how she was getting the money to pay for it."

Looking back at Kyra, he said, "He came home early from work. He went wild when he saw what was happening. The next day she brought me to you."

"But I thought she was going to California with her boyfriend."

Jesse shook his head. "She was going back to New Jersey. I can still remember the telephone number. She'd made me memorize the address and telephone number, just in case, and there was always a nickel in my pocket.... Sometimes she'd take me to places and forget to come back for me. Then, once I was out on the street, I'd have to find someone to dial the telephone for me because I couldn't reach it. If they asked any questions, I always said what I'd been told: 'I'm locked out. My mother's just upstairs. She'll come down and let me in.' No one ever refused. I always hoped someone would get suspicious and call the police, but nobody did." His eyes clicking back into focus, he said, "I was glad when Mario found out. I was scared, because he was so... He beat that one—beat him bloody, then threw him down the stairs. I thought he'd beat me, too. But he didn't. He hit *her*, though. Once, very hard, so hard she fell down. I was glad about that, and even more scared. I *wanted* someone to hit her. But I thought it was my fault, so he was bound to hit me, too. He didn't, though. He just dressed me and gave me a sad look, as if there wasn't a single word he could think of to say to me. Then he turned and started screaming at her— some of it in Italian, some in English. He screamed so hard, I remember seeing the cords standing out in his neck, and his temples were throbbing. And the next day, it was over. He drove us to the bus terminal on his way to work and he said something to me in Italian. Good-bye, I think. Or good luck. I tried for a long time to remember the words so I could look them up. But I couldn't remember." He sighed again and fell silent.

"I wish you'd told me," Kyra said softly.

He looked at her for a long moment, then said, "I couldn't. I was afraid you wouldn't like me anymore."

Drawing him closer still, she said, "Will you tell me something, Jess?"

"You could ask me anything. I wouldn't mind."

She smiled at that and kissed his forehead. "Actually, it's two somethings. At the beginning, why did you sleep every night in the closet? And why didn't you speak?"

Close-to his eyes seemed to grow deeper and darker; his energy was visibly draining away as he thought about how to answer. Then, his voice scarcely more than a whisper, he said, "If no one could see me or hear me, I thought I might be safe. I was trying, in the only way I knew how," he elaborated, "to be invisible."

Dr. Kendall was forced to park several blocks away and was in no mood to deal with the mob she discovered blocking access to the house. Arriving at the perimeter of the crowd, in a voice that would have done a parade ground sergeant major proud, she bellowed, *"Out of my way at once!"* and in the ensuing silence the startled photographers and journalists stepped aside. She was up the stairs and inside the house before they had time to begin wondering who she might be.

"I suggest you ring the police right now," she told Kyra. "They'll put that pack of fools behind a barricade."

"Why would they do that?" Kyra asked, so worn out she could scarcely function.

"Because there's a dying child in the house, for God's sake! Where's your bloody telephone? I'll ring them myself. And what've you done to your hand? I don't care for the look of that at all. Get her some ice!" she told Annie. "I'll see to it once I've dealt with those jackals cluttering up the pavement."

Within an hour, a barricade had been positioned on the opposite side of the street and, with a police officer in attendance, the thinned-down group remained behind it.

CHAPTER 34

"Nothing broken. Just keep that ice on it," Vita Kendall said as she finished examining Kyra's hand. "You need a break," she declared. "You're clearly not yourself."

Seeing the kindness and concern in the doctor's gray eyes, Kyra said, "It's been a rough few days."

"It's only going to get rougher, from your point of view. He's in the end stage. From this point on, Jess will sleep for longer and longer periods—"

"Until he simply fails to awaken," Kyra finished the sentence.

"That's about it. Everything's shutting down."

"But he won't be in any pain?"

Dr. Kendall shook her head. "We'll keep him comfortable. But keeping him comfortable is contingent in large measure on your state of mind, Kyra. Jess's attachment to you... It's formidable, to say the least."

"It's no less than mine to him," Kyra said, her hand going numb from the ice.

"That was obvious from our first meeting," the woman said with a smile. "So get out of here for a few hours. Go for a walk, visit a friend. Find your equilibrium. And don't do any more of this." She indicated Kyra's hand. "You're angry. Anyone would be, under the circumstances. And, believe it or not, I understand how making a new pain helps us deal with the ongoing one. It provides an actual physical focus, lets us turn outward for a time. But it's pointless. All you've got now is a sore hand to go along with your sore heart."

Kyra laughed tearfully. "You're a very smart woman."

"Yes, I am," Vita Kendall agreed. "And I'm a mother, too. Nothing is ever going to be harder than this. So do yourself a favor and get out for a while. You need it, if you're to get through this all in one piece. Now," she said, getting to her feet, "I'll go up and see Jess."

"She's right, you know," Annie said from the counter where she stood, holding a mug of hot tea with both hands. "Robert's not coming until three. Your mum said she'd be here between six-thirty and seven with your dad. She's collecting him from the train. And Joan'll be back once it's dark." She paused, watching Kyra adjust the tea towel of ice wrapped around her hand. "Jimmy's waiting for you to ring him."

Kyra turned to look over at her.

"He's been brilliant the past couple of days," Annie said, as if commenting on the weather.

"Yes, he has," Kyra agreed.

"Ring him. He's set to pick you up in Pitt Street whenever you say."

"I see." Kyra had to smile. "And how am I to get over the fence?"

"Joanie and I rigged a stile. One of the wrought iron garden chairs on this side. And your neighbor, Mrs. Owens, was ever so chuffed to be helping out—loaned us her kitchen step stool for her side. Easy as pie."

"I feel like shit," Kyra said flatly.

"Really?" Annie teased. "I hadn't noticed. Go on, ring Jimmy. He can have his visit with Jess when he brings you back."

"You've got it all arranged, haven't you?"

"Pretty much. Go on, Keer. I'll hold the fort 'til you get back."

Kyra continued to sit at the table, gazing at the elfin woman across the room.

"What?" Annie said. When she didn't get a response, she asked worriedly, "What's wrong?"

"Sorry. I was just thinking about what you said, that we don't meet people accidentally. There's always a reason, but sometimes it takes us a while to see it."

"And what're you seeing?"

"You," Kyra said. "You're a gift."

"Yeh." Annie grinned, then emitted her cartoonlike laugh. "Everybody says so."

"I'm going to ring Jimmy, then go up and attempt to make myself presentable." She deposited the makeshift icepack in the sink before bending to kiss the top of Annie's head. "I love you, you conniving little sprite."

"And I love you, your titanic prominence."

Smiling, Kyra headed for the stairs.

"Have you eaten?" Jimmy asked once Kyra was belted into the passenger seat of the Land Rover.

"No, and I'm very hungry."

"Anywhere in particular you fancy?"

"No. Just someplace discreet."

"All right. We'll bag one of the private dining rooms at Suntory and eat sushi and tempura. And, of course, beautiful soup."

She leaned across the seat to kiss him, then sat back, saying, "There's going to be a houseful of people. We'll have to pick up some food on our way back."

"I'll ring Ginny from the restaurant, get her to arrange it." Glancing over, he asked, "Do you want to tell me how you hurt your hand?"

"Later," she said, looking out at the shop windows as they headed down Kensington Church Street. It was the fourth day of heavy rain and suddenly she longed for sunlight. But at least she was out. And Dr. Kendall was right: it did help. "Thanks for this, Jimmy," she said, looking over at him.

"I'd do anything for you," he said matter-of-factly.

She didn't know how to respond to this. Her brows drew together as she studied him.

"I would," he said, then turned his attention to the traffic.

Not ten minutes after Kyra left, there was a knocking at the front door. Certain it was one of the more intrepid journalists, Annie marched over, opened the door, took in the man standing there—black leather jacket, blue jeans, heavy lace-up boots, a headful of curly pale blue hair, carrying a briefcase—and said, "Piss off!" as she started closing the door.

With a smile that created a dimple in his left cheek, he said in a startlingly upper-crust accent, "Very nicely delivered!"

"Glad you like it. Now piss off!" Again, she began to close the door.

"I'm Stephen Binder, Jess's solicitor. He asked me to stop by."

"Oops. You'd better come in then," she said, grabbing his wet sleeve and pulling him inside. "I'm Annie Cooper. Give us your jacket." She held out her hands for it. "Fancy some tea or coffee?"

"Annie Cooper," he said, placing his briefcase on the floor as he got out of his jacket, gray-green eyes glimmering with amusement. He wore an expensive-looking dark green Shetland V-neck over a white T-shirt. "*Ann-ie Coo-per.* Tea would be lovely."

"*Ste-phen Bin-der,* come to the kitchen."

"Tell me you're not engaged, married or otherwise occupied," he said, following her.

"Aren't you the cheeky one!"

"At least tell me you're over the age of consent."

"Sit there!" She pointed to one of the chairs and went to fill the kettle. "What's this, then?" she asked over her shoulder. "A census?"

"Single respondent," he said, leaning with both elbows on the table, beaming at her. "Very important data."

"I'm probably older than you are. You look about twelve." She hoisted herself up to sit on the edge of the counter.

"I get that a lot," he said. "I'm twenty-eight. And you're what, twenty?"

"Does this routine usually work for you?" she asked, amused.

"Don't know. It's the first tryout. Deadly serious, of course. Because if you are engaged, married or otherwise occupied, I'll be going home today with a broken heart."

"We can't have that, can we? I wouldn't be able to live with myself."

"That's right, you wouldn't. So are you? And if not, will you come out to breakfast, lunch or dinner with me on a day of your choosing?"

"You're a right nutter."

"That's as may be, but will you?"

"We'll see. You not half bad, in a deranged sort of way."

"Don't be fooled. Underneath this gear beats the heart of a true practitioner of the law, in a three-piece from Savile Row, with all the appropriate accessories."

She laughed and said, "Good routine, Binder. It may well work for you. You're sure it's the first tryout?"

"Hand to heart. I adore you."

"Yeh, right." Jumping down from the counter, she set about organizing the tea things. After a few moments she said quietly, "It'll have to wait. I can't be going anywhere now."

"Oh, quite," he said, and she turned to see that his expression had gone sober. "Sorry. That was feckless."

"Not to worry. Known Jess long?" she asked, warming the teapot.

"Almost four years," he said. "He was one of my first clients—and, of course, my youngest. Hired me because he liked my hair, he said. It was green then."

"Blue's better," she said. "So if you're old mates 'n' all, how come you weren't at the launch party?"

"Would we have met then?"

"Most likely. So where were you?"

"Stuck in a jumbo that was four hours late."

"Coming from where?" she asked, spooning tea into the pot.

"New York."

"Another client?"

"That's right. I specialize in entertainment."

"I'll bet you do." She chortled, filling the pot with boiling water. "You probably want a biccie, too. Right?"

"Yes, please, Ann-ie Coo-per."

"Don't grovel, Ste-phen. It's unbecoming to a member of the legal establishment with the three-piece and what-have-yous. Milk and sugar?"

"Just milk, please. How is he?"

Annie looked over. "D'you really care about him or is this just polite chat?"

"When you get to know me better, you'll understand that I don't do polite chat. Jess is my kid brother, my clever uncle and my best mate. I love Jess."

"Yeh," Annie said quietly. "Me, too."

Annie and Joan were upstairs watching TV with Jesse. Kyra and her parents had just finished the Indian dinner Ginny had had delivered to the house when there was an urgent knocking at the front door.

"We saw the *Sun* in Paris this afternoon and got the first flight back," Kyle said the instant Kyra opened the door.

"Wait until you're *inside*, please," Damien said, pushing Kyle through the door. "I'm sorry, Keer," he apologized, giving her a hug. "He's been completely useless since he saw the newspaper this afternoon. Not a word of explanation—" he looked accusingly at Kyle "—just a mad scramble to get back here. I am not fond of your brother at the moment and it has *not* been my favorite day." He draped his wet jacket over the doorknob and went through to greet Richard and Octavia, bending to embrace each of them before dropping into a chair with a sigh. All three of them looked over, waiting to see what was going to happen.

Realizing that they were in for a scene, Kyra draped Kyle's coat over the banister and said, "Let's move out of the hall, please, Kyle." Like a robot, he walked into the living room and stopped a few feet from the dining room. Kyra pulled the sliding doors closed, then remained just inside, watching her brother position himself as if onstage. She hadn't seen Kyle behave this way since they were teenagers: utterly self-absorbed, so caught up in his passion of the moment that no one else seemed to exist for him. It angered her, just as it obviously did Damien who, she suspected, had never before seen this aspect of Kyle's personality. It wasn't attractive.

"Is this *true?*" he demanded of Kyra, pulling the article from his pocket and waving it in her direction.

"Bits of it," she answered, tensed in anticipation of yet more drama. She wished her father would swing into directorial mode and shout "Cut!" But that wouldn't happen. Everyone was waiting to see where the scene was going to go—except for Damien who simply looked travel-worn and exasperated.

"Why has no one ever told me?" Kyle now stood in the dining room doorway about two feet from the table and looked from Kyra to his mother and father, then back at Kyra.

"Told you what?" Kyra asked tiredly. "If you're hungry, Damien, there's tons of food left."

"I'm *very* hungry, thank you. He's been playing the drama queen for hours now. Wouldn't *hear* of stopping for something to eat."

"I'll get some plates." Kyra went to the kitchen, wishing she could just continue right on out the back door; she'd climb over the fence and walk away from the lot of them, sneak back later when the family had gone home. Then she and Annie and Joan could, in harmonious accord, shape themselves into a protective cocoon around Jess.

"Just what is it no one's ever told you?" Octavia asked, as Kyle paced back and forth a few feet from the table. "Could you stop that, please, and sit down?"

"Sorry, no." Kyle kept pacing, the article bunched in his fist.

"What's got into you, for God's sake?" Richard barked. "Sit down at once!"

As if deaf to everything but the noise of his own mental machinery, Kyle kept marching back and forth. "This woman, Jesse's 'birth mother,' referred to *you* as *her* mother," he said accusingly, coming to a stop and pointing at Kyra as she reappeared with plates and cutlery. "And to Jess as your grandson."

"She has done from the outset. I've always considered it a bizarre mistake. Why should it matter that no one told you? I'm really not in the mood for this, Kyle," she warned. "It's been a horrible day, and if you insist on behaving like a glue-sniffing adolescent you'll have to leave. Either calm down and say what you have to say, or go home!"

"But it's *not* a mistake. That's the thing. It's staggering to think it's been almost ten years since you adopted Jesse, and I knew nothing about the circumstances."

"What the hell are you *talking* about?" Kyra demanded. "God, this is tiresome! Really, Kyle, I simply won't indulge you. Get it said or go home!"

Abruptly he swung into the defensive and looked over at her with a boyishly fearful expression. "You'll probably never speak to me again."

Octavia said, "Kyle, you're acting like a madman. Get on with it before one of us strikes you."

"My sentiments precisely," Damien said in an undertone.

"It happened the summer of fifty-four, when we came to stay with you in New York," Kyle told his mother, then turned to Kyra. "You remember that summer, don't you?"

"For God's sake, Kyle!"

"I hung about the theater every day, watching the rehearsals, while you went off to the museums and galleries."

"Kyle," Octavia said impatiently, "get *on* with it!"

"I got involved with the ingenue in your play," he confessed in a rush. "We had an affair."

"Oh, wonderful," Damien murmured, helping himself to some chicken. "It's to be a full-blown melodrama."

"Would you stop the running commentary!" Kyle snapped. "This is very serious."

"I hadn't guessed," Damien said with chilly sarcasm. "However, given what I've had to contend with for the past four hours, I've earned the right to comment."

"Then do it silently!" Kyle said shrilly. "I'm upset enough as it is."

Thinking back, Octavia said, "The boring blonde with the cheekbones who delivered her lines like someone announcing flight arrivals and departures?"

"That's not how I saw her, but yes. She thought I was older than I was." Kyle hurried on, beads of sweat appearing on his upper lip. "And I let her think it. I was having far too good a time. Then, perhaps four or five weeks into the run of the play, we were at her flat on a Sunday afternoon..."

"Kyle!" his father said menacingly, rising halfway out of his chair.

"She told me she was pregnant, that we'd have to get married. I was terrified. In a panic, I blurted out the truth—that I'd only just turned sixteen, that my sister and I were going home in a week's time, and that I couldn't marry her, even if I wanted to, without my parents' permission. To put it mildly, she went off the rails." He wiped his damp palms on his trousers, pulled a handkerchief from his pocket to blot his face, then stood looking at the floor. "She was Catholic. It didn't stop her messing about, but she drew the line at abortion. After she'd had a chance to think, she said there was only one possible solution. She'd take herself off somewhere to have the baby, and give it up for adoption. But I was going to have to help her cover her tracks."

"You stole my wallet and gave her my identification, didn't you?" Kyra asked.

He nodded guiltily, then looked again at the floor.

Keeping her voice low, although she wanted to scream at him, she said, "You bastard, Kyle! How could you *do* that? For years I've been trying to figure out how my name came to be on that loathsome creature's birth certificate.... I could *kill* you! All the misery she caused Jess! God!" She drew in a ragged breath, her chest heaving. "If we'd known from the outset what we were dealing with—"

"—but how was I to know?" he cut in. "If I had known, don't you think I'd have taken my share of the responsibility? I would have." Eyes brimming, he turned to the others, seeking support, but they just stared at him. The tears spilling over, he turned again to Kyra. "I took your wallet," he confirmed remorsefully, "plus some

money I nicked from Mum's bag, and every last penny I had to give
to Lillian to pay her expenses. When we got home I sent her my
savings of two hundred-odd pounds. Then the following January
I wrote to her, enclosing a draft for my fifty pounds of Christmas
money, but the letter came back, marked 'Gone. No forwarding.'"
He used both hands to wipe his face as he looked over at the others. Still they said nothing, and Kyra could only gaze unblinking
at him, her thoughts in chaos as she tried to imagine how this rev-
elation might affect Jesse.

"A few years later," he went on doggedly, "when I was in New
York again, I tried every way conceivable to find her. I checked with
Equity, but she'd gone on honorary withdrawal. The membership
secretary gave me her agent's name, but he had no current address
for her. He told me he'd sent out a small residual check about a
year earlier for a radio advert she'd done, and it had been returned
by the post office. I got in touch with the Screen Actors' Guild and
then with AFTRA. Neither had any record of her. She was gone,
and I didn't know where else to look. I didn't just turn my back on
what I'd done. I may be many things, but I'm not callous. Every
time I went over I tried to locate her. For almost ten years I kept a
private detective on retainer looking for her. But he
couldn't find a trace of either one of them. And finally I had to give
it up. They were gone and I was never going to find them.

"I should have owned up to it, but I was a kid. I'd been vain and
careless, and I was scared. This afternoon, I found out I have a
daughter—a very nasty one, from the sound of it—who casually
turned her son over to the woman she believed to be her mother,
who just happened to be Kyra. Two days after that I was in Connecticut, with Jesse on my lap, reading to the child my sister had
finally managed to adopt, happily thinking of myself as Uncle
Kyle. And all the while I was the boy's *grandfather!*" He laughed
in disbelief, then cried even harder.

Octavia was shaking her head as she found a handkerchief in her
bag and handed it to him. "You should have told us, Kyle. We'd
have been angry, but we'd have made arrangements...." She fell
silent as she realized that had he done that, Jesse probably would
never have come into Kyra's life.

"I was afraid to tell you." He wiped his face and took a shuddery breath. "I'm sorrier than I can say."

Kyra was thinking she had the answer she'd wanted for so long, but it offered no satisfaction. All she could think of was the horror show Jennifer had made of their lives for the past few days. "What the bloody hell were you *thinking?*" she cried, wanting to go at him with her fists.

"But I didn't *know*—"

"You could've told me you'd given some woman my identification. At least I'd have been prepared—"

"For what?" Octavia asked coolly. "Kyle couldn't have known his child would one day show up at your door, believing you were her mother. You're both overreacting."

"Maybe so," Kyra admitted, rounding on her brother. "You were an arrogant, gesturing ass back then, an odious show-off, a pretentious poseur, but I never would've believed you could do something so monumental as giving my identification to another woman and not have the decency to tell me about it! Your daughter, the heroin addict, turned up here a few days ago, planning to cash in on Jess's success, and he gave her two thousand pounds because he felt sorry for her. She took his money, then promptly turned around and sold him to the *Sun* for five thousand more. God, Kyle! You could've spared him so much grief."

"I'm *sorry,*" Kyle said again, stricken.

"Oh, I'm sure you are. It doesn't stop me wanting to beat you about the head."

"What can I do?" he asked miserably. "Tell me and I'll do it."

"For a start, you're going to tell Jess. He deserves to know, and I absolutely will not do this for you."

"I wouldn't expect you to. I've been planning to tell him since I saw the article."

"Look, I know you both feel awful," Damien interjected. "I think we all feel a bit sick, hearing about what's gone on here. But the two of you are going overboard. So Kyle didn't confess at the time. It's a long time later and maybe, just maybe, the timing is perfect. Not only does he deserve it, but I think Jess *needs* to hear Kyle's story."

"You do believe, don't you—" Kyle turned to look at each of them in turn "—that if I'd known about Jess's mother, I'd have told you?"

"We believe you," Octavia said. "Now sit down and eat something. You will not go up to see Jess until you've pulled yourself together. And, Kyra, have a good strong drink or another glass of wine. Kyle was young and stupid, but it can't have escaped you that if he had made a clean breast of it, it's unlikely Jesse would have wound up in your care. You may want to kill him, but your brother inadvertently gave you what you'd always wanted most."

"I realize that," Kyra said. "I do. And by morning I'll have stopped wanting to kill him. But Kyle—" she looked squarely at her brother "—could you, once and for all, finally, please grow up? If you'd come here this evening and simply told us the truth without all the theatrics, it would've been a lot easier on everyone. It's the bloody *performance* we could've done without."

"Hear, hear!" Octavia agreed.

"We're his great-grandparents," Richard said to his former wife, his eyes suddenly bright. "The lad's been rightfully ours all along."

"He's been yours regardless," Damien said. "Rightful or not is irrelevant at this point. Jesse's been happy in this family, he's thrived in this family. *That's* what matters."

"You're right," Kyra said slowly. "That really is what matters."

CHAPTER 35

Annie on one side of Jesse and Joan on the other, the three were sitting on the bed watching *Oliver!*, singing along with the cast. Kyle had to smile at this, reluctant to interrupt. But all three of them looked over simultaneously and Kyle said, "Don't let me disturb you. I'll come back after the film."

"It's all right, Uncle Kyle," Jesse said, pressing buttons on the remote control. "It's a video. We'll finish watching later."

"Any of that Indian nosh left?" Annie asked him, climbing off the bed.

"Tons," Kyle told her.

"Don't talk about it," Jesse begged jokingly. "I'd love some biryani and raita with mango chutney."

"We'll come back and describe every bite," Annie teased. "Come on, Joan. Let's go hoover up the leftovers."

The two young women went out, discreetly closing the door behind them.

"How're you, Monkey?" Kyle asked, crossing the room to sit on the side of the bed close to Jesse. The boy looked small and puffy, as if quantities of air had been injected beneath the surface of his skin. His eyes seemed larger and darker than ever, contrasted to his pallor.

"I'm okay." His voice was several notches below its usual volume. "Just sleepy all the time. Why are you back? I thought you were going to be away until after the first. Is Damien with you?"

"He's downstairs. We were passing a newsagent's this afternoon on our way to lunch, and I saw the front page of the *Sun.*"

"It's all bollocks," Jesse said dismissingly. "I hope you didn't give up your vacation because of that."

"Well, here's the thing," Kyle said, feeling his way into it.

"Ninety-eight percent of it probably is bollocks, but two percent of it's the truth."

"Is that why you've come back from Paris? Because you think something Jennifer said is actually true?" Jesse looked disappointed. "She's never told the truth in her *life,* Uncle Kyle. Keer must've told you she's a drug addict. They're notorious liars. And thieves. They'd take your skin if they thought they could sell it for a few bob. Jennifer would say *anything* to get money."

"So I've heard. But in this instance, she said something she *believed* to be true."

Jesse frowned. "You'll have to explain that. I'm not getting it."

Nervous, Kyle took a deep breath, then began to tell Jesse the story. This time, mindful of Kyra's comments, he stuck strictly to the facts and left out what she'd called his "theatrics."

Jesse listened in precisely the same way he had to the stories that were read to him as a small boy: with complete attention. And as a listener, he always seemed able to hear beyond the words to the subtext, and past that to the speaker's or the writer's intent. It was both satisfying and unnerving to tell Jesse something, no matter how casual, because he appeared to have a special skill at decoding everything—even the spaces between thoughts, the pauses between words; he could read one's mood with alarming accuracy.

As Kyle wound down, unable to help himself, tears again began welling in his eyes, and it was difficult to get out the last of the words. But, finally it was all said. And in the ensuing silence, he felt terribly ashamed, and thought Kyra was right. He had been all she'd accused him of being. "My sister," he told Jesse, "was the one who got the intelligence and common sense, and I got the arrogant stupidity."

"That's not true and it's not fair to either of you," Jesse at once disagreed. "You're very smart.... Will it be all right if I go on calling you Uncle Kyle? It's rather late in the day for me to have to start calling everyone something else."

"Of course, of course," Kyle said quickly.

Starting to smile, Jesse said, "It's like another of the Naughty Little Kyle stories Granny used to tell me. It'd make quite a book."

"Who on earth would want to read it?" Kyle asked, perennially thrown by Jesse's take on things. He was the least predictable person ever.

"Everybody. Especially that lot out there." Jesse hooked a thumb in the direction of the window.

"You're right about that. *They* would." Kyle paused, then said, "I'm so sorry, Monkey." And the tears were back, spilling from his eyes. "I'd never intentionally do anything to hurt you."

"I know that, and it's okay, Uncle Kyle. In fact, it's more than okay. It'll take some getting used to, but it's wonderful to know we're actually related. You mustn't feel badly." He reached over, pulled some tissues from the box on the bedside table and pressed them into Kyle's hand. "You *are* intelligent and you *do* have common sense. You were just young, that's all. I could see myself doing something just like that. I mean, I'm mad for Joanie. These things can happen."

"You're a wonder," Kyle said gratefully.

"No, I'm not," Jesse said. "I just understand how it could happen. You were already confused about what you wanted—your preferences and so forth—so it makes perfect sense that you'd grab a chance like that, thinking it might help you sort things out." He paused a moment, then said, "Crikey! Keer must've gone mental when you told her about Lillian."

"She didn't half." Kyle shook his head, smiling. "She was ready to kill me."

"I'll bet she was!" Jesse smiled, too. Then, his volume diminished now to a whisper, he said, "It's okay, Uncle Kyle. Kids do stupid things. And it wasn't all *that* stupid, if you think about it. I wouldn't be here, would I, if you hadn't fancied that woman. All in all, I think it was a good thing." Jesse looked around the room, then his eyes came back to Kyle. "I've done all sorts of things, met fantastic people, got a book published. I've had a great time, Uncle Kyle, a really great time. So don't feel badly. It's okay."

Octavia and Richard had gone back to her house for the night. Damien was stretched out on one of the sofas in the living room, drowsily reading that morning's *Telegraph*. Annie was upstairs taking a bath and Joan was sitting on the bed, reading the operating manual for the computer, with Jesse curled against her, asleep.

Bundled up in their coats, protected from the rain by the overhang of the back door, Kyra and Kyle were sitting out on the back step, getting some fresh air and a few minutes' privacy.

"Give it a rest now," Kyra was saying. "I know you're sorry, and I'm past the point of wanting to throttle you. What I'm really angry about is Jennifer. She's the one who put that bloody mob outside. I didn't want it to be this way, Kyle. I imagined it would be peaceful, just the family. Now we're smack in the middle of another media circus. It's so unfair to Jess.... It feels like only a year ago that she brought him to me. This tiny, filthy boy. The time's gone so quickly. What was she like, Jennifer's mother?"

"Very pretty, but, in retrospect, I have to agree with Mother. She *did* sound like someone making airport announcements. Of course, I thought she was gorgeous."

"You seemed to have a weakness for beautiful, stupid women."

"I suppose I did. Of course, I was so preoccupied with proving to myself how 'normal' I was, I didn't notice the fine points about the women I took up with."

"For God's sake, how could you not notice? I've had *salads* that were smarter than Beth."

Kyle burst out laughing. "Oooh, that was cruel!"

"But true."

"But true," he agreed.

"So was Lillian stupid?"

"No, just deluded. She thought she'd be a big film star. I certainly didn't think so. But her thinking that is why she refused to have the baby under her own name. She didn't want it catching up to her one day, becoming fodder for the tabloids."

"Obviously, she needn't have worried," Kyra said.

"Well, there was the possibility she might connect with the right people, find herself on the right casting couch at the right time. Stranger things have been known to happen."

"That's also true. Some of the stupidest people any of us has ever met have been film stars. They've got brains like dried peas rattling around in a colander."

He laughed and draped an arm around her shoulders, bringing her against him. "Quite the pair, we are. Forever at odds, and yet I love you more than anyone else, ever. In a way, I've always counted on you, Keer, to keep me honest."

"How?"

"Nothing ever gets by you. You've been the resident reviewer since day one. Not in so many words necessarily, but a look from you and I'd feel like an idiot. It didn't stop me behaving idiotically, because I couldn't seem to help myself. But that look of yours would let me know I was over the top. Sometimes, in rehearsal, or during a run, I'd think of you sitting fifth row center, giving me one of those looks, and I'd immediately start trimming the excess, trying to get to the core of the character, working it from the inside out instead of from the outside in. It helped."

"I'm flattered, Kyle," she said, becoming mesmerized by the steady splashing of the rain and the mellow resonance of his voice. "But don't go overboard. I wasn't a pleasant child to be around."

"We were just young, trying to get through time until we could be adults and have some control of our own lives. Most kids make a hash of it, because it's *hard*. I had so many desires on so many levels, and I felt such a misfit, hiding what I wanted from everyone, including myself, and feeling morally obligated to keep the worst of my classmates away from you."

"You did that?" she asked.

"They were forever begging to visit so they could meet you. I knew they were a pack of randy prats and I certainly wasn't going to set them loose on you. You deserved better."

"That's very sweet. And here I thought you hadn't any feelings at all for me, that I was just...I don't know...an inconvenience. Someone who took the limelight away from you. And I hated it, hated being noticed."

"I had no idea. Isn't it absurd? I was enormously proud of you. You were so independent, so clever, so visibly talented."

"I wasn't independent, I was just lonely. We misperceived each other totally." She took hold of his hand. "What a waste, when we could have been good friends. But I'll tell you this: the longer I know you, the better I like you. Except, of course—" she smiled "—for tonight's performance." She kissed his cheek, then got to her feet saying, "I really must get some sleep. And you should take Damien home, make amends for this afternoon."

Rising, Kyle said, "If there's anything—"

"I know, and I'll ring you."

Flowers and cards, letters and stuffed animals began arriving early the next morning.

Initially, Kyra was touched. She, Annie and Joan found vases for the flowers, then carried the toys and cards up to Jessie. He laughed with delight at some of the creatures and read the cards and letters, saying, "Should I answer them?"

"I don't think it's expected," Kyra said. "People just want you to know they care."

"It's quite something, isn't it?" he said. "Complete strangers taking the time to send flowers and gifts, to write such kind things."

"These people feel as if they know you," Annie said, "cuz they've seen you on the telly and read the book. I reckon that piece in the *Sun* pissed them right off."

"It did me," Joan said softly. "I wouldn't've believed a word of it, Jess, even if I didn't know you."

"We'll let you rest now," Kyra said, shocked at how quickly his energy vanished. His eyes went suddenly dull and his breathing slowed. As the three women watched, Jesse's eyelids fluttered as he tried to stay awake, and then, a moment later, he was asleep.

Annie gathered up the stuffed toys and put them on the desk while Joan arranged the greeting cards on the bookshelves. Kyra looked at them, then at Jesse, wanting to freeze time, to keep all of them here, locked in the moment. "I'll put on the kettle for tea," she said, and started down the stairs as the doorbell rang.

By midday the messengers bringing toys and flowers were arriving in a steady stream. As well, people came to lay bouquets of flowers on the front steps.

"They're turning this place into a bloody shrine," Annie said heatedly. "I'm going to disable the doorbell."

"We can't do that," Kyra said. "I'll write up a notice asking them to leave the deliveries at the door."

"I could print one up on the computer when Jess wakes up," Joanie offered. "I'm learning the word-processing application. He's been teaching me."

"Perfect," Kyra said. "Aren't you clever!"

"Nah." Joan blushed and lowered her eyes. "It's just that Jess knows such a lot and he's ever such a good teacher."

"Obviously," Kyra said, giving her a hug, "you're a good student."

Surprisingly, Joan returned the hug fiercely, murmuring, "You're such a nice mum. I love being here. It's the best place I've ever been."

"You're a lovely girl," Kyra said, her voice unsteady. "We love having you here."

"Yeah?" Joan looked up at her.

"Yeah," Kyra assured her.

Following the exchange, something suddenly started pulling itself together inside Annie's head. It was an insight that was going to lead her somewhere, and she wanted to keep a firm grasp on it so she could study it later, but the doorbell went again and she went marching down the hall, ready to have a go at whoever was there.

"Don't hit me!" Stephen Binder said, one hand upheld, the other filled with the floral offerings he'd gathered from the steps. "I come in peace."

"Get in here, you!" she said, grabbing hold of his jacket and pulling him inside, then relieving him of the flowers. "We're going mental with all the deliveries."

"Hello, Stephen. How are you, Stephen? Lovely to see you again, Stephen."

"Yeh, yeh, yeh." Annie grinned at him. "Hello, how're you, lovely."

"That's better. Hello, Kyra, Joanie!" he greeted them as he got out of his jacket, and the doorbell sounded again.

"Go on 'n' have a cuppa," Annie said, opening the door.

"Obviously, something's got to be done about the flowers and toys," Stephen said, accepting a cup of tea from Joan and sitting down at the table opposite Kyra. "I think a couple of telephone calls will sort this out."

"Calls to who?" Annie asked, coming in with two more bouquets and several toys with cards attached.

"To whom," Stephen corrected her. "A cab driver I know, for one. And Great Ormond Street Hospital, for another. We'll just have them deliver the greetings and reroute the flowers and what-have-you. May I?" he asked Kyra, indicating the telephone.

"Please. We're being overwhelmed."

Stephen swallowed a quick mouthful of the tea and went to the telephone.

As he dialed, Joanie leaned over to whisper to Annie, "He's lovely."

"Yeh," Annie whispered back. "He is."

Kyra got up and walked through to the living room to peek through the curtains at the street. The media crowd had thinned down to a core group of about a dozen. The photographers in the group sprang to attention as a chauffeur-driven Daimler pulled up in front of the house. The driver got out to open the passenger door for a young red-headed boy. He came up the walk and continued on up the stairs. Kyra waited for the doorbell. When it didn't ring, she hurried to the door in time to see an envelope being pushed through the letter box. On some impulse she didn't stop to examine, she opened the door, startling the child.

"Oh, I'm sorry," he said, still holding the envelope. Behind him the door to the Daimler opened again and a handsome elderly woman got out of the car. "I didn't, um, I didn't want to disturb you. I just wanted to leave this for Jesse."

"Are you one of his classmates?" Kyra asked, looking past the boy to the elegant, impeccably dressed female making her way up the walk.

"No, but we did meet in a way."

"Just before Christmas," the woman said, stopping next to the boy. Placing one hand on his shoulder, she extended the other to Kyra. "I am Antonia Owen-Fitzhugh, and this is my grandson, Theodore. We met Jesse at the Ritz."

"Oh, yes." Kyra smiled, returning the woman's firm handshake and admiring her poise. "Jess told me about it. Please do come in."

"We wouldn't dream of intruding," Antonia said.

"It's not an intrusion." Kyra held open the door, saying, "Do come in. I think Jess will be pleased to know Theodore remembered him."

"Is he all right?" Theodore asked quietly, as his grandmother seated herself on one of the sofas.

Dropping down so that she was at eye level with the boy, Kyra put a hand on his arm and said, "He's not all right. But he seems just to be very tired, Theodore. There's nothing to be afraid of."

"Everyone calls me Teddy. And I'd never be afraid of Jesse."

"In that case, would you like to come up with me and say hello to him?"

"Oh, yes, please. We had such a nice chat that afternoon. And Grandmother got me his book for Christmas. It's brilliant. I've read it three times. I feel as if we're friends."

Straightening, Kyra took the boy's hand, saying, "Jess'll be very happy to hear that. We won't be long," Kyra told the grandmother. "Would you like a cup of tea? We've just made a fresh pot."

"Thank you, but no. Lovely watercolor, that," she said, and moved to take a closer look.

As Kyra entered Jesse's room with Teddy, Jess was just waking up. He stared at the boy for a moment, then exclaimed, "I remember you! Tea at the Ritz."

"That's right. I'm Teddy. I was going to drop off this letter but your mother invited us in. My grandmother's waiting downstairs."

"This is super. Come sit down. Did you have a good Christmas?" Jesse was asking as Kyra left and went back downstairs to the living room.

"This is very good of you," the elderly woman said.

"Teddy's a lovely boy."

"Yes, he is," Antonia said. "We're terribly lucky to have him. His parents were killed in a plane crash nine years ago and he's lived with us since then. He got very excited when he spotted Jesse at tea. He'd seen Jesse interviewed on television and was very taken with him. He went on and on about this boy his age who'd actually published a book. So getting to meet Jesse was a thrill for him. And Jesse was so gracious to Teddy, remarkably so. He struck me as a very genuine boy, very kind-hearted."

"He is," Kyra said.

"So, when Teddy saw that frightful piece in the newspaper he was terribly upset, and nothing would do but that he write Jesse a letter and hand-deliver it. I have no idea what he's said in his letter, but he worked at it for hours last night. In his own way, Teddy is also very genuine, and he has the rare gift of natural enthusiasm. Something about Jesse, and the book, too, made a great impression on him. This visit will mean the world to him."

"It'll mean the world to Jesse, too. It puts a human face to the messages and flowers and gifts that have been arriving since this morning."

"Yes," Antonia said thoughtfully. "I can see that you'd need that, under such trying circumstances. Did you do the watercolor?"

"I did. A long time ago."

"It's very like you, I think. Delicate but bold, with wonderful colors. I'm aware of your work as a costume designer, but do you still paint?"

"Not for years and years."

"You should," Antonia declared. "Not many people can transmit such sensitivity with watercolor. It's a fussy medium, doesn't tolerate hesitance."

"You paint?"

The woman laughed. "Very badly, but I can't bring myself to give up trying. So I keep going along to our country house with my paint box in hand, determined each time to get it right. I never do. But I find the effort soothing. You've got to be very focused. It has the desired effect of shutting things out. And sometimes, as I'm sure you well know, we need that."

Teddy came skipping lightly down the stairs and into the room, saying, "Thank you very, very much for allowing me to visit. Jess has given me the telephone number and said I could ring if it's all right with you, perhaps come to visit again."

"It's quite all right with me."

"Come along now, Theodore," his grandmother said, "we must be going." Opening her handbag, she removed a card and gave it to Kyra. "Thank you, my dear. You are every bit as genuine and kind-hearted as your son. It has been a delight meeting you."

"And you." Kyra saw them out and watched as the chauffeur held open the rear door of the Daimler. Teddy offered his hand to assist his grandmother into the car, then turned to wave to Kyra before climbing in after her. The driver closed the door, walked around to the other side, slid in behind the wheel, and the car almost silently drove away.

Back inside, Kyra thought to look at the card, then shook her head in disbelief. The duchess had struck a line through her name and beneath it had printed "Theodore" and their Belgravia telephone number. No wonder she'd been so knowledgeable about technique. The duke and duchess had a famous collection of paintings, and were renowned for their patronage of the arts.

Tucking the card into her pocket she returned to the kitchen where Annie and Joan were putting the finishing touches to a tray for Jesse. They carried it off as Stephen said, "Everything's taken care of. Volunteer cab drivers will collect the toys and flowers and take them to the hospital. And the hospital's organizing volunteers to arrange and distribute everything."

"You *are* good, Stephen. Thank you."

"Who was the boy?" he asked.

In answer, she reached into her pocket and passed the card over to him.

"Oh, I say. I had no idea you knew them."

"I don't. Do you?"

"I've met them a time or two but I've never met Theodore. Know the whole story, of course. Awfully sad. How did he and Jess come to meet?"

"Over tea at the Ritz."

"The world gets smaller and smaller," he said, passing the card back.

"Did Jess ask you to stop by today?"

"To be truthful, he didn't. I came just to be here, if that's all right."

"Lucky for us you did," she said. "The nonstop doorbell was beginning to drive us all bonkers. So, since you're here you can help me put a meal together. And, by the way, don't think I haven't sussed out the *real* reason for your visit."

"It's a curse, being so transparent." He sat back with his arms spread as if preparing to be stabbed.

"Oh, I don't know, Stephen. I think it's quite lovable, really. In my family, revealing one's self has always been a bit dangerous. At least, I used to think so. Now it seems to have become a necessity."

"I'll help in any way I'm able."

"You already have. Now—" she tossed an apron at him "—you can peel the potatoes."

CHAPTER 36

Each day Jesse lost a little more ground, sleeping for longer and longer periods. But when he was awake, he was, for brief periods, almost hyperalert, taking in the slightest details of whatever was going on around him.

Three days later, when the weather turned colder, with the rain continuing to fall nonstop, he asked Kyra, "Is there still a crowd out there?"

"Actually, since yesterday it's been just three or four of the hard-core *paparazzi.*"

"They must be miserable," he said. "Maybe we should invite them in."

"Is that what you'd like, Jess?" she asked, marveling at his generosity.

"If they're determined to stay, perhaps we could give them a cup of tea. And I wouldn't mind meeting them. I'm curious. I mean, they've got to be dead serious to stand out there from morning to night, day after day, hoping for a sellable shot."

"That's true," she agreed. "And if we ask them in, would you like to come down to say hello, or would you prefer to have them come up?"

He thought about that for a moment, then said, "I suppose they'll have to come up. So long as they promise not to take any photos while they're here. I'd hate that."

"I'll send Annie out to have a word."

"You think I'm bonkers, don't you, Keer?"

"No, I think you're truly generous."

"I can't help it. I really am curious."

"I know. It's one of the things I like best about you."

"Yeah?" He smiled. "Know one of the things I like best about you?"

"What?"

"That you let me be curious. Bet nobody else's mother would invite that lot in, no matter how hard their kid begged."

"You're probably right about that." She bent to kiss the top of his head, then went downstairs to talk to Annie and Joan.

"You have *got* to be *joking!*" Annie declared. "He wants to invite that pack of hounds into the house and give the buggers tea, to boot?"

"He does."

"Well, blow me! Okay. If that's what he wants. Joanie, put the kettle on, willya, while I go fetch the thugs."

Kyra laughed and said, "I'll go get Jess spruced up, then hide out in the studio until they're gone."

"He's ever such a kind boy," Joanie said wonderingly, carrying the kettle to the sink. "Anybody else would have a good go at 'em, give 'em what-for. But not our Jess. He's a wonder, he is."

The four men stepped over the threshold warily, as if expecting some mean trick to be played on them. They ranged in age, from the youngest, who looked to be in his late teens, to the oldest, who was probably only in his mid-thirties but had the wearied features of someone at least ten years older. Each of them wore suspicious expressions and were deeply reluctant to leave their equipment in the hall.

"You're not coming in if you don't drop the gear," Annie told them. "Nobody's going to steal it. Just leave it and come have a cuppa. Then you can go up one at a time 'n' meet Jess."

"What's this in aid of, then?" asked the youngest. "Feels like some kind of trick."

"You're not that important, mate," Annie told him. "You're here cuz Jess felt sorry for you, and he's curious to know why you do what you do. So lose the gear, come have your tea, then you'll meet him."

The two photographers who were in their late twenties and appeared to be less bemused and more accepting of the situation at once put down their cameras, removed their sodden outwear and headed toward the kitchen. The youngest, muttering to himself, set his camera down just inside the living room doorway as if by physically positioning it at a distance from the others he was stating that he wasn't like them. And the oldest, a slight, balding man who had hurt, gentle eyes and a tired smile, sighed and said, "I could use a cuppa and that's the God's honest. I was gonna give it up after today, I don't mind tellin' you. The gig's gettin' old, and I feel a bit of a ghoul, hangin' about out there, while the lad's in here enjoying his last few days or hours."

"What's your name?" Annie asked him, gratified to discover he wasn't as offhand and unfeeling as the other three.

"Norm Underhill." He offered her his hand. "Was on staff at the *Standard* nine years, but got made redundant eighteen months back. Can't say I like being freelance, but it's all that's going for now. Weddings, bar mitzvahs. Thing is, the *Standard* hired me freelance to cover this so the other staffers could cover the big breaking stories." His sour expression said what he thought of being paid minimum wage to stand day after day in the rain, waiting for a boy to die.

"You any good, Norm?"

"The best, when it comes to available light," he declared. "Most of the newspaper stuff I did, there wasn't no time to rig up the flash. Those lads—" he nodded at the three men in the kitchen "—they're forever fussing with their meters and what-have-you. Me, I come from the school that taught you to make do with what you got."

"Me, too."

"Yeah, that's right. You're in the business. The lad talked about you at his launch." He smiled at her, and years dropped from his features. "His dreamgirl, or like that."

Annie returned his smile. "Or like that. Listen, Norm, give me your number before you go. I've got some contacts. Might be I could put you up for some location work, doing stills. The money's brilliant, and it's a doddle."

"Yeah?" He brightened at the prospect.

"Sure. Why not?"

"Ta, luv. I'd be glad of the chance, and that's a fact."

The other three men had settled at the kitchen table and were kibitzing with Joan as she set down mugs of tea and a plate of biscuits. Norman looked at Joan, then back at Annie, asking, "Who's your friend?"

"Me mate, Joan. Why?"

"Lovely sweet face she's got, hasn't she?"

"Sweet nature, as well. Come on, have a sit-down, Norm, and I'll fetch you a cuppa."

Each of the photographers had undergone a change by the time they came downstairs after a brief visit with Jess. Quietly, they gathered their equipment, thanked Annie and Joan for the tea, then went back out into the rain.

Norm, who stayed with Jesse a few minutes longer than the others, came back down looking distraught.

"You okay?" Annie asked him.

The man shook his head and bent to pick up his camera and equipment bag. "I bloody hate this," he said thickly. "Hate it! I'd like nothin' better than to pack it in, but I can't afford to. I got two of me own at home—one's seven, the other's nine. He's... This isn't right. It's just not right."

"I'll phone around, see if I can connect you up."

Norm stood for a few seconds, looking up the stairs. "It's not bloody right," he repeated, then looked at Annie and said, "'Preciate the offer, and the cuppa. Ta-ra, then, darlin'," and left, head lowered against the driving rain.

On the evening of the thirtieth, Robert phoned to talk to Kyra. "I've got a little surprise organized for Jess," he told her. "I was hoping it'd be all right with you."

"What sort of surprise?" Kyra asked.

"Something I think he'll like. Do you think you could bring him downstairs to the front door at seven-thirty tomorrow evening? It won't take very long, but I've got everything arranged. And the weather's meant to clear, as well."

"I'm a bit confused."

"I expect he'll want to be dressed, if you can manage it."

"You're being very mysterious, Robert."

"I know, but if I get into any of the details, I might spoil it."

"I see. What should I tell Jess?"

"Oh, anything really. It doesn't matter, just so long as you keep him away from the windows from about seven on, and have him at the door at seven-thirty."

"Okay. No windows, and he'll be at the door."

"Great! Thanks, Kyra. Jess'll like this. I just know he will."

"What's this about?" Jesse asked, as Kyra finished buttoning his shirt.

"Robert has arranged a surprise for you. That's all I know."

"Very mysterious," Jesse said, looking rather pleased as Kyra held the cardigan and directed his arms into the sleeves.

"My words to him precisely."

"By the time I'm finally dressed, I'll be ready to go to sleep." He made a joke of it, but the simple act of getting on his clothes was exhausting. His eyes were darkly shadowed, as if they were sinking deeper into his skull. He could scarcely move his limbs, and Kyra had had to lift him into the tub to bathe him, then had lifted him out again, wrapping him in an oversize bath sheet to dry him while he leaned against her, too weak to do more than try to make a joke of it all.

"Perhaps tonight we'll let you sleep fully dressed."

"I just might," he said.

"I don't think we need to bother with shoes, do you? You'll just wear your slippers."

"Okay." His head hung heavily, only his eyes moving as he watched her drop to her haunches and reach under the bed for his slippers.

"Robert was right about the weather clearing," she said, fitting the fleece-lined leather scuffs onto his feet. "It's a lovely evening, cold enough for snow but not a cloud in sight."

"D'you suppose the weather has something to do with the surprise?"

"I can't imagine why it would," Kyra said, glancing at the clock on the bedside table. Fourteen past the hour.

"I'll bet it does. He probably rang the meteorological service to get the forecast. He leaves nothing to chance. Robert's the most methodical person I've ever known."

"Really?"

"Honestly. He says he's either going to be a mathematician or a lawyer. He hasn't decided yet which. But it fits, doesn't it?"

"Better he be a mathematician," Kyra said.

"Some lawyers are nice. Stephen is."

"True. He is. But Stephen is an exception."

"Robert would be, too."

"You're right. He would be." Kyra stood up and reached for the brush. "Let's have a go at your hair and then we'll be set."

"When's everyone coming?"

"They're already here, love."

"They are? It's awfully quiet," he said, looking over at the door.

"I could shout down and tell them to make some noise, if you like." She smiled at him.

He made a face. "It just doesn't seem very festive, that's all. It *is* New Year's Eve. It's supposed to be hats and horns and lots of noise. It's not a proper festicle without all the carry-on."

"We've got hats, but only Jimmy and Joan are wearing them. The horns are for midnight. And the festicle, complete with all due carry-on, is set to begin after Robert's surprise."

"I hope I can manage to stay awake."

"I'm sure you will, at least for a little while. Ready?" she asked. "It's twenty past."

"Places, please, ladies and gentlemen," he announced importantly. "Places, please. Curtain in two."

"Well, you've got Granny's last A.S.M. down pat."

"He was a *very* serious assistant stage manager."

"Indeed, he was." She smiled again and bent to pick him up. "Just for the stairs. Okay?"

"First the tub, now the stairs. Soon you'll be carrying me everywhere. Makes me feel like a bloody infant," he complained, draping one arm across her shoulders.

"You'd never pass for one."

"Doesn't stop me feeling it, getting carted about like a baby by my mum. I hope no one sees."

"No one will. I'll set you down the instant we get to the bottom step."

"I'm simply to be at the front door?" he asked, as Kyra carried him out of the room.

"That's it."

"Very odd. Do I look all right?"

"You look positively elegant, my dear. Cashmere suits you. Your granny does go for the best."

"I love it," he whispered. "I'd like to sleep in it."

"Then sleep in it," she whispered back. "I would. And Granny would probably find the idea delicious. It's the sort of thing she'd do."

"Really?"

"Really."

"I will, then," he decided, appreciatively stroking the fine, soft wool.

As Kyra set him down at the foot of the stairs, Annie emerged from the living room. "Nice gear, Jess. The cardie's dead posh. You ready for the big surprise?"

"You know what it is?" he asked eagerly.

"Not a clue. Everybody's in there, lined up at the windows. We're all dying of curiosity." She accepted her coat from Kyra and put it on as Kyra pulled on a heavy Aran sweater.

Norm Underhill and the other three photographers watched, bemused, as two vans and an automobile pulled over and parked, one behind the other, just up the road. The van doors opened and boys began scrambling out. A handsome, strapping lad emerged from the automobile and hurried over to talk to the group quietly assembling on the pavement outside the Latimer house.

"What's this in aid of?" the youngest of the photographers wondered aloud, flicking on his flash attachment.

"Dunno," said one of the others, following suit and getting his camera ready.

The tall lad seemed to be the organizer, Norm thought, as the boy quickly and efficiently arranged the dozen others in two rows, according to height. His parents seemed quite content to remain by their car, watching their boy in action. Then the lads all stood to attention, as the outside light went on and the front door of the house opened.

With Kyra supporting him on one side and Annie on the other, Jesse looked out in amazement to see his classmates assembled at the foot of the front walk. At a signal from Robert, the boys began to sing.

"Should auld acquaintance be forgot,
And never brought to mind?
Should auld acquaintance be forgot,
And auld lang syne!"

Glancing around, Norm saw outside lights go on as the front doors to houses up and down the street were opened. Taking in the scene, the neighbors stepped out and joined in the singing. And there—the curtains now open—in the front window of the Lattimer house, were some of the most famous people in the world, the entire Latimer clan, every one of them singing, too. The photo op of all time.

The bloke next to Norm lifted his camera and began to adjust the focus, but Norm put a hand on his arm, saying softly, "Let's give it a miss, eh, mate? Give the lad his private moment."

The younger man stopped and looked at Norm, looked back at the kid in the doorway, at that group in the window, at the boys in the street, and then at the neighbors and said, "Yeah, you're right. I'm for that."

Norm rewarded him with a smile and another pat on the arm, then started to sing along. Having followed this exchange, after a moment's hesitation, the other two lowered their cameras and also joined in; everyone's eyes on the small boy in the doorway whose obvious elation brought more and more voices into the song.

"For auld lang syne, my dear
For auld lang syne,
We'll take a cup o' kindness yet
For auld lang syne!"

Only a few of the neighbors and Richard Latimer knew the following verses; the rest hummed along as the boys sang on.

"And surely ye'll be your pint' stowp,
And surely I'll be mine,

And we'll take a cup o' kindness yet,
For auld lang syne!

We twa hae run about the braes,
And pou'd the gowans fine,
But we've wander'd monie a weary fit
Sin' auld lang syne.

We twa hae paidl'd in the burn
Frae morning sun till dine,
But seas between us braid hae roar'd
Sin' auld lang syne.

And here's a hand, my trusty fiere,
And gie's a hand o' thine,
And we'll tak a right guid-willie waught,
For auld lang syne!"

The last notes faded, and there was a moment of silence. Then the boys began shouting, "Happy New Year, Jess! Happy New Year!" and the neighbors up and down the road called out their greetings, as Jess waved, mustering as much volume as he was able, to say, "Happy New Year, everyone! Happy New Year!"

Kyra and Annie waved with their free hands, their linked arms now holding Jesse upright as he called out to his friends and to the neighbors, finally only able to waggle his fingers. Then, as discreetly as possibly, Kyra maneuvered Jesse inside and Annie got the door closed.

The boys stood for several long moments, gazing at that now closed door. Robert spoke quietly to them as the neighbors went back into their houses, and exterior lights blinked off one by one. The night was suddenly darker. The dozen boys split into two groups, climbed into the pair of vans, and were driven away. Susan and Stephen Forrest crossed the road to join their son, and the three went up the walk and were admitted into the house.

Finally, Norm detached his flash attachment, saying quietly, "Don't know about you lot, but that's it for me. I'm off, and I won't be back."

"Yeah, bugger this," said one of the others.

"Fancy a drink?" the youngest asked the group. "I could do with one, meself."

"And me," said the others, one by one.

Without another word, all four men quickly packed up their equipment.

In five minutes, the street was empty and silent but for the low rumble of a passing taxi in the next road.

CHAPTER 37

Kyra stood staring out the studio window at the patchy gray remains of the snow that had fallen the previous week. The makeshift stile Annie and Joan had created was still in place, a thin crust of snow on the wrought-iron garden chair wedged tight against the fence. It looked odd, she thought, and told herself she ought to go out and move it. But that would mean putting on boots and a coat, and she didn't have the energy.

Turning, she looked around the studio. It looked odd, too; as if it had been years since any work had been done in here. Everything in the entire house had an abandoned air; remnants of some long-ago life. Not yet a month, but it might as well have been a decade. She couldn't seem to acclimate to the silence, the emptiness. Even her clothes seemed unfamiliar; garments that had belonged to someone else. Nothing looked or felt right.

She wandered into the kitchen, thought about making a cup of coffee, at once decided it was too much trouble, and now stopped to take in the details of this room. Magnets still held an old crayon drawing of Jess's to the refrigerator door—a huge-headed, grinning female figure wielding scissors in one hand and what was meant to be a piece of fabric in the other. And down in the corner of the drawing was a tiny, unadorned stick-doll boy figure. On the counter, long-since turned into a container for pens and pencils, sat Jess's old two-handled mug.

The light on the answerphone blinked steadily. She'd allowed the telephone to go unanswered until the tape was full. Her parents and brother, Jimmy and Annie had taken to sending letters by messenger; or one of them would come to the house, calling to her through the letter box, so that she'd open the door and let them in.

She moved now down the hall to the stairs and up, drawn to the bedroom where, again, she stopped and stood looking at the emptied shelves. The computer, the printer, all the disks and manuals had gone to Joan; left to her in Jess's will, along with three thousand pounds to see her through her training course. The stereo system and all the cassettes and CDs had gone to Annie, along with another three thousand pounds. Many of the books and all the computer games had gone to Robert, with a bequest of two thousand pounds.

She looked at the bed, reviewing the ending one more time, still shocked by the finality, the sudden emptiness. Such a fool! she thought, back yet again in the deep quiet of the night, holding Jess as he struggled to stay awake. At the last, he'd tried so hard not to succumb to the sleep that had taken him for longer and longer periods of time. And it had seemed the reasonable, the sensible thing for her to whisper, "It's okay, Jess. Don't fight. Just sleep, love. It's okay." So he'd subsided, and she'd held him. And he'd slept, his breathing slower and slower, until it simply stopped. Thirty seconds, a minute, two minutes. Then she'd been terrified, wanting him to breathe again, to wake up. But he was utterly motionless. Why had she said it was okay? Why had she encouraged him to sleep?

You know someone's going to die; you've known it for months. You tell yourself you're ready; you've prepared in every way for this departure. And yet when it comes, it's such a shock, so jolting. Because no amount of knowledge could ever prepare you for the ending of life, for it simply to stop after a last, slow exhalation. It's ended, yet you wait and wait for the narrow chest to rise, to begin breathing again. You can't know, you can't ready yourself; you shouldn't whisper to a struggling child that it's okay to sleep when there's every likelihood that he'll never wake up, when you've been playing some version of let's pretend that doesn't incorporate any aspect of reality—certainly not the staggering reality of the frail husk of a still-warm, inarguably dead child cradled to your breast.

She kept wanting to redo the ending so that it played out differently, so that they exchanged important words; spoke of their feelings, said proper good-byes. It didn't matter that she'd known he would die, because she'd discovered in the almost four weeks since he had, that a part of her hadn't ever truly believed that he would actually die, or that he'd be the focus of the family's attention at the second funeral service of her adult life that she'd attended with little, if any, awareness of the proceedings. She'd never *really* accepted his death as inevitable. It was a script, with a role she'd played. But the ending, despite her having read and memorized the script, wasn't in any way what she'd imagined.

None of it went according to the plans she'd made. She hadn't expected to send Annie and Joan away the moment Jesse's body had been removed from the house. She hadn't expected to climb the stairs after they'd gone and crawl into Jess's bed and go to sleep for nine solid hours. She hadn't expected to be sitting in the kitchen in the dark eating a bowl of cereal when Jimmy arrived and asked if he could, please, have a bowl, too.

She hadn't expected to send Jimmy away. Throughout the minutes they sat eating their cereal in the dark kitchen, she thought about taking him upstairs to make love. She could taste him, feel him, smell him; she wanted to wrap herself around him like a boa constrictor and squeeze him until they were both gasping for air. But once their bowls were empty and the silence between them grew fraught with unstated thoughts and desires, she surprised herself by saying, "I'll have to ask you to go home now, Jimmy."

"Of course," he'd said quietly. And then, as had become his custom, he'd said, "You will ring me, if there's anything..."

"I will," she'd assured him, then sat on in the dark as he'd donned his coat and went down the hall and out the door.

After it had closed behind him, sending a wave of sharply cold air washing over her, she'd said softly, "Why did I do that? I didn't mean to do that." But, yes, really, she had meant to do that, because she wasn't in love with him anymore. She just loved him. And what she'd wanted was to use him for a time, to close her mind to anything but unadulterated sensation. Which wouldn't have been fair to either one of them.

"We've only got a future as friends," she'd said, finding a peculiar satisfaction in the sound of her own voice in the deserted house. "We might be sexual friends. We might be able to do that. But we'll never be more than friends."

Would that matter? she'd wondered. It couldn't matter. She'd had a husband; she didn't want another one. And a friend seemed to have more value than a lover. So they would be friends. Satisfied with her logic, she'd put the two bowls in the sink and had gone back upstairs to sleep through the rest of the night in Jesse's bed.

Now it was twenty-six days later and while she'd gone back to sleeping in her own bed, she spent an hour or more each day here in Jesse's room. She'd look at Drick slumped sideways on the shelf, or she'd reexamine the contents of the desk drawers. She'd study the rows of books, opening one to read a few lines; or she'd look through his notebooks, not actually reading what he'd written but examining his schoolboy's tidy handwriting. Pages and pages of graded assignments, with comments by his teachers. *Well done, Jess. Nicely done, Jess. A run-on sentence here, Jess.*

She had to keep reminding herself that he'd made the choice, and she was obligated to respect that. But she did wish he could have chosen one of the alternatives, something that would have given him more time. No, given *her* more time. He'd used his time remarkably well, and she had no right to question his decision. She would never know (although she could certainly guess) what had prompted it. But his absence was like a brain injury, something that would heal in its own time, or perhaps not at all. She felt impaired, just as she had when Gary died. That had been, in part, due to the shocking unexpectedness. She'd known this was coming, yet it made no difference. None. Death had dimensions one could never truly comprehend; it was like gazing at the night sky, trying to embrace the concept of infinity. Impossible, unless you were an astrophysicist. Or a mathematician. Perhaps one day Robert would be able to explain the numerical meaning of this to her.

God knows, everyone wanted to assure her she'd displayed wisdom and courage in accepting Jess's decision. They just didn't understand that it had nothing to do with wisdom or courage; it wasn't even a matter of choice. It was what she'd had to do. Everyone also talked about time and how it was needed when it came to loss, to grief. "It has no season," her mother told her. "It just is."

On a visceral level that made sense. The declaration made its way to the core of her brain like a well-thrown dart hitting the bull's-eye. It scored; she felt the penetration. It just didn't have a place in her present reality. She was locked in a state of dismayed wonderment and sought comfort in sleep, in long hot baths, in bowls of cereal eaten in the dark kitchen. Everything else was too much of an effort, and she refused the invitations from Jimmy, from Annie and Joan, from her family, from friends. She had no energy for conversation, couldn't even pay attention to what anyone said. So she remained inside, moving from room to room, now and again pausing to look out the window to see that winter was progressing nicely, thank you. One morning, no doubt, she'd look out and see that it was spring, or summer. That could well happen. She couldn't care. The Tall Princess was, for the present, voluntarily locked in the tower. And the prince was never going to come because she had no wish to see him. She didn't believe in being rescued, never had. You rescued yourself, or you went under. Simple, fundamental.

Shifting, she gazed down the hall at the open doorway to her bedroom which, for the past twenty-six days, had been atypically tidy. The duvet lay neatly over the bed; no abandoned clothes anywhere. She'd even dusted and run the Hoover. Productive lethargy. Leaning against the wall, she wondered what she'd do when she ran out of food. She'd have to go out then, make a quick trip to Sainsbury's to stock up on cereal. But for the moment she still had the better part of a box left; so she was okay.

The house was cold, she realized. Better go downstairs and adjust the thermostat, she told herself. But she didn't move. There was something oriental about the view of her bedroom framed so perfectly by the door; everything very well placed, and the colors lovely and cool. The bed was inviting; she could take a nap. Sleep was, of all her activities, her favorite. Throughout each day she planned how and when she'd take to her bed, to pull the duvet around herself and drift off. She loved sleeping. All kinds of time got used up, entire days, entire nights; big chunks of time surrendered to an alternative reality where everyone was alive and well, walking and talking and making a racket. Sleep was perfection; she had a positive talent for it.

A thumping at the door startled her. Then Annie's voice, bellowing, "Oy, missus. Open the door. You've got visitors!"

"Bloody hell!" Kyra muttered, debating whether or not to respond.

"Don't mess us about, Keer! It's bloody freezing out here and we're not leaving. Come open the door!"

"Damn!" she whispered, feeling guilty, caught out, as if she'd been doing something illicit—which, of course, she had. Grieving was the most illicit of all activities; those caught at it were fated to be given a talking-to. Everyone had comments, advice, idiotic things to say about getting over it, as if death were a virus.

"I'm coming," she said inaudibly, thumping her way down the stairs. "Fat fool," she berated herself. "Can't say no, can't tell anyone to bugger off."

"Open the door!" Annie was shouting, as Kyra unlocked the door and threw it open. "Finally!" Annie said, and turned to signal to a couple sitting in a car parked across the road. "You look very well," she said judiciously, and gave Kyra a hug.

"Who's that?" Kyra asked, turning away and padding down the hall to the kitchen. "Coffee?"

"Definitely," Annie said, draping her coat over the banister. "Better make a pot. That's Stephen and a mate of his from Social Services."

"Social Services?"

"Yeh. I went 'n' did something that's gonna send you mental. But you'll get over it. I guarantee that. You will get over it."

"Oh, Annie," Kyra said tiredly. "What've you done? I'm really not in the mood for any of this."

"I know you're not," Annie said, her tone softening. "The thing is, and I know it's a cliché, but Jess wouldn't've wanted you sitting in here day in, day out, like Miss Havisham."

"Don't go down that road," Kyra warned.

"Sorry, but I'm going. Jess would've hated seeing you this way. It's a bloody waste! Not that you don't have the right to be sad cuz he's gone. You do. We're all sad he's gone. You just can't stay in this house living with his memory, as if the world's ended. It hasn't."

"Hello!" Stephen called from the door. "Is it safe to enter?"

"No!" Kyra called back. "But that's not going to stop you, so you might as well come in." Turning back to Annie, she said, "Why would you presume to tell me what Jess would or wouldn't have wanted?"

"Because he *told* me! Okay?"

"What did he tell you?" Kyra challenged her.

"He told me to make sure you didn't do too much of exactly what you're doing."

Kyra just stared at her.

"It's true," Annie declared. "It's absobloodylutely true! And if you don't believe me, ask Stephen. Cuz he told Stephen the very same thing. He made us *promise!*"

"What? What did he make you promise?"

"To do what we're doing, what we've done."

"Jesus!" Kyra said nervously. She glanced past Annie to see what was going on in the front hall, saw two people fussing with outerwear and turned back. "What have you *done?*"

Having removed his shoes, Stephen came down the hall to the kitchen, saying, "Hi, Keer. Is it okay to turn the light on?"

"I prefer the dark."

"Okay, but I'm going to turn the light on." He did, then stepped aside saying, "This is my friend Maddie. She works for Social Services. And hiding behind her is Peter. Are you going to come out and say hello?" he asked an unseen presence. "Peter's shaking his head," he told Kyra.

"I'd come over there," Maddie said, "but someone's got a very firm grip on my leg." A lean black woman of about thirty, with enormous eyes and a brilliant smile, she said, "Did I hear something about coffee? I'd adore a cup."

"I'll get it started," Annie said, going for the kettle.

Mystified, Kyra watched Stephen lean in behind Maddie and begin whispering to whoever was behind the woman. Kyra looked again at Maddie.

"Peter's feeling a bit shy. We'll just give him a minute. Have you got any juice? I'm sure he'd love some."

Kyra had no idea what might be in the refrigerator. But she went to take a look, finding something terribly familiar about this scene; a sense of déjà vu that had started the instant Stephen had spoken of Peter hiding behind Maddie. "I have some apple juice," she said, lifting it to check the sell-by date.

"Perfect," said Maddie.

"Apple juice, mate," Stephen told Peter.

Automatically, Kyra got a mug and poured in some of the juice. Then, realizing she'd just fixed a child's portion, she carefully set down the juice container, picked up the mug and walked across the room with it, took a step past Maddie and stopped.

Perhaps four years old, Peter had molded himself to the back of Maddie's legs, one hand gripping her so hard that his small knuckles were white. His other arm was in a cast from elbow to wrist, held at an angle by a brightly printed scarf that had been tied around his neck. He had on jeans that were several sizes too large, the cuffs folded so as not to drag on the floor, and a yellow pullover that had seen better days. There was a red-blue bruise all down one side of his face, and his eye was blackened.

Kyra held the mug out to him, saying, "I hope you like apple. It's all I've got."

The boy looked up at her, his head craning so far back it seemed as if he might topple over. "You ain't 'alf big," he whispered.

"I am positively enormous," she whispered back, "but don't tell anyone. They don't seem to have noticed."

"They 'aven't?"

"Silly, isn't it?"

"Yeh. Bloody ridiculous." Letting go of Maddie's leg, he reached for the mug. "I like apple. It's me fave-rit."

"Is that right?"

"Yeh. 'Ate tomato."

"I'll have to remember that."

"Yeh." The boy took a swallow of the juice, then looked up at her again. "'Ow'd you get to be so big, then?"

"Magic spell," she said. "When I was little."

"Crikey! What'd you do wrong?"

"I'm not honestly sure. But I must've done something. Don't you think?"

"Must've done," he agreed, and took another drink. "Am I gonna be stayin' 'ere wiv you?"

"I'll ask. Is Peter going to be staying here?" she asked Maddie.

"If he'd like it and you'd like it."

Kyra turned back to the boy. "It's up to us," she told him.

"I dunno," the boy said. "D'you reckon I'll get a magic spell put on me, too?"

"Oh, no. Only one to a household," she said. "You'll be quite safe."

"D'you tell the troof?"

"Always. I don't tell lies to children. And I never make promises I don't keep."

"'Onest?"

"Honest. Would you like to see your room?"

He gulped down the last of the juice and pushed the mug into Maddie's hand. "I reckon that'd be okay," he said.

"I think you'll like it. May I hold your hand?"

"No more spells?"

"None, absolutely."

"Yeah. Okay, then." He put his hand in Kyra's.

"It's upstairs," she said, leading him down the hall. "There are lots of toys and books, and a telly, too."

"A telly just for me?"

"Just for you. And I think we'll have to see about finding you some clothes that fit, don't you?"

"Yeh," Peter said. "These're 'orrible, ain't they?"

"They are, actually."

"So what's your name, then?"

"Kyra."

"That's a funny name."

"I know. It came with the spell."

"Crikey! You must've done somethin' really, really bad!"

"Maybe. But then again, maybe I did something really, really good."

I would like to thank Toronto's Hospital for Sick Children for their assistance with the research for this book.

BIBLIOGRAPHY

Ahlstrom, Timothy P. *The Kidney Patient's Book: New Treatment, New Hope.* Delran, N.J.: Great Issues Press, 1991.

Brown, Sarah ed. *Prentice Hall Pocket Encyclopedia of Vegetarian Cookery.* London: Dorling Kindersley Limited, 1991.

Carper, Jean. *The Food Pharmacy.* New York: Bantam Books, 1988.

Dobelis Inge N., ed. *Great Recipes for Good Health.* Pleasantville, N.Y.: The Reader's Digest Association, Inc., 1988.

Franklyn, Julian. *A Dictionary of Rhyming Slang.* London: Routledge, 1960.

Gabriel, Roger. *A Patient's Guide to Dialysis and Transplantation.* 5th ed. Lancaster, England: Kluwer Academic Publishers, 1990.

Lindsay, Anne & Associates Ltd. *Lighthearted Everyday Cooking*. Toronto: The Heart and Stroke Foundation of Canada, Macmillan Canada, 1991.

Lumet, Sidney. *Making Movies*. New York: Alfred A. Knopf, 1995.

Rose, Gloria. *Cooking for Good Health*. Garden City Park, N.Y.: Avery Publishing Group, 1993.

Shand, John & Wellington, Tony. *Don't Shoot the Best Boy, The Film Crew at Work*. Paddington, NSW Australia: Currency Press, 1988.

Toomay, Mindy and Susann Geiskopf-Hadler. *The Best 125 Meatless Main Dishes*. Rocklin, Calif.: Prima Publishing, 1992.

TELL THE AUTHOR

Dear Charlotte Vale Allen,
I just finished reading Parting Gifts *and wanted to tell you what
I thought of the book.*

Sincerely,

name _____

address _____

city, state,
zip code _____

(please print)

*If you are reading a library book, please copy this page and
leave it for the next reader.*

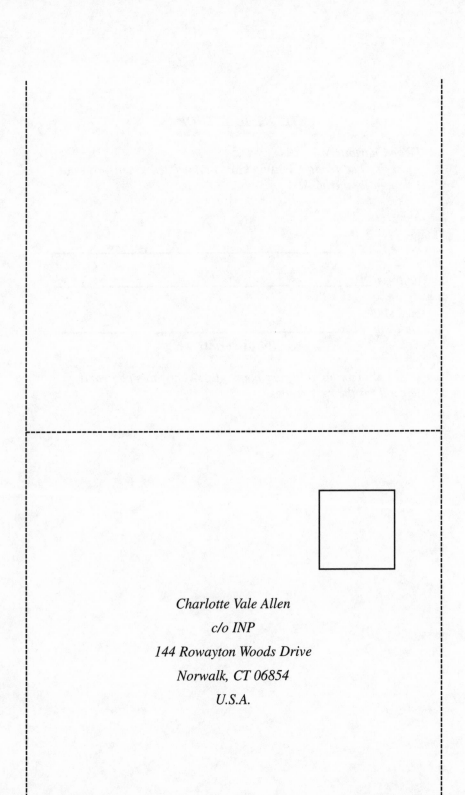

Charlotte Vale Allen
c/o INP
144 Rowayton Woods Drive
Norwalk, CT 06854
U.S.A.

(seal here)

TELL A FRIEND

Dear _____,

I just finished reading Parting Gifts *by Charlotte Vale Allen and wanted to tell you about it because I think it's a book you'll enjoy.*

Sincerely,

_____

Parting Gifts *is published by MIRA Books.*
If your local bookstore doesn't have it,
please ask them to order it for you.

Allen, Charlotte
Vale

Parting gifts

DUE DATE			E129 19.95